The Village Players During the Post War Years

A Narrative History of the Village of Fenton 1946-1950

Cover Photo: Author's wife Marie, with daughter Patricia in her arms and three year old Robert standing at her side. 1948.

Copyright © 2013
Robert G. Harris, Fenton, Michigan

All rights reserved. No part of this book shall be reproduced, stored in retrieval systems, or transmitted by any means without written permission from Robert G. Harris.

ISBN: 978-1-60458-987-0

Printed in USA by InstantPublisher

The Village Players
During the Post War Years

A Narrative History of the Village of Fenton
1946-1950

Robert G. Harris

Dedication

When I began writing this book several years ago, I fully intended to dedicate this book to three of my friends who were "Village Players". They honored me with their insights and the sharing of their personal experiences, thereby aiding my research and writings...however, God has intervened.

While my respect for my three departed friends has not diminished, the passing of my dear wife, Marie, causes me to remember her by dedicating this book to her memory.

Marie and I first met at Fenton High School, when she was a "mere" freshman and I was a "sophisticated" sophomore. About a year after our first meeting, we began a seventy four year relationship; we were "sweethearts' throughout High School and my college years and partners for life after being married in June of 1944. For all of those years, Marie was the love of my life, my best friend and the mother of our children, Robert and Patricia. Now, as I approach the age of ninety years, I expect this book will be the last of my literary endeavors, so I wish to dedicate these humble writings to my beloved Marie...may God bless and keep her, 'till we meet again.

The three friends to whom I also want to remember at this time also died during the time I was writing this book. In the past years, they were valuable assets and among my best consultants. They lived in Fenton and experienced the times and events of which I write. They were significant parts of the fabric of our town and they shared their remembrances with me.

Marge Johnson Kelley was a "farm girl" and getting to school in town was a problem which was solved when she moved in with Lloyd Kelley and his family...and not far from Fenton High School. She worked after school at Mickey's Dairy bar on South Leroy Street. She recalled the shortest distance from the Kelley's house to Mickey's was across the Shiawassee River...however the small bridge across the stream had not yet been built, but there was a fallen tree spanning the water at the location of the present bridge. So, each day she would gingerly walk the tree trunk across the river on her way to and from the dairy.

Marge married Lee, a brother of Lloyd Kelley, who also worked at the dairy. Lee had learned how to make ice cream at Mickey's and in the mid- 1930s. Marge and Lee bought Joe Botticelli's Ice Cream parlor on North Leroy Street. "Kelley's" soon became the "hangout" for all the young people in town. Surrounded by friends, the "Cokes", the Juke Box, the Pin Ball Machine (for those who had extra pocket change) and the friendly personalities of the Kelley's made for some wonderful memories of those high school days.

Paul Botticelli was the eldest of the five children of Joe and Agnes Botticelli...all of the first generation of immigrants to our country. Paul was a 1939 graduate of Fenton High School, where he participated in the sports, student governance and other activities. He was a student of Pharmacy at Ferris Institute (now Ferris State University) when the country went to war and he soon found himself heavily engaged in the fighting in Italy, ironically the homeland of his parents.

Following the end of the war, Paul completed his studies at Ferris. He owned and operated Fenton Drug/Ideal Pharmacy from 1947 until his retirement in 1985. He resided in Fenton all of his life. Paul served on the Fenton City Council and was Mayor of Fenton. He was inducted into the Fenton High School Alumni Hall of Fame. He was a member of St. John the Evangelist Catholic Church, V.F.W. Curtis-Wolverton Post #3243, American Legion and the Fenton Rotary

Paul was one of the "townies"...the youngsters who lived downtown, in the apartments above the family businesses. Paul found humor in telling of how the five Botticelli children would find sleeping in the apartment during the hot summer months intolerable and would seek relief by sleeping on the porch overlooking the alley behind the store. Their building was only two stores removed from the town's most notorious and rowdiest tavern. Almost every night, some of the bar's patrons would find themselves in a dispute and they would take to the alley to settle the matter. Paul said, they provided a "ringside seat" to some of the most interesting brawls...live entertainment for the five Botticelli children!

I can vividly remember the day I delivered a copy of my first book about Fenton (*The Village Players*) to Russ Haddon. It was in the afternoon and there was a chill in the air. I found Russ splitting up some kindling wood in his back yard. As he approached me it became obvious that the chill had affected Russ....he had a tiny stream of mucus dripping from his nostrils. He made some hardy sniffs but it didn't seem to lessen the flow. I had my book in my right hand, cover side up, and as I offered the book to him I was conscious of the drip and made several lateral moves to avoid having the cover soiled.

Now, if all you knew about Russell Haddon was what you learned from the previous paragraph. You would be horribly misinformed. While his last enterprise was operating a tree nursery, he was not the stereotypical "farmer". Nothing could be more further from the truth. Russ Haddon was an educated, intelligent man of many talents and interests. In 1938, Russ Haddon was selected to be the first Director of the new Fenton Community Center. He remained its Director, except for a period during World War II when he served in the U.S. Navy. He was the Director during the "salad days" of the Center...when it was truly the "center" of community activities. Russ' college education was in preparation for a career in education, and later he resigned his position at the FCC to accept a teaching position at his alma mater, Fenton High School. The Fenton community was growing and the people in the Lake Fenton area decided to expand their school offerings and they selected Russ Haddon to be their new Superintendent. He served the Lake Fenton Community in that capacity for sixteen years. He was there as the district grew into a full K-12 system. He later became the Superintendent of the Holly schools and served in that capacity for fourteen years. When he retired as the Superintendent of the Holly schools he retired to his "tree farm".

During his 97 years, Russell Haddon served the community in many other areas, once as a Councilman for the City of Fenton. He was very active as a member of St. Jude's Episcopal Church. At a time when the church was without a Pastor, and while Russ was a student at Eastern Michigan University (then Eastern Michigan Normal College), Russ would come home to Fenton and lead the services as a Lay Reader. Upon his demise, Russ' ashes were scattered throughout the Memorial Garden at the St. Jude's Church. He was a father, an educator, community servant, nurseryman, environmentalist, a devoted servant of his church, and a patron of the local arts.

Table of Contents

Prologue… 1
Act One…the Year 1946 3
    Scene One…the Village Elders 3
    Scene Two…The Gentlemen's Clubs 9
    Scene Three…For Ladies Only 17
    Scene Four…The Village Churches 21
    Scene Five…It's All Business Downtown 25
Intermission….Come Fly with Me! 31
    Scene Six…."Stand Up and Cheer" 37
    Scene Seven…What are the Students Doing? 45
    Scene Eight…Alumni, PTA and the Board of Education 51
    Scene Nine…"The" Fenton Community Center 55
    Scene Ten…"There's a Lot of Recreatin' Goin' On" 59
    Scene Eleven…Items of Interest? 61
Interlude One…The War to End All Wars…No. 2 65
Act Two…1947 71
    Scene One…The Village Council 71
    Scene Two…Doing Business Downtown 77
    Scene Three…The Club Scene…Ladies First! 83
    Scene Four…The Club Scene…for Men Only! 89
    Scene Five…the Veterans and their Ladies 97
    Scene Six…The Church Scene 101
    Scene Seven…The Fenton Community Center 103
    Scene Eight.. "Stand Up and Cheer for Fenton High" 107
    Scene Nine…While the Children Play Games 111
    Scene Ten…Let Us Entertain You! 119
    Scene Eleven…Items of Interest 123
Interlude Two…the Cold War Heats Up! 125

Act Three...The Year 1948 131
    Scene One...The Village Council's "Growing Pains" 131
    Scene Two...Business 137
    Scene Three...Men's Civic Clubs 139
    Scene Four...the Fraternal Lodges 143
    Scene Five...The Ladies Clubs 145
    Scene Six...Fenton's Churches and the Church Ladies 149
    Scene Seven...Patriotic Organizations 153
    Scene Eight...FHS Governance 155
    Scene Nine...FHS Athletics 157
    Scene Ten...FHS Activities 161
    Scene Eleven...Let Us Entertain You ! 165
    Scene Twelve...Other Items of Interest 167
Interlude Three...a World of Upheaval and Unrest 169
Act Four...the Year 1949 173
    Scene One...The Village Council 173
    Scene Two...The Town's Business 177
    Scene Three...The Lady Clubbers 179
    Scene Four...The Men's Clubs 185
    Scene Five...FHS Sports 191
    Scene Six...FHS Activities 195
    Scene Seven...Alumni, PTA and the Board 199
    Scene Eight...Let me Entertain You! 201
    Scene Nine...Items of Interest 203
Interlude Four...the Power Struggles Continue 205
Act Five...the Year 1950 209
    Scene One...The Village Council 209
    Scene Two...Doing Business Downtown 215
    Scene Three...The Town's Churches 219

Scene Four...FHS Sports 223

Scene Five...FHS Activities 227

Scene Six... FHS Items of Interest 231

Scene Seven...Clubs, For Men Only! 233

Scene Eight...The Ladies and their Clubs 235

Scene Nine ...the Veterans and their Ladies 237

Scene Ten...Clubs...Don't Forget the Youngsters..............................239

Scene Eleven...The Fraternal Orders...Plus! 241

Scene Twelve...Let Me Entertain You...Again!...................................245

Scene Thirteen...Items of Interest..249

Epilogue..251

Encore… A Buried Treasure?..255

Appendix One...World War II Honor Roll..259

Appendix Two...FHS Class Rosters 1946 -1950 263

Appendix Three...Cub Scouts 268

Appendix Four...About The Author..275

Prologue…

Almost 13 million Americans were in uniform at the end of World War II. After four years of war, the impulse was strong to dismantle this force. The servicemen's families pressed the government to "bring the boys home," and soldiers overseas demanded an acceleration of the separation process. Within five months of V-J Day, 8.5 million servicemen and women had been mustered out of the armed forces.

And so "the boys came home" and attempted to pick up the lives they had before the conflict. "Coming home" meant going back to school or college, reentering the work force and marrying the "girl left behind"…unless she had found someone new during your absence! Regardless, there was an upsurge in marriages and subsequently a "baby boom".

In the United States alone, approximately 76 million babies were born in those years following the end of the war. In 1946, live births in the U.S. surged from 222,721 in January to 339,499 in October. By the end of the 1940s, about 32 million babies had been born, compared with 24 million in the 1930s.

While there appeared to be no shortage of babies, there was a very large shortage in all kinds of material goods. There was no production of automobiles and large appliances such as refrigerators in the war years. Most of the returning servicemen found an acute shortage in housing. Very little home building had occurred during their time away from home. The baby boom triggered a housing boom, consumption boom and a boom in the labor force.

The transition from military duties to a civilian job was not accomplished without some difficulties. Some of the veterans found upon their return that their previous employer had filled his job and was not willing to make room for him in his business. During the war years, women had entered the work force in great numbers and a large number of them didn't want to return to their pre-war role…they wanted to work outside the home and, consequently, many of the jobs were no longer available to the returning serviceman. Fortunately, the demand for all kinds of products, many not produced during the war years, was exceptionally great and this resulted in an exceedingly large growth in the work force.

Not only had the production of civilian goods been suspended during the war years, but the wages paid to the labor force had not been appreciably increased during that period. Labor was demanding higher wages and the anticipated strike wave began.

Within a month after the end of the war, the number of days lost due to labor strikes had doubled and doubled again within a second month.

43,000 oil workers were out on strike in 20 states in September 1945. Then 200,000 coal miners walked off their jobs. They were followed by 44,000 northwest lumber workers, 70,000 truck drivers in the Midwest, and 40,000 machinists in the San Francisco Bay area. The longshoremen of the East coast ports went on strike along with the workers in the glass and textile industries.

But these strikes were only the prelude to the strikes at General Motors and General Electric. The GM strike idled some 225,000 workers. In January of 1946, 174,000 electrical workers struck, and on the next day 93,000 meat packers walked out. Two weeks later, the steel industry was shut down as 750,000 steel workers struck...the largest strike in the nation's history. The U.S. Bureau of Labor Statistics referred to this era as "the most concentrated period of labor-management strife in the country's history"[*] By the end of 1946, 4.6 million workers had participated in strikes.

The situation prompted President Truman to take actions to bring an end to this nationwide strike movement. The President used a variety of tactics including the use of his War Power authority that was still in effect. When the railroad workers were planning to strike, President Truman seized the railroads and planned to let the Army run them. When the workers continued to strike, the President threatened to draft the strikers. The railroaders backed down and cancelled their plans to go on strike, and continued to work.

When the oil industry was shut down by the strike action of their employees, President Truman seized control of the industry and that action resulted in the workers ending their strike and coming back to work. When the miners defied the government after returning to work and went out on strike for the second time, their union was fined $3.5 million. In most cases, when the government seized other industries experiencing strikes, the workers ended their strike action and went back to work

---

[*] The World War II post-war strike wave:libcom.org

Act One...the Year 1946

Scene One...the Village Elders

It wasn't as if no one expected it...but it was especially noteworthy...when Harry Lemen was elected as Village President for his 15th term. The two local political parties, the Citizens and the Peoples, caucused and presented a full slate of candidates for the village election. The election turnout was one of the largest in years, with some 900 citizens casting their ballots.

Office	Candidate	Votes
President	**Harry Lemen** (C)	442
	Raymond Hunt (P)	352
Clerk	**Burns Fuller** (C))	521
	Lucille Sanders (P)	272
Treasurer	Robert F. Smith (C)	203
	D.R Stiles (P)	549
Assessor	**Irving Gould** (C)	487
	Arthur Barnard (P)	300
Trustees 2 years	**Russell Haddon** (P)	411
	Fred Hall (C)	384
	Charles S. Rounds (P)	372
	Henry Alchin (C)	332
	Wayne Townsend (P)	325
	John Dolza (C)	321
Trustees 1 year	**Elton Austin** (C)	483
	Harold Roshaven (P)	294

The names of those elected are in **bold** print. Those elected joined the incumbent trustees Willard Hatfield and Ray Welch on the Village Council. The popular educator, Burns Fuller, was the winner in the contest for the office of Village Clerk, but only a few months later, resigned when he accepted a new position, which required him to move from his Fenton home. The Village Council appointed Ed Renwick as his replacement.

4 The Village Players Post War

Harry Lemen was the first Mayor of Fenton when it became a City in 1964. He was first elected to the Village Council in 1925 and elected Village President in 1933. He served in that capacity for 34 years. When he retired in 1965 he had served 40 years as a Village or City official. He was born in 1895 in Hartland, Michigan and was orphaned at the age of six. After both of his parents died he lived with his uncle in a three story log cabin on Lake Fenton. He was also known as the proprietor of Lemen's Market in downtown Fenton. In 1964, over 300 people attended a retirement banquet in his honor.

As in the past years the Fenton Village Council was a frugal lot. With the end of the conflict, they were beginning to experience the pressures of a growing community…and the accompanying need for more services and facilities. However, the Village's financial condition in March, 1946 did not yet reflect the changing times. A recapitulation of the Village's finances was the following.

Balance on hand	$ 6,314.23
Receipts for the year	50,319.41
Total Receipts	$62,633.64
Total Disbursements	59,955.80
Gross Balance on Hand	$ 2,677.84

Probably the most discussed subject, that engrossed the Council members for months, was how to honor the veterans. During the war years, the village had placed a large billboard "Honor Roll" on the front lawn of the Fenton Community Center. The "Honor Roll" contained the names of the people serving in the armed services on individual wooden plaques. Each name was painted on a plaque by Grant Wright.

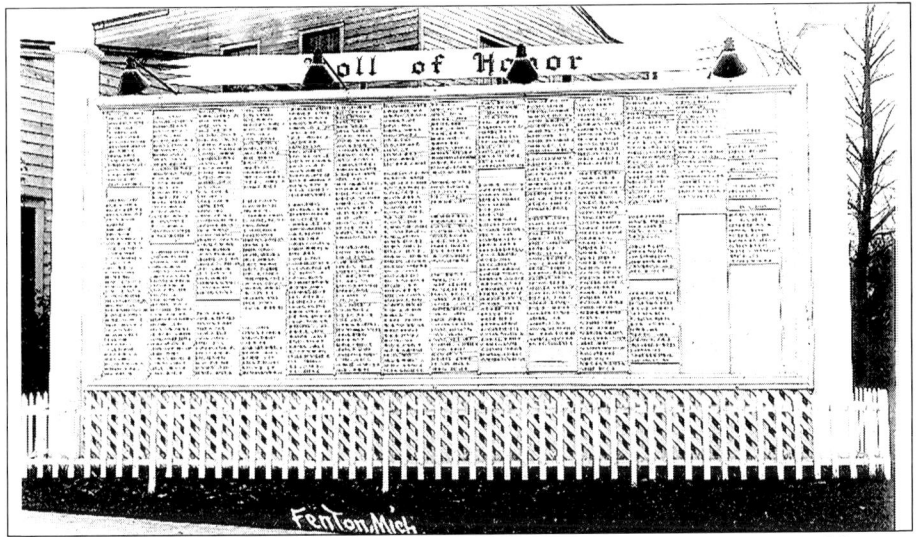

The Dedication Ceremony for the "Honor Roll" was held on Armistice Day, November 11, 1943. Mrs. Myrtle Harris, in her capacity as President of the Patriotic Council opened the program and introduced Mrs. J. B. Obenshain as Mistress of Ceremonies Both the Fenton High School and City Bands were present and played the National Anthem and other patriotic songs during the proceedings

Mrs. J B. Obenshain was an excellent Mistress of Ceremonies, especially when one understands the circumstances in which she found herself. The Dedication occurred only a day or so after the Obenshains learned that their son, Major J.B. Obenshain U.S. Marine Corps, had lost his life in combat in the South Pacific.

The Honor Roll sign was modified several times during the next few years as additional names were added. After the war, the sign was removed and destroyed. In spite of the efforts of the Fenton Museum and its Director Ken Seger, only a few photos of the sign are evidence of its existence.

Eventually, the Council decided to have an enlarged framed picture of the "Honor Roll" billboard placed on a wall in the Community Center for all to see for years to come. It is not certain whether the picture was ever placed in the FCC...at least no one can remember it ever being seen there.

Once the photos of the "Honor Roll" had been taken, the plan was to paint "Welcome Veterans" on the billboard. Similarly, no one can remember ever seeing the new sign. However, the Council did authorize a memorial to the Fenton men who died in both of the World

Wars. This time there is evidence that their directions were followed. There is a bronze plaque bearing the names of those who died in both wars located on Leroy Street just south of the Shiawassee River Bridge in the park area.

The Village did have a "City Band". The City Band played a series of weekly summer concerts in the small park on Shiawassee Avenue, bordered by Park and Elizabeth streets. Howard Park, the music director for the Fenton Schools, also directed the City Band. Longtime Manager Charles A. Simons was replaced by Judson Phillips just before the summer concerts were to begin. Frequent soloists during the concerts were: Marian Alchin-Flute, Bernard Sinclair-Cornet and Howard Bacon-Trombone. The Band played at all of the town's parades and had several "winter" concerts in the Fenton Community Center The band was also a major attraction at the St. John Church's Annual Bar-B-Que..

The City Band was a "low budget" operation. In their annual financial statement, the Band reported a total of $813.10 in receipts with a total disbursement of $731.34. What was most interesting in their report was their properties inventory The Band's Manager; Charles H. Simons listed the following

Inventory of the City Band, March, 1946

25	Uniforms
27	Caps
1	Drum Major Baton and Shako
1	Sousaphone
1	Baritone Horn
1	Alto Horn (upright)
1	Crash Cymbal
1	Director's Metal Stand
24	Folding Chairs
Library	Consisting of Overtures, Selections, Marches, and Popular Music. Estimated value of band property about $1,400.00

As it had done for many years, the Village's Police Department still operated with two full time officers and two part-timers that were available for special events or as relief for the two full time officers. Bob Dode, FHS 38, was the Village Marshall and was joined by Myron Pray. The "part-time" officers were Harold Dode and Lloyd Kelley.

At the time of hiring of Officer Pray, the Council increased the pay for both Dode and Pray from $45 per week to $50 per week. Also with .the hiring of Myron Pray, Bob Dode took the "day" shift and Myron Pray patrolled during the night. Both officers were pleased when the Council also purchased a new 1946 Chevrolet for their use. The Council was duly impressed when the fines collected for parking and traffic violations increased soon after Myron joined Bob Dode on patrol. A total of $243 in fines was collected in the first month both were on the job.

A bit of "Keystone Cops" played out when Officer Dode reported to the Council that the lock on the cell in the jail needed to be repaired or replaced. He reported that in recent weeks he had four "lockups" and four "escapes"!

The Village's Firemen were always the "Pride" of the townsfolk. When the fire siren at the fire station sounded, fellows like Lee Kelley would immediately respond. Lee would turn off the ice cream machine, untie his apron and race to the fire station...Howard Craft, the funeral director, was usually the first to arrive at the station...after all, he was the driver of the fire truck! The volunteer firemen were a very dedicated group and took their "job" very seriously. They enjoyed the camaraderie and often met for dinner at the fire house.

"The Fire Boys" enjoying their monthly steak dinner. L-R Shull Woodworth, Fred Williams, John Bacon, Tom Woodworth, Louis Rector, Howard Craft, Bob Beach, Harry Moore, Claude Cohoon and Lee Kelley Calendar on wall is for 1940.

Scene Two…The Gentlemen's Clubs

Prior to the War, the Men's Fellowship was one of the most active and successful organizations in town. The Men's Fellowship was sponsored by the Methodist Church. However; men of all church denominations were active participants in the series of banquets the Fellowship put on each year at the Fenton Community Center. Soon after World War II began and food rationing was imposed, the Fellowship found it was not possible to obtain the food stuffs necessary to feed 300 men six times a year. Consequently, the Fellowship closed down "for the duration". Late in the year the leadership met and decided to renew their activities in January of 1947.

Two other active men's clubs, the Kiwanis and the XX Club, operated throughout the war years and were very active in community programs and support of the war effort. The Kiwanis had several of its members enter the armed forces, but those remaining continued the club's programs and activities with success.

The XX Club, with its limited membership of only 20 men…and with many of them beyond the "military" age …was able to continue their programs as in the past. Some familiar names from the pre-war days continued to lead the XXers. The officers of the club serving with President John Hoskins were Harry Lemen, Harold Hill, Dr. C. G. Walcott and George Tamlyn.

Now, there was a new club on the scene. The Eagles were organized in October of 1945, and began a very active program of recruiting members and organizing a women's auxiliary. The club was officially known as the Fenton Aerie, No. 2460, Fraternal Order of Eagles (F.O.E.)

In May the Eagles elected Philip O. Crane of Dauner Road as their President. The other officers elected were: Orville (Bud) Azelton-VP, Harold Torrey-Chaplain, Lowery Nash -Conductor, William Strayer-Secretary, James William-Treasurer, Edward Young and Daniel Steele-Guards, Charles Auker-Trustee(3 years), Dennis Watson-Trustee(2 years) and Rolland Sewell-Trustee (1 year).

Not long after the new officers were installed it was time to celebrate their first anniversary. The celebration was held at the Fenton Community Center and featured the initiation of 37 new members.

Congressman William Blackney attended the meeting and congratulated the club on the progress they had made in their first year.

The Eagles continued to "fly" as they leased the upper story of 118 North Leroy Street, the space above the Popular Restaurant, as their new home. They opened the new home in early December after they had completed extensive remodeling. This activity did not interfere with their drive for new members. On Thanksgiving eve, November 27th, they held another initiation ceremony at the American Legion hall at which time they inducted 33 new members. . .

The wives of the members formed the "Eagle Ladies Social Club" and met regularly at the Fenton Community Center. Some of the active members were Mrs. Edward Percival, Mrs. Ralph Robertson, Mrs. Howard Smith, Mrs. Daniel Steele, Mrs. Charles Auker, Mrs. Joseph Oren, Mrs. Dennis Watson and Mrs. Lowery Nash. In December the local club was granted a charter to organize an Eagles Ladies Auxiliary. Consequently, the "Social Club" became the Auxiliary.

The Kiwanis directed their programs to general assistance to the village welfare situation.. They made monthly contributions of $60 to the Fenton Recreation Committee and $5 each week to the High School Hot Lunch project. They also bought clothes, shoes, milk and medicine for many needy families.

One of the fund raising activities to support these programs was to play two basketball games with the Holly Kiwanis...a home and home arrangement. The event evoked several articles in the local paper about having an ambulance, medical doctors, etc on hand for any casualty that might occur during the contest.

Portly businessman Aldrich Locke was one of the starting forwards for Fenton and he was joined by J. C. Peck (owner of the *Rowena Theatre*), Heavy-set Dr. Ralph Ettinger, Ray Hunt (erstwhile politician and insurance man) and the Reverend Wesley Dudgeon of the Methodist Church. They also indicated the game would have "Medical Services" provided by most of the town's Doctors: W. J. Rynearson, R. Ettinger, Navy hero C. G. Walcott and young D.O. Fred Bostick. "Ambulance Services" for the game would be provided by Howard Craft (Funeral Director), Bryan Bowles (Linden's Funeral Director) and the Davis-Graham Funeral Home of Fenton. The "water boy" for Fenton was young D.A. O'Dell assisted by the Village President Harry Lemen The two games were well attended and provided the spectators with many laughs and earned over $500 for each of the Kiwanis clubs.

Several years earlier, some of the townsfolk joined together and developed a swimming beach on Silver Lake which rapidly became the most popular "swimming hole" for the Fenton youth. In June, as the interest in swimming was rising, the Kiwanis recognized that the beach was in need of some work. They gathered together with shovels, picks, hoes and other tools and renovated the area. Several loads of gravel and sand and some manual labor improved the site considerably.

For years, the Fenton High School had excelled in Track and the Kiwanis honored them at an annual luncheon. This year was no exception, when in early July; Coach Ivan Williams brought nine members of the track team to the meeting. Coach Williams commented on each athlete and told of their contributions to the team. Absent members were also mentioned, with credit going to them for their success during the season. Two of the absentees were now serving in the armed services.

In the fall, the Kiwanians were honored on two occasions. First, in August at the State Convention, Aldrich C. Locke, a Charter member of the Fenton Kiwanis, was elected the District's Lieutenant Governor. Then a month later, the Club was pleased to have Edgar A. Guest as their speaker at their Charter night dinner. At the time, Edgar A. Guest was the most popular and the most recognized commentator on Detroit radio as a member of WJR, Detroit.

It was not unusual for the Kiwanis and the XX Club to hold a joint meeting. For the second year, the Football Banquet for the FHS team was jointly sponsored by the XX Club and the Kiwanis. The football banquet was started nearly twenty years earlier by the old Exchange Club, now known as the XX Club, and had been carried on each year since.

Mr. Horace Hitchcock was the master of Ceremonies for the event and Art Valpey, an assistant coach at the University of Michigan was the guest speaker.

. The American Legion and the Veterans of Foreign Wars were aggressively pursuing the returning servicemen to join with them. There were a few new Veterans organizations coming on the scene, the AMVETS for example, but the older organizations were well established in the community and were basically unaffected in their efforts to recruit the Fenton men and women.

One of the principal missions of the both the V.F.W. and the American Legion, was to provide the returning servicemen with assistance with filing any claim with the Veterans Administration. Both the V.F.W. and the American Legion posts in Fenton had a service officer available to help any veteran. The service officer for the V.F.W. in the early part of the year was Oswald (Bob) Utt, who was assisted by Webb Kelleher. When Utt became the Post Commander, he named Norman McNeil as his replacement. The veterans were invited to visit the service officers at the post home located above the Firestone store in downtown Fenton. The Post's Service Officers had undergone special training with the Veterans Administration.

Early in the year, the Veterans Administration reported that nearly half of all the country's cases had been submitted through the Veterans of Foreign Wars. At that time 46,020 claims had been processed by the V.F.W... The Red Cross had handled 25,142, the American Legion 18,661, the D.A.V. did 8,264 and all other organizations accounted for 2,382. In Fenton, both veterans' organizations worked diligently to provide the retuning servicemen the help they needed.

In April, the Curtis-Wolverton V.F.W. Post 3243, elected new officers for the coming year. Oswald "Bob" Utt became the Post Commander. The other officers elected were: Sr. Vice Cmdr-Earl Silvers, Jr. Vice Cmdr-James Nierescher, Quartermaster-Walter Stiff, Adjutant-William Harris, Chaplain-Bryant Hanbey, Advocate-Harry Pokorny, Surgeon-Frank Mytinger, Officer of the Day-Fred Walters, Patriotic Instructor-Emanuel Boilore, Guard-Henry Rosbury, Trustee-Norman McNeil, QM Sergeant-Howard Eble and Service Officer Norman McNeil. The Post reiterated their goal......*Service in War...in Peace...in Comradeship.*

The James DeWitt Post No. 38 of the American Legion established a service center at their home in the Maccabee Building at 115 East Caroline Street. Bernard Weber and Hollis Winn, both World War II veterans, served as the post's service officers.

In July, the Post elected their officers for the coming year. The new Post Commander was Alfred "Frosty" Winter. Others elected to serve were: Sr. Vice Cmdr-Bill Hathaway, Jr. Vice Cmdr-Ian Tanner, Adjutant, Chaplain-Rev. Hartley H. Stockham, Finance Officer-Tom Merrill, Sergeant at Arms-Basil Bowman, Historian-Phillip Crane and the executive committee- Harry Reed and Frank Mytinger.

Both President Truman and Governor Kelly proclaimed the first anniversary of V-J Day, August 14th, as a day for celebration and prayer. The Legionnaires organized a ceremony to again pay tribute to their fallen comrades. The ceremony was held on the front lawn of the

Fenton Community Center. The City Band moved their weekly concert to the FCC and became part of the event. Village President Harry Lemen conducted the dedication of the memorial plaque

In October, after years of occupying their rooms at the Maccabee Building at the corner of East Caroline and Wood Streets, the Legion Post purchased the home of Bert Rollins at the corner of Pine and Roberts streets. After some remodeling, the house became an excellent home for the James DeWitt Post.

The Veterans were able to accomplish much more because of their Ladies. Both the V.F.W. and the American Legion posts had Ladies Auxiliaries. While the Auxiliaries supported the Post's projects, they often had programs of their own. For example, the American Legion women sponsored a Fenton girl to attend the Girl's State held in Ann Arbor. In 1946, the Legion ladies selected Miss Shirley Scott, a Junior at Fenton High School for that honor.

In April, the V.F.W. Ladies Auxiliary elected officers for the coming year. Mrs. Hazel Crystal was elected as the new President. Others elected were: Sr. VP-Edna Pokorny, Jr. VP-Alice Locke, Treasurer-Leda Hanbey, Chaplain-Lillian Goodrich, Conductress- Irene Boilore, Secretary- Naomi Bennett, Trustee (3 years)-Alice Witherell, Trustee (1 tear)-Katherine Walters, Historian-Emma Hall, Musician-Myrtle Harris, Guard-Mary Pasco. Banner Bearer- Violet Harley, Patriotic Instructor-Gladys Dobbs, Color Bearers-Delia Palmer, Edna Bly, Ruby Huff and Henrietta (Hattie) Rohm. The Installation of Officers Ceremony was conducted by Past President Irene Tribbey and assisted by Irene Boilore and Marie Steward.

In the following month, the V.F.W. ladies celebrated their 10th Anniversary. Following the dinner, Village Councilman Charles S. Rounds, representing the Village President Harry Lemen, expressed the gratitude of the town for the many fine works accomplished by the Auxiliary over the past years.

The highlight of the evening was the presentation of the V.F.W.'s Citizenship Medal to Mr. S. F. Beach, the publisher of *The Fenton Independent* for sending his newspapers to the Fenton men and women serving in the armed forces during the war.

In 1942, the Veterans of Foreign Wars had organized an honor degree association entitled the "Military Order of the Cooties", a "fun" organization composed of VFW members in good standing. The ladies of the VFW were soon to follow their men in organizing a companion association for the Cooties. The "Fen–Fun Cootiettes" were formed at that time. In October, the Cootiettes met and elected their officers Chief Grayback-Lelah Stiff, Lady Louse-Agnes Bottecelli; Baby Louse-Marie Allegner; Scratcher-Irene Boilore; Shekel Keeper-Edna Pokorny; Crummy Chaser-Cassie Devereaux; Rustling Louse-Zelma Slover; Louse Hunter,- Henrietta Rohm; Pious Louse- Myrtle Harris; Tightwads-Irene Tribbey and Jackie Tiefer.

The ladies of the James Dewitt American Legion Post held their annual election in late September and elected a woman of the "new" generation as their President. Elizabeth Goodrich, better known as "Betty" was the wife of WWII Marine veteran Howard Goodrich. Betty Goodrich was also a well-liked teacher at Fenton High School for many years. The other officers elected were: 1st VP- Mrs. Shard Faust, 2nd VP- Miss Francis Anible, Secretary- Mrs. Marjorie Lea, Treasurer Mrs. Zella White, Chaplain- Mrs. Della Woodworth, Historian- Mrs. Jean Mytinger, and Sergeant-at-Arms- Mrs. Margareta. .

Mrs. Roy (Lillian) Goodrich, the new President's Mother-in-Law, was the installing officer for the new officers. Lillian was also the member who brought her daughter-in-law into the Legion auxiliary

At Christmas time of 1946, the men and women of the American Legion conducted a program called: "Give to Yanks Who Gave". The mission was to provide Christmas gifts for the veterans confined to the Veteran Hospitals. It was successfully completed when over $200 was raised by the committee to purchase the items for the gift boxes.
.

Sam Casazza

One should not leave our discussion of veterans and their organizations without paying especial attention to a veteran, a member of both the American Legion and the Veterans of Foreign Wars and perhaps the town's consummate veteran.

Sam Casazza lived alone in his cottage on Dart's Landing of Lake Fenton for most of the years he was active in Fenton veterans' organizations. Following the end of World War II, he was joined by his bachelor nephew, Joseph Casazza, after Joe returned from his service with the Army in Italy.

Sam had served in the Army during the Spanish American War with duty in the Philippines. When World War I began, Sam joined the

Army again and served in France during that conflict. It was said that his World War duty with the 38th Division, was as a Mess Sergeant and Sam did nothing to disprove the conjecture. Frequently, it was Sam who prepared the "after meeting" dinner for his fellow veterans and he was often referred to as the "Mess Sergeant".

The author knew Sam Casazza very well and recalls that Sam enjoyed his glass of beer. He could be found at the bar of the Virginia Tavern nursing a glass of beer in front of him. He often appeared to be in a trance, in deep thought or reminiscing. His friends said he was "drifting down the Panay River"...reflecting on his experience in chasing the insurgents in the back country of the Philippines..

In August of 1946, veteran Samuel S. Casazza was awarded a Congressional Medal for his services during the Philippine Insurrection......some 48 years after the event.

History shows that the Cross of Malta, the emblem of the Veterans of Foreign Wars of the United States, is 1,000 years old. Nearly ten centuries ago the Maltese Cross was made the symbol of fighting men who were united by a solemn pledge of comradeship to fight for freedom and to aid the sick and the needy. Those ancient obligations are still symbolized by the Cross of Malta today, for the more than two million former servicemen who are the Veterans of Foreign Wars The Cross of Malta is the symbol of their battles in time of war and of their campaign to defend the God given rights of human beings in time of peace. The Cross of Malta symbolizes the compassion, or sympathy, of those men and women for the needy. It is the sign of services which our contemporary veterans render to help make living a little better for everyone.

There shines the Emblem of The American Legion, it is your badge of distinction, honor and service. It stands for God and Country, and the highest rights of man. Of its several parts, each has a meaning. The Rays of the Sun form the background of our proud Emblem, and suggest that the Legion's principles will dispel the darkness of violence and evil. The Wreath forms the center, in loving memory of those brave comrades who gave their lives in the service of the United States so that liberty might endure. The Star victory symbol of World War I, signalizes as well honor, glory and constancy. The letters U.S. leave no doubt as to the brightest star in the Legion's star. Two Large Rings the outer one stands for the rehabilitation of our sick and disabled buddies. The inner one denotes the welfare of America's children. Two Small Rings set upon the star. The outer pledges loyalty and Americanism. The inner is for service to our communities, our states and the Nation. The words American Legion

Scene Three...For Ladies Only

The women and girls of Fenton would not have had any difficulty finding a group...a club...with which to associate in the year following the end of hostilities.

The Entre Nous and the Bay View women's' clubs, which traced their existence into the last century, were active throughout the War years and they maintained their "prestigious" position as we began the post war era

Late in the year the Bay View Club prepared to celebrate their 50th Anniversary. In the December 26th issue of *The Fenton Independent,* the reporter wrote the following article which is quoted verbatim.

> ***
> Fifty years ago, eight Fenton ladies subscribed for a course of study on ÈThe History of Northern EuropeŠ, published in pamphlet and book form in Bay View, Michigan. Thus, the Bay View Club of Fenton was organized, with members in agreement to meet each Monday during the winter months of the year. Upon completion of the Bay View course, the club continued with miscellaneous programs prepared by members, which carried them in study to every corner of the globe. Gradually the need for social atmosphere became apparent with the increase in membership and the Annual MenŠ Night dinners and Colonial Parties were considered the highlight of the social affairs of the community.
>
> The Bay View Club has always taken an active part in every campaign or project designed to make Fenton a better place in which to live and now has an active membership of 35.
>
> Mrs Grace Gurnes, the only charter member living in Fenton, now serves in an honorary capacity.
> ***

The Entre Nous ladies held their regular meetings throughout the year. Most of the programs found one of the members presenting a paper for discussion. The topics varied from world, national to local affairs. The Christmas party was a very memorable event, when Mrs. Otto Krieger, A world traveler exhibited her doll collection. The dolls were dressed in the styles representing the European countries. One had King George VI in his military uniform. Another was a French peasant couple in typical costumes. All in all it was a "tour de force" of the dressing styles of the European people.

The Child Study Club movement was still very strong in Michigan and Fenton boasted three very active organizations: the Senior Child Study Club (CSC), the Junior CSC and the Pro-To CSC.

Early in the year, the Senior Child Study Club undertook a very interesting and valuable program for all the ladies of our community, even though it was designed for the high school girls. The program was entitled "Points for Poise" and was held in the gymnasium of the Fenton High School. Club President Mrs. Floyd Hartley opened the program which was conducted by Mrs. Beth Frew and Mrs. Arnold Westman Jr. The High School girls directed by Miss Evelyn Northrope , the home economics teacher, presented a play and style show of clothes they made in their classes.

The club elected new officers in March. Those elected were: President- Mrs. August Arndt, VP- Mrs. Dorothy Hodgman, Secretary- Mrs. Maurice Kieft and Treasurer Mrs. Milton Bobier.

In May, it was time for the annual Mother-Daughter Banquet. President Mrs. Floyd Hartley opened the ceremony and called upon Mrs. Harley Stockham to offer the Benediction. The Toastmaster for the event, Mrs. Frank Bachus, presented the following program: Mrs. Immanuel Johnson and her daughter Nan, played a piano duet. This was followed by the traditional exchange of toasts: Katie Armstrong and Janette Edwards toasted the mothers; Mrs. Clarence

Armstrong and Mrs. Robert Edwards returned the toast, by saluting the daughters. The activity was closed with a song by Mary Beth Cotcher accompanied on the piano by her mother Mrs. Paul Cotcher.

As the new school year began, the Senior CSC held their customary luncheon with the teachers as their guests. The group enjoyed a social hour and was entertained by a piano solo by Mrs. Arthur Strom and a reading by Mrs. Russell Haddon.

In May, Mrs. Clarence Edinger finished her term as the Junior Child Study Club President and handed the gavel over to the newly elected President Mrs. Gordon Robbins. Others assuming office for the coming year were: 1st VP- Mrs. Claude Cohoon, 2nd VP Mrs. Ralph Richmond, Recording Secretary Mrs. John Nierscher, Corresponding Secretary Mrs. Don Bristol and Parliamentarian Mrs. Delphin Bender.

The Pro-To CSC, as the other two clubs, met regularly and occasionally held joint meetings as they did when the clubs entertained a visit by the Mrs. C. O. Creal, the President of the State Federation of Child Study Clubs.

If you were interested in music or books, the Fenton Book Club and the Fenton Music Club never missed a beat during the war and kept turning the pages as the new era began

The Book Club did not meet during the summer months, but during their "season" their monthly meetings were well attended. The club met at the Fenton Community Center and their meetings generally featured a guest speaker to review one of the current books and were followed by a tea service. Those attending often included guests or members of other clubs such as the Entre Nous.

At their Annual Meeting the members elected Mrs. Wesley Martin as their President. Others elected were: VP- Mrs. J. C. Peck, Secretary- Mrs. Frank Mytinger and Treasurer Mrs. Frank Wiggins.

The Rainbow Girls were as strong and enthusiastic as ever. As in the years before, as the young ladies reached the entrance age, many were eager to become a "Rainbow Girl". In late May, the Girls installed a new set of officers: Beth Gordon, the outgoing Worthy Advisor, passed her leadership role as Worthy Advisor to Barbara Hyde. Others installed were Jeanne Thorpe, Bonnie O'Berry and Gloria Gordon.

Everything in the
BEST TASTE

That's the town whisper that's being circulated by hosts of satisfied enthusiasts . . . by people, just like yourselves, who have enjoyed the ravishing savor of our

Road House Dinners
AND THE EXTRA-POLITE SERVICE OF OUR STAFF

Daily 5:00 p. m. to 11:00 p. m.
CLOSED SUNDAYS

———o———

Our dining room will accommodate
Banquets and Special Dinner Parties
Arrange with the management
for accommodations

| COCKTAIL LOUNGE |

The HOTEL FENTON DINING ROOM

Ray O'Rielly, Prop.   Telephone 3632

Scene Four...The Village Churches

The Methodist and the Presbyterian congregations both had a change in leadership during this period. The Reverend Dr. J. Stanley Mitchell, who had served the First Presbyterian Church for eight years, announced his retirement in November of 1945. He had been suffering with bronchitis and sinusitis for some time and was advised to move to a more agreeable climate. Dr. Mitchell was considered one of the best orators in the area, and it was a rare occasion when he was not the principal speaker. He was active in the American Legion and the Masons during his years in Fenton.

In February, the Presbyterian Board selected the Reverend Hartley H. Stockham
as their Pastor. Reverend Stockham was a former Army Chaplain who had served overseas in the New Guinea and the Philippines during the war. The Stockhams had two children, a daughter age 14 and a son age 11. The daughter, Nancy, made Fenton her home and her life as a social worker. She was well known and highly respected for her service to the community.

The whole community, not only the Members of the Methodist Church, celebrated the "burning of the mortgage' at the Sunday service of June 20th .The church's District Superintendent, the Reverend Clyde Donald, presided over the ceremony which concluded with the Reverend Donald providing the church's pastor, the Reverend Wesley Dudgeon with the match to set fire to the mortgage.

Fenton's Methodist Church could trace its origin to March of 1837, when six of the founders met in the log house of Levi Warren. Levi Warren owned a large tract of land east of the village and donated the land upon which the church was built. As the *Fenton Independent* reported, *"The story of the enterprise through the years is one of hardship, struggle, disaster as well as progress, achievement, victory"*

On the occasion of a project to enlarge the original building, the walls fell in while excavating, which entailed construction of an entirely new structure. Again in May of 1929, the new church school unit was about to be dedicated when a fire damaged the new addition and destroyed the church proper. In 1930, the Board of Trustees executed a $15,000 loan in order to rebuild the church building The congregation worshipped in the school rooms from 1930 until 1938 because the sanctuary had to go unfinished because of the lack of funds during the years of the Great Depression.

"By various financial methods, individual gifts, and six years of Saturday cafeteria suppers on part of the church ladies, the last bond was liquidated".

The leadership during this period was provided by the pastors, the Reverends Ira W. Cargo and Andrew Butt.. The Trustees during this difficult time were George Petts, Harold Roshaven, Fred Clark, Arthur Bush, John Cox, Eldon Richmond and Clare Severance.

#5 M.E Church Fire May 12-1929

In June of the 1946, the Reverend Wesley Dudgeon, who had served the Methodist Church in Fenton for over seven years, was reassigned to the Church in Mt. Morris and the Reverend Ralph D. Harper was appointed as his successor.

In mid-year we found the major churches in the village were pastored y the following ministers:

St. John Catholic	Reverend Daniel P. Tighe.
St. Jude's Episcopal	Reverend Robert W. Bell
First Baptist	Reverend H.G. Cooper
Trinity Lutheran	Reverend H. C. Kaas
First Presbyterian	Reverend Harley H. Stockham
Free Methodist	Reverend H. E. Leininger

Each of the churches had active women's originations which produced many valuable community and church-related programs. St. Jude's Episcopal Church had their Ladies' Guild, the Methodists had their Women's Society of Christian Women (W.S.C.W.), which was organized into "Bands", St. John supported the Young Ladies Sodality and an Alter Guild, the Presbyterians organized their ladies into "Cornerstones" and the :Lutherans and the Baptists had Ladies' Auxiliaries.

St. Jude's Guild elected Mrs. Arthur Smith as their President and VP Mrs. W.E. McCormack, and Treasurer Mrs. Floyd Coe. In May, the Guild sponsored a "Hollywood Breakfast" at the Fenton Community Center with Aldrich Locke presiding. The chairman for the event was Mrs. Ed Brazier. She was assisted by Mrs. A. E. Hiscox and Mrs. Irving Negus.

The Solidarity of St John Church sponsored a Mother–Daughter Breakfast on St Patrick's Day at the Fenton Community Center. The event attracted a capacity crowd of mothers, daughters and friends. Rosemary Lee chaired the event and was assisted by Helen Weigant, Doris Conarty, Carolyn Lee, June Boilore and Alice Adams

In May, the solemn initiation ceremony was conducted and eleven young ladies were welcomed as new members of Sodality. These were: Dorothy Winters, Katie Armstrong Barbara Swanebeck, Glendera Collins, Rosie Preston, Doris Leese, Violet and Rose Julie, Monica Camp, Helen Jeswick and Phyllis McCormick. June Boilore was in charge of the event.

As it had been for the past twenty years, the St. John Barbecue in July was a welcome community event. In addition to enjoying the beef and ham dinners, those attending enjoyed a concert presented by the Fenton City Band. New games were also enjoyed during the two day event.

When the Reverend Stockham arrived at the First Presbyterian church, he found a very active group of ladies, operating four "cornerstone" organizations. Some of the leaders of the "Cornerstones" were: Mrs. William Gould, Mildred Halstead, Mrs. Raymond Hyde, Mrs. Loula Riedel, and Mrs. Tom McKinley.

Why Invest in a 1947 Model Car When McDANIEL'S are Delivering

New 1948 Kaisers & Frazers

THERE NEVER WAS A RIDE LIKE THIS!

No Car Designed Before the War Can Even Compete with the Ride You Get in a KAISER or a FRAZER

You be the judge! You have driven and ridden in a lot of cars. You know how they ride. Now, get in a KAISER or a FRAZER and *compare the ride!* You're in for a pleasant surprise. For all your present standards of riding quality will become obsolete before you have gone a mile! You will agree that *no car designed before the war can even compete with the* KAISER *or the* FRAZER—for there *never was* a ride like this! You *drift* over rough roads. You *glide* along the pavement. It's a *horizontal* ride—with the *up and down travel* removed.

It's not just a matter of spring design and shock absorbers. Power, brakes, and ease of steering, all play a part. So do superior roominess, extraordinary visibility and extra-low center of gravity—with all the weight of passengers *between the wheels!* But what's the use of telling you *how* it's done! You are interested in the ride. *That* can't be described. It *must* be experienced. So, before you buy *any* car—*compare the ride!*

KAISER

LEARN FOR YOURSELF...

"Compare the Ride!"

McDaniel Motor Sales

608 N. Leroy Street   Phone 4322

Scene Five...It's All Business Downtown

This part of the story might better be titled "Independent Day", for in May of 1946, *The Fenton Independent* published its 4056th consecutive issue of the newspaper. With the May 2nd issue, the publication began its 79th year inexistence.

The Fenton Independent was founded by J.N. Jennings in 1869 and he remained its owner and editor until his son, J.H. Jennings, took over the enterprise for a short time prior to 1908. It was in 1908 that S.F. Beach became its owner and editor. The year 1946 marked the 40th anniversary of the newspaper under his ownership

Sol Faye Beach died on June 9th of this year. His passing was mourned by all in the village for Mr. Beach had played a very significant role in the community life outside the publication of the weekly journal. He was survived by his wife and son Robert. Robert Beach became the editor of the paper.

In August of the year, The Beach family purchased the villages only other weekly newspaper, *The Fenton Courier*. The ownership and management of the *Fenton Courier* had changed several times in recent years and appeared to be having difficulty competing with the more established *Fenton Independent*. As a consequence of this action, the *Fenton Independent* became the sole newspaper source for this book.

S.F. Beach

The Pellett's Department Store was celebrating its 25th Anniversary this year. Pellett's was the largest store in town and offered both men and women's clothing and accessories. George Pellett came to Fenton in 1921 following his service as an Army artillery officer in World War I. After a brief stint in the retail business in Mt. Morris, he came to Fenton and opened his store. Over the years Mr. Pellett had expanded and remodeled the store and its façade.

In mid-year, it was announced that two new buildings were to be constructed and available for occupancy when completed in September.. A four family apartment building was under construction at the corner of South Holly Road and East Street. Mr. Fred Raper, the owner, said the apartment house would be an "attractive, well-built brick building" that will help relieve the housing shortage. On Walnut Street, only a half a block south of the Post Office (then located at the corner of Walnut and Eat Carolina Streets) was the site of the second building project. It was called the "Fenton Professional Building".. "An office building especially designed for professional and business men". Both the apartment house and the office building continue to serve as intended and are occupied at the time of this writing.

The people of Fenton were heard to cry "Please…tell me it's not true" Mickey was selling his dairy and ice cream business! Mickey and Dorothy McBroom had started their dairy business some 23 years before and then added ice cream manufacturing to the enterprise. For years, people would drive for miles to enjoy an ice cream "treat" at Mickey's. The new owner, Mr. Charles Hathaway of Saginaw, promised the quality of product and the excellent friendly service would continue under his ownership.

Another of the established businesses…the O'Dell's Drug Store, marked their 23rd year as a store in Fenton. Additionally, the owner L.M O'Dell was completing his 42nd year in the drug business in Michigan. Son D.A. Odell joined his father in the business following his graduation from Ferris Institute. Another son, Gerald, owned a pharmacy in Clarkston.

It wasn't exactly a "new" business, but Hoskins Restaurant had undergone a complete remodeling throughout and was reopened in October. "Excellent food, cooked and prepared to taste" was promised by the new proprietors Kiley and Wheeler.

A very sociable young man from Byron, William "Bill" Gallagher, decided to open a new business in Fenton….a taxidermy and sporting goods store. Bill Gallagher was a man of many interests and talents. During the pre-war years he headed a "big" band that played in the area.• Bill Gallagher at the piano exuded personality and this personal appeal contributed to his business and social success in future years. Gallagher spent over four years in the Air Corps during WW II, studied Art in Europe and was an enthusiastic and competent hunter. He erected a new building on North Leroy Street at Fifth Avenue to display boating supplies and sporting goods of all kinds. He also provided a service to hunters…a place soon noted for processing deer skins.

• The author played alto saxophone in the band.1939-1940.

In November, the Michigan Bell Telephone Company began work on a new $40,000 telephone building at River and Caroline Streets. The one-story structure would be the first in Michigan built by Michigan Bell in a so-called contemporary architectural style. I was the first to employ radiant heating..

In 1946, as well as it is today and has been for many years, the prosperity of the automobile industry was very important to the welfare of the village and many of its citizens. With the end of the war, the automobile industry found its facilities in excellent condition even improved from their pre-war status. They had been building all types of vehicles and other war equipment and began tooling for automobile production. No automobile's had been built during the war years, so the industry brought out the designs of the 1941 vehicles and began producing "new" old cars. In October, the Buick Motor Division of General Motors in Flint, Michigan, reported that they had produced 23,373 cars during the month of September.. Volume was still restricted by continuing shortages or parts and material and other factors. September production had raised Buick's total 1946 output to 38,037 cars. Before the war, Buick's record month was March, 1941, when production reached 38,913 units.

Many people don't think of their Doctors as being in "business", however it is a business and as with most businesses they maintain "office hours" Early in the year some people complained that all of the Doctors in the Village chose Wednesday afternoons to "take off". If one needed a Doctor during a Wednesday afternoon, there were none available in town! In response to this concern, the town's Doctors got together and published a schedule of who will be available on Wednesday afternoons. The schedule published in December, 1946 was the following.

      Dec 11 …Dr. Walcott
      Dec 18…Dr .Ettinger
      Dec 25 …Dr. Rynearson
      Jan 1…....Dr. Buchanan
      Jan 8…....Dr. Walcott

Since 1938, Dr. R. Noble Peckham conducted his dental practice in downtown Fenton. In August of the year, after 33 month of service in the Navy, Dr. Paul Williams came to Fenton to continue the practice. Dr. Williams soon became an active member of the community

Another veteran of the Navy, Dr. Carl White was released from duty and returned to establish his practice in Fenton, where he had been practicing for several years prior to the war. He took the office space over the Fenton Drug Store, "The Corner Drug Store"...North Leroy and East Caroline. Dr. White was an Eye, Ear, Nose and Throat specialist.

Only a few months later, Paul Bottecelli, a long time Fenton resident, an Army veteran who served in combat in Italy as a Medical Corpsman and a graduate Pharmacist from Ferris Institute purchased the Fenton Drug Company. It was the beginning of a long and successful career in the industry for Mr. Bottecelli.*

Ralph Crawford, Curtis Schupbach and Cedric Whitman, all 1942 graduates from Fenton High School, joined the Army following graduation and upon discharge in 1946 they joined together and purchased the Fenton Concrete Block Company. They announced that they planned to produce a high quality product and do their part in meeting the demand for building materials.

There was considerable business activity in the village in 1946....the following summary is indicative of the volume and diversity of this activity:

- In January, Miss Elda Garnett and he cousin, Marjorie Fritts, opened "Elda's Portrait Studio in the business block of West Shiawassee Avenue.
- In February, Wyman Hardware, a newcomer to the community, installed a new neon sign to the front of his business and completely redecorated the store's interior.
- In March, Warren Anderson, who lives on Dauner Road, announced he is equipped to excavate, dig basements, do hauling and work of that nature.
- About the same time, Mr. and Mrs. E. Stoner, opened a new laundry in the space formerly occupied by the Fenton Floor Covering store on the south side of Leroy in the old Galloway Building

---

* This book is dedicated to Paul Bottecelli, Russell Haddon and Marge Johnson Kelley, See the dedication in the front of this book.

Act One... The Year 1946   29

- Later in May, Mrs. Hazel Parker sold her Downtown Beauty Nook to Alice P. Thompson of Flint. Evelyn Winter and Ruby Brown will continue as operators at the Beauty Nook.
- May 39th marked the opening of two new businesses…Huston Refrigeration Sales and Service and the Fenton Floor Covering. The two companies will occupy the same building at 403 South Leroy Street. ..
- In late May, Mr. and Mrs. C. L. Patten of Detroit, purchased the Fenton Coney Island, changed the restaurant's name to Patten's Grill and immediately began redecorating the store.
- In June, a former Navy cook, W. M. Garrow of Davison, purchased the Log Cabin Restaurant in the 100 block of North Leroy Street and renamed the restaurant :"The Fenton Coffee Shop".
- In July, Arnold "Sonny" Westman Jr., a returned veteran, did some extensive remodeling on his camera shop, the former Tamlyn's studio location.
- In July, Mr. and Mrs. E. M. Donaldson of Flint purchased Bender's Cleaners. The new owners kept the Bender's name, but promised extensive changes in the building, site for the plant and equipment.
- In August, Joe Rogers (one of the Rusinski brothers) took over the new Standard Oil Station at the corner of South Leroy and Ellen Street…just across the street from the Fire Hall. He named his business…Joe's Stand Service!
- A month later, Carol Lea opened the Fenton Resale Shoppe at her residence on north Leroy Street. She would have only women and children's clothing…all clean and in good condition.
- In November, Carrie W. Cornell opened her gift shop at the corner of Caroline and Walnut Streets. The sign outside read "The Treasure Chest".

A & P Advertisement May, 1946

VAN CAMP'S IMPROVED **BAKED BEANS**	16-Oz. Can	9c
RODERTS FRENCH STYLE **GREEN BEANS**	19-Oz. Can	18c
CREAM STYLE **Iona Corn**	20-Oz. Can	11c
ANN PAGE SALAD STYLE **Mustard**	9-Oz. Pkg.	10c
FIFTH AVENUE **Sweet Peas**	20-Oz. Can	17c
BEVERAGE MIX **Fla-Vor-Aids**	3 Pkgs.	10c
ENCORE, Broad or Fine **Noodles**	Lb. Pkg.	19c
JANE PARKER SUGARED **Donuts**	Dozen In Pkg.	15c
SUNNYFIELD CRISP, FRESH **CORN FLAKES**	11-Oz. Pkg.	8c
JANE PARKER APPLE-RAISIN **COFFEE CAKE**	Each	25c
MAKE TEMPTING SALADS—RAJAH **Salad Dressing**	Pint Jar	16c
ALMOND DELIGHT **Cookies**		14c
CREAMY, SMOOTH, SUTANA **Peanut Butter**	Lb. Jar	29c
JANE PARKER CRISP, TASTY **Potato Chips**	½-Lb. Bag	33c
EIGHT O'CLOCK **Coffee**	3 Lb. Bag	59c
COOLING ICED TEA **Our Own Tea**	½-Lb. Pkg.	31c
YLASIC CRISPY **Dill Pickles**	Qt. Jar	29c
NORTHERN **Tissue**	Roll	6c Limited Supply
PALMDALE FANCY ORANGE **Marmalade**	Pint Jar	26c
SULTANA BRAND **Cider Vinegar**	Qt. Bottle	17c

Intermission....Come Fly with Me!

Long before Frank Sinatra invited you to come and fly with him, a fellow named Herman Wessendorf was building an airfield and conducting flight training for those eager to fly way!

Herman Wessendorf was active with the Civilian Air Patrol and a strong proponent of aviation. Soon after the end of World War II, Wessendorf announced the development of an airport, Dauner Field. The field was located just north of Dauner Road and the Village limits and in the area east of Fenton Road (now North Leroy Street and within the present City limits). The airport building was east of the intersection of Fenton Road and South Long Lake Road.

The GI bill provided for pilot training for veterans and it was anticipated that the Fenton Airport would thrive on the training of these veterans. In May, with his partner Raymond Catsman, they began construction of two runways on the property. The North-South runway was 2,400 feet in length and the East-West runway was a bit shorter at 2,200 feet. They had one airplane at the beginning, a Cub trainer, and they engaged the services of Bob Chonoski, a veteran Army pilot, as their primary instructor. It was considered a $20,000 project at the time

It is interesting that the site, the former Dauner family farm, was used for aviation by the Williams School of Aviation in 1914 just before and after the end of World War One. The Williams operation was one of the first flying fields in the State. Today the area is the site of a strip mall and several other business ventures.

. In July, Veteran Dean Winters was the first student to "solo". Within a few weeks before the end of the month, he was joined by Max Kostka, Wayne Wessendorf, Erwin Whitehead, Marshall Brown, Chester Willing, Fred Walters, Fred Bigelow, Percy Way, Delmar Skutt, Garl Albers and Stewart Crego

In the process of earning your private license the students were required to complete a solo cross country flight. . Within a couple of months, the solo flyers named above were joined by many others including Howard Eble, Bob Lorenz, Bob Ireland, Alice Folland, Harry Bush, Bruce Runyan, Mary (Thompson) Locke, Red Warren, Walter Burrow, Don Biggs, William Martin, Jim Foley and Art Goodhue,

32   The Village Players Post War

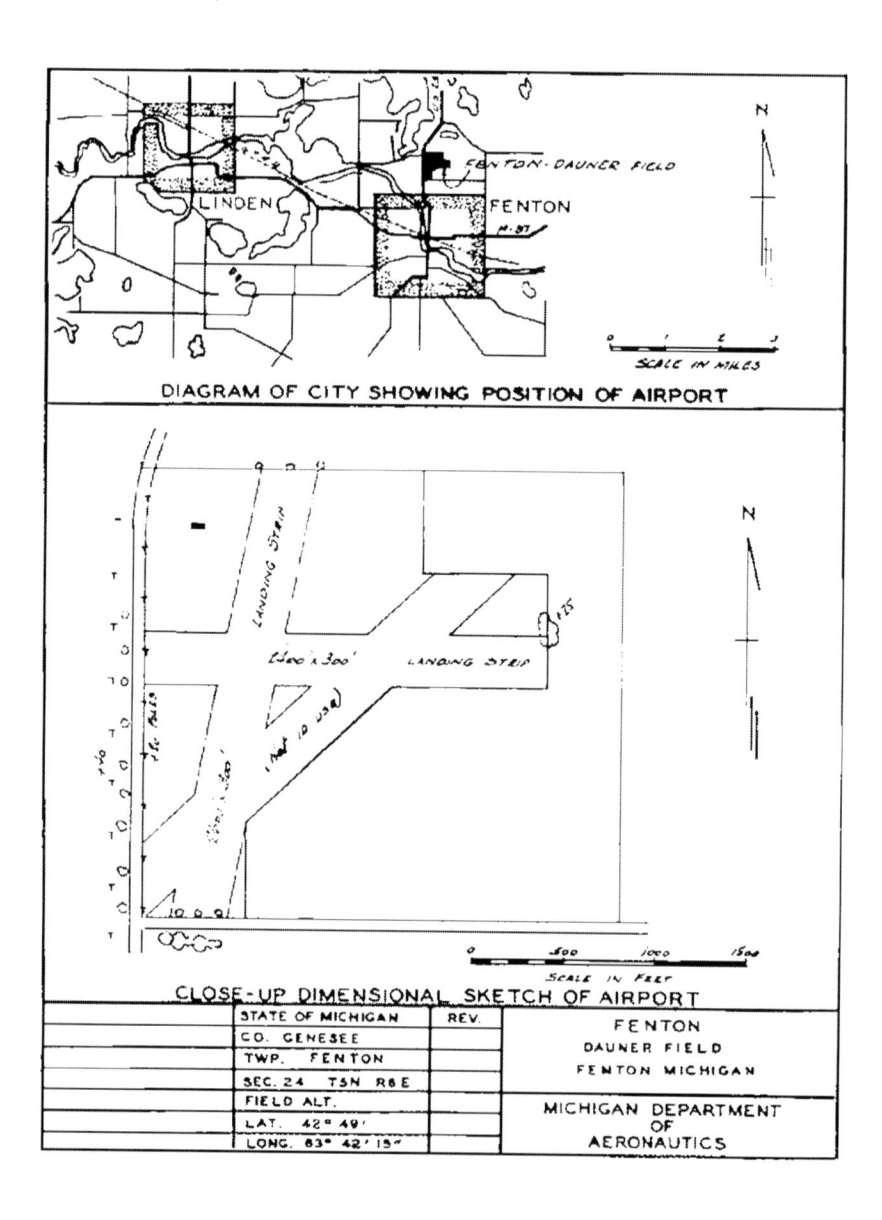

DIAGRAM OF CITY SHOWING POSITION OF AIRPORT

CLOSE-UP DIMENSIONAL SKETCH OF AIRPORT

STATE OF MICHIGAN	REV.	FENTON DAUNER FIELD FENTON MICHIGAN
CO. GENESEE		
TWP. FENTON		
SEC. 24 T5N R6E		
FIELD ALT.		MICHIGAN DEPARTMENT OF AERONAUTICS
LAT. 42° 49'		
LONG. 83° 42' 15"		

Dauner Field was located at the Northeast corner of Dauner Road and Fenton Road (now North Leroy Street). Property is now the location of a shopping mall and other buildings within the Fenton City limits. Source of sketch is the Michigan Airport Directory 1946-1947.

In October of the year, some of the "flyers" joined together and purchased a surplus Army trainer, a BT-13. Members of the "club" were Fred Bigelow, Earl Carmer, Chet Willing, Harry Ephraim, Bob Lorenz, Llewellyn Crystal, Bob Ballard, Don Carnegie and Herman Wessendorf. Within a few months, the group sold the Vultee BT-13 to a group in Flint.

BT-13 Vultee

When their first winter arrived, the activity at the airport slowed a bit, but the cold weather and snow didn't stop Don and Jim Bump from completing their solo flights. Other newcomers starting their programs were Phillip Garvey, Dick Edinger, Howard Ayliffe and Frank McClure. "Old Timers" Chester and Gilbert Hatfield, Graham Peterson and Russell Reynolds continued to fly at Dauner.

Two of the students who earned their Private Pilot's license early were Gerald Neil and Lloyd Ayliffe. In June of 1946, Gerald S. Neil was flying over Mundy Township, northwest of the field, practicing stalls. After stalling the aircraft, the plane began its downward spiral. To recover from the spin, he gunned the engine, but unfortunately, he did not have enough altitude to complete the recovery and he crashed into a wooded area and was killed. Mr. Neil was 24 years old and a veteran of World War II.

Another serious accident involving Dauner Field pilots was in Mid-May of 1950, when Don Carnegie failed to clear some trees at the end of the runway while taking off. The left wing of the airplane hit one of the trees and the plane went into the ground nose down. Don Carnegie escaped serious injury and was fortunate to only suffer some lacerations and cuts. .After treatment by Dr. Ralph Ettinger, he was sent to Hurley Hospital in Flint for observation and further treatment.

Bob Ireland was one of the first to win his Private Pilots license at Dauner Field. In 1949, Bob's wife May (Thompson) was hospitalized with appendicitis and Mr. Ireland had the need for a "baby-sitter" for his daughter, Kathleen. Phyllis Banks was Ireland's regular "sitter" and she was vacationing in St.Ignace, in Michigan's Upper Peninsula at the time, however she agreed to return to Fenton to be with Kathleen during her mother's hospitalization.

Bob Ireland decided to fly to St.Ignace with his daughter and return with Miss Banks. As their plane was approaching Mackinac Island, they were flying in a dense fog when they crashed into the water. No one witnessed the crash; however those on a boat nearby heard the airplane engine and then the sound of the crash. A search of the area did not find a trace of the aircraft or its occupants. To this day, what really happened is a mystery and several searches have been conducted with negative results.

The spring of 1947 brought the rains and the dirt runways became seas of mud and water. The *Fenton Independent* column said they were considering changing the name of Dauner Field to the Dauner Lake and start a seaplane base. But soon the winds came and dried up the runways, so the planes were flying again.

Herman Wessendorf and his instructor John Downing went to Detroit and took delivery of a new PT-26 for the Commercial Flight Training program. The airplane was a red low wing monoplane with a 300 HP Ranger engine that would do 120 MPH. It was equipped with dual instruments, plus landing lights, flaps and a two way radio. It was licensed for both day and night flying.

Several of the local residents, especially in the early days, complained about low flying aircraft, but as time passed, most of the airport's neighbors became adjusted to the "noise". However, the residents of Lake Fenton complained enough for the Michigan Department of Aeronautics to hold a public hearing...but not about the Dauner fliers... but concerning the landing of seaplanes on Lake Fenton

PT-26

In July of 1947, the Michigan State department renewed the license to conduct flight training under the G.I. Bill. According to the Veterans Administration, the flight schools in Michigan were conducting 23% of the G.I. flight training in the nation.

The summer of 1947 found Don Kundinger, Lloyd Steffey, Frank McClure and Harry Ephraim flying their solo cross country flights.

Intermission — Come Fly with Me! 35

Llewellyn Crystal received his private license and as his first flight, he flew his mother, Mrs Hazel Crystal, to Grand Rapids to visit his grandmother who had recently suffered a stroke.

Howard Carlson began his flight training on a Wednesday and soloed on the following Saturday, which was a record time to solo at Dauner. Another "first" was set when Mary (Thompson) Locke was the first female to receive her Private Pilots License at the field.

Another "first" was when Harry Bush, Del Skutt, Fred Bigelow and Glenn Dobbs, who were working on their commercial license, completed their cross-country trips using the radio aids. Walden MacKenzie and Graham Paterson started their commercial training immediately after receiving the Private Pilot rating.

Warren Anderson, who operated an excavating business in Fenton, discovered his plane could be used in his business as well as for pleasure. When one of his machines broke down and he was in need of a new part, Anderson and his wife flew to Aurora, Illinois and returned the same day with the part.

"Old Habits" were found to effect the enrollment of new students. Once the hunting season was over, Don Van Wagoner, Kenneth Manns, Lewis Cummings, Gene Thompson and Bill Feldman signed up for the training program.

The operators of the flying service were very aggressive in their advertising and recruiting. The advertisement on the following page was in almost every issue of the *Fenton Independent* during the year.

It is not known when the flying from Dauner Field came to an end. The Michigan Bureau of Aeronautics reported records on hand did not go back to the time, a search of the internet for "abandoned Airfields" produced negative results. Those individuals who learned to fly at Dauner are for the most part deceased or not to be found in the area, so no direct information is available from the "old" flyers. It is generally assumed that Dauner Filed closed down before 1950, but exactly when is not known to the author.

VETERANS!
Learn to Fly

The U. S. Government Will Pay For Your Lessons

If you served 3 months or more in World War II, you are eligible to receive flying instructions from any approved flight school

Up to $3,000 Flying Time

NO AGE LIMIT—NOTHING DEDUCTED FROM ANY POSSIBLE FUTURE BONUS PAYMENT.

ONLY COST TO VETERANS NOT TO EXCEED $1.50 PER MONTH, FOR INSURANCE, ETC.

SPECIAL FLYING COURSES FOR CIVILIANS

SPECIAL FLYING COURSES FOR CIVILIANS ADVANCED AND BEGINNERS

—•—

Scenic Airplane Rides
$2.50

COMPLETE NEW EQUIPMENT

—•—

See or Call

HERMAN WESSENDORF
DAUNER FIELD

For Further Information
Phone 2-4171 or 2-3297

Scene Six...."Stand Up and Cheer"

"Stand Up and Cheer, Stand Up and Cheer for Fenton High"! The voices of the students and friends seemed even louder than ever before as the FHS teams excelled in all of the varsity sports.

Student reporter Marc Peck had been writing about Fenton High School sports for several years in both of the local newspapers. He was a talented, colorful writer in most respects, but the headlines he used were quite unique. A few examples of his headlines from his articles about the basket ball team in the 1945-1946 season illustrate the point.

* FENTON FACES FLUSHING FRIDAY
* BRAINY BENGAL BUCKET BOYS BATTER BREATHLESS BENDLE
* CAGERS CLOUT CLIO'S CELLAR CREW
* SNIPERS STREAK SOARS TO SEVENTEENTH STRAIGHT
* CAGE CREW CAPTURES COUNTY CHAMPIONSHIP

However unusual the headline may have been, the headlines did tell the story for the 1945-1946 FHS Basketball season. The 1945-1946 Basketball team picked up the winning habits of the 1944-1945 Championship team by opening the season with an astounding 102-17 victory over Swartz Creek. This victory was followed by wins over Howell 57-22 and Flint Technical 25-19.

The team went undefeated, winning 20 games in a row, before losing to St. Joseph in the final game of the State tournament. The Fenton Tigers were the undefeated County Champions for two years in a row and their overall two year record was 37 wins and 2 losses. The 1945-1946 team members were Bob Torrey, Vince Harrison, John Howe, George Howe, Ken Wegner, Ned Jaggi, Bobby Butts, Phil Kelley, Clare Whitman and Don Orthner.

The FHS Basketball "big three"...Vince Harrison, Bob Torrey and John Howe... received recognition for their excellent play during their exceptional season. All three were named to the All County First Team and all three were made Honorable Mention on the *Detroit Times* All-State squad. Vince Harrison was also named Honorable Mention on the *Detroit Free Press* All State team.

FHS 1945-1946 Basketball Team

Front Row: Bobby Butts, Ken Wegner, John Howe, Bob Torrey, Vince Harrison, George Howe.
Second Row: Coach Ivan Williams, Reporter Marc Peck,
Ned Jaggi, Phil Kelley, Clare Whitman, Don Orthner,
Mgr Art Bush, Mgr Alan Niskana

The spring sports always have the weather with which to contend. In 1946, the last recorded snowfall was on March 11th, and the temperatures in April and May were moderate to warm. If it hadn't been for the occasional rainy days, it would have been like "Camelot".

Coach Ivan Williams had a group of talented candidates report for the opening day of baseball practice in early April. Ted Moore, Don Orthner, Bobby Butts and Bill Brabon formed a quartet of experienced outfielders. George Granger, Vince Harrison, Junior Whitman and Bob Cole were experienced infielders. Bob Torrey and Frank Winn were both tested and capable catchers. It was expected that First Baseman Bob Cole would be challenged by Estel Gushwa and Ned Jaggi.

There was some concern about the pitching. Don Orthner, George Granger,, Ted Moore and Jack McKeon were expected to do the pitching. Many of the players had gained considerable experience by playing summer baseball in the American Legion leagues. For example, Bill Brabon didn't earn a letter at FHS in the previous season but playing in the Flint American Legion League for a Linden team, he batted over .400 in playing as their regular right fielder

The team had a very good season with an 11-2 record. However, they lost to the County Champions Bendle 2-0 and had to settle for 2nd place in the conference. The season ended with a On-Loss record of 12-2. Don Orthner was the leading pitcher and Vince Harrison hit for a .440 average to lead the team in hitting. Other "top" batting averages were: Jack McKeon (.420), George Granger (.407), Frank Winn (.370) and Don Orthner (.305).

The schools athletic fields were on the west side, directly behind the school buildings. The area was one large rectangular field extending along Ellen Street to West Street. During the football season, the goal posts and the chalk lines delineated the playing area. Portable wooden benches were provided for each of the two competing teams on opposite side of the playing field. Portions of the field were usually bare of grass, since the "game" field was also the "practice" field.

FHS 1946 Baseball Team

First Row: George Granger, Don Orthner, Jack McKeon, Ted Moore, Estell Gushwa, Bob Butts, Vince Harrison, Second Row: Bill Brabon, Frank Winn, Chuck Franks, Bud Cole, Clare Whitman, .Art Bush

A four-lane cinder track circled the football field and during the spring of the year, the track and field athletes used the facility...however, they did not have exclusive use of the area.

The baseball diamond was positioned in the southeast corner of the large field, with the backstop closest to the school buildings and Ellen Street. The center fielder would be positioned around the fifty-yard line and a trackman would find his way around the track just beyond second base. The available outdoor space was well utilized and while there was some overlapping, no one complained.

It's worthy to note that the 1946 team had to play on the old "diamond" directly behind the school buildings. It was not until the next year before baseball was played on a new "diamond" at the corner of Ellen and West Streets in Phillips Field.

Along with Baseball, the FHS athletes were active with the Track Team. FHS was the defending Regional Champions in Track and the expectations for a successful season were very high.

Just two days before the opening competition with Clio, returnee Ray Steede, who was consistently good for ten points in the field events, suffered a bone separation in his foot while pole vaulting and was lost for the season. Even though Clio swept the filled events, earning all of the 36 points in these events, Fenton won the3 meet by a 68-36 count.

The performances in the meet were indicative of the performances to be repeated throughout the season. Allen Gale won the 440, followed by Dick Perry and Bruce Cornell; John Howe won the low and high hurdles, ran the anchor in the winning relay team; Brother George Howe won the mile going away, followed by Bob Stiff and Allan Niskanen; Vince Harrison won both the 100 and the 220 with Bud Cole and Royce Hyde close behind and Ken Wegner would battle with Chuck Frank and Howard Bacon for the laurels in the 880 yard dash. Others who contributed during the season were Bob Glaspie, Ken Wegner and Maurice Neely.

While they came in second in the Regional meet, mostly due to weakness in the field events, as well as the rain that created some muddy conditions, miler George Howe struggled through the mud to win his race with one of his slowest times.

In the State meet, George Howe won the Mile run in a record time of 4:36.6, his best time ever and a new school record. His brother John didn't win any of his events, but placed in high hurdles and cleared 5 feet 4 inches in the broad jump.

FHS 1946 Track Team

First Row: Allan Gale, Maurice Neely, Ray Steede, Ken Wegner, Phil Kelley, John Howe, Bruce Corneil, Dick Perry, Bob Glaspie.
Second Row: Bob Stiff, Chuck Franks, Frank Winn, Royce Hyde, Vince Harrison, George Howe, Bud Cole, Alan Niskanan

It may have come about because of the ending of the war, but for whatever reason, there was a renewed interest in the game of golf. This interest generated the establishment of a Golf Club at FHS. August Arndt, FHS principal sponsored the club and Shoreacres Golf and Country Club was selected for the site of lessons, practice and competitive matches. It was planned to move to Golf as a varsity sport at FHS if the club was successful. The Club "Pro" Ralph Crane provided his services for the members. The members were Roderick Dexler, Robert Kessler, John Howe, Stuart King, Don Orthner, Marc Peck, Richard Pratt, Jack Reed, Russell Roberts, James Strayer, John Wright and Penrod Wright

Summer arrived and the FHS varsity athletic program for the 1945-1946 came to a close and as the new school year approached it was "Football" that everyone was talking about.

Having won the County Championship for the past two years, winning the third consecutive Crown was everyone's goal for the season. The season started out as if the third Championship was in hand. The team won the first four games of the season beating

Davison, Grand Blanc and Bendle by identical scores of 26-0. Kearsley lost by 20-13, as Fenton's passing attack provided the winning margin. George Howe, who had played Tackle in the 1945 season, was playing halfback this year and set school passing records during the first five games. Unfortunately for George Howe and the team, George chipped a bone in his hip and was lost for the remainder of the season. With the loss of Howe the team lost their potent passing offense, Fenton was tied by Clio and later lost to Bendle by a 7-6 score. This loss knocked them out of the conference lead. Wins over Mt. Morris and Flushing put them in second place and on Thanksgiving Day, Grand Blanc defeated Bendle to win the County Championship. The season ended with the traditional Thanksgiving morning game with Holly....which ended in a scoreless tie.

.FHS 1946 Football Team

1st Row L-R Jim Walter, Penrod Wright, Carl Butts, Jack Groll, Ned Jaggi, Frank Winn, Bernard Sinclair, Bob Glaspie, Bud Cole, Clare Whitman. 2nd Row: Asst Coach Emil Gosseaux, Mgr. Allan Niskanen, Allan Gale, Frank Helms, Jim Bottecelli, Leo Foley, George Howe, Phil Scott, Charles Franks, Vern Clark, Charles Helms, Coach Ivan Williams. 3rd Row: Bill Hill, Dick Perry, Norm Spear, Cline G.Hagerman, Bruce Dorland, Pat Foley, Bill Brabon, Garner Merrick, Bill Freeman, Don Schupbach, Mgr. Jim Lathrop.

"Scat back" Bob Glaspie broke out for many long runs during the season, but was dubbed "bad luck Bob" since on more than a few occasions, his long gain would be cancelled because of a penalty. Bob was an Honorable Mention for the All County team. Receiver Ned

Jaggi was named to the First Team and George Howe, even with playing only five games, was named to the 2nd All-County team.

The team roster included Bill Brabon, Clare "Junior" Whitman, Jim Walter, George Howe, Bob Glaspie, C. Helms, Jim Bottecelli, Frank Helms, Jack Groll, Bernard Sinclair, Leo Foley, Ned Jaggi, Frank Winn, Phil Scott, Bud Cole, Bob Butts, Norm Spear, Bruce Dorland, Allan Gale, , Max Bottecelli, Chuck Franks and Bill Hill

As the 1946-1947 Basketball season began, there was considerable concern as to whether George Howe, the only returnee from last years Championship team, would be able to play this season. But George Howe recovered from his hip injury and played exceptionally well during the season.

The FHS "Tigers" started the 1946-1947 season as if it were a continuation of the previous two championship years. They defeated Swartz Creek 57-5 in the opening tilt but followed with a 27-29 loss to Howell. They regained their winning status by defeating Flint Tech 50-42. Then, after Christmas break, they began playing their conference schedule. How would they fare in the County...time would tell!

Author's Note: The picture below is of the 1947 Graduates positioned in front of the North Entrance to the Fenton High School building. The photo was placed here for no other reason than it was too good of picture of the school entrance to not include in this book. Those of us who attended high school in this building may have forgotten what beautiful architecture these entrances represented...and there were two them. The lintals (the horizontal stone pieces above the doors) have been preserved and it is planned to use them as benches in Alumni Park along side of "The Rock" near Ivan Williams Stadium.

Men

Good Jobs

Are

Available

NOW

at

PONTIAC MOTOR DIVISION

APPLY

Employment Office
On
Glenwood Ave.

Scene Seven...What are the Students Doing?

At Fenton High School, in addition to the election of the Class officers, there were elections for the Student Council. The members of the FHS Student Council planned the dances, the Homecoming Parade, the Carnival, the All-Hi Banquet and other student activities. The FHS Student Council's actions were probably not very different than those of the Student Councils of most other High Schools in the nation, except for one very unusual and suspiciously illegal project

In 1943, C. J. Furlong longtime member of the Fenton School Board, had his eye on the vacant land directly south of the school's athletic field for use by the school. In mid-June, Mr. Furlong, who was then serving as the Board's secretary, learned that the owners, the heirs to the Phillips estate, were about to put the land up for sale. He immediately arranged a meeting with the heirs, Mrs. Julia Hart and Mr. and Mrs. E.A. Phillips,and the administrator of the Phillips estate.

Mr. Furlong told the party of the schools interest in the land for use as an athletic field. He pointed out that the current field was overtaxed by the use of school athletes and the town recreational activities. He requested that the estate propose a sales price so he could take the proposal of purchasing the land to the School Board for their consideration and action.

Within a few days, the Phillips estate declined to sell the land to the schools, but wished to make a gift of this 6-¾ acre parcel to the schools. There were only two conditions for the gift: the land would be used for school athletics and be fenced. The Board accepted the gift and looked forward to improving the land for athletic use. The field was not used for several years but was eventually dedicated as Phillips Field and became the "Home of the Tigers" for several decades to come.*

Now that the war was over, the townsfolk as well as the School Board were in support of the FHS students in their desire to play football "under the lights". Before the war, Grand Blanc High School had installed lights at their football field and their first opponent was the Fenton Tigers. Fenton not only won the game but acquired an interest in playing "under the lights".

---

* The Village Players, Robert G.Harris

The Student Council had established a fund for the purpose of installing lights at Phillips Field; however they were about $1,500 short of the amount required. In early May, representatives of the Student Council met with members of the Kiwanis and XX Clubs to discuss a plan to raise the funds in time to have the lights installed for the 1946 football season.

The plan was for the Student Council to issue certificates of $10 each bearing interest of 1% per year payable on or before five years from June 1st 1946. The townsfolk supported the project and a total of $1,700 was raised The Council planned to pay the entire amount of the loan from the receipts from athletic games. A large increase in attendance at the night football games was anticipated.

The lights were installed in time for the opening game against Davison and the increase in receipts from an increase in attendance at the football games made it possible to repay the total amount of $1,700 plus interest as of December 1st.

```
No 6142            FENTON HIGH SCHOOL            $10.00
                   STUDENT COUNCIL               DATED JUNE 1, 1946
              ATHLETIC FIELD LIGHTING FUND CERTIFICATE
THE FENTON HIGH SCHOOL STUDENT COUNCIL, FOR VALUE RECEIVED, PROMISES, TO PAY TO THE
ORDER OF _____
the sum of _____ TEN and no/100 _____ DOLLARS
ON DECEMBER 1, A. D. 1951, WITH INTEREST FROM DATE HEREOF AT 1% PER ANNUM, ALL BEING PAY-
ABLE AT STATE SAVINGS BANK OF FENTON, FENTON, MICHIGAN.
    This Certificate is one of a series of 150 of like date and and amount, aggregating the sum of $1500.00, issued for the
purpose of financing in part the installation of an adequate lighting system on the Fenton High School Athletic Field,
the payment of said series of certificates, with interest, to be made from receipts from athletic activities.
    The right is reserved to redeem this certificate on the first day of December of any year prior to the stated matur-
ity date, such redemption to be by lot, and in amount to be determined by officers of the Student Council. Payment
of interest in all cases to be made at date of principal payment.
    Issuance of this series of certificates was authorized by action of the Student Council at a special meeting called
for that purpose on May 20, 1946.
```

While venturing into the world of "high finance", the Student Council conducted regular business and organized the annual All-Hi Banquet.. The traditional banquet was held in April and this year's theme was "Holidays". The Freshmen was symbolically represented the "spring season" and the Easter Holiday. The Class selected John Wright to be their speaker at the affair. Summer's Independence Day belonged to the Sophomore and their speaker was Alan Niskanen. The Junior's theme was the third season…and Thanksgiving. Marc Peck was their speaker. And last, but not least (as they say), the Seniors were given Christmas.

The Toastmaster for the All-Hi event was senior Frances Shaw. Mr. Kieft, head of the drafting and manual training departments spoke for the faculty.. Following the banquet, Jack Dowling and his Orchestra played for dancing at the High School Gymnasium

In May, the Junior Class was responsible for the most popular social event …the J-Hop. This J-Hop was not much like the hops in past years. The ballroom at the Fenton Community Center had been transposed into a tropical isle. Hawaiian scenes decorated the walls…. palms, tropical plants and vines were everywhere. A native grass hut had been constructed at one end of the ballroom

All the young ladies were in formal attire and the young men wore their best suit and best shirt and tie. Jack Dowling's Orchestra was again engaged to provide the music for dancing. A record crowd attended the hop, exceeding the attendance of the preceding year which attracted 82 couples. The J-Hop was held at the Fenton Community Center and the ticket cost was $2 per couple.

The class sponsor was Miss Ann Paynich. The committee members responsible for the extravaganza were as follows:

> **Decoration:** Shirley Scott, Jeanne Thorpe, George Howe, Ned Jaggi, Caroline Chidlaw, Dallas Goss, Sally Cowan, Bernard Sinclair, Ethel Davis, Marge Bachus, Floyd Guernsey and Marilyn Hogan.
> **Favors**: Jimmy Edwards, Betty Shields, Barb Hyde, Beth Gordon, Julianne Rounds, Frank Winn and Dick Pratt.
> **Refreshments**: Mary Alice Gordon, Norma Kelley and Sue Harper.
> **Tickets:** Penrod Wright, Connie Standridge, Marion Alchin, Marie Moorman, Bruce Trimmer and Clare Whitman.
> **Advertising:** Marc Peck, Ralph Husband and Bonnie O'Berry.

48 The Village Players Post War

The FHS 1946 J-Hop Grand March at the Fenton Community Center

First Row L-R: Robert Glaspie, Betty Wenderlein, , Penrod Wright, Ann Gudith, Merelyn Burton, Jim Bottecelli, Mildred Miller, and Bruce Trimmer.

Before the end of the year, in November, the Student Council sponsored another "extravaganza"...The "All-Hi Carnival". George Howe was selected as the: Student manager and from all reports he did a very good job...with the help of a lot of active and imaginative helper. Each of the classes and school clubs produced some interesting and some times a unique "sideshow".. There was a concession well stocked with hot dogs, pop corn, apples, soft drinks and donuts and they sold their entire inventory during the event. :

Some of the concession booths in the Gymnasium were as follows: Spill the Milk, Sock the Teacher, Coke Bottle Toss, Basketball Throw, Dart Throw, Penny Toss, Fish Pond and Hit the Dodger.

In the various classrooms other activities were being conducted. These concessions offered a Zoo, Beauty Parlor, Fortune Telling, Dancing, Movies, Hall of Horror, Little Theater, Hobby Show, Baby Show, Radio Studio, Roman Shop, Dog Show and a House of Magic. .

The All-Hi Carnival was very well attended and the proceeds for the event were placed in a fund for the construction of a concession stand at the Phillips Field.

The students ...and the townsfolk...had every right to be boastful of the music program at Fenton High School. Both the Band and the Choral and Choir ensembles were recognized as being first class. In addition as performing as a Marching Band during the football season, the band presented several concerts during the school year. The Annual Spring Concert was held in early May at the Fenton Community Center. Marion Alchin playing the flute and Howard Bacon with the trombone were featured soloists. The highlight presentation was provided with the band playing "Deep Blues" and featuring Bernard Sinclair on the trumpet.

In late March, the Band sponsored a Solo and Ensemble Festival at the Community Center. Keith Stein of Michigan State College served as the adjudicator and rated the various players. Fifteen schools with over 100 soloists, duets, trios, quartets and their accompanists were represented The Fenton band members playing at the Festival included: Bob Wessendorf (tenor sax), Carol Woodworth (cornet), Marion Nash (clarinet), Jerry Hatfield (clarinet), Marion Alchin (flute), Bernard Sinclair (cornet) and Howard Bacon (trombone).

There was much more going on than just "fun and games" at Fenton High School...there was "ah whole lot of learnin': goin' on"!

Many of the radio "jingles" were still playing in the Post-War years. Here are a few of the most popular...

"Pepsi Cola hits the spot,
Six full ounces, that's a lot,
Twice a much for a nickel too,
Pepsi Cola is the drink for you"

"Halo everybody, Halo
Halo is the shampoo that glorifies your hair,
Halo shampoo, Halo"

"Brill Cream, a little dab will do ya,
Brill Cram, you'll look so debonair,
Brill Cream, the gals will pursue ya,
They love to run their fingers through your hair"

"You better get Wild Root Cream Oil, Charlie,
Start using it today,
You'll find you will have a tough time, Charlie,
Keeping all the girls away,
"Hi ya, Charlie",
Get Wild Root right awaaaaaay"

Scene Eight...Alumni, PTA and the Board of Education

The Alumni Association of the Fenton High School was inactive during the war years, but with the end of hostilities they rapidly reorganized and began the practice of having an annual reunion banquet

On the evening of June 14th, over 500 alumni came to the Fenton Community Center for the Alumni Banquet. The number attending required the seating of about 200 people in the hall outside of the Center's auditorium.

Following the dinner, served by the ladies of the Presbyterian Church, the Association President J.C. Peck introduced the Toastmaster, Judge Ira W. Jayne, FHS Class of 1900. Superintendent Clarence Heemstra and two former Superintendents, J. W. Sexton and John A. Dalrymple also were called upon for remarks

John Jennings, Class of 1879, was recognized as the oldest Alumnus in attendance and Miss Bessie Cramer was presented with an orchard in honor of having the longest teaching record at Fenton High School.

On the following Monday, the Association held a meeting at the Community Center at which time they elected a new slate of officers. George C. Paine was elected President. Others elected were: 1sy VP J. C. Peck, 2nd VP Kenneth Pettis, Secretary Thelma Clement and Treasurer Warren Roberts.

The Parent-Teacher Association had been active for several years and had primarily focused on providing "hot lunches" for the students. The P.T.A held regular meetings that were well attended and on occasion would have a program with a outside speakers. In January a Professor Koch from the Education Department of the University of Michigan spoke to over 250 parents and teachers.

Most of the people of Fenton were interesting in having a ice skating area other than the mill pond. In years past, there had been several youngsters who went through the ice in the mill pond. The P.T.A. approached the City Council with the request that the city flood the school athletic field and create a skating area. This was not the first time the field or some other area had been flooded...all efforts were not very successful...it was found that maintaining ice for skating is a difficult task.

At the beginning of a new School year, the P.T.A. made a substantial effort to bring new families and others into the organization, and held a well published "get acquainted" meeting. New members and a renewed interest in the organization was attained..

On December 18th, a special program of Christmas music by the grade children and the FHS Chorus, both directed by Mrs. Lucille Buta, the highly respected music teacher at FHS. The program was held at the high school and was well attended.

The ultimate authority in the Fenton Schools was the Board of Education. There weren't many situations they encountered that they couldn't handle, but in the winter of 1945 the bushy browed leader of the United Mine Workers, John L. Lewis, created a situation beyond their ability to solve. The UAW was on strike in defiance of President Truman and the U.S. government. This prolonged strike caused a severe shortage of coal...and the detrimental effect finally hit the Village of Fenton in late November.

The great majority of the homes and business and public buildings ere heated with coal burning furnaces. Many families were having a difficult keeping warm and finally the Board of Education decided to close the school buildings until they were able to obtain a new supply of coal. In mid-December, they announced the schools would be closed until January 6th. But then....read what student reporter Barbara Hyde wrote in her column "School Daze" in *The Fenton Independent* on December 12th, 1946.

> Never in their lives were the Fenton students so enraged with John L. as they were when the coal strike ended. Of course they were glad to have their homes heated again, but just when Mr. Lewis was actually doing some good---that is forcing the school board to close school 'till January 6th---he called the thing off! As a result we're all back at the grindstone again this week with another six days to go. Oh, the life of a student!

The elections for positions on the Fenton Board of Education never stirred much interest in the townsfolk; consequently, a small group of dedicated men were often unchallenged and served as Board members year after year. Fortunately for all concerned, these dedicated men were also well qualified and the Fenton schools were recognized for their quality education.. Years before the inception of regional certification organizations the Fenton schools were recognized by the University of Michigan and graduates of the Fenton High School would have their high school courses accepted at full faith when enrolled at the University.

Harry A. Lowe was President of the Board with Paul N. Stedman as Treasurer, Clyde J. Furlong as Secretary and members Walter E. Walpole and Harold K. Schaefer. In June the Board elections were held and Mr. Furlong and Mr. Schaefer retained their positions for another three year term. With only 185 votes cast, the challengers Ralph C. Rossman and Alyce R. Cook received 28 and 16 votes respectively

L-R Clarence Heemstra, Paul Stedman, Clyde Furlong, Harry Lowe, Walter Walpole, Harold Schaefer.

The Superintendent was Clarence R. Heemstra and the high school principal was August Arndt. At the time, Mr. Heemstra had served as the Superintendent for thirteen years. Mr. Arndt had served FHS for eleven years, seven years as a teacher of Mathematics which he has continued to teach during his four years as Principal.

During the war years, it was difficult to fill all of the teaching positions at FHS, especially with men teachers. For some time, Mr. Heemstra was required to "double" as the Track coach and Coach Ivan Williams was without an assistant. for Football or Basketball.. With the opening of school in the fall, the Board was pleased to hire Mr. Emile Gosseaux to teach science and mathematics and assist Mr. Williams in coaching.. Others on the teaching staff for the fall semester were: Miss Eleanor Annis, Miss Esther Becker, Miss Hazel Brown, Miss Bessie Cramer, Mrs. Beulah Deweese, Mr. Dwight Fisher, Miss Joyce Haglund,

54 The Village Players Post War

Mr. Maurice Keift, Miss Miriam Kinner, Miss Evelyn Northrup, Miss Tamara Reeves, Mr. Howard Park, Miss Ann Paynich, Mr. Alfred Scholten, Mrs. Esther Stehle, Mr. Ivan Williams Mr. Charles Leighton.

Supt Clarence R. Heemstra

Principal August Arndt

FHS Faculty 1946-1947

1st Row L-R Miss Joyce Haglund, Miss Esther Becker, Mr. C.R. Heemstra, Mr. August Arndt, Miss Tamara Reeves, Miss Evelyn Northrop. 2nd Row L-R Miss Miriam Kinner, Miss Ann Paynich, Mr. Dwight Fisher, Mr. Howard Park, Mr. Maurice Kieft, Miss Eleanor Annis, Mrs. Hazel Brown. 3rd Row L-R Mrs. Lucille Buta, Miss Bessie Cramer, Mr. Emile Gosseaux, Mr. Alfred Scholten, Mr. Ivan Williams, Mrs. Esther Stehle, Mrs. Beulah DeWeese

Scene Nine..."The" Fenton Community Center

Since its beginning in 1938, the Fenton Community Center was "the" center of the community's cultural, recreational and social activities. The center was provided a meeting place for many of the villages clubs and organizations. Since its inception in 1941, the Fenton Kiwanis has held its weekly luncheon meeting at the FCC

During the War years those in charge of the FCC struggled to keep the activity calendar full and exciting...and they did a very good job of it. Russell Haddon had been called to duty with the Navy and Than Chesnut was an excellent substitute Director, with the end of the war and the return of Russ Haddon, the FCC was rejuvenated and 1946 promised to be a really good year!

The FCC Director Russell Haddon\ was assisted by a citizen's volunteer group, the Community Council, which was comprised of 53 representatives from the various churches and civic organizations in the village. It was important to "revitalize" the Community Council in view of the many new requests for services, such as the Village Council asking for a street to street investigation to find rooms, apartments and buildings suitable for conversion to dwellings. .A Federal Agency asked for assistance in the collection of food and funds for the war ravaged, undernourished nations. Locally, a group was asking for a comprehensive study of adult education and the establishment of a representative group to plan courses of study and training for adults. It wasn't like the "'ol days"...many more and diversified activities were being expected.

"Than" Chesnut

Russell Haddon

In May, the Community Council met to elect new officers and plan their programs for the coming year. Douglas Clarke, a veteran and active in P.T.A .and other civic activities was elected President. Don Bristol, a representative of the Methodist Church was named Vice President. Mrs. G.L. Wright, a Charter Member of the Council, was sleeted as

Secretary-Treasurer. Mrs. Wright\ had been mainly responsible for the community health program which secured Fenton's nurse.

After much deliberation, the Council organized to conduct a "self study" of the village. The entire community program of adult education, recreation, inter-group relations, civic progress and other community matters were included in the study. The Council was assisted in the survey by the University of Michigan. The information gained from the survey was used in planning the programs for the FCC.

As a direct result of the study, the FCC offered a new public service..."Rooms for Rent". The FCC maintained a registry of available housing in the area.

The town's recreational programs were organized by, or with the assistance, of the staff at thee FCC. The summer recreational program was the most comprehensive of these recreational programs. It included a "tot lot", day and night tennis and shuffleboard, swimming at Silver Lake and other activities located at the Center, school facilities and other community venues. In the six years of operating the "tot lot", there had never been so many youngsters to sign up for the activity. A total of 192 "tots" enrolled for the five day per week program.

The "Adventure Series" of lectures, sponsored by the Kiwanis and Isaac Walton League, were just a few of the many talks and presentations conducted in the Center's auditorium. The Music Club and others often sponsored musical recitals. When it came to music and dancing, both "modern" and square dancing attracted many of the townsfolk.

With the coming of warm weather, the locale of the recreation programs moved from the confinement of the buildings to the out-of-doors. The two tennis courts were available for playing and the lighting for night playing began in May. There were lessons for "beginners" or refreshers for the "old timers". Tennis had not yet become one of the favorite sports for the young people, so most of the players were "beginners".

With the opening of a newly constructed badminton court behind the FCC in April, another activity was made available.

The Hiking Club met and organized for their summer activity. The Club, which first met in 1939, meets at the Center every other Sunday afternoon and goes hiking. Sometimes it is "'round the road" route, other times it is "cross country" trek 5or 6 miles long.

Act One... The Year 1946   57

The perennial favorite with the people of all ages was table tennis. Three tables were set up in the Recreation room Brad Hoffman was in charge of the Friday night competition for the adult men, which was reported to become very intense upon occasion.

There was a Social Committee for the FCC which was responsible for the social recreation, which included Saturday night modern dances and other special occasions. The Committee President was Edison Stiles with Elmer Nellett as the Secretary-Treasurer. The matter of engaging an orchestra for the Saturday night modern dances resulted in hiring Dick Smale and his Orchestra. Dick Smale was a 1941 graduate of FHS and an Army Air Corps veteran.

There was one Saturday night in December when Dick Smale\ had to keep his trombone in its case…the coal shortage finally hit the FCC. The newspaper headlines read: "COMMUNITY CENTER DARK LAST SATURDAY NIGHTŠ

The Fenton Community Center

Each year the Community Council conducted a fund raiser drive to support the many activities at the Center. In a February a public meeting was held to review the annual budget. The committee asked the villagers "Do you believe that Fenton should continue to support the Community Center, School Nurse, Summer Playground, bathing Beach, Boy and Girl Scouts?

The Community Fund Drive Committee was headed by George W. Pellett as its President. Mrs. Claude Sinclair and Eugene Cooley served as Secretary and Treasurer, respectively. Other Directors were E. C. Reid, Mrs. Pasco, Arthur Becker and J.C. Peck. The drive was conducted from October 28th to November 5th and exceeded its goal.

What Things Cost in 1946:
Car: $1,400
Gasoline: 21 cents/gal
House: $12,500
Bread: 10 cents/loaf
Milk: 70 cents/gal
Postage Stamp: 3 cents
Stock Market: 177
Average Annual Salary: $3,150
Minimum Wage: 40 cents per hour

1946 RCA 621-TS (Pre-war design)

1946 Ford Automobile

Scene Ten..."There's a Lot of Recreatin' Goin' On"

The young men of Fenton...and some not too young...were unabashed sports enthusiasts. If they were not intensely following the High School teams they were playing the games. In the winter it was bowling or basketball, in the spring and summer it was baseball or softball and football watching in the fall.

For the older folks it was largely and spectator sport. There were the college teams...University of Michigan and Michigan State College for football primarily, and the Detroit Tigers baseball team was followed with great interest.

The local baseball team was called the Fenton Merchants. The list of merchants and businessmen in town who purchased a complete set of "suits" for the team included almost everyone in town. The townsfolk rooted for the home team and attendance at the home games was small but vocal. The Merchants played in a league that included Linden, Gaines and Durand and the completion was keen.

The two Hunt brothers, Vern and Bob, were very active in most sports, but particularly baseball. Vern did a lot of the pitching and Bob did a lot of the hitting. Lyle Neely was both a good pitcher and a fine hitter. The team drew upon many of the current or former high school players such as Vince Harrison, Jack Hartley, Al Turco, Bruce McLenna and Lyle Neely. Others on the team were Lyle Bumstead, Jesse Pasco, Harold Foley and Art Brown.

The Fenton Softball League was organized under the leadership of Chairman Don Burdick with over 35 players attending the organizational meeting The nominating committee headed by Vern Hunt presented a slate of officers for election. Those elected were President Howard Craft, and VP Odie Wilhoit. Bruce Marsh was elected as the Business Manager.

During the season over 90 players were involved and the game attendance was about 75 spectators per game.

The Fenton Softball league champions were the Hunts. Vern and Bob Hunt sponsored and played on a team in the league. Other teams in the league, in the order of their finish, were; Hartland, Long Lake, Kiwanis and the Lutheran Church.

There were two winter bowling leagues available to men bowlers. There was the Inter-City Bowling League and the Genesee Tool Bowling League. Their seasons ended in May with the winning teams being Bill's Barber Shop (i.e. Bill Marshall who later in the year was elected as Genesee County Sheriff) in the Inter-City league and the Fenton Eagles in the Genesee Tool league.

In September, the Booster League was comprised of twelve teams as follows: Green Lantern,- Cobblestone Tavern-John Havilland; Hoffman's- John Hockett; Joe Pasco's Team,-; Cobblestone Service,-Joe Cappo; Smith\ Photo, Howard Craft; Fenton Concrete Block,-Herb McKinley; Lutheran's Men's Club,-Carl Tisch; Mickey's Dairy-Don Burdick; Seeburg Amusement,-"Deke" Shivley; Michigan Bean Co.-Arnold Westman Jr. and Woodworth Brothers-Tom Woodworth.

Not all the games being played were taken as serious as the American Legion Donkey Baseball game. This was not the first time the Donkey baseball was played in town, but this year the Donkeys arrived with new equipment...a modern lighting system and loud speakers. The "Championship" Industrial Tool team (they won the last game) was managed by Bryan "Slim" Hanbey and his experienced lineup included H. Loomis, O. Stanley, Tar Foley, M. Bass, K. Henry, J. R. Strom,, C. Levendowski, B. Ireland, D. McKinley, j. Martin, J. Phillips, E. Soper, F. Bachus, B. Moss, B. Runyan, Geo. Baker, Tom McKinley, Virgil Zoll, C. Copeman and D. Durfee.

The challenger's team, managed by Tommy Chappell is made up of veterans....Army, Navy, Marines and Coast Guard. Chappell designated Ruth Dollis as his pitcher...Others on the team were Dwight Lee, Jerry Dollis, Bill Dode, Freddie Johnson, Francis Trimmer, Chet Willing, Raleigh Carpenter, Duane Loomis, Ruth Dollis , Russell O'Berry and Bob Wales

Over five hundred spectators witnessed the most comical gamed ever played on a Fenton diamond. The Veterans team defeated the team from the Industrial Tool Company. By as score of 4 to 1...but who was counting? There were several protests by the losing team as some players rather than ride the donkeys., picked up the small animals and carried them as they ran the bases.

Scene Eleven...Items of Interest?

In reviewing the papers of the day, there were several articles that peaked my interest...

- Men with sagging middles, men needing active exercise to keep in condition, and men who enjoy a little volleyball competition or playing are invited to meet with fellow in similar circumstances the High School gym on Wednesday, nights at 8 o'clock.
- ...the theft of Benito Mussolini's body ...confessed by a man in custody...he would turn over the body if he was assured by police that the corpse--exhumed from a Milan potter field--would be buried in the family plot ...police said "no deal".
- X-raying of the high school students, ninth through twelfth grades, in all County High Schools was completed this week...In Fenton, where there is 328 high school students, 238 or 72.8 percent were X-rayed.
- Mr. M. E. Hinkley, local jeweler, received a broken wrist when he fell on the sidewalk in front of the A.J. Phillips Public Library. As a result he was unable to work...Mr. Hinkley claims he notified President Harry Lemen on the day of the accident that the sidewalk was slippery and needed to be cleaned. He filed a claim with the Village for $343.13.
- Jim Thomson, son of Postmaster and Mrs. Clark Thompson, completed his second year as a regular tackle on the Championship football team of Staunton Military Academy. He is 6 ft. 2 inches tall and weighs 235 pounds.
- A great many men will be pleased to learn that the dinners and programs of the Men's Fellowship will be resumed in January, 1947. These pleasant and profitable gatherings were for several years a monthly feature during the winter months, but owing to wartime restrictions were discontinued
- The Men's Fellowship has a baseball attraction as guest speaker, Davey Jones, an old-time baseball star of the Detroit Tigers. In 1907-08-09, Davey Jones, the brilliant Ty Cobb and the great slugger, Sam Crawford comprised the outfield for the Detroit Tigers.

- Last Saturday, Joe Skinner dropped by the Independent office, wearing his discharge button and fresh from the demobilization center. Since his arrival in Fenton, Joe was unable to find his family who had moved during his absence. After many phone calls, he managed to locate his family in Grand Blanc. Joe has spent many months overseas and was mighty glad to see Fenton, and after the delay, to be united with his family.
- Dr. R. Noble Peckham, who opened his Fenton practice in 1938, has qualified as an oral surgeon and will join Dr. F. Thorald in Flint. Dr. Paul Williams of Royal Oak will continue the practice here begun by Dr. Peckham
- "It couldn't have happened in a more difficult place" says President Harry Lemen, on commenting on a water repair job taking place at the Fenton Fire Hall. Last Friday, men busied themselves attempting to reach and repair the water line which .rested several feet below the surface and directly under the cannon mounted in the fire hall lawn. It was necessary to remove the cannon and with a power shovel remove a large quantity of dirt, which partially blocked the main street
- *(The cannon, a large Civil war Naval "Parrot" Gun now is located in the Oakwood Cemetery. "Main" Street was and is South Leroy Street.)*
- **"Quick thinking of Dick Eble Saves Life of Youngster"** A group of youngsters were playing on a dock on the south end of Lake Fenton, when Boy Scout Dick Eble noticed that young Dickie Irvine had jumped into fifteen feet of water and did not come up. Eble plunged in the water and brought Irvine out of the water and place him safely on the dock. Dick Eble is the son of Mr. and Mrs. Howard Eble and Dickie Irvine is son of Mr. and Mrs. William Irvine of Flint.
- The local Army recruiter stated today that the new Regular Army can now offer you security beyond comparison of any job you may now hold in civilian life. The man that enlists or reenlists in the Regular Army is guaranteed this material security:

  1. He is assured of hi pay each month at the following rate.
     7th Grade (Private) $50.00
     6th Grade (Private First Class) $54.00
     5th Grade (Corporal) $66.00

4th Grade (Sergeant) $78.00
3rd Grade (Staff Sergeant) $96.00
2nd Grade (Technical Sergeant) $114.00
1st Grade (Master Sergeant) $138.00

With a 5% increase on base pay for each three (4) years prior service, up to a maximum total of a 50% increase after 30 years service.

- There were seven drownings in Genesee County by August of 1946 and unfortunately Royal L Lynch of Alpena was drowned in Lake Fenton when a canoe in which he was riding capsized. Lynch had served four years in the Armed Forces and was a student at the University of Detroit at the time of the accident.
- Eight students from Fenton are enrolled at Western Michigan College. They are: Thomas L. Becker, Roy G. Wise, Francis C. Trimmer, Eugene N. Powlison, Kenneth R. Trimmer, Wayne P. Townsend, Frederick H. Johnson and Dwight A. Lee. Also, Alton G. "Fuzz" Marshall is enrolled as a graduate student in Public Administration at Syracuse University.
- Miss Clara Davis, FHS Class of 1940, left New York on the ship *Wisteria* on August 17th bound for Tokyo. Miss Davis was one of 1400 girls who will serve as U.S. Government secretaries in Seoul, Korea and Tokyo, Japan.
- William Bowman, 26, son of Marcella Bowman published his composition "You Belong To Someone Else".. Mr. Bowman wrote both the words and music.
- Grandmother Kathleen Runyan's Memoriam for her Grandson Francis Robert Runyan, FHS "41, remembered he had
- died on October 1, 1943 with the Marines in the South Pacific. (Later Bob Runyan was one of the first to be returned to the United States for burial).
- Leon J. Pavey is serving aboard the USS Brownson, one of 13 ships of Task Force 63, the Navy's expedition to the Antarctica. The expedition will explore the Antarctica for approximately four months, training personnel, testing equipment and developing techniques for maintaining bases in frigid areas.

- A letter to the Editor of the *Independent* pointed out that on Wednesday's afternoons all of the town's Doctors had "closing hours".. Consequently, those in need of a medical attention would not find a Doctor available. As a result the town's Doctors arranged for one Doctor to be on call every Wednesday afternoon and published the "duty roster" in the December 5th issue. Drs. Walcott, Ettinger, Rynearson and Buchanan were listed in the schedule.
- The National Debt, as of today, is 278 Billion Dollars and the debt limit was set by Congress at 200 Billion Dollars. It can be hoped that we can rapidly approach the time of a balanced budget. (Excepted from Weekly Report of Congressman William Blackney)
- After blizzards in March, the summer was an extremely dry season, which caused some severe water shortages. The Villagers were cautioned on their use of water and to be aware that fire could cause damages resulting from the shortage of water.
- Fenton residents again have the opportunity to support a local man for a county office and have this community, which is the largest outside of Flint, represented. William R. "Bill Marshall, well –known citizen of Fenton, seeks nomination for the office of Sheriff on the Republican ticket. "Bill" has lived in Fenton for 21 years. For many years he ran a barbershop (*and is also known as a fishing enthusiast.*)
- The wheat program announced by the government will mean continued skimping on bread, meat, beer and whiskey for over a year to help feed hungry people abroad. Furthermore the bread will continue to be "dark" and it will come in small loaves. . (August 22, 1946)

Interlude One...The War to End All Wars...No. 2

At the end of World War II, vast regions of Europe and Asia had been reduced to ruins. All parts of the world were in turmoil. The colonies of the European countries were in an upheaval as the people actively supported the movements for independence and freedom from the control of foreign nations. Millions of Germans and Japanese were forcibly expelled from territory they formerly called home. These were the "displaced persons" who because of their religion, ethnicity or politics were driven out of their homes. Millions of people were also "displaced" as a result of the war damage.

Sudeten Germans make their way to railroad station in Liberec, Czechoslovakia for movement to Germany.

Family members were separated and wandered about searching for their kin. The Allied forces became occupiers, taking control of Germany, Japan and much of the territory they formerly controlled

Soon the control of the occupied territories was divided among the Allies with the Soviet Union taking over all of Eastern Europe, including the Eastern part of the capital city of Berlin. They installed Communist "puppet" governments in these nations and actively supported the overthrow of monarchs to be replaced by communist leaders in countries like Bulgaria and Romania. As Winston Churchill described it, an "Iron Curtain" had fallen across Europe, dividing West from East.

It is estimated that when the war began in 1939, the world population numbered about 2 billion.. Over 80 million people...about 4% of the world's population ...were killed in the war. The leaders of the allied nations were determined to take the necessary steps to prevent the possibility of another world conflict. The League of Nation, founded in the aftermath of World War I. had proved to be ineffective in preventing a world conflict, and was allowed to close shop, only to be replaced by a new worldwide organization of states, the United Nations.

The name "United Nations" was coined by President Roosevelt in early 1942 when 26 nations agreed to stand together to continue the fight against the Axis powers. It wasn't until June of 1945, before representatives of 50 countries met in San Francisco to draw up the charter for the new organization...the United Nations.

In January of 1946, the General Assembly and the now famous Security Council, met in London for the first time. I wasn't until October of 1946, before the U.N. met in New York, then at Hunters College. In December, the U.N. accepted a gift of a six-block tract of Manhattan property from John D. Rockefeller, Jr. to be the site of the U.N. headquarters.

The growing tensions between the Soviet Union and the Western Powers, principally the United States, soon became known as the "Cold War" The U.S. Ambassador to the Soviet Union, George Kennan, sent his "Long Telegram" to the State Department, in which he reported the Soviet regime was "functionally insecure, opposed to the U.S. and held designs on the world for violent destabilization". The "Cold War" continued for decades until it ended with the collapse of the Soviet Union during the Presidency of George H.W. Bush.

The Allies established an International Military Tribunal to address the "war crimes" committed by the Nazi regime. The Tribunal met in Nuremberg, Germany and in September of the year, found 22 Nazi leaders guilty of war crimes. Twelve of the war criminals were sentenced to death by hanging. All twelve of the convicted Nazi were hanged except for Hermann Goering, who cheated the gallows by taking a deadly poison the morning before the hanging was scheduled. A similar tribunal acted in the Pacific theatre where the Japanese responsible for war crimes were tried, convicted and punished.

While the American people were struggling with shortages, labor strife and the turmoil created by the return of millions of servicemen to civilian life, there were several "ugly" racial incidents during this period.

President Truman made significant advances in the area of civil rights, but was not able move the Congress to consider major civil rights legislation. The President issued Executive Orders that desegregated the Armed Forces and forbid racial segregation in government employment. He also created a Commission on Civil Rights A U.S. Court ruled that race-based housing restrictions were illegal. These restrictions were put in place after WW I and resulted in "ghetto" like communities such as Watts in Los Angeles.

In spite of the positive action in the civil rights arena, their were racial riots in several cities, such as the one in Columbia, Tennessee in February of 1946 that killed two people and wounded many more. Long before the incident with Rosa Parks, Irene Morgan of Virginia was jailed for refusing to give up her seat in a bus. As a result of this arrest, the Supreme Court struck down Virginia's segregation statute on interstate busies

It was reported that lynching in the South approached the record 1918 level as Negro GIs returned and sought the rights for which they were fighting. One of the more brutal episodes occurred in July of 1946, in Monroe, Georgia, when two Negro couples were killed by the Klu Klux Klansmen. The FBI investigation named 55 suspects in the lynching of Roger and Dorothy Malcolm and George and Mae Dorsey, however no one was ever charged with the crime. Dorothy Malcolm was pregnant. One may suggest it was not until the administration of President Lyndon Johnson that any significant civil rights legislation was considered.

Because of the intense war effort, significant progress had been made in the sciences and technology. The American people saw changes in everyday life that were unimaginable in the pre-war years. There had been enormous advances in technology, medicine and communications as well as the weapons for war.

The United States was the sole atomic power and it continued to refine its weapons. In July, the U.S. exploded a 20 kiloton atomic bomb at the Bikini Atoll in the Marshall Islands. There was some apprehension about exploding an atomic bomb with some fearing it would set off a nuclear chain reaction that could destroy the planet.

A test nuclear explosion as part of Operation Crossroads in the Bikini Atoll. Marshall\ Islands on July 25, 1946.

However, our scientists pointed out that the energy released by any one of the major earthquakes every year is about 1,000 times as much as the Bikini bomb. Over the next twelve years, the U.S conducted 67 nuclear tests in the Bikini and Eniwetok area. The research for the development of the atom bomb also led to other discoveries such as learning more about radiation that were applied to x-ray technology.

The medical profession now had new advanced medicines and methods of treating injuries and diseases as a result of the demands of warfare. Penicillin and new antibiotics were now available to the people

The Germans had introduced a jet powered aircraft in the latter days of the war and in post war area, the jet aircraft was being viewed as the future for commercial as well as military airplanes. Radar applications for navigation and commercial air control were directly applicable from their wartime use. It is also interesting to note that the first of man's contact with the Moon was accomplished in January of 1946, when the U.S. Army bounced a radar signal off the lunar surface

While television had been developed before the war, in the post war era, the commercial use of television blossomed. In October, 1946, the RCA Corporation offered a table model "sight and sound receiver" for $225. Other companies were soon producing their sets and over 7,000 sets were sold in the year and commercial TV was established and on it's way!

This Television set, selling for $100, has a 5 x 7 inch screen.

   It wasn't long before many store windows would have one or two television sets glowing in the evening hours. It was quite common to see a small group of citizens standing on the sidewalk watching this small eerie bluish picture on the display TV set. The first person in the neighborhood to buy a new television set, was soon surprised by the number of new friends he had acquired and were anxious to join him and his family to view "Uncle Milty" on Tuesday nights

   Today, it is difficult to conceive of fighting a world-wide war without the use of a computer, or a copy machine or any one of the many items of office equipment now commonly accepted and not considered anything unusual. But, it wasn't until February of 1946 until the Electronic Numerical Integrator and Calculator, considered the first computer, was unveiled. The ENIAC filled an entire room, weighed 30 tons and had 17,488 vacuum tubes. It was designed for the U.S. Army for the purpose of calculating the trajectory of artillery shells. The ENIAC was the beginning of what is now the modern computer technology. It is difficult to believe, but today's average calculator has more computing power than that of by the ENIAC.

Yes, things were a 'changing!

Everything in the BEST TASTE

That's the town whisper that's being circulated by hosts of satisfied enthusiasts . . . by people, just like yourselves, who have enjoyed the ravishing savor of our

Road House Dinners

AND THE EXTRA-POLITE SERVICE OF OUR STAFF

Daily 5:00 p. m. to 11:00 p. m.
CLOSED SUNDAYS

—o—

Our dining room will accommodate

Banquets and Special Dinner Parties

Arrange with the management
for accommodations

| COCKTAIL LOUNGE |

The HOTEL FENTON DINING ROOM

Ray O'Rielly, Prop. Telephone 3632

Act Two…1947

Scene One…The Village Council

As the New Year began, the town's leaders were faced with many problems… new and old. The Village was growing at a rapid pace. Bob Beach, Editor of the Independent, wrote *"Since the close of World war II, Fenton has been experiencing a "Building Boom" at least comparable to or greater*\related to the growth of the village, many were "old" and the result of the lack of funds and attention during the war year. But before the Council could address these concerns, there needed to be an election!

The two local political parties caucused and placed a complete slate before the electorate.

Office	People's Party	Citizen's Party
President	Harry Lowe	Harry Lemen
Clerk	Lucille Sander	Bradley Hoffman
Treasurer	John Weidman	Edgar Weber
Assessor	Bruce Marsh	Irving Gould
Trustees	Raymond Hunt, Shull Woodworth and George Tamlyn	Elton Austin, Wayne Townsend and Raymond Forsyth

The election didn't arouse much interest within the village with less than 300 citizens casting their votes. Most of those voting cast a straight ticket for the Citizens party candidates. All of the Citizens party candidates were elected. Elton Austin received the largest number of votes of any of the candidates with 242. Wayne Townsend and Ray Forsyth joined the incumbents Elton Austin, Fred Hall, Russell Haddon and Charles Rounds as members of the Village Council.

As President Harry Lemen began his 16th term in office, in the first council meeting with the new trustees, the two new members, Townsend and Forsyth, evidenced their independence when they dissented on a vote to purchase a 1 ½ Ton truck for the village. Trustee Townsend stated his position saying "Why not purchase a truck big enough and heavy enough so grading and snow plowing can be done properly". The Village Engineer Neidermeier reported the Village already owned a small gravel truck, however it has stopped running since the truck's radiator fell off.

.The Village contracted with the Gould Engineering Company to prepare the plan for the Villages "Post War Project" program. The project provides Federal funds to finance local projects postponed because of the war. Fenton's post war program included installing 7000 feet of storm sewer in the western part of the Village and approximately 8,320 feet of sidewalks in various areas of the town.

With the increase in downtown business came the problem of finding a parking space. The Village had instituted two hour limit on parking and had been enforcing the limit...as indicated by the increased revenue from fines for parking violations. Now the Council was considering Parking Meters as a solution for the parking problem. The installation of parking meters in downtown Fenton aroused a lot of interest and discussion among the farmers and villages. The *Fenton Independent* placed a ballot in an issue to assess the public's attitude. Several hundred ballots were returned with an overwhelming "negative" on parking meters.

Two of the town's most well-known citizens, Hoyt Glaspie and H. Rabezzana, wrote a letter to the Editor concerning this matter. In part this is what they wrote: *"Fenton is one of the best and most delightful villages still in existence; homey and charming in its ways; an oasis of peace and beauty; it gives one that sense of* HOME TOWN *that the standardized towns have entirely lost. Why spoil it with parking meters when there is no necessity for them?*

Councilmen Townsend and Forsyth did a complete study on the issue but the only actions was the acceptance of President Lemen's recommendation to mark the parking spaces and enforce the tow-hour parking ordinance

The issue lay dormant until early December when the Council reacting to the recommendations of the Street Committee, established a one-hour parking limit on Leroy Street from Elizabeth Street to First Street. The two-hour limit would remain for Caroline and Roberts Streets. (Roberts Street is now named Silver Lake Road.)

On March 1st, the Finance Committee reported to the Cpincil on the Villages finances. They reported the following:

Balance on hand March 1, 1946	$ 2,677.84
Receipts doe the years	71,246.06
Total Receipts	$73,923.89
Total Disbursements	68,461.89
Gross Balance on hand	$ 5,462.01

For several years, the townsfolk had noticed the Oakwood Cemetery was not in very good condition. The Oakwood Cemetery Association did not have adequate funds to bring the cemetery grounds back to its once beautiful state.

Consequently six of the nine members on the Cemetery Board presented the Council with idea of turning the ownership of the cemetery over to the Village of Fenton.

The twelve stockholders of the Cemetery Association met and voted 9 to 3 to offer the ownership of the Cemetery to the Village. All that needed to be done was for the Council to accept the responsibility of ownership. No action was taken at this time *(November)* and the consensus was that the issue would be placed on the spring ballot.

Charles Bussey, a member of the Cemetery Association Board, wrote a letter to the editor of the *Independent*, in which he expressed his desire for the Village Council to accept the gift of the cemetery. He stated *"It would be a source of pride to Fenton and its citizens"*. Mr. Bussey was the brother–in-law of Mary Rackham and a member of the Board of the Rackham Foundation.

Garbage collection was a "big thing" in Fenton ever since the "City Dump" had moved out of the area now occupied by the Fenton Community Center to a location on the Village limits south of town. This year the council accepted the lowest bid and awarded a contract for the collection and disposal of the towns garbage.to Russell Meyer and George Kirk. Meyer and Kirk maintained a fleet of trucks and planned to carry out the work in accordance with the schedules set by the Village Health and Sanitation Committee. The low bid was for $3,000 per year.

In June the Village Assessor Irving A. Gould reported a gain in the Village's tax revenue of $92,195. He attributed the gain largely to the construction of new homes in Fenton. The euphoria of this welcome news lasted until the first Council meeting in December.

At the meeting, Hugo Theisen, Chairman of the town's Water Commission, cited the need for the present water rates to go up to cover the costs of needed improvements and new wells. Mr. Theisen, along with John Collins and James Reagan, members of the Water Commission, pointed out the increasing need to provide service for the new homes. In addition, the costs of equipment to do this work and the higher labor costs make an increase in water rates essential.

At the next meeting the Village Council authorized an increase in the water rates from $2.50 to $4.00 with collection to commence in February, 1948.

In January of the year, Robert Dode, Fenton's Police Department, made his report to the Council concerning the Police activities for the past year. Officer Dode reported the following:

- Held 39 prisoners overnight for prosecution the next day. Compared to 14 in 1945
- 4 convicted of drunk driving
- 7 convicted of reckless driving
- 1 convicted of carrying a concealed weapon
- 1 convicted of larceny from an automobile
- 21 auto accidents compared to 22 in 1945
- 1 killed compared to 2 in 1945, 10 injured compared to 15 in 1945.
- 1 pedestrian injured compared to 6 in 1945
- Issued 206 parking tickets, 53 in 1945
- Issued 91 moving violations, 38 in 1945
- Issued 116 tickets- improper lights, 48 in 1945
- 2 Break & Entering, 2 in 1945
- 381 Red Lights, 184 in 1945
- 1 auto stolen and recovered, 2 arrests made.
- Collected $1,379.87 in fines. $400 in 1945
- Miles driven for year: 21,936

Act Two 1947

Other items of interest in the Village Council:

- The American Legion representative, L. A. Wilson and Hoyt Glaspie, appeared before the Council to re-submit a request for the approval of a permit to serve liquor at their new Legion home. Eventually it was approved, but a permit to serve liquor at their dances was denied..
- Frank Seger, caretaker of the Village dump, was allowed to sell the items he could salvage from the dump to supplement his salary. Mr. Seger appeared before the Council requesting a $5.00 a month raise At the time he reported that his policy in the future was "cash and carry" since several "customers' had failed to pay as promised.
- The Council established a "General Office" in the Fire Hall at the corner of S. Leroy and Ellen Street. This office would do the clerical work for Fire, Police and Water Departments and Village Engineer. A Mrs. Folts of Detroit was hired to supervise this office. Her salary was set at $25 a week.
- The headline read NEW NEON SIGNS WILL BRIGHTEN LEROY STREET". The Council approved for four local businesses to erect new neon signs at their establishments.
- "At last action has been taken to remedy Fenton streets"…so the newspaper reported. Finally the Village had several of the streets "tarred". "It was sorely needed, and now that it has been done, let's keep it that way"
- Citizen Clifford Stanley and others were successful in get the State Conservation Department to "stock" the Mill-Pond with fish. 1,200 Perch 4 to 6 inches were planted along with 1,00 Walleye at 6 to 8 inches and 500 Bass of varied sizes.
- In early June two of the local businesses, the Fenton Independent offices and the Poppy and Lauer farm implement store. The thieves stole $254 from Poppy and Lauer, Nothing was missing at the newspaper office
- Fenton's Fire Department…all volunteers…elected their officers at an April meeting. Those elected were: President Lee Kelley; VP D. Shiville; Secretary-Treasurer Howard Craft; Chief Shull Woodworth; Chief H. More; Fire Marshall F. Williams; and Engineer Howard Craft.

- In order to discourage the installation of septic tanks in the Village, the Council decided to not pay a share of the installation of septic tanks after September 1st. The Village would reject payments for septic tanks being installed by property owns and builders.
- Clark Thompson received his permanent appointment as Fenton's Postmaster. Mr. Thompson lived in Fenton since 1908, graduated from FHS in 1915 and served as a Deputy Sheriff for eight years. During the GM strike he was shot in the leg during a demonstration at the Chevrolet Plant.
- The first of the summer concerts of the City Band was held on July 2nd on the back lawn of the Fenton Community Center; The Wednesday night concerts continued through the summer. However, the attendance was less than it had been in prior years. Finally, Charlie Symons and Judson Phillips attended a meeting of the Village Council to suggest why people were not attending as they had in the past. According to Symons and Phillips crowds of two or three hundred attended when the concerts were played in the Shiawassee Avenue Park Now, in the rear of the FCC only a few attend. The issue was not resolved at that time. The discussion turned to the fact that the twenty man band cost the Village $823 in 1946.
- In November, Officer Myron Pray tendered his resignation. A search began immediately for his replacement. After interviewing the final twelve applicants, the Council accepted the recommendation of the Personnel Committee and hired Gilbert Hatfield.. Mr. Hatfield was a veteran of WW II and had served in the U. S. Constabulary in Berlin.
- In December, the Consumers Power Company warned the people of Fenton about the possibility of interruptions in electrical service. To minimize this possibility, the company is asked customers to conserve electricity, especially between the "peak" hours of 5:00PM and 6:00 PM.

Scene Two...Doing Business Downtown

The streets were full...full of snow...the *Rowena* and the stores were all closed...even the Fenton Hotel and the Virginia Bar were shut down...the whole town and its hinterland were isolated from the "world"!

It had been a "bad" winter for the area...snow and more snow...but when the blizzard hit it was "very bad". The 40 miles per hour winds moved the snow into huge drifts which closed the roads and made it impossible to travel in a car and very difficult to move about on foot.

The Telephone company used a horse and bobsled to move its repairmen around in an attempt to find the downed lines...which were snow covered and much more difficult to locate than downed lines after a "regular" storm with high winds The bus lines, the Short Lines and Greyhound, were not able to serve Fenton for three days..

No traffic existed, mail was not delivered, school busses were unable to make their rounds schools were closed, stores were without bread, milk trucks were not able to deliver, folks were forced to literally hibernate until the storm subsided and the plows could operate. Stalled cars on the streets and highways made plowing difficult.

Dr. "Buck" Buchanan, a horse enthusiast, hitched up one of his horses to a sleigh and made his house calls around Fenton and he even travelled into Tyrone Township.

..Bob Beach wrote in his editorial in the April 17th issue of the *Fenton Independent*..."For the benefit of the readers outstate and those who bask in the sunshine of warmer climes...and too...to warn Fenton folks who plan to return for the summer, this article is written. We Fentonites doubt that there will be a summer. Upon awakening this morning) the villagers found, to their sorrow and disgust, the ground again covered with snow.".

A little bit of snow wasn't going to stop the local businessmen from doing business! The town was growing, more products were becoming available as the peace time industry had moved from tanks airplanes and guns to refrigerators, television and new automobiles.

As Warren Roberts, local manager of the Consumers Power Company, reported, In an eight month period, thirty-four residential meters were installed in Fenton along with eleven new commercial meters. During the same period, the lake areas around Fenton had ninety-eight residential and 17 commercials hookups.

Lumber companies in Fenton had sold out of the r building materials they could acquire and had back orders for more,/ And the building "boom" continued.

Many of the new built homes in Fenton were in the north part of the Village. The homes were small but well-built and were generally snapped up by returning servicemen Some of the builders given credit for the building the homes in that area were local builders Lyle Tuttle and George Brown. The State Savings Bank of Fenton has provided much of the financing for the veterans home purchases.

The building program, has in a large measure, relieved the housing problem in Fenton, especially for the returning veterans. It has been said that it boosted Fenton out of the "small town" class.

Winglemire;s Furniture Store on East Caroline Street felt the need for more display and storage space and to meet this need they built a two story building on Walnut Street just around the corner and behind the Maccabee Building.

Even when the snow was flying, Leon Tice, a young Fenton man, was busy constructing a new building next to the Hamburg Inn on North Leroy street. When completed he opened a new Grocery and Meat Market.

Black's Dairy built a new retail store just west of the Shiawassee River on the north side of Caroline Street.

At the corner of North Road and North Leroy Streets, Lyle Tuttle constructed a new building to be "Johnnies Grill"., a restaurant and a retail store..

Jack and Vi Foehr, owners of the popular Green Lantern Tavern at corner of South Long Lake and Torrey Roads, were also engaged in some building. But not to their choice! They had experienced a fire that required substantial rebuilding. During the rebuilding, The Green Lantern set up temporary operations in the old Bayport Hotel on Lake Fenton.

The town merchants were not only building new structures, but many of them were remodeling and generally improving their stores.

The Wismer-Wright Chevrolet dealership had completely remodeled their building across the street from the Fenton Hotel. During the war years, the building had been used as an annex to the Genesee Tool Company and during that time had been filled with tool making machinery.

Many changes were made to both the interior and exterior of the downtown stores. For example:

* Attorney Maurice Matthews office on South Leroy Street and was shared by Realtor Julia Sweeny, moved temporarily across the street into the former Winglemire Annex, until the remodeling could be completed.

* Fred Smith, new owner of the William Brothers Store installed a new and modern front to his store located just north of the Rowena Theatre.

* Across the street at Gould's Market, the entire main and upper fronts were rebuilt for a nicer and more attractive appearance.

* George Pellett, owner of Pellet's Department Store, purchased the adjoins building south of his present store, the former Winglemire Annex and built display windows in the front of the store. The remainder of the build was used for storage with plans to expand into the space in the future.

* Theisen Motor Sales remodeled their whole store on Roberts Street (now Silver Lake Drive) with new floor space for both show room and service departments.

Not only were the local businesses involved with improving their positions. The Bell Telephone Company moved into their new building at the corner of River and West Caroline Streets and soon thereafter made an instantaneous changeover to their newly installed equipment. The old equipment had been located over the Fenton Hardware Store (corner of South Leroy and Caroline Streets) for years.

The change in the telephone equipment also required a significant change for the telephone customers. All of the telephone numbers had to be changed. The Bell Company issued new directories with the new numbers and when the new equipment came on line, all of the new telephone numbers changed. Surprisingly, the change went off with no "hitch".

Because so many of the townsfolk were dependent for work on the automobile industry, when Buick expanded their facilities in Flint, it was of great significance to the Village of Fenton. Buick had essentially built a whole new plant. It comprised 17 new buildings and more than 2 million square feet of new floor space for manufacturing, assembly, forge and shipping. The new facilities were estimated to allow for production of over 500,000 Buicks per year. Prior to the war, Buick's peak production was about 378,000 cars annually.

Mr. and Mrs. McDaniel opened a new building on North Leroy Street in 1946, to house their Kaiser-Frazer automobile dealership. After one year, they reported they had sold many cars and were filling orders as rapidly as possible.

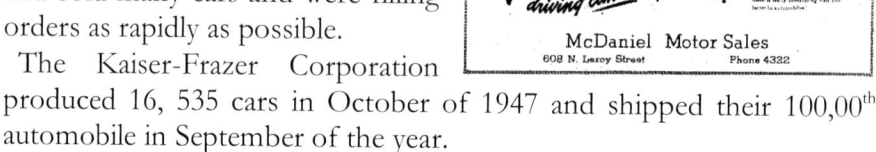

The Kaiser-Frazer Corporation produced 16,535 cars in October of 1947 and shipped their 100,00[th] automobile in September of the year.

Late in the year, George W. Pellett, owner of the town's largest store, and Albert H McClatchey, a Detroit Realtor, purchased the property around Russell Lake in Tyrone Township. Russell Lake had been enlarged to a lake of 100 acres some 20 years before by Judge Gillespie of Pontiac, from whom Mr. Pellett and Mr. McClatchey purchased the property. The property was comprised of the lake and the lands surrounding it, in all some 480 acres. An additional 25 acres was purchased from Albert Donaldson of Tyrone Township. The total of 508 acres completely surrounded the lake. Control of the entire lake allowed the owners to make the restrictions covering the use and building development of the land.

No boat liveries, no overnight cabins, no business of any kind detrimental to the property owners and no sub-standard buildings would be allowed. The new owners expected the first parcels of land would be available early in 1948.

Russell Lake was renamed Lake Tyrone to identify it more naturally with the area of the Tyrone hills surrounding it

In October, Mr. and Mrs. J. O. Nelson, longtime gasoline and oil dealers in Fenton, sold their entire business, which included the large bulk station and five retail stations in the area, including the one located at the corner of River and Roberts Streets. (Roberts is now Silver Lake Drive) to Cities Services. Johndean Jacobs and Jim Smith continued to operate their station as the local Cities Service outlet.

Some of the other events that make news in the business community during the year were as follows:

- Mr. Billmeier purchased the photo studio formerly known as the Tamlyn's, from Mr. Smith. Mr. Smith and Arnold Westman Jr. shared the store, with Mr. Smith operation the studio and Mr. Westman providing other photo related services. Mr. Billmeier and Mr. Westman continued that arrangement and shared the space.
- The Van Fossen family operated the Fenton Floral Company for fourteen years and then sold it to W. J. (Johnnie) Nierescher in August of 1947.
- The South Side Grocery changed ownership again in 1947. Frank Young, who purchased the store from Eugene Cooley a year before, took on a partner, Sherman Wilson, who was employed by Mr. Cooley and Mr. Young acquired an interest in the business, which was renamed Young and Wilson.
- The new Professional Building on Walnut Street acquired a new
- tenant when the Fenton Loan Company located their offices in ther building.
- One of the town's popular "hangouts" changed hands when Wes Sanford took a job at the Romulus Air Base and sold "The Deck" to Dayton Churchman. "The Deck" was located in the triangular area at Main and North Leroy Streets. (Main Street is now Grange Hall Road).
- Mickey's Dairy made news when the owner Charles Hathaway announced the incorporation of his business. Elton Austin, who had been employed as office manager became a stockholder and was elected Secretary and Treasurer of the new firm. Other officers were President Charles Hathaway and VP Verna Hathaway.
- The Williams Brothers Appliance Store was sold to Mr. and Mrs. Fred Smith of Flint. Bob and Jack Williams had opened their store soon after the end of the war.
- The former residence of Mr. and Mrs. Frank Algoe was sold to Mr. And Mrs. Kenneth Jameyson of Flushing. The large home on the corner of Shiawassee Avenue and Adelaide Street was opened as a convalescent home. The first patient at the home was Mr. Allen Dunton of Fenton,
- In November, Mr. and Mrs. Dick Murray, formerly of Flint, opened "Dick's Place", a coffee house

- In late November Mr. and Mrs. Arthur W. Embry, who lived over the former Hoffman's Store on South Leroy Street, opened a store known as the Fenton Packing House Market. The store was located about two miles south in Tyrone Township. The market had the latest in equipment and featured custom butchering, smoke and sugar cured meats.

There were many anniversaries celebrated during the year:
- "Bud" Leetch who managed the Byerly store in Fenton for eleven years, opened his new market on South Leroy Street just two years ago and was celebrating the anniversary.
- Pellett's Department Store had been in business in Fenton for 26 years.
- James H. and Robert W. Obenshain, Fenton residents for five years, had purchased the Don Alchin's market in the 100 block of South Leroy Street one year ago and were celebrated their First Anniversary.
- Mr. and Mrs. Wyman were celebrating their Second Anniversary of their hardware store, the successor to Colvin's Hardware Store.
- E. B. Mitts held a two day "open house" at the Mitts Greenhouse to celebrate the fiftieth year in business in Fenton. The greenhouse was first built in 1897 by George Bridson, later sold to Henry Adams and then purchased by Mr. Mitts in 1936. It was originally named the Fenton Green house and was the first to be built in Fenton. In 1947 it was the largest in the number of cubic feet in Genesee County.

Scene Three…The Club Scene…Ladies First!

The two oldest women's club in town, the Bay View and the Entre Nous continued to be the most prominent and prestigious clubs in town. Their membership was composed of the wives of the men considered the "movers and shakers" in the Village. The other clubs, such as the Child Study Clubs or the Rebekahs the veteran auxiliaries, were project driven or companions to the men's organizations

On January 6th, the Bay View Cub celebrated their fiftieth anniversary with a meeting at the Fenton Community Center. The club President Mrs. G. L. Whittle gave a brief welcome, after which the past and present activities of the cub were reviewed by Mrs. C. W. Whitman, Mrs. C. E. Rolland and Mrs. James Thompson.

A display of past programs and club photographs of the past years was presented.

Members of the Entre Nous were, as well as other friends, were special guests. Further, the Entre Nous furnished the floral decorations.

Mrs. F. A. Chapin and Mrs. C. E. Rolland poured the tea and Mrs. C. W. Whitman and Mrs. J. R. Barbour cut the three layered Golden Anniversary cake.

Because of the many years of membership were named Honorary Hostesses. Those so honored were: Mrs.\ C. E. Rolland, Mrs. James Thompson, Mrs. A. G. Wright, Mrs. W G. Whitman, Mrs. F. A. Chapin, Miss Edith Hadley, Mrs. E. E. Crane, Mrs. C. G. Morehouse. Mrs. J. M. Stewart, Mrs. B. G McGarry, Mrs. J. R. Barbour and the only living Charter member, Mrs. Grace Gurnes.

Other members of the Bat View Club were Mrs. E.C. Reid, Mrs. Myron McGlynn, Mrs. R, H. Hyde, Mrs. N. H. Alexander, Mrs. E. R. Sluyter, Mrs. Clark Thompson, Mrs. M. Scott, Mrs. A. E. Wolcott, Mrs. C. H. White,

In March the Club held their annul election of officers…The membership re-elected the incumbents: President Mrs. Whittle, VP Mrs. McGlynn, Secretary Mrs. M. Scott, Treasurer Mrs. White and Mrs. Walcott as Parliamentarian.

It was "Showtime" for the members of Entre Nous at their meeting in February. After a short business meeting, President Mrs C. A. Damon turned the program over to Mrs. Russell Haddon, Mrs. Eugene Cooley and Mrs. Leon Pavey.

Mr. Howard Bacon favored the group with a trombone solo "Willow Echoes", followed by Miss Nancy Bower who sang two solos, "The Man I Love" and "Where My Caravan Has Rested". Both were accompanied by Carol Alchin on the piano. Mrs. Leon Pavey gave a review of the current Broadway plays and their personalities.

Next on the program was a humorous one-act play "Consolation" directed by Mrs. Haddon. The cast consisted of members: Mrs. Russell Lince, Mrs. Lynne Avery, Mrs. Al Fessler, Mrs. Eugene Cooley and Mrs. Haddon.

In April, the Entre Nous celebrated their Fiftieth Anniversary at a noon luncheon at the Fenton Community Center. A table decorated with yellow snapdragons, daffodils and daisies, provided the byBay View Club, was centered with the Anniversary cake.

President Mrs. C. A. Damon introduced Mrs. Dora Morehouse who presided as the Toastmistress and told of the origin of the club and past history.

Past Presidents present were: Mrs. N. H. Chesnut, Mrs. George MacNeal, Mrs. George W. Pellett, Mrs. D. S. Frackelton, Mrs. Kleber Merrick, Mrs. Louis Riedel, Mrs. Clarence Heemstra and Mrs. DeForest Arrand.

The committee in charge of the Anniversary luncheon was chaired by Mrs. Burns Fuller and consisted of the following members: Mrs. Lynne Avery, Mrs. Burton Baker, Mrs. Harry Adams, Mrs. Ernest Hungerford, Mrs. W B. Hoey, Mrs. Charles Lea and Mrs. Leon Pavey.

Other club members were: Mrs. Aubrey Butler, Miss Maude Morris, Mrs. Lloyd Hunt, Mrs. Ed Blazier and Mrs. Wesley Martin

Out-of-town guest were: Mrs. Sheldon LaTourette of Hartland, Mrs. DeForest Arrand of Flint, Mrs. Walter Conrad of Detroit and Mrs. Roger Leestma of Ann Arbor.

Mrs. Eugene Cooley then entertained with two excellent readings. The meeting was closed with Mrs. Haddon's reading entitled "Friendship"

The Child Study Clubs continued to be very popular in Fenton, as well as the State of Michigan. The Senior CSC was led by their President Mrs. August Arndt. Other members included Mrs. Floyd Hartley, Mrs. Maurice Kieft, Mrs. Ivah Rolland, Mrs. Donald E. Chase, Mrs. Jack Lea, Mrs. Burnette Rogers, Mrs. August Arndt, Mrs. Ernest Tirrell, Mrs. P. Cotcher, Mrs. Frank Bachus, Mrs. Kleber Merrick, Mrs. Robert Edwards ., Mrs. Clarence Armstrong, Mrs. Thor Nielsen, Mrs.

Arthur Sorenson, Mrs. Claude Sinclair, Mrs. Dorothy Hodgman, Mrs. Owen Meier, Mrs. Elmer Nellett, Mrs. Arnold Westman, Mrs. Don Alchin, Mrs. David Frew, Mrs. Charles Averman, Mrs. Ivan Williams, Mrs. Roy Wood, Mrs. Louis Riedel, Mrs. Lowell Swanson, Mrs. George Pellett Sr., and Mrs. Emile Gosseaux.

At their meeting of January 29th, Miss Nancy Bower offered a vocal selection and Miss Carol Alchin a piano solo.

On March 11th, the Senior CSC elected new officer for the coming year. Those elected were: President Mrs. Maurice Kieft, VP Mrs. Dorothy Hodgman, Corresponding Secretary Mrs. Owen Meier, Treasurer Mrs. Elmer Nellett and Press Reporter Mrs. Arnold Westman.

Each year the Senior CSC presented a Mother–Daughter Banquet. This year was the 29th Annual Banquet and the theme was "The Big Top", consequently the decorations included many clown faces and clusters of balloons. As was the custom, Miss Marjorie Bachus, Miss Martha Swanson and Miss Virginia Edwards gave a toast to the mothers entitled "Tight Rope Walkers" and Mrs. George Pellett W. Sr. responded on behalf of the mothers with a toast to the daughters entitled "Tis not Easy to Train".

The October meeting, the first meeting of the new club year, the Senior CSC entertained the teachers of the Fenton Schools. The new President Mrs. Maurice Kieft became the "teacher" and the teachers her students. The program was prepared by Mrs. Kieft and a committee composed of Mrs. A. Arndt, E. Tirrell, P. Cotcher and E. Gosseaux.

At their meeting on May 1st, the Junior Child Study Club elected Mrs Claude Cohoon as their President for the coming year. The meeting also featured a "Youth Forum" in which several young people participated in a lively discussion of problems of current interest. Those participating were: Betty Burton, Pauline Francis, Marcia Schupbach, Nelson Curtis Jr., Donald Dexter and Franklin Werner. .

The program was arranged by members Mrs. Judson Phillips, Mrs. Ed Renwick, Mrs. Howard Reasner, Mrs. Lynn Welch and Mrs. Robert Lutz.

The Pro-To Child Study Club in February featured the presentation of two papers: Mrs. Mort Patten presented "Eating Habits and Problems" and Mrs. Roy Buffmeyer offered "Praises and Awards". Their meeting was hosted by Mrs. Kenneth Wilhoit and assisted by Mrs. Chet Hillis

At the Pro-To CSC meeting in May, the club elected their officers for the coming year. The resets were : President Mrs. Mort Patten, VP Mrs.

George Kidder, Recording Secretary Mrs. Ralph Rheingans, Corresponding Secretary Mrs. Robert Sleeman, Treasurer Mrs. Leon Robinson and Parliamentarian Mrs. Champ O'Heron.

The Fenton Music Club and the Fenton Book Club were also very popular and the members of each club were most likely members of both and either the Entre Nous and Bay View

Traditional Yuletide festivity dominated the December meeting of the Music Club hosted by Mrs. Lynden Avery in her home. The meeting opened with all present signing "Joy to the World" and would have been followed by an exchange of gifts. However, the exchange was replaced by a collection to be used for European Relief.

Miss Alice Van Atta conducted wide-ranging program using the many talents of the members.

A Nativity scene with Miss Leah Merrick as Mary, as the Club Chorus sang "The Slumber Song"

Mrs. Donald Smale read "The Christmas Story", A Spanish story "Mary Treads on Snow" and a Danish story "It was a Peaceful, Holy Christmas Eve"

The Club's Chorus sang several Carols from around the World. The members of the Chorus were: Mrs. Emile Schucter, Mrs. Charles Woodworth, Mrs. Irving Negus, Mrs. Edward Blazier, Mrs. Herbert Gardner, Mrs. Maurice Kieft, Mrs. John Legg, Mrs. Ernest Tirrell, Mrs. Henry Alchin, Mrs. Nierescher and Mrs. Arthur Strom .Miss Alice Van Atta provided the piano accompaniment.

Miss Van Atta presided over the Wassell Bowl and was assisted by Mrs. John Dolza, Mrs. Blazier and Mrs. Roy Polson.

In January, the members met at the Flint home of Barbara (Barnes) Syring. Barbara was a member of the club and had recently married Byron Syring, a frequent Baritone in many of the productions in Fenton.

The program for the evening was given by Mrs. Beulah Belford whose beautiful soprano voice impressed those in attendance. Mrs. Belford was accompanied by Mrs. Emily Hixson.

The members prevailed on Mr. Syring to sing several numbers to complete a fine musical evening

In May, one of the meetings was devoted to the study of the music of George Gershwin   The meeting was hosted by Mrs. L. E. Blazier and the program conducted by Mrs. Donald Smale.

Following the musical program the club elected officers for the coming year. Those elected were: President Mrs. Arthur Strom, VP Mrs. John Dolza, Recording Secretary Miss Mabel Van Atta, Corresponding Secretary Mrs. Lynden Avery, Treasurer Mrs. Maurice Kieft, Librarian Mrs. William Parish and the Board of Directors: Mrs. Robert Bell, Mrs. W Skillen and Mrs. Donald Smale.

The Club was interested in all kinds of music and in March, they invited Alexander Znamenskuy, a priest of the Russia Orthodox Church, and a singer of repute, to provide a program of Russian folk art and church songs. Following the program two ladies from Flint, attired in Russian dress served tea in a Russian manner

In June, the Music Club sponsored a concert at the Fenton Community Center featuring Mr. Romeo Tata, a violinist from Michigan State College. Mr. Tata played brilliantly and responded to the audiences request with several encores

The Music Club was especially blessed to have Miss Alice Van Atta as one of its members. Miss Van Atta was a very accomplished musician She was at home with the piano and the organ. She was a member of St. Jude's Episcopal Church where she played the organ on Sunday and any other special occasion. She was also consider the "premier" music teacher in town.

In early November, Miss Van Atta presented a program on the music of Brahmas for a club meeting. The program featured duo-piano numbers with Mrs. Elmer Westman and Miss Van Atta, a piano quartet of Mrs. John Legg and Mrs. Harry Bush At the First Piano and Mrs. John Dolza and P. Rerish at the Second Piano.

On April 23rd, the Fenton Book Club elected officers for the coming year. Those elected were: President Mrs. Russell of Linden; VP Mrs Jack Obenshain; Recording Secretary Mrs. C. H. White; Treasurer Mrs. Wiggins; Program Chairman Mrs. Martin; Tea Hostess Mrs. James McKinley. Following the election Mrs. .Harold Schaefer presented a book review. Tea was served by the members from Linden: Mrs. Ralph Garratt, Mrs. Byron Evans, Mrs. A. Lind and Mrs. Fred Kirshman.

The meeting of Fenton Book Club in late November was not as "Grandeurs" as that of the Christmas meeting of the Music group, but after the discussion of several new books, tea was served by the hostess .Mrs. Frank Mytinger.. Others attending the meeting were Mrs. Charles Lea, Mrs. Walter Walker, Miss Effie Bishop, Mrs. Irving Negus, Mrs.

Harold Perkins, Mrs. P.W. Perish, Mrs. W J. Parker, Mrs. C. White, Mrs. D. A. O'Dell, Mrs. Don Phillips, Mrs. Myron McGlynn, Mrs. W Hoey Mrs. Lralie Whittle and Mrs. James Cohoon.

The Favorite Rebekahs, the "favorite" ladies adjunct of the local I.O.O.F. (the Oddfellows) met in January to install their new officers for the coming year. The new officers were: Noble Grand-Grace Russell, Vice Grand- Myrtle Swanebeck, Secretary Grace Wright, Recording Secretary Maxine Zimmer, Treasurer Marvel Burden, Past Noble Grand- Wilda Achin, Chaplain Della Woodworth, Guardians Stella Roberts and Zola Simmons, Conductor Phyllis Warner and Musician Wanda Butts. Members serving in other capacities were; Esther Lord, Phoebe Rector, Minnie Moore and Allie Parker.

What Things Cost in 1947:

Car: $1,500
Gasoline: 23 cents/gal
House: $13,000
Bread: 12 cents/loaf
Milk: 80 cents/gal
Postage Stamp: 3 cents
Stock Market: 181
Average Annual Salary: $3,500
Minimum Wage: 40 cents per hour

Scene Four…The Club Scene…for Men Only!

The "Eagles Have Landed" and were doing very well in attracting new members, many of whom lived in the community but were employed outside of the immediate area

The more established men's clubs…Kiwanis and the XX Club…continued to attract the "movers and shakers" in the community.

The Kiwanis membership included most of the "downtown" businessmen. Undoubtedly, the noon luncheon meeting at the Fenton Community Center was convenient for those members.

The XX Club's membership, which they limited to only twenty members was, for the most part, downtown business men. While the club members sometimes exclaimed the club was not burdened by the obligations of national and/or International organizations, they did join with the Kiwanis on some local projects. They were for the most part a social "knife and fork" club.

The Eagles, the newest of the international connected, service clubs, generally attracted the men from all walks of life. They got off to a fast start and their activity level did not seem to diminish,

The Men's Fellowship, which was not technically a "club", was a community activity which attracted hundreds of men to their series of banquets The program had to "shut down" during the war years because the rationing of food made it almost impossible to hold a banquet for a couple hundred diners. Now, the Men's Fellowship was re-organizing to present their traditional six banquets during the tear.

In August an energetic group of young men of the community decided there was work to be done and they were willing to do it! The group became affiliated with the International Junior Chamber of Commerce and received its charter at a banquet at the Fenton Community Center on October 9th.

The forty men group of young men , ages 21 to 36, elected the following as their officers: President John Neirescher, Vice Presidents Robert Lutz and Jim McKinley, Secretary Ray Cummings and Treasurer Bill Searight.

The Board of Directors elected was: For One: Year-Wayne Wessendorf, Paul Bottecelli and Robert Obenshain. For Six Months: Ward Waite, Kenneth Harris and Stanton Miner.

The speaker at their Charter Night banquet was Paul B. Bagwell of Michigan State College and Vice President of the United States Junior of Commerce.

Before the end of the year, in the less than three months, the Jaycees (by which they were most frequently called) had successfully completed the following projects

- Received the Village approval for the erection of street signs...and paid for by fund solicited from the Fenton merchants.
- Sponsored a play by the Village Players at the Community Center.
- Sponsored a "huge" Christmas parts at the Community Center at which a gift was presented to each child attending, showing of two hours of comedy movies, Had a "Jolly 'ol' Aldrich Saint Nick" (Aldrich Locke did his usual jolly Santa!), so all the children could visit with Santa.

Santa's helpers included: Mr. and Mrs. Warren Anderson, Mr. and Mrs. Rolland Covert, Mrs. Emile Gosseaux, Mr. and Mrs. Robert Obenshain, Mr. and Mrs. Evar Strom, Mr. and Mrs. Ward Waite, Mr. and Mrs. James Cohoon, Olin Flick, William Searight and Bill Strom.

It was a Merry Christmas for the newly formed Jaycees...they provided a Christmas gift for the Village with new streets signs and a wonderful Christmas party for the town' youngsters.

The other newcomer group...The Fenton Aerie, Fraternal Order o Eagles...only a couple years old...continued to be active, especially in recruiting new members...for both the Aerie and its Ladies Auxiliary

In May at the Aerie's home in downtown Fenton, above the Popular Restaurant, the election of officers for the coming years was conducted. Those elected were: Worthy President Joseph Oren, VP Orville Azelton, Chaplain Harold Torrey, Treasurer Gerald Durand, Conductor Edward Youngs, Inside Guard Wilbur Case, Outside Guard Anton Horvath Jr. and Trustee Phillip O. Crane

Mr. Crane joined incumbents Charles Auker and Earl Shiville on the Board. Rolland Sewell continued as Secretary since he was serving a three year term.

The Eagles' Ladies Auxiliary held a joint installation of new members and an election of officers on December 9th.

Fifty-two new members from Fenton, Linden and Holly were initiated at this meeting. The election results were as follows: Madame President Martha Miner, Jr Madam President Mildred Steele, VP Dorothy Ebmeyer, Chaplain Thelma Oren, Secretary Jessie Nash, Treasurer Virginia Calkins, Guards Margaret Torrey and Beatrice Shiville, Conductor Marie Steward and Trustees: Josephine Auker, Catherine Dreyer and Mary Young.

For the third consecutive year, the Fenton Kiwanis continued to be the major service club in town. In the six years since the club was founded, the people of Fenton, and the surrounding area had been well served by this group of men.

During the winter of 1945-46, the Kiwanis sponsored a basketball program for boys from grades 7 through 12. 125 boys participated in the program conducted by FHS Coach Ivan Williams. The youngsters met on Saturday mornings and were instructed in the fundamentals of the game and then played games in the afternoon. The older boys played their games on Monday evenings. Two leagues were formed and trophies and medals were awarded at the end of the season.

The Kiwanis sponsored Boys Basketball program was in addition to a social recreation program of dances, outdoor sports, parties and dramatics directed by Tamara Reeves.

For several years the Kiwanis had conducted a "Field Day" at the Shore Acres Golf Club on Torrey Road, west of Lake Fenton. Consequently, on July 16th, the Kiwanis and their "paying" guests indulged in a day of fun , with lots of golf, followed by a dinner at the club house. The term "paying" guests is used because the event was a major fund-raiser for the club. All those participating contributed to the fund which supported the clubs many projects.

Chet Hillis, Club President and Chairman of the "Field Day" pronounced the event a "big success".

Typical of the regular meetings was a presentation by a member but mostly, by invited speakers. One such meeting in September had Dr. M. Owen of Michigan State Collage speaking on "Inflation".

For the first time, the club sponsored a concert. Violinist Leona Flood performed to a capacity audience at the Community Center on the evening of October 17th. In the afternoon, preceding the concert, Miss Flood met with school children. She captivated her audience of school children by telling stories about her violin, its history and qualities.

In celebration of their Sixth Anniversary, the club held their Charter Night dinner at the Fenton Hotel. The members and their ladies enjoyed the "magic show" program, but the "fun" part was reserved for the latter part of the evening.

Each lady received a flower and a box of candy. Other prizes were also given: Mrs. Hillis, Mrs. Bowles and Mrs. Whittle each received a basket of groceries; Mrs. Taylor a new hat; Mrs. Curle received the prize award of the evening…a "Paris Creation"…presented by Aldrich Locke. The "Creation" was a waste basket decorated with a string mop, dish cloths and a funnel to represent a new hat. Needless to say…"A good time was had by all".

On November 11th, many of the Kiwanians got up about 3AM and headed for the Community Center and began preparing stacks of pancakes for the large crowd expected to come to their "all you can eat" Annual Pancake Breakfast…and they were not disappointed!

The Kiwanis elected their officers for the coming year in late November. Those elected were: President Leslie Whittle, VP John Millington, Treasurer Elmer Westman and the new members of the Board of Directors were: Ray O'Reilly, Warren Roberts, Dr. Paul Williams and Robert Beach.

In early December the Kiwanis Club honored the Fenton High School football team at a noon day luncheon at the Fenton Community Center. Coach Ivan Williams introduced each member of the County Class "B" Championship team.

The guest speaker for the event was Howard Auer of Flint Central High School. His talk was enjoyed by the members of the club and the boys in attendance

The final club activity of the year was their annual effort to raise money for the Goodfellows by selling the Goodfellow's paper to the citizens traversing the roads and streets of the town.

The Men's Fellowship had reorganized and planned a series of meetings for their "Spring Session".

The first meeting of the series was held on evening of January 29th at the Fenton Community Center. The subscribed membership for this new revitalized organization numbered over 250 men and almost all of them attended this initial program.

Wilfred Irwin, the Prosecuting Attorney for Livingston County and a former FBI operative was the guest speaker. In addition, a popular male quartet, the "Three Flints and a Lighter" provided the musical entertainment.

The second meeting was a Father-Son Banquet, held on March 17th at the FCC. The members reported that the "new" Fellowship was already exhibiting some of the old momentum and enthusiasm for the program. The attendance for the event was over 330 men and boys.

The highlight of the evening was a talk and a demonstration of shooting by Corporal Lester Coykendell of the Michigan State Police. A local quartet provided the musical entertainment and the dinner was served by the ladies of the Methodist Church. Than Chesnut planned the event.

The last meeting of the "Season" was the traditional "Ladies Night" and it was held on the evening of April 14th at the Fenton Community Center. As expected, the event was attended by over 200 men and women.

The Fellowship met in April to plan the programs for the 1947-1948 series of banquets. It was decided to hold five meetings, one each month during the season. The FCC agreed to sponsor the meetings and allow them to be held in the FCC building.

At this meeting, the following officers were elected: President Ed Mitts, VP Warren Roberts, Secretary Avery Loucks and Treasurer Otis Furman. Than Chesnut was charged with continuing to provide the fine meals the club had been enjoying.

Judge Frank McAvinchey, Judge of Probate in Genesee County was the Guest speaker the Men's Fellowship's first meeting of the new season. The evening of November 10th heard Judge McAvinchey expound on Michigan's new "Community Property Act". As the Judge explained this new law every citizen and should be understood by everyone. Well over 200 Fenton men attended the banquet to hear the Judge. The men of the XX Club served as the waiters and the food was prepared by the ladies of the Methodist Church.

The Fenton Chapter of the Isaac Walton League was noted for its annual "Wild Game Banquet". This event was held in mid-December and, this year, was held in the basement of the Methodist Church. About 100 persons were present including members, their families and guests to partake of the delicious venison and moose meat. The game was provided by several of the club members. Mrs. Don Bennett and her crew were credited with preparing the sumptuous fare.

Jim Foley, the chapter President acted as Toastmaster and Bob Lutz, the VP, offered the words of welcome. The program featured Dennis Haver of Detroit, a big game hunter, lecturer and photographer. Mr. Haver provided a very interesting and educational color movie of fishing and moose hunting in Canada.

Bill Freeman and Lemen Shelby, two of Fenton's young men, spoke of their summer experience at the Michigan United Conservation Camp in Allegan. Their stay at the camp was sponsored by the local chapter of the Isaac Walton League.

Fenton's "noted" quartet consisting of Ryan Strom, Grant Wright, Lynn Welch and Lee Kelly, rendered several numbers that were enjoyed by those assembled...and left them wanting more!

Earlier in the year, the club had cosponsored, with the Kiwanis, an appearance of Ben East, a very popular lecturer on Michigan Wildlife, in particular, and the "Outdoors" in general. Ben East had appeared in Fenton many, many times in the past and always attracted a large audience for his shows. This time Ben East's program was about Alaska..."the Great Land". The pictures shown were of Alaska's great reindeer herds, blue foxes, wildflowers and the Alaskan seal herd.

The Masons continued to occupy the top two floors of the building housing the State Bank of Fenton and the photograph/camera business of Arnold Westman Jr. and Mr. Billmeier.

While this Scene is titled "...for Men only!", when we discuss the activities of the Masons, we need to include the Order of the Easter Star. The O.E.S. is the largest fraternal organization in the world to which both women and men may belong. Worldwide, there are over 500,000 members. Consequently, just forget the "...for Men Only!" admonition as we recall the activity of the Fenton chapter of the Eastern Star. On the evening of October 30th, the members of the Fenton O.E.S. gather at the Masonic Hall for "supper" and the installation of officers for the upcoming year. Over two hundred members and guests were in attendance.

The outgoing Worthy Matron, Alice Peterson, hostess for the evening, introduced the musical part of the program which included duets by Moreen Peterson and Gladys Knight and a piano solo by Jerry Hatfield. The program featured a solo by Harriet Mortimore Toomey of Detroit and a 1922 Fenton

High School graduate. Mrs. Toomey concluded the assembly by singing "The Lord's Prayer".

The installing officers were: Carolynn Pellett, Zella White, Gene Armstrong, Luella Patterson and Alma Hall (Organist).

The elected officers were: Worthy Patron Willard Hatfield, Worthy Matron Sadie Galloway, Associate Patron Charles Wyman and Associate Matron Marion Bristol. Others elected were: Ruth Sinclair, Ida Mae Miller, Elsie Thorpe, Mary Alice Davies, Carrie Cummings, Avis Hough, Benita Roshaven, Martha Hatfield, Helen Richmond, Lavina Welch, Mary Butts, Elizabeth Day, Eleanor West and Edgar Weber. Others reported to be in attendance were: Mattie Hiscox, Arch Peterson and Ray Cummings.

In mid-December the Fenton Lodge the F. & A. M. (Free and Accepted Masons) installed their officers for the new year. Those elected were: Worshipful Master Willard Hatfield, Senior Warden Bruce Marsh, Junior Warden D. R. Stiles, Treasurer K. Weber and Secretary Judson Phillips. Others elected to other positions were: Harold Otto, Avery Loucks, Myron Richmond, Guido Bassler, Sidney Smale and Francis Gray.

One should not overlook the Fenton Grange. This organization was largely subscribed by the people in Tyrone and Fenton Townships, and those were likely to be in farming. On October 16th, the Fenton Grange elected their officers for the upcoming year. Those elected were: Master-Warren Logan, Overseer Bert Moyer, Lecturer Claire Rossman, Steward Ralph Rossman, Asst. Steward John Rossman, Chaplain Anna Galloway, Treasurer Helen Swanebeck and Secretary Carrie Logan. Others elected to offices were: Ray Bradshaw, Mildred Moyer, Wilma Unger, Bertha Chapman, Pearl Johnson and Rita Bradshaw. *(Authors note...Obviously the "...Men Only!" tag does not apply with the Grange)*

Admittedly not a very good picture, but this is the town's Santa Claus"...Aldrich Locke ...dressed in his finest.

When Aldrich Locke was the owner of a gasoline station, a young Harold Barden remembers being in the front seat of his father's automobile while "gassing up" at Locke's station. Invariably Aldrich would come to the car and lean in and exchange some pleasantries with Harold's father. When Aldrich would place his forearms on the window opening on the passenger side, his hand would be very close to young Harold's face. Harold remembers being attracted by the gold Masonic ring Mr. Locke wore.

For many years, Aldrich Locke was the best "Santa Claus" in town. He had a very handsome costume and an especially well made set of "whiskers". Not just the ordinary "fake looking" ones, but a set that looked very, very real. "Santa" would set up in the Community Center and the town's young children would line up for the opportunity to tell "Santa" exactly what they wanted for Christmas.

Young Harold Barden was one of those youngsters and when his turn arrived, he mounted "Santa's" knee. As he was about to answer "Santa's" inquiry as to his wishes, he noticed "Santa" was wearing a beautiful gold ring...just like Mr. Locke's. He knew then who this "Santa" really was!

Scene Five…the Veterans and their Ladies

The Post War years were active ones for the veteran organizations and the competition for new members was brisk. The Veteran of Foreign Wars, as their name conveys, were interested in joining those veterans who had served outside of the United States in a combat zone. The American Legion, which traced their heritage to World War I and the veterans in France, did not restrict their membership…all veterans of the services were eligible to join the Legion.

There were several "upstart" organizations also vying for recruits….The Amvets was one of these new associations that were eager to find a home in Fenton.

The James DeWitt Post of the American Legion had established their home in the Maccabee Building at the corner of East Caroline and Walnut Streets for many years. This year they acquired the home of Bert Rollins at the corner of Robert and Walnut, just around the corner from the Maccabee Building. After several months, in which the members remodeled the house to better serve the needs of the Post and their members, the new home was available and ready to occupy. Beginning on February 15th, all activities were held in the new home.

L.A. Wilson and Hoyt Glaspie appeared before the Village Council to re-submit the Legion's request for a club license for the sale of liquor to its members. Eventually the request was approved, but a request to serve drinks during a membership dance was denied.

In June, during the baseball season, the Legion sponsored an excursion to Detroit to attend a Detroit Tigers baseball game. This time the group traveled by train and they picked a good day to be "take me out to the ol' ball game". The Tigers were playing a double header against the New York Yankees on July 20th.

This year, as in years past, the Legion Post selected a girl to attend the Wolverine Girls State on the campus of the University of Michigan in Ann Arbor. Mrs. William Hathaway, Girls State Chairman for the Post, announced that Miss Rose Mary Howe had been chosen.

On October 2nd, the Legion's Auxiliary held their election of officers for the coming year, Those elected were: President Ida Foust, VP Jeanette Hathaway, VP Lelah Bradley, Secretary Florence Winn, Treasurer Jacqueline Steffy, Chaplain Lillian Goodrich, Historian Mildred Brancheau and Sergeant at Arms Margaret Durfee.

The veterans of the American Legion and their ladies were not ones to forget the servicemen confined in the Veterans Hospitals, so in November they conducted a "Gifts To Yanks" campaign in preparation for the Christmas season.

The Legion, along with the VFW post, was not prepared to have the recognition of the end of World War I go unnoticed. Since there were no apparent plans to recognize the ending of that war, the two veterans groups got together and organized a parade on Armistice Day, November 11th. The American Legion and the VFW members and their ladies auxiliaries were led by the Fenton High School Band for a march from the Legion Hall to Memorial Park. Memorial Park was the lawn in front of the Phillips Library, which is now the Fenton Museum. Following the ceremonies at the Park, the marchers returned to the Legion Hall for a Pot Luck dinner. The evening was reserved for dancing at the VFW Hall.

On March 6th, the Veterans of Foreign Wars, the Curtis-Wolverton Post #3243, elected their officers for the upcoming year. Those elected were; Commander William G. Harris, Sr. Vice Commander Edward W. Kelleher, Jr.Vice Commander Hollis Winn, Quartermaster Walter Stiff, Chaplain Thomas Brennan, Surgeon Frank Mytinger, Post Advocate Harry Dobbs and Trustee Orville Utt. *(Authors note: It's a privilege to relate that the new Commander was my father...as of this writing he is the only member to be elected as Post Commander on three separate occasions)*

William G. Harris

In April the Post celebrated their 12th Anniversary with a dinner and dance. Bill Gallagher and his Orchestra provided the dance music. *(Authors note: As a high schooler, I played alto sax in Bill Gallagher's Band).*

In May, the Post sponsored the "Big Radio Jamboree Show". The performers were from a popular radio show which featured country and western music of the Kansas City Ramblers. The show was held at the Fenton Community Center for two nights, May 15 and 16.

Probably the most significant event of the year was when the VFW Post purchased the land for their new home. The site was situated on North Leroy Street just beyond the village limits at that time. Emmanuel "Dick" Boilore, the Chairman of the Building Committee, reported the construction of a new hall would begin next spring. The land is located just south of the Locke's Gas Station and has a frontage of 150 feet. The current VFW building is located on this property.

The VFW Ladies Auxiliary held the installation of their new officers in April. The ceremony was conducted by Lelah Stiff, the outgoing President and Myrtle Harris provided the piano music for the installation. Those installed were the following officers: President Edna Pokorny, Sr. VP Alice Locke, Jr. VP Katherine Walters, Secretary Naomi Bennett, Treasurer Lela Hanbey, Chaplain Lydia McCormick, Conductress Doris Huff, Guard Mary Pasco, Trustees: Hazel Crystal, Irene Boilore and Myrtle Harris. Others elected to other positions were: Delia Palmer, Pauline McNeil and Alice Locke.

The Auxiliary held a Bazaar in September to raise funds to support their Hospital program. Hospital Chairman Myrtle Harris said the profits from the Bazaar would go for the most worthy of causes, caring for the needs of the disabled veterans.

On November 19th, the Post and the Auxiliary members held a Christmas party for the children, many of whom would have little for Christmas.

The auxiliary also joined with other Auxiliaries in Michigan in a program that purchased a carload of Gerber's Baby Food which was enough to feed 500 babies all winter.

The "fun" degree of the VFW was the Military Order of the Cootie and their auxiliary was the Cootiettes. Both organizations had very unusual names for their officers' positrons. The "real" cooties were constant companions for the Army during World War I in France, hence the array of names are associated with this experience.

The Cooties elected the following: Seam Squirrel Emanuel Boilore, Blanket Bum Bob Utt, Hide Gimlet Joe Rosbury, Quartermaster Harry Pokorny, Shyster Walter Wilhoit, Sky Pilot Walter Stiff and Hospital Chairman Isaac Stiff.

Their compatriots, the Cootiettes, with the "cootie" related names for their officers held their election in late October. Those elected to the offices with the "funny" names were: Chief Grayback Agnes Bottecelli, Lady Louse Zelma Slover, Baby Louse Myrtle Harris, Scratcher Irene Boilore, Shekel Keeper Edna Pokorny, Pious Louse Lelah Stiff, Louse Hunter Katherine Muce, Tightwad Leda Hanbey and Marie Wagner.

The Amvets Post 135 was organized on April 8th at the Fenton Community Center. A group of about twenty young veterans of WW II felt the need for the new, younger veterans of the war to form a new organization. The spirit of comradery of the younger veterans had stayed with them after they had returned home and to the life of a civilian.

At their first meeting they elected Ben Cloud as their Commander and the following officers; Secretary Robert Turco and Treasurer Curt Schupbach. Others in attendance at this meeting reported in the *Fenton Independent* (last names only...ugh) were: Amundsen, Foley, Helmboldt, Cunningham and Landis.

At their third meeting in mid-May, the membership had grown to twenty-eight and serious planning and organization was underway. The plans included forming a bowling team for league completion in one of the summer leagues. However most of the discussion during the meeting was about naming the post after one of Fenton's fallen soldiers.

After an evening of discussion the group chose to name the post in honor of two of Fenton's sons lost in the war. The post was named the "Weigant-Zabitch Post 135".

Robert Weigant, an Army Paratrooper and a graduate of Fenton High School, Class of 1943, lost his life in combat in Belgium in 1944 as the Allied Forces were making a push to cross the Rhine and drive into Germany.

Melvin Zabitch was in the Army in the Philippines when the Japanese invaded that country. He was in a hospital at the time and was captured by the Japanese and placed in a labor camp. When General MacArthur's troops landed to retake the Philippines, the Japanese decided to load some five hundred prisoners on a ship and send them to labor camps in Japan. The freighter transporting the POWs was moving in a northerly direction along the coastline when it was torpedoed by one of our submarines and sank. Only a few of the POWs made it to shore and were rescued later. PFC Melvin Zabitch was not one of the survivors

Scene Six...The Church Scene

It was an unusual year for the church pastors. Reverends H.G. Cooper, Robert Bell and H. C. Kaas left their Fenton Churches for other positions. In June, Reverend Cooper resigned as Pastor of the First Baptist Church after 20 months to accept a pastorate in Gypsum, Kansas. It wasn't until September before the Reverend Hugh Woodside accepted Fenton's call and left his church in Canada. The Woodside family moved into the parsonage adjacent to the church.

The Episcopalians lost the very popular Reverend Robert Bell in late November, when the pastor accepted the leadership of the Calvary Episcopal Church in Saginaw. During his five years in residence, the Reverend and his wife had been active in the town's community life. The Episcopal Diocese did not designate his replacement for another six months, so the congregation conducted the Sunday services with visiting clergy and lay readers during this period.

Another popular clergyman left Fenton in December when the Reverend Kaas and his wife announced they were moving to Riley, Michigan to assume the pastorate of the nearby St. Peter's Lutheran Church.

The "work" of the Church continued throughout the year in a very traditional manner. The Presbyterian women, organized in four groups, called "cornerstones", met on a regular basis and conducted their various "good works" projects. The leaders of the Cornerstones this year were: # 1- Mrs. DesJardins and Mrs. Harry Faling; #2- Mrs. Lee Kerton; #3- Mrs. Herb Roberts, Mrs. Leonard and Mrs. J. C. VanDoorn; and #4- Mrs. C. A. Leetch, Mrs. Tom McKinley and Mrs. Roy Buffmeyer.

St. Jude's Episcopal women were members of the "Guild". In May the elected their leaders for the year: President Mrs. William Scott, 1st VP Mrs. Burns Fuller, 2nd VP Mrs. Douglas Clark, 3rd VP Mrs. James McKinley Jr., Secretary Miss Thelma Clement, Treasurer Miss Effie Bishop. Other Committee members were: Mrs. Frank Mytinger, Mrs. Aldrich Locke, Mrs. Edmund Gould, Mrs. Robert Obenshain, Mrs. Floyd Chapin, Miss. Flora Davis, Mrs. Harriet Harris, Mrs. Marion Moore and Mrs. Ed. Blazier.

The Methodist women were organized in "bands", four in number, and met on a regular basis to conduct their church work and community projects. Among the leaders for the year were: Mrs. Cora Dittalock Mrs. Ed Burden and Mrs. Henry Alchin. In late September, between 125 and 150 church members attended the Dedication of a new Church parsonage where Mrs. Clair Abbott sang a very appropriate song... "Bless this Home".

The St. John Catholic Church was the sponsor of a young ladies society..."Sodality". Sodality's Christmas Ball was an annual affair that the members and community enjoyed immensely. A solemn reception of new members was held in mid-May. The new members were: Eleanor Anthes, Eleanor Dunn, Joan Dreyer, Clare Foley Clara Hubert, Marie Jacobs, Mildred Jacobs, Kathryn Matthews and Norma Bauer. Annie Vincent was in charge of the ceremony which included selections of the Sodality Choir under the direction of Mrs. Lawrence Marklund. The Reverend Dennis P Tighe delivered the sermon.

In July, the townsfolk had the pleasure of attending St. John's annual Bar-B-Que. Those who had attended enjoyed a delicious turkey dinner, the Bingo, Rodeo and many other events.

The Trinity Lutheran Church, Main Street

Scene Seven...The Fenton Community Center

Of the many programs offered at the Fenton Community Center, it seemed the most popular with the adult population of the Village was the Adventure Lecture Series.

For example, in early March, over four hundred persons attended the Adventure Series lecture by Dennis Cooper, a former Air Force Major who had recorded his experiences in the Pacific theatre and now presented a very interesting illustrated lecture entitled "From New Guinea to Japan with the Fifth Air Force". Many of those who attended the lecture at the Fenton Community Center said this presentation was the "best ever". Major Cooper, a former Intelligence Officer, spoke for two hours using both colored motion pictures and hand painted slides.

In the last lecture of the 1946-1947 Adventure series, Flint Attorney Louis D. McGregor, an inveterate world traveler and hunter, presented a colorful talk about "Mexico". As a "bonus" for the two hundred or so attending, complimentary tickets to the Ben East lecture on April 22nd were offered. Ben East, a familiar and frequent lecturer in Fenton, was the Field Editor for the "Outdoor Life" magazine.

The 1947-1948 Adventure Series began on October 19th with the appearance of Henry Hedges with "The Southwest Pacific". Mr. Hedges, a Chicago Engineer, was a Seabee in the Southwest Pacific. During this time, he filmed the people of Bora Bora and his movies were "breathtakingly beautiful" and portrayed the Polynesian way of living.

The November program was with "Slim" Williams on "The Yukon Trail Blazer". According "Slim's" publicist he was a "world famed international trail blazer and wolfdog musher". Again, the FCC Auditorium was filled to capacity.

The December show marked the return of Dennis Cooper, now a Detroit teacher. Mr. Cooper's topic on this occasion was "Isle Royale Vacation". Again, he had large and enthusiastic audience in excess of three hundred persons

For the last eight years, the Community Center had conducted a Summer Recreation Program. With this experience, the FCC was able to offer a very expansive recreational program, one that met the varied needs of the participants. This expanded program was aided by the cooperation of the Student Council, the FCC's Social Committee, Old Time Dance organization and The Village Players. Activities began on June 30th and ended on August 15th. Some of the activities were:

- Mrs. Jerold Pasco had two special interest groups…Grades 5 and 6 and Grades 7 and up. The groups participated in overnight hikes, canoe trips, softball, campfires and photographing. Other activities were dictated by the interests of the children.
- For those that enjoyed creative play, Miss Miriam Kinner offered a variety of things to make and skills to learn. Articles made of plastic metal, fabric; leather and clay were made by the boys and girls.
- The athletic minded boys played in a softball league two nights a week. They played handball, badminton and ping pong at the Center.
- Swimming was available for all attendees other than those in the Tot Lot.
- After the second week of the program, an attendance report was published.

Girls Recreation	25
Boys Recreation	127
Tot Lot	271
Swimming	122

Two other services offered by the FCC were appropriate for the times: Job Service and Veterans Counseling.

The Job Service staff added another function in July when they began to assist in "ride sharing". They found that there were a significant number of auto workers without reliable transportation to the Flint auto plants. Therefore they began publicize their willingness to bring drivers and riders together.

The primary function of the Job Service was to have job applicants registered along with employers hiring needs. In the summer the area farmers were appealing for part-time or full-time farm workers no experience necessary!

The Job Center reported in July, that they had applicants with the following skills: Men: Carpenters, Laborers, Clerks, Linesman, General

Office, Truck Drivers, Sales and Machine Operator. Women: Clerks, Waitress, Stenographer, Practical Nurse, Housework and Child Care.

Both the American Legion and the Veterans of Foreign Wars in Fenton had a Service Officer who was trained to help veterans with problems, such applying for medical assistance, VA home loans and all conceivable inquires with which the veteran has communicating with the Government agencies. Apparently, the Village thought the need was so great, that they asked the FCC to establish a Veteran's Counseling Service. Its mission was to help veterans in their employment, education and other problems. In July, a month of typical activity, the FCC reported the following:

>Number of Veterans Served
>   Spanish American War.......... 1
>   World War II....................30
>   Next-of-Kin......................2
>Tyoe if Contacts
>   New Veterans...................19
>   Repeat Veterans.................21
>   New Next-of-Kin................2

The Community Center was "the" place in town to dance. The "Summer Dance Calendar" was published in the *Fenton Independent* in mid-June. Old Time Dancing was very popular with the "older folks" and "swing" was "in" for the younger crowd The Band's motto was "Swing and Sail with Dickie Smale"

SUMMER DANCE CALENDAR
SATURDAYS
FENTON COMMUNITY CENTER BALLROOM

MODERN DANCES	OLD TIME DANCES
9:30—1:00	9:00—1;00
Dick Smale's Orchestra	Music by Louis Gage
June 21	Caller, John Martin
July 5 and 19	June 14 and 28
August 2, 16, 30	July 12 and 28
	August 9 and 23

Admission 60c
"Nothing to sell but a good time"

The FCC Board of Directors held their annual meeting in September and elected Otis Furman, the assistant Cashier at the State Savings Bank, to serve as a Board member, filling the vacancy resulting from the death of Charles S. Crane. Board members serve until age 70 and are a self-perpetuating administrative body, charged with the handling of the operations of the Community Center. At their meeting, the Board returned Harry Lemen to the office of the President and Don Alchin as Vice President. George Paine became the new Secretary replacing Elton Austin who held the office for 6 years. Otis Furman was selected as the Center's Treasurer.

On July 22nd, Mary A. Rackham, the widow of Horace Rackham, died after a long illness. Mrs. Rackham was the daughter of Dexter Horton, a veteran of the Civil War and a prominent citizen of Fenton in the 1800s. Mrs. Rackham was born in Fenton on September 1, 1864 and graduated from the Fenton High School in 1887. Her husband was a friend, attorney and early investor of Henry Ford. With the success of Henry Ford, the Rackhams acquired considerable wealth with which they generously supported many projects. They established the Rackham Foundation, and in 1938 provided the funding for the building of the Fenton Community Center and the Fenton Municipal Building (better known as the "Fire Hall").

As a "human interest" sidelight, one should know about the story Ivah Rolland enjoyed telling. It was Ivah's birthday and her mother-in-law, Mrs. Frederick G. Rolland the former Margaret Eddy was holding a party for Ivah at her residence.

One of the guests was Mary Horton Rackham. Margaret Rolland and Mary Rackham had been schoolmates in their younger years and were lifelong friends.

Ivah recalled that sometime during the gathering, Mary Rackham said she was considering making a substantial gift to the Village of Fenton. She asked Ivah what she thought the village needed most of all. Ivah said her response to Mrs. Rackham was that the town needed a "community house", a place where the town's people could gather.

Sometime later, the Horace H. Rackham and Mary A. Rackham Foundation made a gift to the Village of Fenton to build a "Community House". Ivah Rolland enjoyed telling her friends the Community Center was "her Birthday gift"!

What a fine gift...one that keeps on giving!

Scene Eight.. "Stand Up and Cheer for Fenton High"

After two exceptional seasons of Basketball, the expectations for the 1946-1947 team were very high. After all some of the "stars" of last year's team were returning for their senior year. Clare Whitman, Ned Jaggi, George Howe, Charles Helms and Marc Peck were the returning seniors that created the "great expectations".

The season had its "ups and downs" especially after opening the season with a smashing 57-5 win over Swartz Creek, but losing to Howell, Holly and Beecher were real "downers".

But in spite of these disappointments, the team was the Champions of the Genesee County League making it three in a row for FHS.

George Howe and Ned Jaggi were the team leaders with Jaggi establishing the new school scoring record with 171 point during the season. Howe was close behind scoring 132 points.

The season record ended with 11 wins and 4 losses after the team "checked out" in the first game of the District Tournament losing to Orchard Lake St. Mary by the score 29-25.

FHS 1946-1947 Basketball Team

Front Row L-R Walter Tobin, Jack Reed, Ned Jaggi, George Howe, Chuck Helms, Marc Peck   Back Row L-R Ken Herrick, Clare "Junior" Whitman, Jim Bottecelli, Frank Winn, Pat Foley, Mr. Ivan Williams, Mr. Emile Gosseaux.

FHS Track Team 1947

1st Row: Marc Peck, Charles Helms, Dick Perry, Allan Gale, George Howe, Bud Cole, Frank Winn, Robert Glaspie. 2nd Row: Frank Helms, Leo Foley, Charles Franks, ????, ????, Royce Hyde, Coach Ivan Williams. 3rd Row: Sam Hunter Mgr., Jack Orritt, Walter Tobin, ?, ?, ?, Floyd Guernsey, Mgr.

The Trackmen of FHS had an outstanding season by being the 1st place winners in the Genesee County League meet. They placed third in the Regional meet and first place in the dual meets with Clio, Bendle and Grand Blanc. When it came to the State meet is when the FHS athletes shinned, especially miler George Howe and Chuck Helms. George Howe won every race he ran taking County, Regional and State honors for the second year in a row...fastest miler in Michigan's High Schools for those two years in all classes. Chuck Helms became a State Champion by winning the 880 with a time of 20:04.4. [1]

The Baseball team had a so-so season going 4-4 with too many "rainouts" interrupting the rhythm of the season. Frank Winn, Mike Harrison Jerry Durfee, Frank Helms, Pat Foley, Bud Gale, Lemen Shelby, Jim Bottecelli, Vince Messinger and Max Bottecelli were the lettermen for the season.

---

[1] Michigan High School Sports Assoc. Records

Everyone was back in school and "it was time for some Friday night football!" Coach Ivan Williams had a several veterans returning and the prospects of a winning season were good.

As the season progressed the team exceeded all expectations, going undefeated until they lost to Beecher in a hard fought contest on the opponent's home field. The team got back on the winning track and won their last three games which included the traditional Thanksgiving game with arch rival Holly High School.

This was the third consecutive year in which the Fenton football teams had defeated Holly, so the Holly Herald Trophy found a home in the FHS trophy case.

The attendance at the home games may have proved that "everyone likes a winner". The home crowds exceeded 2000 at each game. The team's supporters also traveled to the away games in surprising numbers. The *Fenton Independent* remarked after the team played Bendle on their turf with a large contingent of Fenton rooters in the crowd "Not many years ago Fenton couldn't get that many to attend home games to say nothing of those played out of town"

Phillips Field, the home of the Tigers, now had some new bleachers which would provide game seating for 1200 to 1300 fans. For many it would be the first time, when attending a home game, they did not have to stand along the sidelines.

The site now had a Fieldhouse which provided a locker room for both teams and a food service to provide drinks and snacks As the rules provided at the time, there was no "platooning" so a player would be on both offense and defense. Jim Bottecelli at right end, who drew much praise for his defensive prowess, also found success in receiving a pass from his younger brother, Quarterback Max Bottecelli. The team also had a "specialist" in Darwin Dager...a place kicker. Dager had a fine season, however his debut wasn't his best effort...he missed on his first extra point in the Bendle game. Running back Chuck Franks was injured, a broken collarbone, in that game, and Lemen Shelby stepped in and proved to be an excellent replacement. In the Clio game, Shelby ran for 75 yards in only 8 carries. The two guards, Frank Helms and Cline Hagerman received recognition for their solid defense on several occasions.

The starting lineup for most of the year was as follows: LE-Pat Foley, LT-Phil Scott, LG-Frank Helms, C-Bruce Dorland and Warren Robinson, RG-Cline Hagerman, RT-Dick Locke and Leo Foley, FB-Rick Rockman, QB-Max Bottecelli, LHB-Charles Franks and Leman Shelby, RHB-Bill Hill and Dick Perry. Eight Fenton players were selected for the All-County team. Those selected were: First Team-Cline Hagerman, Leo Foley and Rick Rockman; Second Team-Jim Bottecelli and Bruce Dorland; Honorable Mention-Phil Scott, Frank Helms and Max Bottecelli.

FHS 1947 Football Team

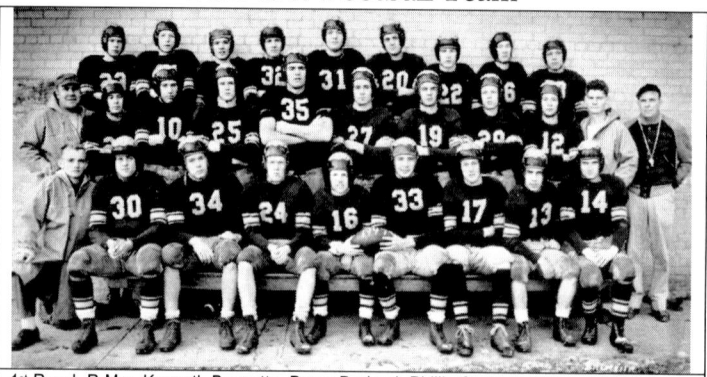

1st Row L-R Mgr. Kenneth Bennetts, Bruce Dorland, Phillip Scott, Ed Bjorling, Bill Hill, Jim Bottecelli, Wallace Robinson, Don Schupbach, Dick Perry. 2nd Row L-R Coach Ivan Williams, Bill Auker, Norm Spear, Chuck Franks, Leo Foley, Rick Rockman, Cline Hagerman, Leman Shelby, John Wright, Mgr. Art Bush, Asst Coach Bill Cowan. 3rd Row L-R Jerry Durfee, Garner Merrick, Max Bottecelli, Frank Helms, Dick Locke, Pat Foley, Dick Rynearson, Sam Hunter, Vince Messinger.

Scene Nine…While the Children Play Games

Running a school district was serious business and the Board of Education was comprised a group of serious men headed by their long time President Harry A. Lowe. With their guidance the Fenton schools had conducted an excellent academic program, accredited by the University of Michigan, and generally recognized by the community as being of top quality. The Board had managed the district's financial affairs very well providing the funds to maintain the facilities and employ a well-qualified teaching and administrative staff. The Board was frugal but not "penny-pinching". They were concerned about their employees who stood by during the war years when funds were short and the demands high. In their meeting of late June as they were completing their budget for the coming school, in which they had planned to increase each teacher's salary by $300, the State Legislature increased the distribution of funds to the school. This allowed the Board to increase the amount for each teacher from $300 to $500.

Salaries for the 1947-1948 would now begin at a $500 increase of the salaries of 1946-1947. Under the new schedule, beginning teachers would draw $2400 with an increase of $100 each year. The newspaper reported that "The present schedule is a generous one. It is in line with trends that are not only statewide, but national as well." The following is a list of those contracted for the 1947-1948 school year.

Kindergarten-Eleanor Munn & Lois Strom
1st Grade-Leta Clay & Della Gardner
2nd Grade- Iola Ireland Pasco & Jean Kunk
3rd Grade-Alice Hillman & Zella Pyne
4th Grade-Mary Hoffman & Fritzi Lipp
5th Grade-Huldah Bousu & Marie Saupe
6th Grade-Jean Holloman & Alice Wheaton
Art-Eleanor Annis
Music-Lucille Buta
Commercial-Bessie Cramer & Jean Gordon
Jr. Hi English-Ellen Adams
English-Joyce Haglund & Rebecca Zankl
Shop-Maurice Kieft
Science Miriam Kinner

Soc. Science & English-Anne Paynich
Science & Math-Emile Gosseaux
Geography-Dwight Fisher
Home Econ.-Evelyn Northrup
History-Athletics-Hubert Cowan
Instrumental Music-Howard Park
Latin & English-Hazel Brown
Jr. Hi Math-Esther Stehle
Science & Math-Charles Leighton
Boy's P.E.& Coach-Ivan William
HS Principal * Math-August Arndt
Superintendent-Clarence R. Heemstra
Secretary-Dorothy Hodgman
Janitor-Odie Wilhoit, Edward Warner
  & Ray Seger

As the schools opened in the fall, Fenton schools were experiencing an unanticipated increase in enrollment. The total enrollment was 1066, of which 514 were in the lower grades and the remaining 552 were in high school. Accommodations were at a premium with two classes meeting during the lunch hour. Kindergarten enrollment estimates were much too low and in general it was recognized that the time was rapidly approaching when the old buildings would no longer be able to provide the space required to meet increasing enrollments.

The Parent-Teachers Association, the PTA, continued to be active during the year. In early May, the PTA held their annual election and the following individuals were elected to serve. Eldon Burton was elected President and for the High School, the Reverend Harley Stockham was elected "Father", Mrs. H.O. Dexter the "Mother" and the "Teacher" was Mr. Charles Leighton. For the Junior High, Carl Tisch was elected "Father", Mrs. D. A. O'Dell the "Mother" and Miss Alice Hillman the "Teacher". (All the Fathers, Mothers and Teachers were also Vice Presidents). Mrs. Don Bristol was elected as the Secretary and Robert Lutz was named the Treasurer.

In October, at their first meeting of the new school year, President Burton outlined the objectives for the year, one of which was to develop a large membership through presenting interesting programs and good fellowship. The attendance at the opening meeting exceeded 150 interested parents and teachers.

The Student Council was another governmental body in the school operations. To the author, it is surprising to learn of the authority this group possessed. An earlier Student Council had conducted the sale of "bonds" to the public to raise the funds for the installation of lights on Philips Field. The bonds were to be repaid within five years from the revenue received for admission to the night football games. The Student Council anticipated a major increase in this revenue because of the games being played a night when more of the public could attend...and they were right! The attendance at the games was considerably higher and the bonds were paid off in the first year.

Now, the Student Council recognized the need for a "field house" to accommodate rest rooms, snack bar and space for the teams to assemble. Since the previous "bond" sale had worked so well, in June they offered a $4,500 bond sale and with the help of the Kiwanis, XX Club and the State Savings Bank, the project was fully subscribed in record time. In July the construction of the building began and it was completed in time for the football season.

FHS Student Council 1946-1947

!st Row: Rosemary Howe, Jeanne Kelley, Allen Niskanen, Shirley Scott, George Howe, Robert Glaspie, Barbara Swanebeck, Barbara Petty. 2nd Row: Ronald Millington, Charles Kuehn, Carol Hartley, Norma Kelley, Mr. August Arndt, Violet Petry, Michael Harrison, Max Bottecelli. 3rd Row: Garner Merrick.   Frank Helms, James Bottecelli, Charles Helms, Ned Jaggi, Edward Louden.

The President and Vice President of the Student Council were elected in the spring of the year for the upcoming school year. Representatives of each class were elected each semester. Consequently, the leaders of the Student Council for the first part of 1947 were in the class of 1947 and are those pictured above.[2] The officers were President George Howe, Vice President Allen Niskanen, Secretary Shirley Scott and Treasurer Robert Glaspie.

Fenton High School had not only distinguished itself in athletics but was well respected for its music program. Both the band and the chorus, under the direction of Mr. Howard Park and Mrs. Lucille Buta, had established a well-deserved reputation for excellence.

The Chorus entertained the student body at several assemblies and the community with their presentations at the annual Christmas and spring concerts. During this year the chorus also entered District competition and earned a "ticket" to the State Contest at East Lansing where they were recognized for an excellent performance The Chorus also participated in the Hartland Music Festival for the first time.

The Chorus elected the following officers: President Jack Pellett, Secretary Joy Durand, Librarian Nancy Bauer and Accompanist Carol Alchin.

---

[2] Picture from *The Fentonian 1947* Courtesy of Cecelia (Colburn) Terry '47

114   The Village Players Post War

FHS Chorus 1946-1947

1st Row L-R: Mrs. Lucille Buta, Norma Foley, Mildred Miller, Nancy Bauer, Venetia Standridge, Martha Swanson, Mary Alice Gordon, Carol Alchin, Lois Hungerford, Marian Alchin. 2nd Row: Lois Jean Nichols, Joyce Durand, Frank Helms, George Howe, Bernard Sinclair, Edward Bjorling, Jack Pellett, Phyllis McCormick, Virginia Swartz. 3rd Row: Virginia Hall, Eleanor Anthes, Clare Cooper, Harold Rockman, Charles Helms, Clark Patton, Robert Walsh, Carol Eddy, Barbara Reed. 4th Row: Betty Heron, Irene Sherwood, William Freeman, Richard Locke, Eugene Bently, Marva Edwards, Deloris Finger, Jane Stanovich.[3]

FHS Choral Choir 1946-1947

1st Row L-R: Mrs. Lucille Buta, Venetia Standridge, Norma Kelly, Nancy Bauer, Mildred Miller, Mary Alice Gordon, Carol Alchin, Lois Hungerford. 2nd Row: Frank Helms, George Howe, Bernard Sinclair, Edward Bjorling, Jack Pellett.[4]

---

[3] Ibid.
[4] Ibid

The Fenton High School Band was the "heart beat" of the student body. The Band played at all of the school events; assemblies, football games (home and away), basketball games and school and town parades. Under the direction of Mr. Howard Park, the band also played for the Villages' annual Christmas Concert and their Spring Concert at the Community Center. The Band was also invited to play at the State Fair from August 29th through September 7th.

FHS Band 1946-1947

1st Row L-R Barbara Ireland, Janis Anderson, Phyllis Roberts, Walter Hungerford, Jerry Hatfield, Mildred Miller, Marjorie Hoyle. 2nd Row: Conrad Krankle, James Frank, Marion Nash, Leroy Young, Thomas Stephens, Frank Winn, Carolyn Fisher, Erma Muchler, Eleanor Harper, Edward Louden. Robert Wessendorf, Donald Griswold, Lee Merrick. 3rd Row: Dorothy Hoyle, Charles Turner, Darlene Jarvis, Kenneth Herrick, Arlin Horvath, Betty Watkins Bruce Dorland. Marion Alchin. Lyle Harper, Bruce Collins, Howard Bacon. 4th Row: Howard Park, Carol Alchin, Jane Hodgman, Joyce Orritt, Lois Torrey, Harold Rockman, Bruce Champlin.
Members Absent: Joyce French, Martha Moyer, Donald Butcher, Jack Pellett, Jean Kuzukos, Robert McKenzie.

(Author's Note: The "Band" picture was not included for identifying the band members as much as it was to show the "gymnasium"...this is where basketball games, assemblies, dances, plays, public meetings and many other events were held.)

116 The Village Players Post War

The Fenton Community Center was the site in March for the Second Solo and Ensemble Festival sponsored by the FHA Band. A number of bands from the surrounding region participated in the competition. Members of the band also participated in the State Solo and Ensemble Festival. At the Honor Assembly in June the following individuals were recognized for the performances at these Festivals.

FHS Festival Solo	State Festival Solo	FHS Festival Ensemble	State Festival Ensemble
Donald Griswold	Marian Alchin	Jerry Hatfield	Kenneth Herrick
Jerry Hatfield	Carol Alchin	Janice Anderson	Skip Horvath
Marian Alchin	Howard Bacon	Conrad Krankle	Leroy Young
Howard Bacon		Walt Hungerford	
		Skip Horvath	
		Leroy Young	
		Kenneth Herrick	

It was a lot like "once in a blue moon"...during the year there were two Senior Class Plays during the year. In the Spring, the Class of 1946 presented "The Old School Spirit" on the evening of April 24th at the Community Center. The players also did a matinée performance for the grade school children. In her weekly column "School Daze" in the *Fenton Independent,* Barbara Hyde pronounced it an "Excellent Performance" and said it was the "best I've seen". It did play to a packed house and the audience was quite effusive in applause and praise. The play was directed by Mrs. Russell (Sybil) Haddon and had the following students in the cast: Dallas Goss, Norma Kelley, Dick Pratt, Bob Wessendorf, Cecelia Colburn, Penrod Wright, Martha Swanson, Venetia Standridge, Merelyn Burton, Ann Gibney, Frank Winn, Jeanne Thorpe and Charles Helms.

The Senior Class for 1948 chose to have their Senior Play on the evening of December 11th at the Community Center. The play was "West End High", play that looked at the lives of a group of likeable young people of high school age. The play was again directed by Mrs. Haddon. The Senior students in the cast were: Royce Gearheart, Leo Foley, Nancy Bauer, Rosemary Howe, Ed Bjorling, Vic Guernsey, Peg Richmond, Ray Coyne, Nancy Schleicher, Holly Walpole, Ann Loomis, Rosemary Jacobs and Danna Bronson.

The All High Banquet and the Junior-Senior Banquet were traditional events which were held each school year...and year 1947 was not an exception. The All-High Banquet was held on Friday evening, April 18th at the Community Center. The theme for the Banquet was ""The Races of Mankind". Freshman Violet Petry spoke of "The Negro Race", Max Bottecelli, a sophomore, talked about The Red Race", "The Yellow Race" was the topic presented by junior Carol Hartley and the senior spokesman, Gerald Dougherty's topic was "The White Race".. Penrod Wright was the Toastmaster and the faculty speaker was Mr. Alfred Scholten.

Following the Banquet, there was dancing in the Gym at the High School until two in the morning. Glen Mallack's orchestra provided the music...and as the saying goes..."a good time was had by all".

A month later the seniors were the quests of the Juniors at the annual Senior-Junior Banquet.

. The affair was held at the Community Center and the theme was "Bon Voyage" and the decorations, invitations and programs carried out the theme. As it had been in the previous banquet the mothers of the junior students prepared the meal and the junior's father served as the waiters

The evening's Toastmaster was Bill Hill and Rosemary Howe was the speaker for the Juniors. Marjorie Bachus responded for the Seniors. Entertainment was provided by Mrs. Buta' "Choral Group" and Mr. Emil Gosseaux played several piano selections before Carol Hartley, Leo Foley and Jim Bottecelli presented a "Giftatory" to the Seniors. Music at the dance that followed was by Ralph Crawford's orchestra.

It was Homecoming on October 10th and while the football game with Kearsley High was important there were other events that were equally exciting...such as the Bonfire on Thursday night followed by the snake dance through the downtown...and as the newspaper urged the townsfolk to get there position on the street early to watch the festive youth...snaking through the streets.

The Homecoming Queen was crowned under the lights on Phillips Field before the kickoff for the game. The candidates for Queen, which were nominated by each class, were: Seniors-Loretta Shelby and Janet Huston; Juniors-Barb Swanebeck and Barb Petty; Sophomores-Violet Petry and Joyce Orritt; Freshman-Lea Weesner and Lucille Hubert. After the student vote the final five were-Huston, Shelby, Petty, Swanebeck and Hubert They rode in a yellow convertible to the center of the field where Superintendent Clarence Heemstra announced the name of the Queen and presented Barb Petty the crown and a corsage. Following the game there was a dance at the Community Center.

118 The Village Players Post War

"Togetherness" Time for old friends to "party"...It's 1947, and the location is the dance hall in Russellville...From left to right around the table...Ken Trimmer and Jean , Bob Turco, Elmer Schupbach, Louis Trimmer, Marnie and Pete Hartley, Lois (Searight) Putnam and Ray Putnam, Jim Durfee, Barbara (Glaspie) Johnson, Joyce ("PeeWee" Glaspie Crawford and Ralph Crawford, Lillian and Curt Schupbach. (There appears to be 92 beer bottles on the table !)

Scene Ten...Let Us Entertain You!

The *Rowena* was the only movie theater in town, but it showed "first run" movies! Unlike the theaters in many small venues, the *Rowena* had an "uncle" in the business. J.C. Peck, the owner-manager of the theater was a member of an industry committee that made the decisions on the distribution of the movies in this region. Consequently, "Jaycee" always made sure the "first run" theatres included the *Rowena*.

The local theater group decided to change their name again! Over the years they had been the "mimes", "the drama club", "the little theatre group" and once before "The Village Players". Regardless of the name, the small group of local thespians were active again in 1947. As the newspaper reported, their aim was "to have a good time putting on a good show which will entertain others".

The Village Players selected "Ladies of the Jury" as their first production of the new year. Rehearsals began in February and the show was held at the Community Center on April 0th and 10th before a "full house". The President of the Village Players, Mrs. Russell Lince. and the Director, Mrs. A. Johnson, were praised for an excellent cast selection. The cast included: Mrs. L. A. Wilson, Mrs. Jay Davis, Elizabeth Pedersen, Peggy Macdonnell, Mrs. Emile Gosseaux, Mrs. Joseph Oren, Chris McGarry, Robert Shields, Alan Macdonnell Jr., Elmer Strom, Ryan Strom, Alan Macdonnell Sr., William Gallagher, Earnest Tirrell, Dean Winter, Russell Lince, Burt Meyer, Sibyl Haddon, Lynn Winter, JoAnn Sneath and J. A. Johnson.

A "Guest in the House" was the show for October 23d and 23th. The play was presented at the Community Center to another "standing room only" audience. The Junior Chamber of Commerce sponsored the Village Players in this production. This three-act comedy was directed by Earnest Tirrell, who was assisted by Mrs. Russell Lince. The cast included: Mrs. Herman Wessendorf, Sue Lowe, Mrs. L. A. Wilson, Mrs. Fred Rollins, Mrs. Kenneth Wood, Bob Smith, Ryan Strom, Wilbur Strom, Burt Moyer, Mrs. Russell Haddon, Marion Churchill, Mrs. J. A. Johnson and Grant Wright.

The "Christmas Show" at the Community Center was a musical variety show organized by the Village Players and directed by Mrs. Robert Smith. It was called "Farced-Fetched" and included an array of local musical talent. Santa Claus made an appearance to the delight of sthe parents and their children in attendance. The show ended with a community sing that "revved up" the holiday spirit.

In April, "Uncle Jack" Hutchkiss introduced his "Dancing Dolls". The "Dolls" were a group of children, at the beginning all under two years of age, whose specialty was "old fashioned" dancing. Later they accepted children a few years older. They also had a flair for performing in public. In a few months the group had over forty members. They made their first public appearance at the V.F. W. Hall on April 30th and in the months to follow were booked by many organizations. The "Dolls", dressed in formals and evening clothes, made an appearance at the I.O.O.F. Hall, where over forty "dolls" performed a Grand March to the awe of those in attendance,

Their repertoire expanded beyond square dancing as time went on, and soon included Spanish dancing and other pleasing dance skits. Some of the children who were "Dancing Dolls" were: Donald Burke, Jimmy Bauer, Dale Clark, Nancy Joslyn, Ida Hartsough, Fred Schulte, Donna Banks, Marjorie Joslyn, Joan Parkin, Rex Roberts, Ann Zamble, Richard Graham, Janie Bently, Nancy Fraser, Anne Zankl, Sandy Black, Donna Black and Sandra Nelson.

Everyone loves a parade...and the people of the Village of Fenton were not an exception The National holidays found the city band leading the way to Memorial Park (in front of the A.J. Phillips Library) or to Oakwood Cemetery. However there were a couple of parades that were different.

It was mid-August and the town was experiencing a heat wave, with temperatures around 100 degrees, when the "Motorless Parade" was held. It was the second annual Motorless Parade which marked the end of the summer playground activities. Following the parade, the town's youth were invited to participate in a "talent show" at the Community Center. Ron Millington was the Master of Ceremonies for the talent show and the Kiwanis provided prizes for the best talent

The town celebrated Halloween each year. The parade started at the high school on Adelaide Street and after traversing Adelaide, Mill, South Leroy and Caroline Streets, ended up in Philips Field under the lights. Youngsters of all ages were invited to parade and to be judged for the best costumes. The City Band led the way and as you would expect..."a good time was had by all".

The donkeys were back in town in 1947! In January, they were involved in a basketball game at the FHS gym before a crowd of over

600. In September, the Donkeys played baseball on the FHS diamond under the auspices of the American Legion. The event attracted a crowd of several hundred who witnessed a very different kind of baseball.

By 1947, the townsfolk had returned to their pre-war year-around sports programs. In the fall it was men's basketball and both men and women's bowling leagues. With the coming of the warmer weather, it was baseball and softball that received the most attention

As the year began the basketball league was finishing up the portion of their program that began in the latter part of the previous year. The league was composed of four teams from Brighton and Fenton. The teams were: Fenton Concrete Works, Industrial's CIO, Brighton #1, Brighton #2 and Sugden's Irregulars. The Fenton team's players included many former FHS players. Bob Torrey, Bud Madden, Duane Loomis, Bob Ireland, Brad Hoffman, Garner Merrick, Ralph Crawford, Bill Brabon, Curt Schupbach, Bruce McLenna, Bob Hunt, Don Orthner, Larry Sugdenand Bass were some of the Fenton fellows who were playing.

The league President was Elmer F. Hunt and the Chairman of the FCC Recreation Committee was Bruce Marsh. Any Fenton area man, including the rural and resort districts, were invited to participate. The Fenton Schools provided the use of the gym and showers at no charge. The league also had the assistance of FHS Coach Ivan Williams. The league play ended in May and the league was reconstituted in the following November for a new season.

There was still some snow on the ground, when in March, the Fenton Recreation Committee through Elmer F. Hunt put out a call to the baseball enthusiasts in Genesee County, of Fenton's intention to organize a County Wide Baseball league for the 1947 season. Consequently, by May, five teams in addition to the Fenton Merchants team, began league play. The teams were from Gaines, Clarkston, Holly, Linden and Byron. It wasn't until October before the season concluded with the Gaines team winning the honors, with Fenton closely behind. For the most part, Fenton's pitching chores were handled by Don Orthner and Harold "Tar" Foley. Some of the Fenton players were: the catcher Art Brown and Vern Hunt, Lyle "BoBo" Neely, Claude Kirkey and Lyle Bumstead. The Merchants star pitcher young Don Orthner went 9-1, pitched ten complete games with his only loss to the league champion team from Gaines

For those that preferred softball, there was a league formed that had six teams from...all from the Fenton area. The team names were: the Independents, Tyrone, American Legion, Long Lake, Eagles and Concrete Block Co.. They played a full schedule through July and the teams were very competitive, with the league lead changing frequently, but in the end, the team from Tyrone nosed out the Independent tame by ½ game and the third place American Legion team by 1 ½ games.

The "new" Fenton Recreation finally dropped the "new" in their name and rightfully so, they were the only Bowling Alley in town. .

The ladies bowled in the Fenton Recreation Ladies League with twelve teams: Fenton Drug Co., Genesee Tool, Fenton Five, Woodworth Brothers, Mitt's Greenhouse, Craft Funeral, Linden, Fenton Home Grocers, Fenton Recreation, Michigan Bean, Nina' Beauty Shop and Motorettes. In the fall of 1947, the league began a new season and the some of the teams were replaced. The Genesee Tool, Fenton Five, Craft, Fenton Home Grocers, Fenton Recreation and Nina's were replaced with Cecil's, Gallagher Sport Shop, R & B Taxi, The Misfits and Julia Sweeney Realtor. Some of the leading ladies were Folland, Miller, Petts, Dager, Cheesboro, Dobbs, McWain, Dode, G. Woodworth, Gottman, Erickson, Foley, J. Graham, Stander, Stiff Stevens, Carnegie, Steele and Nelson. (Sorry, no first names available.)

For the 1946-1947 season the men participated in the Inter-City League and/or the Booster League. The Inter-City and Booster leagues each had twelve teams. When the two leagues reorganized for the -1947-48 season there were twelve teams were in the Booster league.

The Inter-City league teams were: Virginia Tavern, Poppy & Lauer, Farmer's Gas & Oil*, Bill's Barber Shop, Theisen Motor Sales, E & A Electric*, Cobb's Cleaners, Johnnie's Nursery, Gould's Market*, Lee Lumber Co., Martin Motor Sales and Cross & Welch Dec*. As above, those teams marked with an asterisk replaced the Local 633, Porter's Service, Fenton Hardware and Linden Creamery teams of the previous season. The top bowlers were H. McKinley H. Roberts. Jerry Pasco. M. Burdick, R. Richmond, S. Kirshman, U. Terras, L. Weigant Doug Gould, Robert Dode and D. Theisen.

The townsfolk had a lot of opportunities to enjoy life...and they did!

Scene Eleven...Items of Interest

- In January, the Greyhound Bus began service from Fenton to Detroit. It joined the Short Lines which had been serving the Fenton –Flint for years.
- Miss Clara Davis sent a note home reporting she is working with the U. S. Army in Seoul, Korea
- Mr. and Mrs. Stanley were spending the evening with Mr. and Mrs. John Chapman, playing a game of Pinochle. Mrs. Stanley was a beginner, and was not very familiar with the game. During the evening as she picked up the hand just dealt to her...and what? Right Aces! "Beginners luck" said Mr. Stanley.
- Around 2 AM the morning of September 20th, a motorist rounding the curve at Leroy and Mill Streets, ran into a fire hydrant and broke it off at ground level. Village Engineer Jim Reagan, enjoying a healthy sleep at the time, was aroused to plug the line and restore the water supply the residents in the area. It was not for several days that Mr. Reagan located a spare hydrant in Lapeer and was able to get everything back to normal.
- A peaceful Sunday evening in September was harshly interrupted when neighbors discovered the home of Mr. and Mrs Bud Azelton on South Long Lake Road ablaze. The Azeltons were not at home at the time. By the time the Fenton firefighter arrived the home was completely consumed. Their pet dog and birds were victims of the fire.
- Early Sunday morning in November, fire was reported in the Fenton Floor Covering Store at 403 South Leroy Street. (The area in now called "Dibbleville".) The Fenton fireman battled the blaze and prevented the fire from spreading. even though at times the flames shot into the air enveloping the adjacent buildings. Both the main and second floors of the store were completely destroyed. The loss was estimated to be $20,000.
- In the early morning in March, fire destroyed Barney's Hamburg Stand on the corner of the Fenton-Flint Road and North Long Lake Road. The Fenton Fire Department were summoned, but because of the weather...the worst blizzard in years...and upon arrival were too late to be of much service.

- Fenton Firemen were called to the home of Mr. and Mrs. Helquist4 at 1685 Denton Hill Road one evening in early January when a fire was discovered in a back room. The neighbors came with buckets of water and snow to hold the blaze until the Firemen arrived. The flooring and the joists were damaged and the loss was estimated at $1,000.
- The Grand Trunk experienced another fatal accident, when Arthur F. Finney was killed as he lay on the tracks just west of Torrey Road. The Engineer of the freight train saw Mr. Finney laying face up on the tracks ahead, but was unable to stop the train in time to avoid him.
- Eleven of the girls graduating in the class of 1947 earned "B" or better grades throughout their four years at FHS. They were: Shirley Scott, Marian Alchin, Beth Gordon, Betty Lou Shields, Mary Alice Gordon, Ruth Ann Bailey, Marjorie Bachus, Mildred Miller, Barbara Comstock, Barbara Hyde and Jean Thorpe.
- The Girls from the Class of 1934 held a reunion at the home of Gladys Abbey Peterson on Scott Lake near Pontiac.
- The American Legion Baseball excursion to the Tigers game happened on the day the Tigers broke their attendance record at Briggs Stadium (Tiger Stadium named after is owner at the time Walter Briggs)
- Presidential candidate Thomas Dewey made ripples in the town, when he came to dinner with his brother in-law Dr. Hutt of Holly. To counter the boasting Hollyites, Fenton reminded them that Fenton was closer to Governor Dewey's home town of Owosso than Holly.

Interlude Two...the Cold War Heats Up!

With the end of the war, the nations of the world looked forward to a period of peace and cooperation. The United Nations had been formed to facilitate this international trust and cooperation and by doing so, prevent future conflicts. However they were sadly disappointed as the Soviet Union consolidated its control on the countries of Eastern Europe and was installing a Communist government in each of the countries they occupied, forming a "bloc" of all the countries captured by the Red Army when driving the German invaders out of central and Eastern Europe. New Soviet satellite states rose in Poland, Bulgaria, Hungary, Czechoslovakia, Romania, Albania, and East Germany.

There was a mutual distrust between this Eastern bloc and the West, the United States and its allies. It was a clash of ideologies that eventually turned into a nuclear arms race and was dubbed the "Cold War". Presidential confidant Bernard Baruch coined the term "Cold War" in a speech saying "Let us not be deceived -- we are today in the midst of a cold war."

The tensions between the East and West were further exasperated when the United States implemented a comprehensive aid program for the distressed nations of Europe...the Marshall Plan. The Soviet Union feared the US was attempting to consolidate its influence in Europe.

The US emerged from the war economically superior and richer than any of its allies or enemies. Further, the leaders of US were determined to make the US the center of the postwar world economy. Consequently by providing aid to the free nations of Europe furthered this goal. In April of 1948, the Congress appropriated 13 Billion dollars for the Marshall Plan. They also approved $1.8 Billion for the reconstruction efforts in Japan.

Geo. C. Marshall

The increasing economic and political clout of the United States in Western Europe and the USSR in Eastern Europe shifted the balance of power from the former imperial powers of Western and Central Europe to the United States and the USSR. U.S. policy in post-war Germany until July 1947 had been to not help the Germans in rebuilding their nation. The Allies' plan was "Industrial disarmament" and to destroy Germany's capability to wage war by complete or partial de-industrialization.

In July 1947, President Truman accepted the position of many of his advisors that economic recovery in Europe could not go forward without the reconstruction of the German industrial base. Germany had received some U.S. aid through other programs and after 1948 West Germany became a minor beneficiary of the Marshall Plan. Volunteer organizations had been forbidden to send food to the German people, but the prohibition against sending food packages to individuals in Germany was rescinded in June of 1946.

In 1947, a civil war broke out in Greece between the American-supported royalist forces and a communist-led force. The U.S. launched a military and economic aid program for Greece and neighboring Turkey. This aid helped the royalist forces emerge as the victors.

In March of 1947, President Harry Truman proclaimed that the U.S. would provide aid to promote democracy in defense of the "free world", the principle became known as the "Truman Doctrine". Truman reasoned that if "totalitarian regimes" were allowed to coerce "free peoples," they would represent a threat to international peace and the national security of the United States.

One of the international "tinder boxes" was to be found in the Middle East…the region referred to as Palestine. Palestine was governed by the British as a mandate and their authority was being challenged by militant groups of Zionists who were determined to establish as Jewish State in the biblical home of the Jews.

The Zionist movement planned to bring thousands of displaced European Jews to this new nation of Israel. The British policy was to deny this influx of displaced Jews to the area. On several occasions the British Navy intercepted ships loaded with European Jews. During this upheaval, the most notorious and extremist group of rebellious Jews in Palestine was the Stern Gang (Hebrew: "Fighters for the Freedom of Israel). Extremely anti-British, the group repeatedly attacked British personnel in Palestine. They attacked airfields, railway yards, and other strategic installations in Palestine. After the creation of the state of Israel in 1948, the actions of the gang, which were not supported by the moderate leaders of the Jewish community in Palestine, ended. The Stern Gang was founded after a split in the right-wing underground movement Irgun Zvai Leumi. The Irgun Zvai Leumi, was the forerunner of the erut ("Freedom") Party The Irgun (Hebrew: National Military Organization) committed many acts of terrorism against the British, whom it regarded as illegal occupiers, and it was also violently anti-Arab. Irgun was active in the organization of the immigration of European Jews into Palestine.

The third militant Zionist group was Haganah, (Hebrew: "Defense"), representing the majority of the Jews in Palestine. The Haganah was organized to combat the attacks of Palestinian Arabs against the Jewish settlements. The Haganah's policy of self-restraint resulted in very moderate activities, at least until the end of World War II. It opposed the terrorist activities of the Irgun Zvai Leumi and the Stern Gang.

When the British blocked unlimited Jewish immigration, the Haganah became a terrorist organization and began bombing bridges, rail lines, and ships being used to send the "illegal" Jewish immigrants back to Europe. In 1947, the United Nations' partitioned Palestine. The partition allocated land to the provisional government of Israel. The Haganah served as the defense force of the new Jewish state; It successfully defended the new nation and defeated the forces of the Palestinian Arabs. With the creation of the State of Israel in 1948, the Haganah became the Israeli army.

The decolonization of the European "empires" following World War II created many "hot spots" of international concern. Britain's "biggest" possession was India and the move for independence in India was one that could not be denied. Consequently, in August, India gained independence after some 200 years of British rule. Britain partitioned the subcontinent into India and Pakistan based upon the religion of the people in those sections. Independence in Pakistan and India led to bloody conflict and thousands died

However France had a problem with their colony of Indo-China where they had no intention of relinquishing control. The rebellious activities in French Indo China were to have dire consequences for the French but also for the United States in the mid-1960s.

During the war, Japanese forces occupied French Indo China. A unit known as the Viet Minh, led by Ho Chi Minh, fought the Japanese during their occupation and was supported by China and the Soviet Union. Ho Chi Minh had led the opposition to the French prior to WW II, and with the end of the war, continued to press for Independence from the French. Following a major defeat, the French agreed to negotiations with the Viet Minh. These negations led to the partitioning of the country, Viet Nam, into two parts. North Vietnam was led by Ho Chi Minh and became a Communist state and the Viet Minh became the Viet Cong. Emperor Bao Dai assumed control of South Vietnam. The agreement called for elections at a later date which would unify the country. The elections were never held because of a distrust for Ho Chi Minh by the non-Communist Nations concerned.

About the same time, a similar action was occurring on the Korean Peninsula. The peninsula was governed by the Korean Empire until it was annexed by Japan after the Russo-Japanese War in 1910. It was divided into Soviet and American-occupied zones in 1945, after the end of World War II. North Korea refused to participate in a United Nations supervised election held in the south in 1948, which led to the creation of separate Korean governments for the two occupation zones. North and South Korea each claimed sovereignty over the whole Korean Peninsula, which led to the Korean War of 1950. The Armistice Agreement of 1953 ended the fighting; but the two countries are officially still at war against each other, for a peace treaty was never signed. Both states were accepted into the United Nations in 1991.

The United Nations, now headquartered in the United States, was the beneficiaries of a gift of a large parcel of land in New York City along the East River as the site of the future home of the United Nations.

There was a considerable amount of concern, especially in the Congress, about the presence of Communists in America's government and the motion picture industry. FBI director J. Edgar Hoover warned that communists had launched "a furtive attack on Hollywood" 12 years earlier. President Truman was not as fearful of a Communist takeover as others in Government; however, yielding to public pressure, he signed an Executive Order requiring all federal employees to swear allegiance to the United States as a condition of employment...a "loyalty oath".

A month later, the Attorney General's office produced a "List of Subversive Organizations". It included about a hundred organizations and schools considered "adjuncts of the Communist Party".

About the same time the House of Representatives established the Un-American Activities Committee (HUAC) for the purpose of hunting for Communists in the film industry. In October, the House Un-American Activities Committee convened in Washington for public hearings. The Committee named several Hollywood persons as having Communist leanings, among those named were: Katherine Hepburn,

Charles Chaplin and Edward G. Robinson. Screen Actors Guild President Ronald Reagan, testified that communist sympathizers never controlled the Guild and he declined to identify anyone as a Communist.

A group of movie stars, including Danny Kaye, Humphrey Bogart and Lauren Bacall, formed the Committee for the First Amendment to counter the "witch hunt" by the Congress Spokesman Danny Kaye claimed that the motion pictures did not contain Communist propaganda.

The nation's attention was drawn to a new phenomenon when a pilot reported the sighting of a "flying saucer" near Mount Rainier. This incident was hardly noticed until the following month when an object crashed near the Army Air Force base at Roswell, New Mexico. While the Army explained the incident as the landing of a weather balloon, the eye witnesses insisted it was some sort of "alien" spacecraft.

The speculation that it was a "flying saucer" was enhanced when the local newspaper the *Roswell Daily Record* reported the Army had captured a "flying saucer". Again, the Army claimed it to be the debris of a "harmless high-altitude weather balloon". Almost twenty years later the Air Force reported that the wreckage was part of a "device to spy on the Soviets".

Yet another "phenomena" was occurring at the same time. It was the rapid growth of the television industry. By the time of the telecast of the World Series, it was estimated that over 15,000 television sets were in use in the United States.

The Congress opened up for television in January and the telecasts of the Congress "in action" was available to viewers on the east coast, specifically, Washington, Philadelphia and New York City It wasn't until October 5th before President Truman's address from the White House was televised.

There were many other advances in technology, most likely the result of the emphasis on science and technology during the war, Radar, one of the most significant developments during the war, now found an application in commercial and private aviation. In December, William Shockley of Bell Laboratories announced the invention of the transistor. Headlines in the *Fenton Independent* reprinted from a news agency, proclaimed "Radios without Tubes a Possibility".

We had recovered from the shock of seeing an airplane flying without a propeller and we were only partly surprised when Air Force test pilot

Charles E. "Chuck" Yeager flew the experimental Bell X-1 rocket plane and broke the sound barrier with a speed of Mach 1.07 for the first time over Edwards Air Force Base, Calif., which was then called Muroc Army Air Field.

The nation had experienced a period of labor unrest following the end of the war and the Congress wrestled with what should be done to bring order in the world of labor. In June, the Congress passed the Labor Management Relations Act also known as the Taft-Hartley. The Act which provided for an eighty day "cooling off" period for strikes considered to be endangering to the public health and safety. President Truman vetoed the Taft-Hartley Act, but had his veto overridden by Congress. The act declared the closed shop illegal and permitted the union shop only following a majority employee vote.

No other President before President Roosevelt had served more than two terms in office and the Congress considered addressing the issue but nothing was done at that time to impose term limits on the office. It wasn't until 1951 when the Twenty-First Amendment to the Constitution was ratified. The amendment stated "no person shall be elected to the office of President more than twice".

In September, the National Security Act became law creating the Department of Defense and unifying the Army, Navy and newly formed Air Force. James V. Forrestal was the first person appointed Secretary of Defense. The Act also established the National Security Council and the Central Intelligence Agency. In view of America entering the "Atomic Era", the U.S. Atomic Energy Commission was established and Physicist Robert Oppenheimer was appointed chairman of the General Advisory Committee.

Baseball had once again gained the public's interest as many of the pre-war stars had returned to the game along with some very talented rookies. Jackie Robinson was one of these highly talented rookies who was signed by the Brooklyn Dodgers of the National League. Jackie Robinson was the first black player in the Major Leagues and he proved he belonged by being named the "Rookie of the Year". Not long after Jackie Robinson's debut, the Cleveland Indians of the American League signed Larry Doby...the first black player in the American League.

The baseball world was excited about the opening of the baseball season and it was "Babe Ruth Day" at Yankee Stadium as baseball fans honored the "Bambino". The Babe was suffering with cancer. Two months later, on August 16, 1948, Babe Ruth died.

Act Three...The Year 1948

Scene One...The Village Council's "Growing Pains"

It was said the Village of Fenton was growing faster than most other communities of its size. As more homes were built, new businesses started, more and more demands were laid on the Village government. In the previous year, the Village had purchased a new 2-ton truck, a road grader, snow plow, loading machine for gravel and snow, new police car, $300 for new stop signs, $1,000 of black top for streets, paved two miles of streets, installed one mile of sanitary sewer, ½ mile of storm sewer, six blocks of sidewalk construction and numerous other repair jobs. In addition, the village now had a full time engineer on the payroll.

The Council had accomplished a lot and managed to stay within their budget. The village was also nearly debt free after paying down $3,500 on the Sewage Disposal Plant obligation. As mentioned before, the village leaders, whomever they may have been throughout the years, were a frugal lot to say the least. "Pay as you go" was their creed....long before others coined the phrase.

However, the costs of running the village were threatening to exceed the available income. Many of the newly built homes were not yet on the tax rolls, but the demand for services was "now". Therefore, the majority of the council agreed to borrow funds in advance of the anticipated increase in tax revenue from new construction. The Council authorized the borrowing of $9,990. This was to be received from three notes each of $3,300 to be executed in February, March and April, if necessary. They were short term notes to be paid in August, September and October of the year.

This "deficit spending" received some criticism in the local paper and among some of the townsfolk who followed the "goings-on" of the Village officials. The opponents of the Council's borrowing money for operations voiced the lack of "stability" in the body. Bob Beach, the editor of the *Fenton Independent* authored these remarks in his weekly column: *"During the last year so little thought was given to stability that the village is now operating on borrowed money and exceeded their budget by several thousands of dollars"* *"This fact alone is evidence that it is a matter of great importance to select men of ability and keen judgment to handle affairs of the village"*

The Village Players Post War

"It was not necessary for the Village to borrow last year to meet payrolls and bills until taxes began rolling in. Somehow they managed. This year something went wrong. Not so much thought was given to "stability".

The release of the Village's Treasurer's report on February 22nd the Village budget was very "tight".

Receipts:
Receipts in General Fund	$3,252.07
Receipts Misc. Sources	684.41
Borrowed from State Bank	3,300.00
Fire Runs Rebated	46.58
	$7,313.06

Disbursements:
Current Bills	$2,566.50
Supplies	3.60
Pay Roll	510.50
Pay Roll#2	558.50
Total Disbursements	$3,639.10
Balance in General Fund	$3,673.96

But the Council seemed more concerned with the "parking problem" than "stability". The perceived problem of parking on downtown Leroy Street was the topic of discussion at many of the Council meetings in the early months of the year. In earlier times they had considered placing parking meters on the street, but wisely backed off this idea as the natives began to look around for their pitchforks. (Only kidding!). Now they had passed an ordinance restricting parking on Leroy streets two business blocks to one hour. Several citizens appeared before the Council protesting one hour was much too short. Others argued that if someone intended to shop longer than one hour, let them park around the corner. But the Council bought the argument for a longer time and changed the parking to a two hour limit...with the proviso that the streets would be actively policed for those who overstayed the limit.

Reacting to a petition signed by 123 citizens, the Council summarily terminated the waste collection contract of Mr. Myers over the strong objection of Trustee Russell Haddon who suggested the lack of due process in the firing.

February found the two local political parties caucusing to prepare a slate of officers to present in the March 8th election. The Citizens party nominated the following slate: Village President- C. E. Ross, Clerk-

Brad Hoffman, Treasurer- Ed Weber, Assessor- Irving Gould, Trustees- Dr. W. F. Buchanan, Evar Strom and Henry Alchin. Conspicuous by its absence was the name Harry Lemen. President Lemen was completing his 16th term in that office. Was "deficit spending" the reason his party passed him over?

The People's Party presented their slate as follows: Village President – J. J. Weidman, Clerk- Edison Stiles, Treasurer- William Baldwin, Assessor- George Burr and Trusteed-C.S. Rounds, Don J. Bristol and Harold Roshaven. Soon after the announcement of the slate, Mr. Weidman withdrew and was replaced as the party's candidate by Harold Hill. Mr. L.F. Moore also replaced Mr. Baldwin in the Treasurer's spot on the ticket.

The many friends of Harry Lemen supported his announcement that he would once again run as a "sticker" candidate for the office of Village President for his 17th term, in that office. Once before, his party had passed over him and he successfully ran for the office as a "sticker" candidate. The odds were that he would do that again. Harry Lemen was highly respected by the people of Fenton.

In the election, votes were cast for four candidates for Village President and Harry Lemen -up C. E. Ross. Others elected were: Clerk- Brad Hoffman, Treasurer- Edgar Webb and Assessor- Irving Gould. The Trustees elected were: Evar Strom, Dr. W.F. Buchanan and Don Bristol. In September, Brad Hoffman resigned in order to attend Michigan State College. He was replaced as Village Clerk by Edison Stiles.

It is interesting to note that a resident needed to be registered with the Village Clerk to vote in Village elections and with G. C."Gus" Lutz, the Township Clerk, in order to vote in County, State and National elections.

Russell Haddon was the first Director of the Fenton Community Center and returned to that position after a stint in the U.S. Navy during WW II. He served two years as a Village Trustee and had recently resigned as FCC Director to accept a position on the Fenton High School faculty. Later Russ Haddon served 16 years as the first Superintendent of the new expanding Lake Fenton School District. Later he served as Superintendent of the Holly schools before retiring to his nursery and tree farm.

Mr. Haddon did not run for reelection to the Village Council and had an open letter published in the *Fenton Independent* which was very unusual for a "politician" in those days...or ever. The complete letter follows:

Confessions of a Councilman

No public official should leave office without openly confessing his obvious inadequacies and little publicized failures as an elected representative of the taxpayers.

I feel I must bare my soul to the disillusioned and disappointed public which so generously elected me two years ago. It is hoped that this may be a guide to the voters in selecting councilmen in the March 8th election.

Without duress or compassion (and being a lame duck, this is easier to do) the following admissions are set forth:

...to have spent the entire budget and forced the village to borrow on its 1948 taxes (this is open conspiracy with Councilman Rounds who, with the writer comprise the majority of the seven man legislative body, according to a recent published article)

...to have accepted a bribe: a two pound box of chocolates-assorted, Sanders, from Wells Paving Company for Christmas.

...that the annual $50.00 councilman's stipend was accepted with only token resistance.

...to have further upset the budget plans by permitting the Parks Department to be the only department with an unused balance.

...to have brazenly questioned the existence of the Water Department inventory.

...to have been one of the political bloc which hired a trained, experienced engineer.

...to have supported the construction of one too many sewers.

...to have foolishly insisted on regular reports from the Water Commission.

...to have been sentimental in business by considering a retirement plan for city employees and establishing personnel standards, wages and incentives.

...to have thought the parking "problem" not a problem.

...to not having agreed to the firing of the garbage man without allowing him to defend himself.

...to have asked if an employee could be a member of the board which employs him.

...to have intimated that there could be "programs of stability" as long as two "liberals" control the vote in a seven man body.

...to have dared to say "no" to a women's group.

...to have missed two council meetings and three committee sessions to teach the youngest son his father's name.

...to have stubbornly insisted that this community needs a city manager type of of government unless retired, capable men who have only the problems of the civic welfare to wrestle, can be put into office.

...to have avoided the consequences of these "irregularities", conspiracies, pressures, briberies, dereliction of duty and immature decisions, by declining nomination for a risky second term.

Signed, Russell Haddon

The Council placed a referendum on the Mach 8th ballot proposing that the Village accept ownership of Oakwood Cemetery. The Council had already voted to accept the ownership from the private foundation .but they were advised to submit this issue to the public since it would incur additional costs the taxpayers, these costs were estimated to be about $2,000 a year. The voters responded overwhelmingly in support of acquiring the cemetery.

From all reports the cemetery was in terrible condition Overgrown with weeds and no evidence of any substantial maintenance for several years. Recognizing the enormity if the cleanup problem, the Council asked the towns originations and the general public to come to the cemetery on Saturday and bring their rakes, lawnmowers and other tools and help restore the appearance of the cemetery to its former beauty. The Fire Department, the Junior Chamber of Commerce and other groups, pledged to turnout in force and help the townsfolk in the cleanup. With the coming Saturday the people turned out in large numbers and did an excellent job in improving the appearance of the cemetery grounds. More work was needed but it was an outstanding effort by the people of the Village and an excellent demonstration of the pride in the community.

Now that the cemetery was the property of the Village, a governing board for the cemetery needed to appointed. A rare bit of a "keystone cops" routine occurred in appointing the members of the cemetery board. There initial appointments to the board were: E. C. Reid, Fred Hall and Ward Wortman. A special meeting on the following night was required whom both Mr. Hall and Mr. Wortman declined their appointments to serve The Council then name Howard Craft and Roy Wood to serve on the board.

Jim Reagan, one of the Village's most respected employees was forced to resign because of ill health. Mr. Reagan had served 21 years as the Water Engineer. His assistant, Dave Klinger replaced him.

Hugo Theisen, Chairman of the Water Commission, reported they had been able to recondition an old well formerly considered to be of little value and now have a stream sufficient to meet present needs.

In January, before the council "solved" the parking problem on Leroy Street, those needing "long term" parking were creating another problem that the Fire Marshall Fred Williams brought to the attention of the public and the Council. Driveways were being blocked and alleys jammed with cars, as the drivers were attempting to find parking off of

Leroy Street. "Drastic action will be taken" said Williams "if these violations occur in the future."

The "fire boys" were the favorites of the town's people. They appreciated these volunteers and took pride in how professional they were in the performance of their duties. Each spring the Fire Department would elect their officers for the coming year. In April they elected Lee Kelley-President, Deke Shivile-VP, Howard Craft-Secretary, Shull Woodworth-Fire Chief and Harry Moore his Assistant.

It wasn't something they wanted to do, but the pressure on the present budget required the Council to act. In mid-June, the Village Council approved an increase in the property taxes. The rate was set at $30.00 per thousand dollars of evaluation. This was an increase of $6.00 from the existing rate of $24.00 per thousand. In the breakdown of how the taxes were used, the largest increase was for debt service. jumping from $2.00 to $7.00. The explanation for the increase was that the increases were in line with what the rest of the country was experiencing and that in Fenton "a considerable amount of work (was) being accomplished."

In the middle of winter, the Council received numerous complaints about the door-to-door salesmen who were moving through neighborhoods bothering the housewives with their high pressure sales tactics. .

(Author's Note: I can't let this topic pass without relating a real life story. Years ago a friend of mine confessed to being one of those "pesky" door-to-door salesmen. Upon returning home after the war, he took a job selling a new product... a plastic tablecloth. It was in the middle of winter and the temperature was hovering in the mid-teens as he went from house-to-house attempting to sell this new plastic product. At one house, the lady was interested in the tablecloth, but she asked to see it unfolded. So my friend unfolded this four foot square, bright red and white checkered plastic to its full glory The lady looked the table cloth over and finally decided not to buy it and politely stepped back into her house leaving my friend with a very stiff and inflexible sheet of plastic. The cold environment had stiffened the plastic and he could not refold the tablecloth without it breaking...it was very brittle. What to do? He had to carry this 4' x 4' piece of frozen plastic, like a sail in the wind, about two blocks to the nearest gas station. After a few minutes in the warmth of the station house, the plastic returned to its pliable state and he was able to fold the sheet and place it back into its package. He had learned his lesson...never unfold a plastic sheet in cold weather!)

Scene Two...Business

One measure of business activity can be the growth and expansion of telephone service. In that respect the Michigan Bell was very active in providing expanded service to its users. In February, they announced plans to install over 20,000 new phones in the rural areas of the State. In the rural areas in the past year, Michigan Bell had installed about 14,000 new phones, 20,000 poles, 9,000 miles of wire and 435 miles of cable continuing hundreds of wires.

One of the main objectives of expanding services to the rural areas was to reduce the number of parties on one line to eight or fewer. Nearly 3,000 such party line reductions were made in 1947.

They were also planning to create "extended area exchanges". These extended area exchanges would permit users to call nearby exchanges without paying toll charges. In spite of these developments, the number of persons on the waiting list for new phones was about 13,000. Many of those on the list were in the Fenton area. However, there was good news in November, when the new service allowed users in Holly and Fenton to direct dial others in the neighboring town without paying toll charges.

Bob Beach, the editor of the *Fenton Independent,* the town's weekly newspaper, said to him "it seems more businesses are making changes this spring than in past years". The Woodworth Brothers put a new front on their store, the former location of the Fenton Covering store, which was destroyed by fire last year, has a new front and Pellett's Department store acquired the Oddfellows Building next door and were busy remodeling the building and incorporating it into the original store. Frank Vosburg was remodeling the former Log Cabin Inn, the Fenton Hotel added space and redid the cocktail lounge, Kroger's erected a new neon sign...the largest one in town, Theisen Motor Sales had a new display room and offices and Bill's Barber Shop had a new front with a large display window. Many more new fronts were planned and just about every merchant freshened up his store front with new paint

There were some changes in ownership in the business community during the year. In April, Chester D. Hillis (everyone called him "Chet") bought out John B. Hoffman, his co-owner of Hoffman's Farm Supply Store on Ellen Street just east of the Fire Hall. The Truchan name returned to the grocery business in Fenton, when brothers Charles and Vince Truchan bought the market on West Caroline, just west of the bridge. The Truchans had owned a grocery store on the South Side (now called Dibbleville) prior to the war. It is interesting to note that the part owner of this same store, now called the South Side Grocery, sold his interest in the business to a Mr. Greer. It was reported in the newspaper that while Mr. Greer is not very well known in Fenton, his wife, the former Betty Brunson, is a "Fenton girl" and very well known in town. The newspaper article went further in its reporting to assure its readers that Mr. Greer "will be found to be a fine young man". Would the New York Times ever be so "small town" nice?

Upon returning from the war, Curtis and Elmer Schupbach and a couple of their friends went in the concrete block making business. There were nine children in the Schupbach family and their father had supported the family as a salesman...actually a "peddler". Everyone in town knew Mr. Schupbach and he was respected and well liked. However, he never had a store, so his "boys" decided to build one for him. So Curtis and Elmer and Don, their younger brother, built a 40 x 60 foot building on Fenton Road (now North Leroy Street) across the street from Aldrich Locke's gasoline station. The building was made with concrete blocks and steel. The building was designed by Don Schupbach and most of the construction work was done by the brothers. Today, at the time of this writing, the building is occupied by the Pittsburg Paint Store.

A new building was completed a 113 Mill Street in December and was owned by Mr. Richards, an experienced electrician. He named his business the Warren Electrical Service and he planned conduct general electrical contracting and specializes in renewing electric motors.

In July, the *Fenton Independent* included the following article:

> The latest thing out" says Bill Strayer, proprietor of the Barber Shop, North Leroy Street. Bill proudly points to his automatically shoe shining equipment. All you have to do, says Bill, is drop a nickel and hold your foot up to the machine, it does the rest. Either black or brown, and a good job for 5c. No tipping required. The machine operated for nearly two minutes. Ample time for the average pair of shoes

Scene Three...Men's Civic Clubs

Since the organization of the Fenton Kiwanis Club in 1941, the residents in the Fenton community had benefited from the Kiwanis programs which improved the environment...both physical and social ...and enhanced the quality of life for the townsfolk of all ages. The members of Kiwanis were, for the most part, the businessmen of the town. Their lunch time meetings were held in the Community Center, generally within walking distance for most of the members.

In August of 1947 an energetic group of young men formed the Fenton Junior Chamber of Commerce and got off to a fast start. The Jaycees accepted men, ages 21 to 35, and because of their youth they tackled a number of programs that involved "hands on" work.

The Jaycees elected the officers for the new club year starting on July 1st. Those elected were: President James J. Cohoon, 1st VP William Searight, 2nd VP Rolland Covert, Treasurer Thomas Faull and Secretary Edison Stiles. Arnold Billmeier and Wilbur Strom were elected to the Board of Directors and Don Bristol was selected as the State Delegate. In October, Rolly Covert resigned in order to accept out-of-town employment and Paul Bottecelli was appointed to succeed him .Evar Strom was appointed to the Board to replace Bottecelli. The other Board members were Wayne Wessendorf, Robert Obenshain, Ward Waite, Kenneth Harris and Stanton Miner.

The J.C.C. began their program of placing street signs at the street intersections throughout the town. The street signs, erected on a steel post, were of wood construction and had the street name in large letters. Their first effort erected twenty-nine signs one Sunday afternoon. The cost of each sign was about $20.00 and the post was set in two feet of concrete. The intersections still without signs were to be installed as funds became available.

The Jaycees continued to move rapidly from one project to another, sponsoring a Tiger Baseball excursion in August. The Greyhound bus was loaded for the trip to Briggs Stadium to watch the Detroit Tigers play the New York Yankees.

The traditional Pioneer Picnic was threatened by a lack of support and J. C. Peck prevailed on the Jaycees to step up and continue this Old Timers event. But it wasn't all fun and games for the group. The Jaycees took the lead in soliciting for the Fenton Community Fund Drive. The Community Fund supported the Boys Scouts, FCC's

Council of Social Agencies, Girl Scouts, Community Nurse, FCC Recreation Committee and Salvation Army.

The last week in October was the First Anniversary of the J.C.C and the members celebrated the event with a dinner at the Community Center. The speaker for the evening was Joseph Anderson, the General Manager for the A.C. Spark Plug Company in Flint. William Baldwin led the community singing and the local quartet of Lee Kelley, Grant Wright, Ryan Strom and Lynn Welch gave a few musical selections. The organization started with 43 Charter members and now had 65 members. The dinner was also the occasion to elect William Dode, George P. Pellett . and Charles Leighton to serve on the Board.

Christmas was approaching and the Jaycees finished the year by holding their second Christmas party at the Community Center which was attended by 1,154 children of ages one through nine. Sergeant Legree, the famous "Singing Cop" from Flint provided the entertainment. The party was not the only activity for the Jaycees during the holiday season. Weeks before Christmas, the Jaycees were busy decorating the town by stringing lights and stars across the streets and decorating the lamp posts with Christmas trees.

The Kiwanians were some of the strongest supporters of the Jaycees and they looked upon the Jaycees as an excellent source of new members. When the Jaycee reached 35 years of age he was called an "Exhausted Rooster" and was pushed out of the J.C.C. and was just "ripe" for the picking by the Kiwanis

As the year began, the Kiwanians were led by their President G. Leslie "Duke" Whittle, 1st VP John Millington, 2nd VP Dr. William M. Taylor, Treasurer Elmer Westman, Secretary Ronald J. Butler and Immediate Past President Chester D. Hillis. The Directors were: Robert Beach, Claude Cranston, Ray O'Reilly, Warren Roberts, Dr. W. J. Rynearson, Dr. Paul Williams and Dr. C. H. White.

The Annual Football Banquet for the FHS team, held in cooperation with the XX Club had Michigan State's new Head Football Coach Clarence "Biggie" Munn as the guest speaker. The hosts and Coach Munn congratulated the team on tying for the County Class "B" Championship.

The club conducted a "White Elephant" sale in July a fund raising event and gained over $1,000 from the items donated to the Kiwanians by the villagers. Ray O'Reilly, the popular proprietor of the Fenton Hotel, was the Chairman for the event which was held in the large lot just south of the Leroy Street Bridge over the Shiawassee and adjacent to the farm implement store of Poppy and Lauer. (Property now occupied by the Fenton Post Office). All of the proceeds from the sale were given to the Underprivileged Children's Fund to use in Fenton and nearby area.

In early August, the Kiwanians held their Field Day, a golf outing fund raiser, at the Shoreacres Golf Club on Torrey outing, which Road, west of Lake Fenton. This event was a yearly provided recreation and raised funds for the Underprivileged Children's Fund.

Club officers for the coming year were elected in late October and resulted in John Millington being elected to serve as President. Others elected were: VP Carl Lind, Treasurer Warren Roberts and Board members R. B. Graham, Dr. Buchman, Dr. Ken Harris and D. A. O'Dell.

In November, the Kiwanis cooperated with the Genesee County T.B. Association to provide free chest X-Rays to the people of Fenton. This program was supported by the sale of Christmas Seals

The year came to a close with the members on the streets of Fenton selling the Goodfellows edition of the *Fenton Independent*. The issue told of the clubs activities and raised funds for the Underprivileged Children.

The twenty members of the XX Club continued to support selected programs such as the lecture series at the FCC and worked with Kiwanis on several occasions. The XXers enjoyed their monthly dinner meetings and socializing with their colleagues. In August, the club met at the Lake Fenton cottage of Dr. Noble Peckham and welcomed the report of Pat Foley and Max Bottecelli about their experience at Boy's State

The Men's Fellowship had returned "with a vengeance" to the town's social scene. After sitting out the war years, the Men's Fellowship revival now accounted more than 250 members. The Fellowship sponsored dinner programs during the fall and winter of the year. In On February 2nd, the Father-Son Banquet was held at the Fenton Community Center. With 323 in attendance, Arthur L. Compton, the General Secretary for the Flint Y.M.C.A., was the featured speaker for the event. Fellowship President Ed Mitts, opened the festivities by paying honors to the following individuals: Thomas Moorman, the oldest father at age 85; Pete Moorman, oldest son at age 49; Duane Theisen , youngest father at age 21; Bruce Helmboldt, youngest son at age 29 months and Grant Wright and Phillip Foley, fathers with the most sons present...3.

The evening's entertainment included th singing of Sergeant Wilburn Legree, Flint's "Singing Cop"; a Son's Quartette composed of Don Forsyth, John Wright, Bud Curtis and Jack Pellett; Clowning Don Adams, a local entertainer and an instrumental trio with Warren "Bones" Logan, Emile Gosseaux and Carryl Church.

VP Warren Roberts was the program chairman and J. L. Standridge led the group singing.

In August the Fellowship announce the new season would have one additional meeting for a total of six dinners Secretary Avery Loucks confirmed that the veteran "Commissary expert" Than Chesnut had agreed to providing six "vitamin loaded squares per member". The membership dues for the season were set a $3.75.

The six program dates and speakers were scheduled as follows:

October 11	Gordon Atkins, Y.M.C.A. Boy's Farm
November 8	C.P. Mehas MD, TB Sanitarium.
December 6	Judge O. Z. Ide, Detroit
January 17	Aldrich Baxter, Attorney, Detroit
February 28	Father-Son Dinner
March 28	Ladies Night

On October 11th, Gordon Atkins appeared as "advertised" and spoke about working with juvenile delinquent boys from broken homes that live at the Y.M.C.A. Boy's Farm. Following the "Corn Beef and Cabbage" supper, Billy Baldwin entertained with recitations and led the group singing.

Dr. Mehas, the Medical Director for the Oakland County Tuberculosis Sanitarium delivers a dramatic message at the meeting of November 8th and Judge O. Z. Ide told of his war experiences as an Army Judge Advocate during the last meeting of the year 1948 on December 6th.

With the Methodist ladies doing the cooking, Than Chesnut supervising the food preparation and George Tamlyn directing the kitchen "gang", those attending received what was promised...."a vitamin-packed square meal"

Scene Four...the Fraternal Lodges

In 1948 there were basically three fraternal organizations in Fenton...the Masons and their affiliated societies-the Order of the Eastern Star and the Rainbow girls; the Independent Order of Oddfellows (I.O.O.F.) and the Fraternal Order of Eagles. Fraternal organizations are generally defined as groups "whose members are usually bound by oath and who make extensive use of secret ritual in the conduct of their meetings." and have secret gestures and handshakes.[5]

The Fenton Aerie 2460 of the Fraternal Order of the Eagles, the newest lodge in town, held their annual election in May and the retiring President Joseph D. Oren announced the following elected: Worthy President Orville Azelton, VP Harold Torrey, Chaplain Roland Sewell, Conductor George Roberts, Secretary Gerald Durand, Guards Harold Britten, Dewey W. Barnes and Trustee Anton Horvath.

Fenton Hotel owner, Ray O'Reilly was the M.C. for the Annual Father-Son banquet in June. The Eagles' Hall was filled to capacity for the dinner... As is the custom, the Sons offered a toast to the Fathers and the Fathers responded in a similar manner. Howard Bacon did the honor for the sons and George Anglen toasted the sons. Dennis and Jay entertained with piano and vocal solos. Bennett Lake was the site for the annual picnic in mid-August. The day was full with games for both young and old and hot dogs and ice cream was available all day long. It was an opportunity for he members to relax and enjoy themselves after a year of community projects.

The Oddfellows sold their building to George W, Pellett which allowed the Pellett Department store to expand, but the Masons still occupied the second and third floors of the building on the northwest corner of Leroy and Caroline Streets. All of the organizations related to the Masons used this space for the meetings an s other activities. All of the orders held elections and installed new officers for the coming year.

The Fenton lodge of the F & AM, the Masons, held their ceremony in late December and the following Masons were installed: Worshipful Master Willard Hatfield, Senior Warden Bruce Marsh, Junior Warden C. Judson Phillips, Treasurer D. R. Stiles, Secretary E. Weber, Chaplain Graham Paterson, Senior Deacon Harold Otto, Junior Myron

---

[5] From Wikipedia, the free encyclopedia

Richmond, Stewards Sidney Smale, Francis Gray, Kenneth Latta, John Ruckel, Tyler and Harold Wells.

The Order of the Eastern Stars, held an installation in November and elected Worthy Matron Marian A. Bristol, Worthy Patton Charles E. Wyman, Associate Matron Elsie Thorpe, Associate Patron Nelson Thorpe, Secretary Mary Mathews, Treasurer Ida Mae Miller and Conductress Mary Alice Davies. Other elected were: Martha Hatfield, Lucella Patterson, Avis Hough, Doris Adams, Elvira Wyman, Mary Butts, Lilly Londul, France Richmond, Helen Richmond, Lillian Bruder, Edward Bruder, Florence Zoll, Carrie Cummings, Marjorie Watters, Lucille Alden, Gertrude Gordon and Dorothy O'Neil.

The Rainbow Girls held their installation in September and selected Worthy Advisor Elaine Ireland and Worthy Associate Advisor Laquite Huet to lead them in the next year. Others elected were: Nancy Bly, Lena Dixon, Marion Bruder, Peggy Walraven, Luella Beebe, Betty Marsh, Donna Fisher, Janet DuBois, Jane Little, Nan Johnson, Martha Moyer, Barbara Bender, Beverly French, Nannette Stiff, Ann French, Pat Moyer, Verna Cooper, Darlene Jarvis, Carol Adams, Marcia Welch, Donna Alpaugh, Mary Stephens, Carolyn Fisher, Joan Irvin, Janice Wright and Marjorie Piddington. The program for the event had a solo by Carol Walden and a piano solo by Betty Van Gidder

The Oddfellows sold their two story building immediately south of Pellett's Department Store in the first block of South Leroy Street and were planning to build a new building in the near future. The Oddfellows and the Rebekahs continued to meet in the club's quarters in the second floor as Mr. Pellett, the new owner, expanded his store front to include the first floor of the building.

In June the I.O.O.F installed the following officers: Noble Grand Emil Strom, Vice NG Earl Seger, Secretary Charles Truchan and Treasurer George Anglen. Others serving were: Laverne Gleason, Henderson Graham and Fred Slover.

The Famous Rebekahs elected: N.G. Margaret House and Vice NG Wilma Kelly. Others were: Hazel Crystal, Lucille Bradley, Marvel Burden and Florence Robbins. Members included: Myrtle Swanebeck, Mrs. Lou Rector, Mrs. Ed Lord, Mrs. Pete Morea, Mrs. Roy Welch, Mrs. Wm. Henderson, Mrs. Charles Truchan, Mrs. Floyd Zimmer, Mrs. Florence Robbins and Mrs. Edgar Burden.

Scene Five...The Ladies Clubs

"The more things change...the more they stay the same" [6] The towns' two oldest clubs for women continued as they had for the last several decades   The Entre Nous and the Bay View met on a monthly basis, generally in the home of one of the members, where they would enjoy some sandwiches and tea and discuss the topic of the day. Most of the discussions followed a presentation of a research paper on the topic by one or two of the members. Occasionally, an outside speaker was invited to speak on a subject of special interest to the group. Both groups attracted the wives of the town's businessmen or those in school, church or government leadership positions   The women in the clubs were often leaders in their own right and along with the husbands of others, the club membership were among the town's "movers nd shakers". The club often took on projects to improve the quality of living in the community and joined with other organizations in community fund raising and support of theater and lectures at the Community Center.

The Entre Nous ended the year 1947 with a musical program hosted at the home of Mrs. H. R. Gardner. Misses Sandra Seal and Barbara Ross offered piano solos and Mrs. P. W. Parish and Mrs. John Dolza played selections on the piano and Novachord. The singing was provided by Mrs. W H. Skillen and Mrs. Jesse Powlison. Mrs. Eugene Cooley and Mrs. Russell Haddon dramatically reviewed the play "Deep are the Roots". Following the program tea was served by Mrs. George Pellett Sr.. The January meeting was hosted by Mrs. Lloyd Hunt and the topic for discussion was presented by Mrs. Burton Baker, Mrs. Frank Mytinger and Mrs. Lynden Avery.

The Entre Nous elected new officers in April and named the following: President Mrs. Ernest Hungerford, VP Lynden Avery, Secretaries: Mrs. Eugene Cooley, Mrs. Fred Ulch and Mrs. W B. Hoey, Treasurer Mrs. Frank B. Mytinger, Auditor Mrs. Kleber Merrick and Parliamentarian Mrs. Dora Morehouse. The new officers were inducted by the out-going President Mrs. C. A. Damon.

The gaily decorated home of Mrs. L.A. Riedel was the scene for the annual Christmas luncheon. Each member contributed package of food

---

[6] The proverb is of French origin and was used by the French novelist Alphonse Karr (1808-90). It also appears in George Bernard Shaw's 'Revolutionist's Handbook' (1903).

to be used by the Council of Social Agencies in packing Christmas baskets for the needy. Mrs. Wesley Martin chaired the event and was assisted by Miss Maude Morris, Mrs. Walter Walpole, Mrs. Arthur White, Mrs. L. E. Hungerford, Mrs. Frank B. Mytinger and Mrs. Lynden Avery.

The Bay View Club was led during the year by Mrs. Floyd Chapin, Mrs. Mrs. J. B. Obenshain, Mts. C. H. White, Mrs. G. L. Whittle, Mrs. Gorton Milliken, Mrs. R. G. Brown and Mrs. McGlynn.

The Child Study Club movement in Michigan was still very strong and in Fenton the three clubs were very active. The Senior Child Study appeared to be the "leader of the pack", perhaps it was only the tille "Senior", but the club did sponsor the annual Mother-Daughter Banquet which experienced a very large attendance and was supported by the two other CSC in town. The Senior CSC traveled to Holly for a joint meeting with the Holly CSC and in April joined in a meeting of all CSC in Fenton at the Community Center. It was the CSC annual "Guest Night" and those assemble heard Miss Francis Martin of Central State College (now Central Michigan University) speak on "Creative Living".

The annual Mother-Daughter Banquet was held on May 8th at the Community Center and was attended by over 280 mothers and their daughters. The dinner was served by the ladies of the Eastern Star and followed by an elaborate program with the "Story Book Land" as the theme. The back entrance on the stage was a large edition of a Mother Goose book, and the fabled figures entered the stage through an open page. Following the traditional toasts with Miss Carol Hartley toasted the mothers and Mrs. Emile Gosseaux responded for the mothers, the pageantry of the evening unfolded. The Mother Goose characters were played by Julie Tirrell, Sally Jo Meier, Mary Alice Graham, Mary Beth Cotcher, Diane Bobier, Jane Arndt, Patricia Rolland and Mary Kieft. Miss Nancy Bauer sang "Over the Rainbow" and "Some Day My Prince Will Come".

Gifts were presented to the oldest mother present, Mrs. Bensen Mitts, the youngest mother present, Mrs. Scott Mitts and to Mrs. Floyd Hartley, who was one of three mothers having three daughters present. The others were Mrs. Arthur Senecal and Mrs. Ray Hagerman.

Those CSC members who were responsible for the banquet were: Toast Mistress Dorothy Hodgman,. Kerber Merrick, Mrs. Elmer

Nellett, Mrs. Charles Leighton, Mrs. Howard Park, Mrs. Ernest Tirrell, Mrs. Arthur Sorenson, Mrs. C. G. Walcott and Mrs. Thor Neilson.

The Junior Child Study Club was only "junior" in name being well organized and active with their programs. Mrs. Wayne Wessendorf hosted a "surprise" program in April that was planned by Mrs. W F. Buchanan and Mrs. Donald Dunn. The ladies put on a play..."It's a Woman's Privilege"...for the members. Stars in the production were: Mrs. Ed Renwick, Mrs. Wayne Wessendorf, Mrs. John Nierescher, Mrs. Henry Alchin, Mrs. Clair Field and Mrs. Howard Reasner. Refreshments were served by the hostess assisted by Mrs. Claude Cohoon.

In May, the club met at the home of Mrs Ed Bretzke and elected their officers for the coming year. Those elected were: President Mrs. Ralph Richmond, VP Mrs. Robert Lutz, Secretaries Mrs. Charles Walker and Mrs. W F. Buchanan, Treasurer Mrs. Judson Phillips and Parliamentarian Mrs. Eugene Cooley.

The club closed their club year with a dinner meeting at the home of Mrs Buster Bender. The program included a discussion of "Tuberculosis", led by Miss Raymond of the Genesee County Social Agency.

The activities of the Pro-To Child Study Club paralleled thos of the two older CSC in town. In May, the Pro-To CSC met at the home of Mrs. William Gamble to elect their officers for the coming year. Those elected were: President Mrs. Chester Hillis, VP Mrs. Sam Angus, Secretaries Mrs. Don Burdick and Mrs. Willima Gamble, Treasurer Mrs. Dennis Watson and Parliamentarian Mrs. William Patton.

In mid-September, a group of young ladies met at the home of Mrs. JamesMcDevitt for the purpose of organizing a new Child Study Club. In early October, the group met again and at the home of Mrs. P. W. Parish and adopted a constitution, elected their officers and named the club the Novus CSC. Those elected were President Mary McDevitt, VP Irene Hunt, Secretaries Pauline McNeil and Dorothy Smale, Treasurer Irene Parish and Auditor Jeanne Peabody.

In December the club met at the home of Mrs. Ruth Dode at which time all member brought dolls they had dressed for the Old Newsboys Association of Flint. The dolls were judged by Carol Lea, Elizabeth Lutz and Jean Burdick, representatives of the Senior, Junior and Pro-To CSC respectively. First prize went to Rita Conley and second to Betty O'Grady. Refreshments were served by the hostess assisted by

Mrs. Catherine Hemboldt. Plans for a Christmas Party at the home of Mrs. Irma Parish were formulated.

For those ladies whose interests were in books and music, they found two very active groups dedicated these areas. The Fenton Music Club sponsored concerts, recitals and general musical programs. These programs were held at the Community Center and were well attended by the local citizens. Their meeting in April was held in the home of Mrs John Dolza where the members and their guests were entertained by Mr. Joseph Hunter, Bass Baritone, from Flint. Miss Alice Van Atta accompanied Mr. Hunter on the piano. Others active in the club were Mrs. Don Smale, Mrs. William Skillen, Mrs. Lynden Avery, Mrs. Ernest Tirrell and Mrs. Stanley Peabody

The Book Club met monthly, generally at the home of one of the members, but on more than one occasion, they met at the Community Center The meeting at the Center in April, the last meeting for the club year, was also the time for electing new officers for the coming year. Those elected were: President Mrs. Russell Judson, VP Mrs. J. B. Obenshain, Secretary Mrs. Carl H. White and Treasurer Mrs. Frank Wiggins. At the meeting the program consisted of the presentation of a review of a new book by a visitor or a club member. On this occasion, Mrs. E. F. Bacon of Flint reviewed "No Trumpets before Him" by Nelia Gardner White. (Why do "experts" from out of town always have three names?)

An English professor wrote the words, <u>Woman without her man is nothing"</u> on the blackboard, and directed the students to punctuate it correctly.

The men wrote: **"Woman, without her man, is nothing."**

The women wrote: **"Woman! Without her, man is nothing."**

Scene Six...Fenton's Churches and the Church Ladies

The people of Fenton were blessed with an array of Christian congregations, including all the major denominations, from which to select to practice their religion. There were very few, if any, villagers of the Jewish faith and the nearest synagogue was in Flint. If any of the old timers had heard of a mosque or Islam, it was probably from a movie or the reading of Arabian Nights. Yes, the townsfolk were followers of Christ and a goodly number of them were avid church-going Christians.

The Baptists, Episcopalians, Methodists and the Presbyterians had located their churches in the "downtown", while the Roman Catholics built their field stone church across the railroad tracks "way out" on North Adelaide Street and the Lutherans placed theirs on Main Street near the eastern village limits. The Christian Science society's place of worship was on East Rockwell. The Free Methodists Church was at Shiawassee and East Streets. The Fenton Bible Class met at South Holly Road and Pine Street. The Fenton Seventh Day Adventists met every Saturday morning at the Fenton Community Center. Some of the villagers attended the service of some outlying churches, such as: the Tyrone Community Presbyterian Church, the Long Lake Community Church and the church at Hallers Corner.

First Baptist Church
Ellen and Walnut Streets

The Ladies Auxiliary of the Baptist Church was active in both the church and the community during the year. Their leaders, elected in April, were President Mrs. George Koan, 1st VP Mrs. W Runyan, 2nd VP Mrs. R. Irwin, 3rd VP Mrs. E. Mead, Secretary Mrs. Albert Wood, Treasurer Mrs. A. Salmers and White Cross Mrs. Bloomer.

The Trinity Lutheran started the year with the dedication of a new parsonage on Orchard Street adjacent to the church building. The Reverend A. A. Klein and his family were the first to occupy the new home. Soon thereafter, the evening of May 14th, the annual Mother –

Daughter Banquet was held in the church building. Springtime was the theme and the decorations were all light a bright.

Mrs. H. Woodward Jr. served as the Toastmistress for the evening and Mrs. Anton Sorenson greeted those assembled and Mrs. A. Klein offered the Invocation. The Traditional Toasts were offered by Phyllis Neilsen . Others involved in the program were: Mrs. Carl Tisch and her three daughters, Gail and Pearl Gulch, Mrs. C. Jubelt and Mrs. Otto Schutt.

The Methodist women continued to be organized in smaller groups, called "bands", which, while working on church-wide projects, had their own agendas. The leaders of the Bands for this year were: Band #1- Mrs Elva Bowen, Band #2-Mrs. George Petts, and Band #4- Mrs. John Mortimore.

The Methodists found their "young adults" organizing an "Intermediate Fellowship" in April. The new group elected their officers and the following were named to serve: President Margaret Hartley, VP Charles Harper, Secretary Jim Standridge, and Treasurer Ann Bush. Others serving were: Joy Russell, Gail Hagerman and Gary Zoll. Church sponsors for the new group were: Mr. and Mrs. Richard Edinger, Mr. and Mrs. Wayne Roddy, Mr. and Mrs. Arthur Bush and Mrs. Hartley.

Our Lady's Sodality of St. John's Catholic Church, an organization for young women, accepted new members at a reception in late May. Ann Boilore, Lucille and Anna Mary Hubert, Amata Cook, Betty Van Gilder, Bethany Bush, Beth Reinke and Anna Marie Kudlinger were the new inductees.

In September, the Sodality elected officers for the coming year. Ann Camp was elected to serve a second term as Perfect and the following were elected: Vice Perfect Carolyn McCarty, Secretary Eleanor Dunn and Treasurer Joan Dreyer. The officers from the past year were Vice Perfect Elizabeth Foley, Secretary Celine Camp and Treasurer Ann Foley.

Miss Camp appointed Mary and Rose Preston, Bethany Bush, Amata Cook and Bernice Schoemaker to various committees. Eight new pledges were introduced at the meeting their first meeting. They were: Barbara Foley, Katheryn Lince, Mary Lou Hillis, Donna McMicheal, Louise Turco, Betty Hajec, Gloretta Hogan and Elise Pollidan.

Sodality May Reception May 1948[7]

Front Row L-R Elizabeth Foley, Anne Camp, Celine Camp, Ann Foley
Others identified in picture: Barbara Swanebeck, Anna May Hubert, Betty Jane Smith, Clara Hubert, and Cecelia Colburn (Left on 3rd Row), Ann Carter, Joan Dreyer, Mary Jean Dunn, Monica Camp and Amata Cook.

The Annual Christmas Ball was held at the Community Center, and the Sodality members and their guests dance to the music of Brahm Ward and his Orchestra, one of Flint's finest. The committee chairmen for the affair were Carolyn McCarty (Publicity), Eleanor Dunn (Decorations), Joan Dreyer (Tickets) and Ann Camp (Orchestra). Patrons for the party were Mr. and Mrs. Don J. McGuire, Mr. and Mrs. Herman St. Martin, Mr. and Mrs. Deane Cox, Mr. and Mrs. D. E. Newcombe and Mr. and Mrs. Linus Bush.

St. John's Annual Barbecue was held on July 3rd and 4th, and in addition to the delicious food, the event featured various rides and games provided by the Cote Amusement Company. All proceeds from the event went to the School Fund. Father Tighe expressed the hope that building a church school could begin later in the year.

---

[7] Sodality picture provided by Cecelia (Colburn) Terry '47

Earlier in the year, January 21st, the Parish held its first Mardi Gras at the Fenton Community Center. The event featured dancing, card games, plenty of good food and an opportunity to raise funds for the school fund. Those involved in the planning and operation were Co-Chairs Catherine Trollman and Phillip Foley. Committee Chairs were Elisabeth Foley, Anna Camp, Mary Groll, Bob Gearhart and Berniece Schoemaker.

In the absence of a pastor, St. Jude's Guild handled much of the business for the congregation. Guild President Mrs William Scott and her members did very well in this leadership position. They conducted a pancake breakfast on Shove Tuesday, a parish supper and the annual parish picnic successfully.

Father Daniel Patrick Tighe[8]

In December, the Guild elected the following officers: President Mrs Burns Fuller, 1st VP Warren Roberts, 2ndVP Mrs. Marion Moore, Secretary Miss Thelma Clements and Treasurer Miss Effie Bishop.

In years end, we found the major churches in the village were pastored by the following ministers:

St. John Catholic	Reverend Daniel P. Tighe.
St. Jude's Episcopal	Reverend Alvin H. Hanson
First Baptist	Reverend H. Woodside
Trinity Lutheran	Reverend A. A. Klein
First Presbyterian	Reverend Hartley H. Stockham
Free Methodist	Reverend H. E. Leininger
Methodist	Reverend Ralph D. Harper

---

[8] Photo provided by Mary Jean (Dunn) Reselige

Scene Seven...Patriotic Organizations

Two active patriotic women's organizations in Fenton at this time were the Women's Relief Corps and the Daughters of Union Veterans. Both organizations were associated with the Civil War and the Union veterans of that conflict. In Fenton, the two organizations, W.R.C. and DUV, joined together for their meetings and many of their functions. Many of the women were members of both organizations. These patriotic organizations express purpose was to perpetuate the memory of the Grand Army of the Republic..

In January, the two organizations met for a joint installation of officers. The DUV's officers were: President Dorothy Griswold, Sr. VP Hazel Crystal, Jr. VP Hattie Coats, Secretary Phoebe Rector and Treasurer Ruby Anglen. Others elected to serve were: Bertha Chapman, Florence Goodell, Olive Parker, Kate Hempstead, Marie Steward, Ida Brunson, Allie Parker, Edna Sommers, Oreanna Johnson and Mary Strom.

The installation of the new officers for the WRC followed with the induction of President Ruby Anglen, Sr. VP Blanche Faling, Seigrid Strom, Secretary Violet Vandercook and Treasurer Kate Hempstead. Others elected to serve were: Bertha Chapman, Rolla Moore, Marie Steward, Florence Goodell, Hattie Coats, Allie Parker, Carolyn Mortimore, Mary Mitchell, Gladys Kinne, Esther Lord and Olive Parker.

The VFW engaged the Cote Amusement Company to operate a carnival for a week in June. The Carnival was set up in the vacant lot off East Caroline Street near the Railroad Depot. The earnings from this event went to the Post's building fund.

On April 11th, the Post members installed their officers for the coming year. Webster Kelleher was elected as the Post Commander. Robert "Bob" Beach was named Senior Vice Commander and William "Bill" Gallagher was selected for Junior Vice Commander.

The VFW Auxiliary held their annual election of officer s in early March. Those elected were: President Alice Locke, Sr. VP Pauline McNeil, Jr. VP Doris Huff, Secretary Rita Conway, and Treasurer Leta Hanby. Others serving were: Lydia McCormick, Edna Bly, Mary Pasco, Edna Pokorny, Hazel Crystal, Irene Boilore, Delia Palmer, Margaret Durfee, Violet Harley, Emma Hall, Lillian Goodrich and Myrtle Harris.

The "fun" organization of the VFW, "The Military Order of the Cootie" was active in support of those hospitalized veterans. The men were organized as Caraboa Pup Tent 32 and their ladies as the Fen-Fun Cootiette Club 105. The names given to the officers were generally derived from the experiences of the "doughboys" in France, where many suffered from an infestation of "cooties". The men elected the following: Seam Squirrel Joe Rosenburg, Blanket Bum Webb Kelleher, Hide Gimlet Bob Utt, Hungry Nit William Harris, Custodian of the Crummy Duffle Bag Walter Stiff, Sky Pilot John Hauritz, Jimmy Leggs, Harry Pokorny and Provost Marshall Emmanuel Boilore.

The Fen-Fun ladies elected Chief Grayback Zelma Slover, Lady Louse Myrtle Harris, Baby Louse Edna Pokorny, Shekel Keeper Lelah Stiff, Scratcher Irene Boilore, Pious Louse Agnes Bottecelli, Crummy Chase Irene Tribbey and the Tightwads Marie Wagner and Cassie Devereaux.

On July 29th, the James DeWitt Post, held their annual election of officers. Those elected to serve were" Commander Harold Freeman, Sr. Vice Commander L. A. Wilson and Jr. Vice Commander Phillip Crane, Others elected to serve were: Reverend H. h. Stockham, Stanley Harter, Dave Bard, Bryant Hanby and Tholand Vreeland.

The Legion's Ladies elected the following; President Jeannette Hathaway, 1st VP Rose Harrington, 2nd VP Hazel Shaw, Secretary Florence Winn, Treasurer Elsie Brancheau, Chaplain Della Woodworth, Historian Elisabeth Goodrich and Sergeant-at-Arms Harriet Angus. The Executive Committee consisted of Lillian Goodrich, Mary Pasco and Luella Gould.

Joe Bottecelli chaired this year's Baseball Excursion for the American Legion. The train left the Fenton at 9AM and the revelers were met by a al bus in Detroit and taken to Briggs Stadium to see Detroit Tigers play the Chicago White Sox. .Those attending paid a total of $4.50...which included the cost of the train trip and the seat at the ball park.

The Legion women conducted a safety campaign and as part of the program ran a "slogan" contest for youngsters. The winner was a nine year old, fourth grade student Richard Webb. His winning slogan was : Safety Pays With the Lives It Saves". Other winners were Jon Vrbensky, John Gordon, Carl Schroeder, Bob Lutz, Charles Bumstead, Susan Miller, Jeri Rusinski, Mary Jean Dunn and Bethany Alexander. Mrs. John Turco was the Auxiliary's Chairman for the event.

Scene Eight...FHS Governance

In October, after over sixteen years as a member of the Fenton School Board, Harry Lowe tendered his resignation. Mr. Lowe had served as the Board President for the past thirteen years and had devoted himself diligently to the betterment of the school system. Many improvements could be credited to his administrative ability. After a stint in the hospital, he resigned because he was unable to devote the time and attention the duties required. Harold K. Schaefer was elected as President and Paul N. Stedman was selected to fill the vacancy on the Board. The school election had been conducted in July and incumbents Paul N. Stedman and Walter E. Walpole were defeated and newcomers Dr. Noble Peckham and William J. Nierescher joined incumbents Harry Lowe, Harold Schaefer and Clyde Furlong

Harry A. Lowe

The Parents-Teachers Association also experienced a record attendance at their meeting in January, when over 170 parents and teachers attend their meeting. At their last meeting for the year, over 100 attended and elected their officer for the coming year. Outgoing President Eldon Burton conducted the meeting which elected the following for 1948-1949

John Dolza	President
S. A. McCullan	Father VP-Grades
Mrs Howard Reasner	Mother VP-Grades
Mrs Thurman Kiesling	Mother VP- High School
Mrs. Jerold Pasco	Teacher VP-Grades
Mrs Harry Adams	Teacher-High School
Maurice Kieft.	Treasurer
Mrs. Donald Dunn	Secretary

While Student Councils are often perfunctory bodies, "something to keep the natives subdued", the Student Council at Fenton High School actually did some "governing". They made many major decisions effecting student life at the school. The Student Council officers for the year were: President James Botticelli, Vice President Barbara Swanebeck, Secretary 1st Semester Rosemary Howe, Secretary 2nd Semester Gloria Gordon, Treasurer Max Botticelli and Reporter Pat Watt. The Advisor was August Arndt.

156 The Village Players Post War

FHS Student Council 1947-1948

1ST Row L-R   Peggy Walraven, Carol Alchin, Rosemary Howe, James Botticelli, Max Botticelli, Barbara Swanebeck, Carol Hartley, Carol Adams. 2nd Row L-R Alan Burdick, Michael Harrison, Sharon Kelly, Violet Petry, Gloria Gordon, Mr. Arndt, Janet Breckenridge, Holly Walpole, Donald Griswold Victor Guernsey. 3r Row L-R James Clark, Ronald Millington, Conrad Krankel, Garner Merrick, Harold Taylor, Samuel Hunter.

FHS Faculty 1947-1948

1ST Row L-R   Mrs. Lucile Buta, Mrs. Stehle, Miss Evelyn Kinner, Clarence Heemstra, Mrs. Rebecca Zenkl, Miss Jean Gordon, Mrs. Ann Kean. 2nd Row L-R Dwight Fisher, Miss Eleanor Annis, Mrs. Ellen Adams, Miss Bessie Cramer, Mrs. Hazel Brown, Mrs. Miriam Kinner, Miss Joyce Haglund, Howard Park. 3rd Row L-R Charles Leighton, Emile Gosseaux, August Arndt, Bill Cowan, Ivan Williams, Maurice Kieft.

Scene Nine...FHS Athletics

As the year began the Tiger Basketball team had won their first game versus Howell and lost the second outing with Flint Tech. The expectations for a winning season were not high even though the last three seasons had been exceptionally successful. With only two returning lettermen, Jim Bottecelli and Pat Foley, the team played to a 7-7 record for the season. After winning their first league game with Grand Blanc, the fans were overly optimistic which resulted in a "packed house" for their second league game with Davison. The demand for tickets was so intense the school had to announce that the attendance for the game would be limited to 500. The locals were disappointed when FHS lost by the score of 39-27. The highlights of the mediocre season were found by defeating arch-rival Holly on two occasions.

FHS Basketball Team 1947-1948

1st Row L-R Bruce Dorland, Vince Messinger, Chuck Franks, Jim Bottecelli, Pat Foley. Max Bottecelli, Harold Taylor. 2nd Row L-R Coach Ivan Williams, Skip Horvath, Leman Shelby, Butch Helms, Garner Merrick, Bill Hagood, Asst Coach Bill Cowan

The baseball team began their practices in early April with over 30 candidates reporting the first day. Many veterans were in this group, with Mike Harrison and Vince Messenger, the "keystone combination", at Shortstop and Second Base, returning from a stellar season. Pitcher

Pat Foley was expected to have an exceptional season as was Max Bottecelli as his receiver. Others expected to be keys to a winning season were: Bill Edinger, Lemen Shelby, Jerry Durfee, Bill Marsh, Dick Rynearson and Garner Merrick. Freshmen Darwin Dager and John Judson played and did not disappoint Coach Cowan. Unfortunately, Fenton ended the season with a five win-three loss record,. The team was led in batting by Mike Harrison (.480), Max Bottecelli (.400), Vince Messinger (.379), Pat Foley (.357) and John Judson (.277).

FHS 1948 Baseball Team

1st Row L-R Bill Freeman, Max Bottecelli, Pat Foley, Vince Messinger, Jim Bottecelli, Jerry Durfee, Bill Hagood, Darwin Dager. 2nd Row L-R Mgr. Hans Jothan, Bill Hoey, Mike Harrison, John Judson, Bill Marsh, Garner Merrick, Glen Anderson, Bill Edinger, Walt Hajec, Coach Bill Cowan

The FHS Track team had a moderately successful season and sent four members to the State meet: Dick Berry in the 440; Chuck Franks, 1947 State Champion in the 880; Frank "Butch" Helms in the 880 and Ron Watts in the mile. Unfortunately none of the four were able to win a medal. Dick Berry set a new school and Regional record in the 440 yard dash with a time of 53.8. Interestingly, in doing so, Dick bested the record time of his brother Bob who ran the dash in 53.9.

Those lettering in Track this year were: Chuck Franks, Dick Perry, Sam Hunter, Royce Hyde, Ron Watts, Royce Gearhart, Jim Clarke, Cline Hagerman, Frank Helms, John Wright, Ken Watts, Mark Crane, Chuck Kiesling, Frank Wegner, Leroy Young, Jim VanCleve and Bill Edinger.

While the football team failed to win the Conference title as they had in the previous year, they posted a respectable 6-2-1 record and paced third in the County league. There were problems with injuries and ineligibility during the season which probably had some detrimental effect, but the two opening games with Howell and Holly raised everyone's expectations. The Tigers defeated Howell by a score of 33-0 and arch-rival Holly by 51-0. The two losses were to Kearsley 6-0 and Mt. Morris 12-0.

Frank "Butch" Helms (Guard) was selected for the All-County First Team and Darwin Dager (End) made the Second Team.

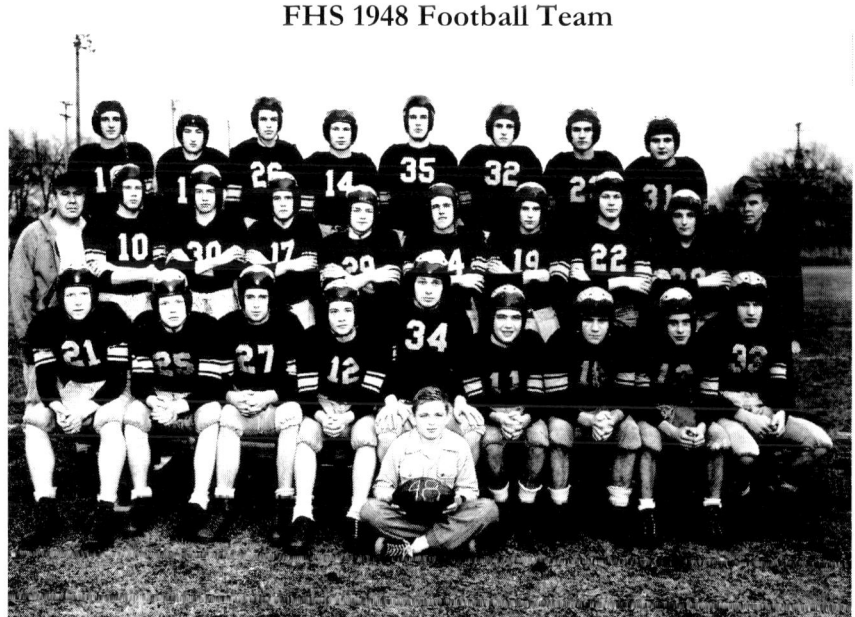

FHS 1948 Football Team

1stRow L-R Garner Merrick, Leman Shelby, Dick Stanley, John Wright, Gene Bentley, Max Bottecelli, Frank Helms, Bill Hagood, Dick Rynearson, Mgr. Dick Moorman, 2nd Row L-R Coach Williams Jerry Durfee, Jim VanCleve, Jerry Palmer, Martin Foley, Dan Foley, Bill Edinger, Glen Anderson, Paul Petty, Coach Cowan 3rd Row L-R Arlin Horvath, Don Frew, Dave Thornton, Robert Cutler, Lyle Harper, Darwin Dager, Ken Herrick. *Absent:* Pat Foley, Roger O'Berry, Dick Locke

160 The Village Players Post War

The distaff side of the student body was also active in sports. Members of the G.A.C.(Girl's Athletic Club) participated in a number of sports including softball, tennis, bowling, volley ball, badminton, touch football, socker and basketball. The Club met two times each week to plan their Activities. The Faculty advisor was Coach Bill Cowan. An advisory board composed of Lucille Hubert, Clara Hubert, Lorena Marsh and Ruth Young, all representatives of their class, also contributed to planning the Club's activities. The Club officers for this year were President Barbara Petty, Secretary and Treasurer Watt.

G.A.C. 1948

1st Row L-R   Dorothy Swartz, Lorena Marsh, Barbara Petty, Bobbie Ireland, Sis Ireland, Mamie Young, Pat Watt, Ann Loomis, Lee Merrick, Lucille Hubert, Mr. Cowan. 2nd Row L-R Mildred Carmer, Sheila Rossman, Mildred Jacobs, Janet Breckenridge, Eleanor Dunn, Joan Dreyer, Mary Jean Elrich, Esther Barton,
3rd Row L- R Darla Goss, Jeannine Turner, Frances Orcutt, Marie Jacobs, Verna Cooper, Jean McNab, Ann Kudlinger, Marilyn Bass, Joyce French, Marion Nash, Beverly Geister

Scene Ten...FHS Activities

The students of Fenton High School were very, very active outside the classroom. In addition to the sports teams and student politics, the Band and the Chorus were making music and helping to round out the academic experience

The FHS Band had an outstanding year,, following in the path of the bands of recent years. The Marching Band was present at the home football games and was a source of great pride for the students and the community. The highlight of the year was the Bands appearance at the Michigan State Fair for the third year. The Band played a concert after which the Fair's Music Director presented the Band with a trophy for their outstanding performance.

FHS Band 1947-1948

The Chorus presented the musical comedy "Pickles" at the Community Center in early February to an overflow crowd. The Chorus and all vocal music activity at FHS, and the entire school system, was under the direction of Mrs. Lucille Buta. Mrs. Buta came to the Fenton schools in the Fall of 1944 and quickly became recognized, not only for her musical acumen, but also for her for her positive influence on not only those students in her classes, but for all the others in attendance at FHS. Ralph Steward, FHS '56, was one of Mrs. Beta's students from his days in Middle school through his high school years. He credits Mrs. Buta for inspiring him to make career in music education. Mr. Steward retired after eighteen years teaching musical at FHS. When asked for some descriptive adjective to describe the diminutive Mrs. Buta, he suggested a few..."formidable, challenging, unique, admirable, demanding, a perfectionist, respected..." Most of all..."she knew her stuff"

162   The Village Players Post War

FHS Chorus 1947-1948

1st Row L-R   Nancy Schleicher, Evelyn Zeibig, Nancy Bauer, Holly Walpole, Donna Schutt, Marguerite Richmond, Jean Kelley, Barbara Burton, Dorothy Swartz, Phyllis McCormick. 2nd Row L-R   Beth Hungerford, Marjorie Green, Sharon Brill, Edith Wise, Pauline Francis, Marva Negus, Esther Barton, Donna Bronson, Carol Eedy, Carol Alchin, Betty Smith. 3rd Row L-R   Virginia Hall, Lorraine Hungerford, Monica Camp, Martin Foley, William Freeman, Max Fox, Gerald Graham, Victor Guernsey, Ruth Young, Marvel Edwards, Alice Moorman, Rosie Preston. 4th Row L-R   Grace Folland, Norman Spear, Royce Gearhart, Edward Bjorling, Phyllis Scott, Leo Foley, James Botticelli, Raymond Coyne, Pat Auker, Robert Tinker, Lois Goodrich.   Director Lucille Buta.

It is safe to speculate that almost every student enjoyed music even though they didn't participate in the Band of Chorus. Throughout the year there were many school sponsored dance, but the "big one" was the J-Hop. This semi-formal dance, sponsored by the Junior class, was held in the Community Center on the evening of April 30th.

Junior Class Officers Leading Grand March of J=Hop 1948

Act Three... The Year 1948

The theme for the J-Hop this year was "Gay Paree" Unlike the practice of the past years, only students will be allowed to purchase tickets. This restriction was necessary to allow sufficient space in the room to conduct the traditional Grand March. The Grand March was led by Class VP Frank Helms, Treasurer Jerry Durfee and Secretary Diane Loehne. The J-Hop was attended by 93 couples.

The Junior Committees for the event were: Tickets-Chairman Jerry Durfee, John Wright, Lorena Marsh, Elaine Ireland, Eleanor Harper, Nancy Stockham and Marie Stephens; Decorations: Barbara Swanebeck and Jane Gamble: Favors: Chairman Mariam Bruder; Refreshments: Chairman Barbara Petty; and Publicity: Carol Alchin, Diane Loehne and Jerry Durfee. Carl Stoll and his seven piece orchestra, including a vocalist, were engaged for the event.

The students loved to dance, but banquets also peaked their interest. The Annual All-High Banquet had 285 students in attendance The general theme was music with reach class representing some of the recognized styles: popular music, folk songs, jazz, and the classics. The Toastmaster for the evening was Jim Clark, who introduced the class speakers: Jim VanCleve-Freshmen Ron Millington-Sophomores; John Wright- Juniors; and Gloria Gordon-Seniors. The Faculty speaker was s Charles Leighton. Entertainment at the banquet was provided by Carol Jones and Carol Walden who sang and Harold Taylor who read a skit. The dinner was followed by a dance at the at the school gymnasium.

The Senior play this year was "Skyroad", which was set in the Cleveland Airport in 1932 when the "stewardesses" was very new The play was directed by Mrs. Russell "Sybil" Haddon and the cast included Elaine Ireland, Marve Edwards, Dorothy Swartz, Carol Alchin, Eleanor Harper, Garner Merrick. Marion Eastman, Don Dunn, Jane Gamble, Barbara Swanebeck, Bruce Gillespie, Harold Taylor, Les Kent, Carolyn Fisher and Kent Bennetts.

Cast of "Senior Play "Skyroad"

Why Invest in a 1947 Model Car When McDANIEL'S are Delivering

New 1948 Kaisers & Frazers

CHECK THESE KAISER AND FRAZER FACTS BEFORE YOU BUY ANY NEW CAR!

✓ Both cars are 100% postwar... in body and chassis design... in engineering, as well as in beauty of line... in color and upholstery, in appointments... in every smartly styled detail!

✓ Both cars are built in America's only 100% postwar automobile plant... Willow Run is the last word in production efficiency... equipped with war-developed tools and methods for high-precision, quality manufacture. Chassis and bodies are built complete on the industry's longest, newest, production lines.

✓ Both cars are built by Kaiser-Frazer Corporation, an organization of seasoned experts in every phase of the automobile industry, headed by Henry J. Kaiser and Joseph W. Frazer.

✓ Both cars have innumerable special features... like built-in ventilation... seats more than 5-feet wide... extraordinary vision in all directions... 27 cu. ft. of luggage space under rear deck... safety push-button door openers... special insulation... fresh air heat... unusual service accessibility... and...

Both cars are serviced with genuine factory parts, wherever you go, by one of the *four largest* dealer organizations in the world.

CALL ON YOUR NEAREST KAISER-FRAZER DEALER AND TAKE A RIDE!

McDaniel Motor Sales
608 N. Leroy Street   Phone 4322

Scene Eleven...Let Us Entertain You !

The *Rowena* remained the only movie theater in town but the Holly Theatre, also operated by J. C. Peck, was active and was joined by a theatre in Linden. So, the movie goers had little difficulty finding a "show" to attend. However, movies did no supplant the townsfolk's desire to see the local thespians doing their thing.

The local theatre group, *The Village Players,* led by their President Ryan Strom, produced their first play of the season on May 16th. The play "The Whole Town's Talking" was directed by Mrs. J.A. Johnson at the Fenton Community Center to a "full house" of enthusiastic theater goers. The cast was headed by Wilbur Strom with Burt Moyer, Jacqueline Roberts, Thelma Rolland and Ronald Swartz. Others in supporting roles were: Nettie Wood, Bob Smith, Janet DuBois, Carol James, Madeline Wessendorf, Raymond Coyne, Jane Wilson and Diane DuBois.

The Fall production of the *Village Players* occurred on October 24th at the Community Center when the play "Adams Evening" was presented to an enthusiastic audience with an evening of laughs, mixed with suspense. The leading roles were played by Royce Downey, Tim Smith, Nettie Wood, Ryan Strom, Zella Gosseaux, Elmer Strom and Jacqueline Roberts. The play was directed by Bill Strom.

Another group "The Dancing Dolls" hit the stage on several occasions and was always well received by those in attendances. This group of young dancers included the following: Danna Black, Patsy Wood, Warren McKeusir, Bettie Black, Janie Bently, Nancy Fraser, Joan Parkin, Sandra Nelson, Jimmie Bauer, Mildred Geister and Sharon Geister. Pianist Junnie Standridge was also a member of the group.

Some of the younger men in the community chose to get their "kicks" from renewing their active participation in Football. The Fenton Independent Football Association was formed in September and fielded a football team named the *Independents*. The team was sponsored by the Fenton Independent and the Ray Hunt Insurance Agency. The football squad was, for the most part, composed of former players at Fenton High School. Those listed as original members were: Bill Brabon, Mel Schupbach, Bob Torrey, Phil Kelley, Jim Durfee, Harold Dennison, Walter Fisher, Phil Scott, Clare Whitman, Pete Hartley, Jim Walters, Dick Black, Rick Rockman, Bob Butts, Chuck Franks Vince Harrison, John Howe, George Howe, Bob Glaspie, Russ Reynolds, H. Rockman,

Jim Thompson, Don Schupbach, George Granger and K. Trimmer, Others joined the team as the season progressed.\ The team remained undefeated through the first five games of the season, defeating Rose Malicki's Detroit team 13-12, Hamtramck 26-0, Tecumseh 19-12, East Detroit's Vogue A.C. 33-0 and the Bay City Blazers 23-6 . They ended the season with 7 wins and 4 losses and second place in the State League. The townsfolk had found discontinuance of the rational Thanksgiving Game between Fenton and Holly High Schools to be real "bummer" until they learned the Independents would play Howell on the holiday on Phillips Field.

Chuck Helms was the only player to experience a serious injury. Helms was hospitalized after leg surgery. There was no insurance to cover any injury and for the next couple years, various groups conducted fund raising events to help him pay his hospital bills.

The Tri-County League opened their season in April with the two Fenton entries, with the Merchants and the American Legion playing each other on the home field. As in past seasons, the team from Gaines and the Merchants were contending for first place throughout the season, and finally won the crown by one game over the home team. Pitchers Charlie Conklin and Don Orthner led the Merchants with the support of Jack Hartley, Mike Harrison, Vince Harrison, Al Turco, Bob Hunt, Claude Kirkey, Art Brown, Vern Hunt, Lyle Bumstead and Vince Messinger,\. The Fenton Legion team ended last in the standings in spite of some excellent pitching by Pat Foley and Dick Edinger and hitting of Pat Foley (.500), Dave Bard (.499) and Bud Madden .375).

It seemed the "Boys and Girls" ...participants in the town's bowling leagues were doing their "thing" throughout the year, but in reality, serious bowling was during the winter season. The Bowling Association had two men's leagues, the Inter-City League and the Booster League, each with the standard 12 teams. Some of the bowlers participated in both leagues. The Eagles also sponsored a 12 team league and the Fenton Recreation Ladies League met the needs of the enthusiastic women bowlers and had 12 teams participating.

At the end of the season, each league enjoyed their Banquets and at the end of the 1947-1948 season he leaders were the Virginia Tavern (Inter City), Mickey's Dairy (Booster) and Cecil's (Ladies).

Scene Twelve...Other Items of Interest

- Charles C. Davis FHS '19 was awarded an "Oscar" by the Motion Picture Academy for his technical contribution to film making.
- The Dancing Dolls said farewell to their leaders, Margie and Nancy Justin who moved away from Fenton.
- Mr. and Mrs. William Stocken and Mrs. Emma Howell were injured in an auto accident on Christmas day. Mr. Stocken and Mrs. Howell were hospitalized in Pontiac.
- In late March, a three year old boy fell through the ice near Crane Wood Landing on Long Lake (Lake Fenton) and was rescued by 12 year old Donald Lonsbury.
- Fire, of an undetermined source, destroyed one of the barns behind the old Baptist Home. Firemen battled the place all night.
- In July, Boy Scout Dick Eble saved young Dickie Irvine from drowning when Irvine jumped into deep water and failed to come to the surface. Eble plunged into the water and brought the young man to the dock at the south end of Lake Fenton.
- Than Chesnut travelled to the Rose Bowl with the U of Michigan Football team....newspapers referrd to him as "Rosebowl Than" and he took some Michigan apples with him. For years Than would deliver apples to the U of M football team and the band on games day.
- In March, the ten residents of the Hamilton Apartments were aroused during the night by fellow resident George Paine who found the building on fire. The building, at Sinclair and High Streets was completely destroyed.
- Tradegy struck in March when Donald Williams, a 4 year old toddler, walked into the side of a moving truck on Poplar Street (now Silver Lake Rd). The little fellow died in his attempt to join other children across the road

- For the first time in six years, the Fenton Girl Scouts sold "Cookies". Two groups sold a total of 916 boxes with Patsy Haviland (105) and Mary Jean Dunn (44). The top sellers.
- President Truman had a balcony built off his second floor bedroom. The balcony will allow the President to sit and relax outside of the public view. The cost of the balcony was $15,000.
- The Fenton Kiwanis and XX Club sponosred Pat Foley and Dick Rynearson at the Wolverine oy's State at Eaat Lansing.
- *The Fenton Independent* installed a modern press replacing the press that served the newspaper for 27 years printing over 3,3510,000.
- The Bell Telephone Labs announced radios without vacuum tubes and play instantly when turned on are now a possibilty with the invention of an entirely new electoinc divice, the "transistor".
- Beginning in November, Fenton and Holly telephone users will be able to make unlimited calls between the two exchanges without paying any toll charges.
- A state-wide drive by the shoe retailers ..SOS ..."Share Our Shoes", have collection barrels at Bobier's and Pellett's. The shoes will go to Europe to where 200 million pairs are needed
- In July, the *Independent* ran the following want ad:

> $5,000. Lake Fenton all-year home, school bus by door, 2 bedrooms, large living rom, spacious kitchen, bath and utility room, good well screened proch. $1,000 down and balance easy.

What Things Cost in 1948:
Car: $1,550
Gasoline: 26 cents/gal
House: $13,500
Bread: 14 cents/loaf
Milk: 86 cents/gal
Postage Stamp: 3 cents
Stock Market: 177
Average Annual Salary: $3,600
Minimum Wage: 40 cents per hour

Interlude Three...a World of Upheaval and Unrest

The "Crimson Tide" was on the move...and it wasn't the Alabama football team that had the peoples of the free world concerned. The Soviet Union had begun the "Communization" of those countries in their sphere of influence.

The governments of the countries of Eastern Europe were rapidly being replaced with Communist regimes. In the early months of 1948, the non-communists in Czechoslovakia struggled to maintain their positions in the government, but were soon forced out of office.

Even the highly respected President, Eduard Benes, eventually resigned, citing poor health, and was replaced by the communist Prime Minister Klement Gottwald. Benes found his "poor health" only a few months after his Foreign Minister and nationalist leader, Jan Masaryk, was found dead, dressed in his pajamas, below his bathroom window.

In Europe, sixteen nations joined the Marshall Plan's economic cooperation organization. However, the Soviet "bloc", which included Czechoslovakia, Poland, Hungary, Romania and Albania, declined. Finland also deferred to avoid antagonizing the Soviet Union.

In the Far East, the Soviets were supporting a communist government in North Korea. They had occupied the northern part of the Korean peninsula after declaring war on Japan, just days before Japan's surrender. The United Nations had proposed an election for all of Korea and move towards a unified government, but the North Koreans balked and the election was held in South Korea only. In the South Korean election over 85% of the eight million eligible voters went to polls.

Both the North and the South Koreans produced their own Constitution and their form of government. The formation of their separate countries occurred on the same day. On April 8th 1948, both the Republic of Korea (South Korea) and the Democratic People's Republic of Korea (North Korea) proclaimed their status as a nation.

The Soviets tightened their control of Eastern European communists to combat the increasing nationalistic independence activities in their countries. At a meeting of the communist nations, the Cominform, Yugoslavia was expelled from the organization for their independent communist agenda.

Other Communist take overs were occurring in other parts of the world. The Chinese Communists were gaining control of Manchuria and capturing large quantities of U. S. war materiel intended for the forces of Chiang Kai-shek, the leader of the Chinese. Nationalists

In the East Indies (Indonesia), the Dutch were attempting to hold on to their colonies and fighting a Communist inspired insurgency.

In some instances the "threat of communism" was used as the rational for a government take over. In Venezuela, a three-man military junta overthrew the democratically elected government, declaring the action as a "democratic necessity in the face of Communist influence"..

The Communist Party in the United States was making "small waves"...such as their leader Max Weiss' comments in an edition of the *Communist Monthly*; He wrote that the Soviet Union was "the most advanced democracy the world has known". In July of 1948, the U.S. Federal government indicted each of the members of the governing board of the Communist Party USA for advocating "destruction of the government of the United States by force and violence".

The Soviets expressed displeasure with the way the Allied Nations...the United States, France and Great Britain...were dealing with Germany and cut off all rail and road routes to West Berlin, which was deep in Soviet controlled East Germany and occupied by the Allies. Thus the "Berlin Blockade" began. The Allies began the "Berlin Airlift" and for over a year transported all goods, including coal, into West Berlin.

Following the action of the United Nation's General Assembly, the National Council "representing the Jewish people in Palestine" met and established the nation to be called Israel. However, the unrest and fighting continued as Egypt, Transjordan, Lebanon, Syria, Iraq and Saudi Arabia went to war against the new nation.

President Truman was serving in the last year of his term in the office he assumed upon the death of President Roosevelt. President Truman was not hesitant to speak out against the conduct of the Soviet Union and at a joint session of Congress in March of 1947, he blamed the Soviets for the Communist takeover of

Czechoslovakia and asked the Congress to enact a universal military training program and a new Selective Service bill.

It was an election year and President Truman was opposed by the Republican candidate, Thomas Dewey, a former Governor of New York. Truman made a whistle-stop train trip across the nation, speaking at the many stops from the platform at the back of the train. The nation's polling organizations, including the well-respected poll of the *Literary Digest* predicted Dewey would defeat the incumbent in the election. On the night of the election, the *Chicago Tribune*, being very confident in the polling predictions "Jumped the gun" and published an edition with a blazing headline...**DEWEY DEFEATS TRUMAN**. The U.S. polling organizations were embarrassed and apologetic about their methods. The *Literary Digest* ceased publication.

President Truman had two other opponents in addition to Thomas Dewey,. The former Vice President, Henry Wallace ran as the Progressive Party's candidate, and campaigned against the hostility toward the Soviet Union and captured 2.4 % of the votes, The "Dixiecrat" candidate Senator Strom Thurmond carried four states: Louisiana, Mississippi, Alabama and his home state of South Carolina, but garnered fewer votes than Henry Wallace. Most of the citizens learned of the campaigns from the newspapers and the radio since Television was still uncommon

During the short time he served as Vice President, Harry S. Truman saw President Roosevelt, infrequently and was not told of the development of the atomic bomb or the strained relations with Soviet Russia. With the death of President Roosevelt on April 12, 1945, he inherited all these problems... and many others He was reported to have said "I felt like the moon, the stars, and all the planets had fallen on me."

Within a short time, President Truman was required to make some of the most crucial decisions in the nation's history. After V-

E Day, the war against Japan was in its final days, Japan rejected the U.S. offer to surrender. The President understood an invasion of the Japanese Islands would result in a great number of casualties for both the invaders and the Japanese people. Consequently, he ordered atomic bombs to be dropped on those cities devoted to war work. Hiroshima and Nagasaki were bombed and the Japanese surrendered..

He presented to Congress a 21-point program, proposing the expansion of Social Security, a full-employment program, a permanent Fair Employment Practices Act, and public housing and slum clearance. While his predecessor, President Roosevelt had the New Deal", Truman's program became known as "the Fair Deal".. President Truman took the lead in negotiating a military alliance of Western nations, the North Atlantic Treaty Organization (NATO) which was established in 1949.

The President was known for his fiery speech and use of mild profanity, especially in his dealing with the press and the Republicans. He was often encouraged by his supporters with "Give 'em Hell Harry!".. The President's response was "I never give them hell, I just told the truth and they thought it was hell". He did not shy away from accepting responsibility and proclaimed this with a sign on his desk reading "The Buck Stops Here"

He decided not to run again and he retired to his home in Independence, Missouri. at age 88, he died December 26, 1972, at the age 88.

- Congressman William Blackney reported the curent strength of yjr Armed Forces as compared to strenght on V-E Day: Army from 6 Million vs 560,000; Navy 3 1/3 Million vs 494,00' Air Force 2.3 Million vs 336,000; and Marines 500,000 vs 79,000.

Act Four...the Year 1949

Scene One...The Village Council

As the New Year opened, the Village leaders had a lot "on their plate" but they had little, if any, knowledge of the significant events to unfold which would certainly affect their future. The question on the regulation of downtown parking still troubled the council members, the downtown businesses and the public in general. Previously they had set a two hour limit for downtown parking, but it had not been well received by the townsfolk. In the first meeting of the year, Trustee Charles Rounds boldly offered a motion to return to the one hour limit which was to be aggressively policed. The motion passed unanimously. Well, now the parking problem was solved...or was it?

In late February, the two local political parties, the Citizens Party and the People's Party, caucused and presented their slates for the upcoming Village election. The Citizens Party offered President Harry Lemen, Clerk Elton Austin, Treasurer Edgar Weber, Assessor Irving Gould and Trustees Merton West, Wayne Townsend and Harry Wykes. The People's Party's slate presented President A. C. Locke, Clerk Robert Obenshain, Treasurer Charles Walker, Assessor John Weidman and Trustees Elmer Westman, Earnest Tirrell and Charles Dager.

There was a record turnout of voters for the Village election which saw the People's Party candidate, Aldrich C. Locke elected as the Village President. Aldrich Locke garnered 668 votes to Incumbent Harry Lemen's 255. Only Elton Austin, Edgar Weber and Irving Gould from the Citizens slate were elected. In photo, Harry Lemen, on left, congratulates Aldrich Locke on his victory.

The defeat of Harry Lemen for the Village Presidency was somewhat of a surprise since Mr. Lemen had served in the office since 1933 and was highly respected and well-liked by the townsfolk. On the other hand, Aldrich Locke was also highly respected and well-liked...after all who couldn't like the town's "Santa Claus"? Perhaps it was just time for a change?

The newly elected Councilmen Elmer Westman, Ernest Tirrell and Charles Dager would join the incumbents Dr. "Buck" Buchanan, Don Bristol and Evar Strom to form the new Village Council.

The new Village President and the newly constituted Village Council was immediately challenged by the "cash flow" problem, as will the continuing problem of meeting the growing needs of a growing community without sufficient revenue to meet those needs. The immediate problem of insufficient funds on hand was met by transferring $1,300 from the Paving Fund to the General Fund, with, of course, the return of the moneys as soon as other funds are available. Clerk Elton Austin advised that before the tax collection in July, there would be at least two substantial revenues due the Village-the Gas and Weight Tax and the Sales Tax. So, with the financial problem solved for the moment, the President Locke assigned members to serve on six committees: Purchase and Finance; Streets and Parks; Health, Sanitation and Sewer; License and Lighting; Personnel; and Fire and Public Buildings.

President Locke also appointed Clifford B. Dye to serve as the Village Attorney. Attorney Dye had served the Village in that capacity for the past three years and his appointment was unanimously approved by the council members.

A short time after assuming the office Aldrich Locke came down with the mumps. It was hard to tell that he had the mumps because of his portly build, but Aldrich confirmed it was the mumps. Being unable to attend the council meeting at the time, Mr. Locke tuned to the technology of the day and kept an open phone line with the council so he could keep abreast of the proceedings.

The new Village governors were as frugal as its predecessors...they were "tight" with the money The financial situation of the Village was published on March 1st showed the following:

Balance on Hand March 1, 1948	$ 4,822.84
Receipts for the Year	110,684.06
Total Receipts	$115,506.90
Total Disbursements	112,761.90
Gross Balance On Hand	$ 2,745.00

As the locals were striving to meet the needs of the community, Fenton's representative in the U. S. Congress, William Blackney was reporting in his weekly column in the *Fenton Independent* as follows:

> "Our Spendthrift Government: In the Federal Fiscal Year just ended, the government shows a deficit of $1.8 Billion. For the new year, President Truman and the Treasury Department estimate the deficit will total $873 Million. But last January they guessed the deficit would be only $600 Million...only 1/3 of what it proved to be. They could be just as wrong this year. In fact, it is estimated the deficit might run as high as $5 Billion."

Many of the issues which once confounded the Council, such as whether to the village should take possession of a neglected Oakwood Cemetery or whether to install parking meters along Leroy Street or who should be awarded the garbage collection contract had been resolved to everyone's satisfaction. The Oakwood Cemetery was now in excellent condition, the parking problem, perhaps the *perceived* parking problem, had been set aside to everyone's relief and a responsible company had been awarded the garbage collection job. The downtown merchants were especially pleased since now their trash would be picked-up twice a week from the alleys behind their stores. Previously, each business had to contract for the service on their own.

The three major problems confronting the new Village President and the Council were Sewers, Water and Streets.

For the past decades, Fenton's streets were, for the most part, unpaved. Each year the Council would arrange for the "oiling" of selected streets which would generally solve the dust problem for the residents along these streets for at least one season. This year the Village engaged a firm to treat West Street, North Adelaide Street, Sixth Street, North East Street and East High Street with a "triple seal street coating". $10,000 was approved for this "super" oiling job. The Village also continued the project, which began the year before, to build two miles of hard surfaced streets each year. The project also included the wideneing of the paved streets from 13 to 20 feet.

The State Highway Department repaired the bridge over the Shiawassee River on South Leroy Street during the summer. The bridge was originally built in 1906 by two Fenton residents, Hamilton and Morehouse. At the time the street was of gravel and there were no sidewalks. The State rebuilt the foundation and the east wall of the structure, built sidewalks and paved the road over the bridge. The original beauty of the structure was not disturbed and remains the same to the present time.

Sanitation had not always a principle concern of the Village Council but with the closing of the downtown "city dump" (to provide for the building of the Community Center in 1938), the building of more sanitation sewers, the restrictions on the installation of septic tanks and providing garbage collection sanitation had become a priority concern

Perhaps these sanitation issues were so "big", they had overlooked the public toilet at the corner of Adelaide and Caroline Streets. The residents in the vicinity of the toilet had filed petitions over the years to have the toilet removed. The property on which the toilet stood was owned by Dr. Sleeman of Linden. The Council promised to look into the matter. It is not known when the toilet facility was removed, but it was!

For years the townsfolk had suffered because of an inadequate sewer system. Bob Beach, the Editor of the *Independent* had recently become a homeowner and had experienced what others had been experiencing every time there was a heavy rain. Some very strong editorials expressed his anger and frustration about the urgent need to build sanitation and storm sewer system. He expressed the thought that the taxpayers were willing to go into debt to provide this system. President Locke and the Council members were very aware of the problem and along with Village Engineer Downey began to work on a plan to correct the situation.

The Water Department, generally financially "underwater", made an interesting discovery in December. They had pumped about 30,000,000 gallons of water during the last quarter of the last year. After checking the billing for the water provided the users, during that period, they found that they had only billed for 7,000,000 gallons. Where did the other 13,000,000 gallons go?

Scene Two...The Town's Business

Most of the business news seemed to be related to the automotive industry. In January, long-time auto dealer Hugo Theisen, whose lot was located on Roberts Street (now West Silver Lake Road) in the first block west of the intersection with North Leroy Street, announced the purchase of the Hannah's Auto lot near the Village limits on North Leroy Street. It appeared as if the Theisen Motor Sales was expanding its business but .only two months later, in March, Theisen sold out to Amuel M Kirk of Flint. Kirk's Sales and Service's Grand Opening was held in conjunction with the showing of the new 1949 Plymouth.

The McDaniel Motor Sales had opened two years earlier and represented the new Kaiser-Frazier company. The Fentonites, as well as the people throughout the country, had not seen a "new" car during the war years and the new auto maker sold all the cars they could produce in their Willow Run, Michigan facility. Bill and Clara McDaniel had the Kaiser Frazer agency in town and it was a surprise when General Motors announced the McDaniel Motor Sales would become a Buick agency. The McDaniels said they would soon have new Buicks in the showroom at 608 North Leroy Street. They would also continue as a sales and service agency for the Kaiser-Frazier automobiles until a new agency was appointed.

The Lanning Brothers, who had been in the oil business for several years, had recently acquired the Packard agency and had several models on display at their business,. Not to be outdone, so it seemed, the Western Auto Store at 117 South Leroy Street, the next door neighbors to the Methodist Church, announced they were selling the new "lightweight" Crosley cars and trucks. The Crosley vehicles included the "world's lowest-priced station wagon, a convertible and a two-door sedan. The Convertible delivered in Fenton for $1,039.96, which included Federal and State taxes, license and title. Earlier in the year, the Wismer-Wright Chevrolet Company, located at 305 North Leroy Street (just across the street from the Fenton Hotel), purchased the service station just south of their facility, which was owned and operated by Floyd Hartley. George Wright said the property would be included in the company's plans for expansion of their business.

In late June, the community experienced the closing of the Genesee Tool Company, one of the town's industries. During a two-day auction, the plant was essentially dismantled as piece by piece, the machinery and equipment was moved out of the building. Genesee Tool Company had been a thriving war production plant producing machine tools for the British before the United States had entered the conflict. In the early years of the war, the German submarines were sinking ships headed from the United States to Great Britain in such large numbers that the tools mad by the Genesee Tool were produced in triplicate, crated in three individual shipments with each shipment loaded on a separates ship for its voyage to Great Britain. As the *Fenton Independent* lamented "Many in Fenton, for years to come, will refer to the Genesee Tool Company as the place where they did their part *(in the war effort)*".

Other items of interest in Fenton's business world were:

*   The Shell Oil Company built a 75,000 gallon bulk plant 320 feet along the Grand Trunk railroad, east of the Depot. The plant was managed by the Lanning Brothers.

*   Louis Riedel completed 25 years as Manager of the Michigan Bean Company elevator in Fenton.

*   Don Alchin returned to the grocery business with the opening of his new store at the corner of Silver Lake Road and Adelaide Street. Mr. Alchin operated a grocery store on South Leroy Street for years before selling the business to the Obenshains.

*   Billmeier's photo shop offered the new "View Master". The View Master shows three dimensional Kodachrome views of interesting points in the United States and the world.

*   Larry Hamady opened his "Pure Food Market" on Fenton Road (now North Leroy Street) at the village limits.

*   Mrs. Mary Butts wife of the late Carol Butts, announced that she will continue to operate the Felton Memorial. Her three sons will also participate in the business.

*   The management of the Industrial Tool Company entertained their employees with a dinner at the Fenton Hotel.

*   The "Deck" at the point of Main Street and First Street , opposite the Fenelon Hotel, a popular sandwich shop, was reopened by their new owners William "Bill" Marshall and Fred Brunson. Two weeks later Mr. Marshall sold his interest to his partner, Fred Brunson.

*   Mrs. Irene (Graham) Imhoff became manager of the popular Hamburg Inn. The former manager, Ed Giles, left to cut meat at Obenshains Market.

Scene Three...The Lady Clubbers

In these pre-TV days, the glory era of clubs continued. If anyone in Fenton could not find a club or organization to meet their needs, that person wasn't really trying. Both men and women had a variety of fraternal, veteran, hobby, political, special interest and social organizations active in the community.

The two long standing Women's clubs, the Bay View and Entre Nous, continued their active presence. The Bay View club was led by their President Mrs. Don Smale. Some of the most active members were: Mrs. Anson Walcott, Mrs. James Stewart, Mrs. W H. Skillen, Mrs. Clark Thompson, Mrs. Earl Breckenridge, Mrs. Don McGuire, Mrs. Fay Anderson, Mrs. Fred Corneil, Mrs. E. C. Reid, Mrs. Robert Brown and Mrs. Johnny Nierescher. Similarly, the Entre Nous continued meeting on a weekly basis, usually in the home of a member, discussing issues of current or historical interest.

The Entre Nous was led by Mrs. L. Hungerford. Some of the active members were Mrs. Frank Mytinger, Mrs. L. A. Riedel, Mrs. C. R. Heemstra, Mrs. L. E. Blazier, Mrs. Arthur Watts, Mrs. Maude Morris, Mrs. David Limbach, Mrs. Claude Sinclair, Mrs. Walter Walpole, Mrs. Clifford Phillips, Mrs. Charles Lea, Mrs. Lynn Avery and Mrs. Elroy Herrick.

The Child Study Cub movement continued to be very strong throughout the State and the four clubs in Fenton were active parts of the Michigan Child Study Association.

For the most part, the four Fenton clubs met every two weeks in the home of one of their members. The program for the meetings was usually a discussion of a topic related to child care. The meetings usually included light refreshments. On occasion, the four clubs would come together and sponsor a program at the Fenton Community Center. One occasion was when the four clubs entertained the CSCs of Howell. The guest speaker was Mr. Victor Anderson of Flint's Whaley Home. The meeting was attended by the Mrs Lyle Price, President of the State Association.

The Annual Mother–Daughter Banquet was held in May and attended by over three hundred women.

In October, the Senior CSC elected officers for the next year: President Mrs. Elmer Nellett, VP Mrs. Howard Park, Secretary Mrs. Arnold Westman Jr., Treasurer Mrs. Donald Chase, Other members of the Senior CSC are listed below:

> Mrs. Ivan Williams, Mrs. Leo Miner, Mrs. Carl Tisch, Mrs. Clark Hagerman, Mrs. Charles Lowe, Mrs. Ivah Rolland, Mrs. Sterling Torrey, Dorothy Hodgman, Mrs. Thomas Faull, Mrs. Burnette Rodgers, Mrs. Maurice Kieft, Mrs. Thor Nielsen, Mrs. Owen Meier, Mrs. Ernest Tirrell, Mrs. Carver Walcott, Mrs. John Lea,

Mrs. Floyd Hartley, Mrs. Claude (Ruth) Sinclair, Mrs. W H. Gordon, Mrs. David Frew, Mrs. Douglas Gould and Mrs. Kleber Merrick.

The Junior CSC operated in a manner similar to the Seniors, The club met every two weeks in the home of one of their members. Light refreshments were in order, but on occasion, they shared supper together. Each member, in turn, would research a topic of interest and present her findings to the membership. Some members of the club are listed below:

President Mrs. Ralph Richmond, Mrs. John Verbensky, Mrs. Henry Alchin, Mrs. Clair Field, Mrs. Charles Walker, Mrs. John Millington, Mrs. Sue Watts, Mrs. W F. Buchanan, Mrs. Elwood Ellsworth, Mrs. Eldon Burton, Mrs. Paul Williams Mrs. Howard Reasner, Mrs. Wayne Wessendorf, Mrs. Gordon Robbins, Mrs. Millie Dode, Mrs. Dorothy Peckman, . Mrs. Elaine Wright, Mrs. Edith Neidermeier, Mrs. Lavina Welch, Mrs. Margaret Hoekesma, Mrs. Linda Cohoon, Mrs. Marjory Nierescher, Mrs. Elsie Dunn, Mrs. Ralph Richmond, Mrs. Harold Dode and Mrs. Lynn Welch.

The Pro To Child Study Club met in May and elected their officers. Those elected were President Mrs. Sam Angus, VP Mrs. Harold Schleicher, Recording Secretary Mrs. Al Seelye, Corresponding Secretary Mrs. Roy Buffmeyer, Treasurer Mrs. Chester Hillis, Parliamentarian Mrs. George Kidder, and Mrs. Ray Gleason.

The newest CSC in Fenton was named the "Novus" CSC and even though the club was relatively new in town, they were very active in the community. Most of their meetings were of the same program type as the other CSC, however, perhaps the highlight of their program year was when they had their husbands as their guests. The ladies were well prepared to "roast' their male counterparts with song parodies and "dumb" husband jokes. It was an evening of fun and one that the men didn't expect but would remember.

In late April, the Novus members elected their officers for the coming year. Those elected were: President Mrs. Howard Goodrich, 1stVP Mrs. Harold O'Grady, 2nd VP Mrs. Ben Alger Jr., Rec. Secretary Mrs. Leo Helmboldt, Corr. Secretary Mrs. John Block, Treasurer Mrs. Robert Hunt and Auditor Mrs. Stanley Peabody. The outgoing President was Mrs. James McDevitt. Some of the members of the club were:

> Mrs. Morris Winacuff, Mrs. Roy Goodrich, Mrs. Peter Parrish
> Mrs. Lowell Merrill, Mrs. Zola Simmons, Mrs. William Dode Jr.,
> Mrs. Norman McNeil, Mrs. Paul Bottecelli, Mrs. Clifford Abbey,
> Mrs. R. E. Covert,

The Oddfellow's women, the Favorite Rebekahs...began the year with their officers being Noble Grand Margaret House, Vice Grand Wilma Kelly, Secretaries Lucille Bradley and Hazel Crystal and Treasurer Marvel Burden. In December, well ensconced in their new meeting hall, the Rebekahs elected officers for the year 1950. They were: Noble Grand Wilma Kelly, Vice Grand Jacqueline Steffey, Secretaries Marie Morea and Stella Roberts and Treasurer Betty Horton. During the year, some of the other members were the following:

> Maud Reed, Susie Dart, Clara French, Ollie Parker, Esther Lord, Phoebe Rector, Lena Barnes, Jean Burdick, Florence Robbins, Ruby Anglen, Beulah Moore, Violet Bachus, Elizabeth Miller, Ida May Hall, Stella Brabon, Della Woodworth, Minnie Moore, Mary Butts, Clarissa Zimmer, Grace Russell, Emily O'Berry, Myrtle Swanebeck and Wilda Alchin.,

The Order of the Eastern Star celebrated their 59th Anniversary in 1949 with a dinner at the Fenton Community Center. Over 300 members and guests, representing other Masonic orders, were in attendance. The Anniversary committee, led by their General Chairman, Mrs. Julian Bristol, was composed of the following members:

> Mrs. Nelson Thorpe, Mrs. Warren Logan, Mrs. John Davies, Mrs. Charles Wyman, Mrs. Maurice Matthews, Mrs. Clarence Miller, Mrs. Willard Hatfield, Mrs. Frank Galloway, Mrs. Alex Hiscox, Mrs. Edwin Adams and Mrs. J. C. White.

In early November, the O.E.S. installed their officers for the coming year. Those selected to serve were: Worthy Matron Mrs. Nelson Thorpe, Worthy Patron Mr. Nelson Thorpe, Associate Matron Mrs. John P. Davies, Associate Patron Mr. Edward Bruder, Secretary Mrs. Claude Sinclair, Treasurer Mrs. Clarence Miller, Conductress Mrs. Willard Hatfield and Associate Conductress, Mrs. Carol Butts.

The Rainbow Girls installed their new officers in September. Lois Dixon was selected as the Worthy Advisor. The other officers were: Miriam Bruder, Joyce French, Luella Beebe, Janet DuBois, Janice Nash, Pat Moyer, Ann Kiesling, Betty Marsh, Doris Hagood, Martha Welch, Nita Edinger, Janice Wright, Carol Adams, Pat Eldridge and Sue Martin.

The installing officers were: Bonnie O'Berry, Beth Gordon, Barbara Nancy Bly, Ethel Davis, Bonnie Hyde and Darlene Jarvis.

The Ladies Auxiliary of the Eagles held their first Mother-Daughter Banquet in May. Mrs. Aldrich Locke was the Mistress of Ceremonies, Marion Nash gave the Toast to the Daughters, and Miss Esther Boyce toasted the Mothers. The entertainment was provided by the singing of Sharon Curtis.

There was a long standing interest in Books and Music in the Fenton community. The Book Club and the Music Club continued to flourish in the Post-War years, with the clubs sharing many members.

The Book Club met every month, except in the summer months, in the Community Center. The program at the meetings generally featured a guest speaker who reviewed one of the current books, followed with a tea service   The attendance generally was between 70 and 90 persons, members and guests. The presentation was   The Club elected their officers in May and the following were elected" President Mrs. Carl White, VP Mrs. William Hoey, Treasurer Mrs. Carl Lind, Secretary Mrs. Art Watts and Program Chairman Mrs. Faye Anderson.   Some of the active members were:

> Mrs. J. B. Obenshain, Mrs. Walter Walpole, Mrs. W W. Martin, Mrs. Henry Alchin, Mrs. Earl Brackenridge, Mrs. John Dolza, Mrs. Fred Cornell, Mrs. Arthur Watts, Mrs. Don Smale, Mrs. Frank Mytinger Mrs. Marjorie Davis, Mrs. Claude Sinclair, Miss Marjorie Davis, Mrs. A. J. Pettis, Mrs. Bruce Gregory, Mrs. Carleton Lauer, Mrs. Fred Willard and Mrs. Earl Leslie,

The Fenton Music Club's routine varied from the Book Club in that they generally met in the home of one of the members and on occasion would sponsor an artist's performance at the Community Center. These musical programs were open to the public. For example, in February, the club sponsored a recital by Violinist Marian Custer Coley, of Michigan State.

Miss Alice Van Atta, an accomplished organist and pianist, and a member of the club, presented several musical programs during the year. These programs were both educational and entertaining, in that Miss VanAtta would provide a sketch of the composer's life along with playing his music. A frequent guest of the club, was Harriet Mortimore Toomey, formerly of Fenton, now of Detroit and recognized for her excellent singing voice.

In October, the club held their election of the officers for the coming year. Those members elected to office were: President Mrs. John Dolza, Secretary Mrs. John Legg, Treasurer Mrs. Ann Woodward and Program Chairman Mrs. Maurice Kieft. Other members were:

> Mrs. Russell Loomis, Mrs. Clifford Philips, Mrs. E. C. Reid, Mrs. Earl Breckenridge, Mrs. Donald Smale, Mrs. F. W. Parrish, Mrs. Emille Schuster, Mrs. Ernest Tirrell, Mrs. Frank Mytinger, Mrs. Don Alchin and Mrs. Irving Negus.

As one might expect, the Veteran's organizations were very active following the influx of new members...veterans of World War II. Only the Women's Relief Corps and the Daughters of Union Veterans failed to gain members as a result of the recent conflict. However, the W.R.C. and the D.U.V. continued to meet together and often share projects[9] and officers. The Fenton D.U.V. was named after Lucy C. Blanchard, a Union Army nurse, who lived in Fenton after the Civil War ended.

In January, the two organizations met and installed new officers for the coming year. The D.U.V. was installed by Ruby Anglen, who was then serving as the Department of Michigan's President. Those installed were President Hazel Crystal, VP Allie Parker, Jr. VP Florence Goodell Sr., Chaplain Bertha Chapman and Treasurer Ruby Anglen, Other active members were: Edna Sommers, Anna Galloway, Kate Hempstead, Phoebe Rector, Dorothy Griswold, Marie Steward, Ida Bronson and Bessie Pratt.

The W. R. C. officers were installed by Mrs. Esther Bard. Those installed were: President Ruby Anglen, Sr. VP. Blanche Faling , Jr. VP Seigrid Strom, Secretary Violet Vandercook and Treasurer Kate Hempstead, Other active members were: Marvel Burden, Holly Moore, Rita Carmer, Esther Sord, Allie Parker, Marie Steward, Florence Goodell Jr., Edna Sommers, Mary Mitchell and Hazel Crystal.

---

[9] The Monument in Fenton's Oakwood Cemetery was erected in 1906 by the W.R.C. in memory of the unknown soldiers and sailors from that community who died in the Civil War in service of their country. In 1926, a boulder with a bronze tablet in memory of Union veterans of the Civil War was placed in Library Park (The area in front of the building now serving as the Fenton Museum). The memorial was erected by the Lucy Blanchard Tent No. 25, Daughters of Veterans,

The April installation of officers was a Joint installation for both the Post and its Auxiliary and it was attended by many of the officers from the Michigan Department of the V.F.W.

For The Ladies Auxiliary: President Pauline McNeil, SrVP Doris Huff, JrVP Lillian Goodrich, Treasurer Leda Hanbey and : Naomi Bennett, Edna Bly, Lelah Stiff, Rita Conway, Myrtle Harris, Irene Boilore, Mary Pasco, Agnes Botticelli, Delia Palmer, Kathryn Stanley, Dorothy Alvesteffer, Hazel Crystal, Violet Harley and Irene Boilore.

The V.F.W. Auxiliary celebrated their 13th Anniversary with a dinner at which Village President Aldrich Locke was the main speaker. Other notable events during the year were their celebration of Hattie Rohm's 74th Birthday, a party for Fenton's Gold Star Mothers, and visits to the Veterans Hospitals (at which time they distributed articles of clothing, cigarettes and other gifts to the hospitalized veterans). In November, the Legion's Ladies Auxiliary elected their officers for the upcoming year. These elected were: President Rose Harrington, 1stVP Elsie Brancheau, 2nd VP Betty Horton, Secretary Ilda Faust and Treasurer Betty Goodrich. Others elected were: Della Woodworth, Lillian Goodrich, Maude Reed, Grace Wright, Zella White and Ruth VanAlstine.

One of the Auxiliary's fondest programs was the contest for the best poster promoting the sale of "Poppies". Both the ladies of the Legion and the V.F.W sold poppies on Poppy Day, but the Legion ladies sponsored the poster contest. The winners of the contest this year were: High School class-(1st) Marcia Schupbach and (2nd) Jerry L. Durfee; 7th to 8th Grades- (1st) Patricia Rossman, (2nd) Linda Schupbach and (3rd) Frank Piccinni; 4th thru 6th Grades-(1st) Foster Gillespie, (2nd) John Gordon and (3rd) Mary Lynn Dolza.

At Christmastime, both the men and the women worked together to supply gifts for the hospitalized veterans. Mr. J. C. White and Mrs. Harry Reed were Co-Chairman for this year's project.

This scene cannot close without mention of the "Fen-Fun Cootiettes"... the female counterpart to the V.F.W. degree organization...the "Cooties". The ladies followed the men by assigning titles to their club offices related to the WW I experience of the "doughboys" with the pesky varmints...Cooties. In November, the "Cootiettes" elected their officers. Those elected were: Chief Grayback Myrtle Harris Others were: Edna Pokorny, Irene Boilore, Agnes Botticelli, Lelah Stiff, Zelma Slover and Irene Tribbey.

Scene Four...The Men's Clubs

The "club" which had the largest membership was the rejuvenated Men's Fellowship. As in the past, the Fellowship conducted six, meetings during the year. In February, the meeting was the Father-Son Banquet and ended their season with the Ladies Night Dinner in April. The officers serving in the 1948-1949 were re-elected for the upcoming year at the April meeting. The officers were: President Warren Roberts, VP Sidney Smale, Secretary Avery Loucks, Treasurer Ray Hunt and Steward Than Chestnut.

Those clubs which would be considered as "civic" clubs included the Kiwanis, the XX Club and the "Jaycees"...the Junior Chamber of Commerce.

The Kiwanis was organized and began meeting at the Fenton Community Center almost before the plaster was dry. The Kiwanis, who met on Tuesdays at noon.. a luncheon meeting ...which was very attractive for the business men in the downtown?

In January, the officers of the Fenton Kiwanians were: President John Millington, 1st VP Carl R. Ling, 2nd VP John Hillis, Treasurer Warren Roberts and Secretary Milton Bobier,. The Board of Director members were: Dr. W. F. Buchanan, R. B. Graham, Dr. Kenneth Harris, D. A. O'Dell, Ray O'Reilly and Dr. Paul Williams. G. Leslie Whittle was the Immediate Past President. In October, the club elected their officers for the upcoming year. Those elected were: President Carl Lind, VP Stanley Johnson and Treasurer Warren Nateria, Board members Dr. Fred Bostick, William Gallagher and Tom Wilde joined incumbents R. B. Graham, Dr. Ken Harris, D. A. O'Dell and Dr. W. F. Buchanan.

A "Key Club", sponsored the Kiwanis was organized in the Fenton High School. The new club elected Ronald Millington as their President and Edward Louden as their Vice President. Other members of the club were: Don Griswold, Tom Stephens, Jerry Bassler, John Loomis, Jerry Hatfield, Rodney Bly, Dave Thorton, Charles Turner, Kenneth Herrick, Frank Wegner, Lyle Harper and Mike Harrison.

The Fenton Kiwanians were not only interested in the older boys, and for some time had sponsored Boy Scout Troop No. 112. In October the Kiwanians met with the Scout adult leadership to reorganize for an expansion of the Scouting program in the community.

The Kiwanis conducted four fund raising events during the year in order to provide the funds for the many programs they were conducting. The "big" summer fund raiser was the Field Day at the Shoreacres Golf and Country Club, on Torrey Road. The money earned at this event was placed in the Underprivileged Children's Fund. The Club also conducted a New England Dinner and a Pancake Breakfast to raise funds for the fund.

The Kiwanians also sold "Goodfellow" edition of the *Independent* to raise funds to purchase Christmas food baskets and other gifts for the poor. They sold 2,200 papers for over $700.

The men of the "no agenda" XX Club kicked off the year with the election of officers, following a dinner prepared by the women of the V.F.W. Auxiliary. Dr. Carter G. Walcott was elected President and the other officers so honored were 1st VP C.J. Phillips, 2nd VP C. E. Wyman, 3rd VP R. F. Smith, Treasurer E. C. Reid and Secretary C. H. Thompson.

The Jaycees, whose members were 35 years of age or younger, were a very active group in the community. Among the many community projects conducted by the Jaycees during the year, the two most remarkable projects were for the Fourth of July and the Christmas celebrations.

In July, the headlines in the *Fenton Independent* told the whole story.

Gala Plans Are Made For Fenton's 4th of July: All day Schedule Completed By Jaycees

This huge undertaking by the Jaycees included a Children's Parade in the morning, Prizes were awarded for the most attractive pets, best decorated bike, and other similar competitions. The Fenton and Holly firemen held a water battle on the old FHS athletic field and there were games for children and for ladies. The Ladies competition included a "husband calling contest". In the early afternoon there was a Double header Ball game. The Fenton Kiwanis battled the Fenton Jaycess in the first game and the Fenton Merchants took on the Holly Merchants in the second contest. (Fenton Won!)

In the evening, there was a parade for the "Queen" that included the City Band, Fire and Police, Veterans, etc., all preceding the Queen and her Court in their convertibles. The Parade ended up at Walnut and Caroline where the block on Caroline to Leroy Street had been blocked off for a: Street dance. It was then when Miss Bonnie O'Berry was crowned as "Queen of the Fourth of July". Members of her court were Misses Joan Stewart, Edinger and "Skip" Hartley.

The Jaycess second major undertaking was the Christmas Celebration. For this, the Jaycees held two parities for children. The younger children, ages up to year nine, were entertained at the Community Center, where over 500 youngsters found games, movies candy and apples galore and best of all, Santa Clause came and those children, who cared, could sit on his knee and tell him what they wanted for Christmas. The older children partied at the *Rowena* Theater. About 400, ages ten through twelve, enjoyed candies, gifts and a movie at the theater

It wasn't enough to hold parties for the town's children, but the Jaycees also did all of the street decorations for the Village. The leaders of the Jaycess for the year were James J. Cohoon, Edison Stiles, Royce L. Downey, Harold Dode, William Dode, Clayton Moorman, William Searight, Charles Leighton and Thomas Faull.

In May, the Fenton Jaycees won a State–Wide competition when they were recognized as for "showing the greatest amount of diversified service in their community". Then President James Cohoon accepted the Henry J. Giessenbier Trophy on behalf of the Fenton club.

The Fraternal organizations...F. & A. M. (Masons) O. E, S. (Order of the Eastern Star), I. O. O. F. (the Oddfellows...Independent Order of Oddfellows) and the Eagles (the Fraternal Order of Eagles) were active in Fenton dumg this period. The women were organized somewhat like auxiliaries to the men's clubs, for example the Rebekahs were associated with the (Oddfellows),

The Oddfellows had sold their Leroy Street building to their next door neighbor, Pellett's Department Store, but continued to meet in their old place while a new h0ome was being built. Shortly after Labor Day, they moved into the new premises. The new building was located on Poplar Street (now Silver Lake Road) just west of the Shiawassee River where it passes under the road. It was a two story structure and the Oddfellows used the upper floor for their meeting room and the main floor as a "dining room". The building now serves as a business location, no longer an Oddfellows meeting place. According to the club's Noble Grand, Emil Strom, at the time, the Oddfellows had been in Fenton for over fifty years. But times were changing and within a few years the Fenton club, along with their Favorite Rebekahs, was disbanded.

The Masonic family continued to prosper during the post-war years and enjoyed their meeting rooms on the northwest corner of Leroy and

Caroline Streets. The Masons occupied the upper two floors of the three story building above the State Savings Bank.

The Eagles, the youngest fraternal organization in town, was active in community affairs, but still had time enough to have some fun. The "Millionaire's Party" January was such a success that they held another one in March. The "big" winners at the first affair were Mrs. Harvey Walters, Mrs. Cleo Steward, Charles Auker and Kenneth Latta.

The Izaak Walton League of America is a national non-profit organization dedicated to protecting the soil, air, woods, and water of the United States. There were many men in the community that were active hunters and fisherman and, in general, were avid outdoorsmen. .Consequently, the local chapter was well subscribed.

For years, the club sponsored a Wild Game" dinner The "cook" prepared an assortment of the recent conquests for the table. However, their "Family Day" outing found the meal being prepared in a more traditional mode by the wives with a "pot luck" dinner.

The highlight of the "Family Day" was trapshooting with team competition. Bow and Arrow shooting was also on the schedule.

In the Fall, the club held a "Turkey Shoot" at their lodge on Hickory Ridge Road. Everyone could take a chance on winning a Turkey for Thanksgiving. Fifty entrants competed and the winners were John McCormick, Warren Roberts and Bill Hathaway. Those sportsmen preparing for the hunting season had their rifles tested and sighted by rifle expert Gene Buckingham of Runyan Lake. Some of the active members of the club were:

> Harvey Swanebeck, Charles Baker, William Gallagher, C. F. Hathaway, Evar Strom, Basil Chapel, Lloyd Kelley, Walter Lawson, Henry Alchin, Walter Arnold, James Bentley, Nelson Curtis

The established veteran organizations in town continued to be the American Legion and the Veterans of Foreign Wars posts. Each were active in their pursuit of the veterans of WW II and in recent years, each organization had sponsored events that were becoming annual affairs and which "most" of the Villagers enjoyed.

The American Legion sponsored a "Baseball Excursion" to see a Detroit Tiger game. The participants travelled as a group to and from Detroit. The trip was probably more enjoyable than the game itself. Considering when going by bus, there was usually a small keg of beer in the aisle for the passengers to tap during the trip.

The V.F.W. would bring one of Michigan's travelling Carnivals to Fenton in the summer and set them up in a vacant lot adjacent to the Railroad Depot. This year a group of citizens, mostly residents in the nearby housing are, petitioned the Village Council to deny any request to license a Carnival in that area. The petitioners claimed the noise, traffic congestion and unsanitary conditions created by the event were unacceptable. The council's response was to have each party meet and arbitrates the problem. However for this year, the V.F.W. found another solution.

Having procured land just north of the Village limits for the purpose of building a meeting hall, the Carnival found the vacant lot an ideal location. Carnival Chairman Mike Bly was pleased to report that the club profited very well and the money was placed in the Post's Building Fund.

The V.F.W. election of officers in April, evidenced a "changing of the guard", the arrival of the next generation into leadership roles in the organization. With the election of Norman McNeil as Commander, Senior Vice Commander Leo Alvesteffer and Junior Vice Commander Francis Maehese...all veterans of World War II...the Post's leadership had welcomed the next generation.

The April installation of officers was a Joint installation for both the Post and its Auxiliary and it was attended by many of the officers from the Michigan Department of the V.F.W.

These installed in their new offices were: For the Post; Commander Norman McNeil, Vice Senior Commander Leo Alvesteffer , Junior Vice Commander, Francis Marchese, and: Frank Mytinger, Earl Robinson, Harold Huff, Hollis Winn, Harry Dobbs, William Carlson, William Gallagher, Sam Casazza, Walter Stift, Arthur Wolverton, Warren Boilore, Jack Conway, Henry Rosbury, R.B. Graham, Norman Reed and Emmanuel "Dick" Boilore.

The Fenton Patriotic Council, made up of representatives from the patriotic, civic and fraternal organizations in Fenton, met in April and elected their officers. Those elected were: President Bryant Hanbey, VP Harold Torrey Jr., VP Jessie Nash and Secretary-Treasurer Ruby Anglen. The Council coordinates the patriotic events during the year.

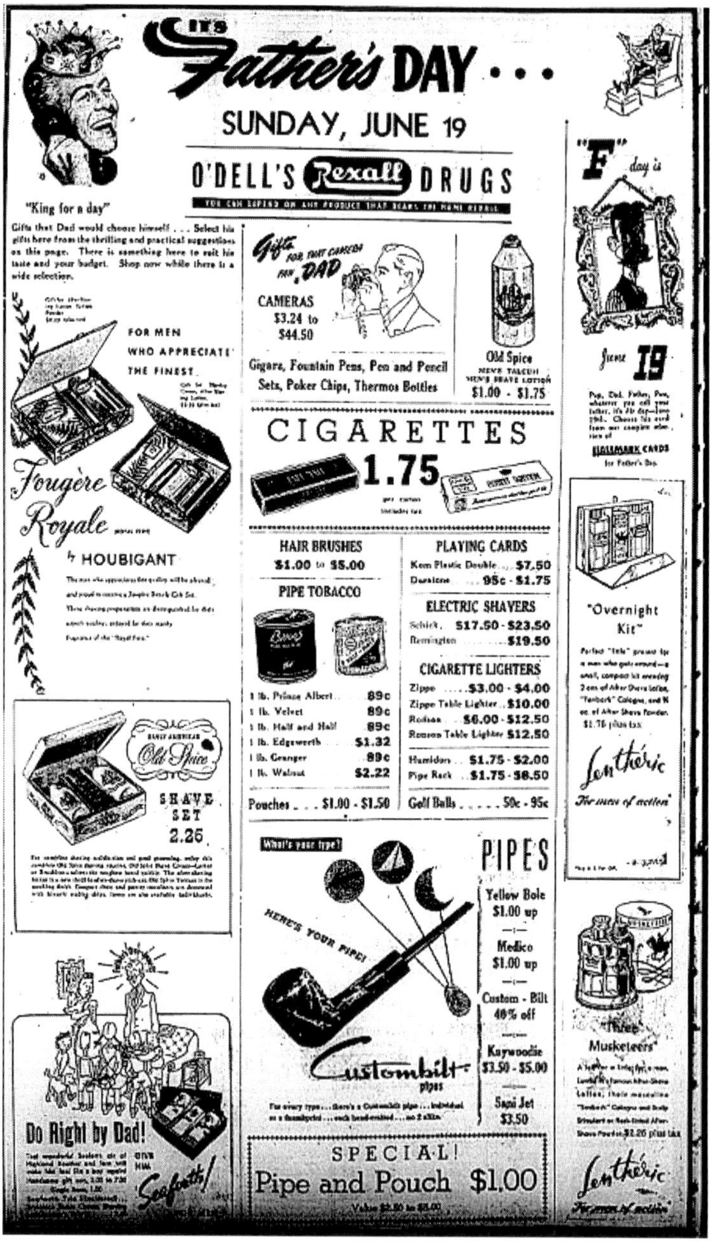
It's Father's DAY . . .
SUNDAY, JUNE 19
O'DELL'S Rexall DRUGS
"King for a day"
Gifts that Dad would choose himself . . . Select his gifts here from the thrilling and practical suggestions on this page. There is something here to suit his taste and your budget. Shop now while there is a wide selection.
FOR MEN WHO APPRECIATE THE FINEST
Fougère Royale
by HOUBIGANT
Gifts for that camera fan, Dad
CAMERAS $3.24 to $44.50
Cigars, Fountain Pens, Pen and Pencil Sets, Poker Chips, Thermos Bottles
Old Spice
$1.00 - $1.75
"F" day is June 19
HALLMARK CARDS for Father's Day
CIGARETTES
1.75
HAIR BRUSHES
$1.00 to $5.00
PIPE TOBACCO
1 lb. Prince Albert 89c
1 lb. Velvet 89c
1 lb. Half and Half 89c
1 lb. Edgeworth $1.32
1 lb. Granger 89c
1 lb. Walnut $2.22
Pouches . . . $1.00 - $1.50
PLAYING CARDS
Kem Plastic Double $7.50
Duratone 95c - $1.75
ELECTRIC SHAVERS
Schick $17.50 - $23.50
Remington $19.50
CIGARETTE LIGHTERS
Zippo $3.00 - $4.00
Zippo Table Lighter $10.00
Ronson $6.00 - $12.50
Ronson Table Lighter $12.50
Humidors $1.75 - $2.00
Pipe Rack $1.75 - $6.50
Golf Balls . . . . . 50c - 95c
"Overnight Kit"
$1.75 plus tax
Lenthéric
For men of action
Old Spice
SHAVE SET
2.25
What's your type?
HERE'S YOUR PIPE!
PIPES
Yellow Bole $1.00 up
Medico $1.00 up
Custom - Bilt 40% off
Kaywoodie $3.50 - $5.00
Sani Jet $3.50
Custombilt pipes
"Three Musketeers"
Lenthéric
For men of action
Do Right by Dad!
GIVE HIM
Seaforth!
SPECIAL!
Pipe and Pouch $1.00

Scene Five...FHS Sports

The 1949 FHS Football team was not expected to have a winning season since only five lettermen were returning. However, Coach Williams put together a team that beat Holly 20-0. Defeated Mt. Morris in the Homecoming game 20-6 and over-all ended the season with a 6-2-1 record. Quarterback Glen Anderson, Bill Edinger (LH), Lyle Harper (LE), and Bud Cutler (RG) were selected for the All County Second Team

FHS 1949 Football Team

1st Row L-R Bill Edinger, Jerry Palmer, Glen Anderson, Frank Wegner, Ken Herrick, Bill Foley, Roger O'Berry, Martin Foley, In front, L-R Mgrs. Leroy Smith, Jim Chene, Don Hatfield. 2nd Row L-R Coach Ivan Williams, Jim VanCleve, Lyle Harper, Dave Thornton, Bud Curtis, Dean Moore, Ron Bruder, Darwin Dager, Paul Petty, Ray Durant, Coach Bill Cowan, Don Frew. 3rd Row L-R Dick Burley, Bud Cutler, Tom Stephens, Dave Simpson, Conrad Krankel Ron Rounds, Tom Moorman, Larry Lisk

The Basketball team was favored by the return of several players from the previous season and consequently enjoyed a very successful season winning 12 and losing only two games. After a slow start the team won eleven games straight before losing their last game to Grand Blanc 32-28. Pat Foley and Mike Harrison led the team in scoring. They were joined in the starting five by "Skip" Horvath, Garner Merrick, and either Bill Hagood or Frank "Butch" Helms. The Tigers played arch rival Holly twice during the season and beat them decisively both times, 40-23 and 46-16.

FHS Basketball Team 1948-1949

1st Row L-R Frank Helms, Garner Merrick, Pat Foley, Frank Wegner, Bill Hagood, Mike Harrison. 2nd Row L-R Asst. Coach Bill Cowan, Vince Messinger, Max Bottecelli, Bill Edinger, Ron Millington, Bill Freeman, Coach Ivan Williams absent: Skip Horvath, Dick Moorman Mgr., and Bob Zankl Mgr.

FHS Baseball Team 1949

Front L-R Mgrs. Dan Hatfield, Leroy Smith, Dick Moorman 1st Row L-R Bill Hagood, Glen Anderson, Vince Messinger, Mike Harrison, Pat Foley, Max Bottecelli, Darwin Dager, Bill Edinger,   2nd Row L-R   John Judson, Bill Freeman, Ray Durant, Dick Rudduck, Harry Schulte, Dean Moore, Frank Helms, Jerry Durfee, Jerry Bender, Coach Bill Cowan

The Baseball team was a "winner" from the first time they took the field. FHS had one of the best high school pitchers in high school baseball in Pat Foley. Foley had two no-hitters in his six game league season in which he recorded 106 strikeouts in 57 innings. The Tigers were the undisputed Champions of the County League. As reported in the *Fenton Independent*, Vince Messinger and Mike Harrison were a snappy infield combination and Max Bottecelli was exceptional in catching Pat Foley.

FHS Track 1949

1st Row L-R   Ken Latta Mgr., Dave Thornton, Jerry Palmer, Bruce Gillespie, Jerry Bassler, Jim VanCleve, Lyle Harper, Bill Foley. 2nd Row L-R Bud Cutler, Tom Moorman, Ron Bruder, Dick Locke, Dave Simpson, Tom Stephens, Bill Edinger, Coach Ivan Williams. 3rd Row L R   Jim Pardee, Richard Kiest, Dan Carmody, Mark Crane, Bill Bass, Larry Lisk, Don Griswold.

The team was led by Jim Van Cleve who starred at the 100 and 220 dashes. On occasion Mark Crane showed some "George Howe" style as a miler finishing near Howe's school record times. Other top performers were Bill Edinger in the pole vault, Lyle Harper in the high jump, Bill Foley and Dave Thornton in the hurdles, Jerry Palmer in the 440, and Dick Locke in the shot put. Others who earned their varsity letter were Bill Bass, Richard Kiest, Bruce Gillespie, Larry Lisk, Robert Cutler, and Dave Simpson.

SCIENTIFIC LUBRICATION

Our modern, fully equipped Lubrication Department is prepared to lubricate your car correctly

$1.00
Any Make or Model

OPEN 7 A. M. till 2 A. M.

WISMER-WRIGHT CHEVROLET CO.

Phone 3278

Scene Six...FHS Activities

As in the past years, the students were actively engaged in a variety of activities. The Student Council was busy conducting the election of officers, planning social events, fund raisers, banquets, Homecoming and a myriad of other issues that required their attention.

In January, the first order of business for the Student Council was the election of officers for the second semester of the school year. Under the rules, the class Presidents and the President and the Vice President of the Student Council were elected to serve the whole school year. All other members were elected to serve one semester. Consequently Garner Merrick and Alice Walpole, Student Council President and Vice President respectively, were serving the full school year.

The new council consisted of the following: 9th Grade-Sandra Seal, William Bass and David Stockham; 10th Grade-Jean Millington, Jerry Bassler and Don Griswold; 11th Grade-Conrad Krankel, Janet Breckenridge, Kenneth Herrick and Ron Millington; 12th Grade- Max Bottecelli, Nancy Stockham, William Hoey and Harold Taylor.

The Student Council set some very high goals for itself. They sponsored the Carnival in March expecting to raise sufficient funds to purchase a communication system for the school that would "broadcast" announcements to all parts of the building. The "Carnival" was well attended and the profits were sufficient to purchase the system.

On April 8th, the Annual All-Hi Banquet was held at the Community Center. The theme this year was "The Four Freedoms" as proclaimed by President Roosevelt during World War II. Nancy Stockham was the Toastmaster for the event. The Seniors represented "Freedom of Speech" and their speaker was Don Dunn. Mike Harrison spoke on "The Freedom of Religion" for the Juniors. David Thornton represented the Sophomores on "The Freedom from Want" and Freshman Sandra Seal spoke on "The Freedom from Fear". Following the banquet, the attendees turned to dancing with E. Cowan's Band providing the music.

The Student Council was responsible for scheduling the Student Assemblies. An example of the quality of their selections was in March, when they procured Richard Carradine of the famous acting family, to present a program on "Scenes from Shakespeare".

196 The Village Players Post War

The Homecoming activities surrounding the football game with Mt. Morris this year were what the FHS students enjoyed every fall. The big bonfire and rally the night before the game, the snake dance through downtown, the parade with floats from each class and several organization, the crowning of the Homecoming Queen and the dance following the game were all eagerly awaited and enjoyed by all. The committee chairman for the Homecoming activities were: Don Griswold, Ron Millington, Conrad Krankel and Mike Harrison.

It was not surprising to find the FHS Vocal Music groups rated highly. Mrs. Lucille Buta's program had been rated highly for the past several years. In April, the A Cappella Choir participated with 26 other school groups in a Vocal Festival at Flint's Central High School. The FHS choir was rated as Excellent , thereby qualifying for the State Festival.

Mrs. Buta was an inspirational leader and former students in her program remember her as both demanding and fair. In September of the year, members of her 1947-1948 chorus met at her home for a "reunion". The group enjoyed singing songs, the "Barber Shop Quartet" and the solos by Ray Coyne and Pat Auker.

FHS 1948-1949 Chorus

1st Row L-R Mrs Lucille Buta, Joyce Helmboldt,, Shirley Stanley, Carol Walden, Norma Bauer, Barbara Petty, Jane Lodgman, Velma Wolverton, Betty VanGillder, Carol Alchin, Diane Loehne, Beth Hungerford. 2nd Row L-R Rosie Preston, Mildred Jacobs, Esther Barton, Betty Burton, Pat Bronson, Nancy Stockham, Jean Steward, Phyllis McCormick, Nona Young, Janice Anderson, Lorraine Hungerford, Ida Cook. 3rd Row L-R Pat Auker , Vince Messinger, Pat Foley, Walt Hungerford, Jerry Hatfield, Bill Edinger, Kent Bennetts, Dick Stanley, Nelson Curtis, Max Botticelli. . 4th Row L-R Frank Helms, Dick Fessler, Bob Tinker, Dave Firestone, Gene Bentley, Lee Kent, Dick Locke, Kenneth Kidder, Bill Foley, Martin Foley, Charles Turner, Bruce Collins.

Act Four...the Year 1949   197

While it seemed as if the Vocal music program was receiving most of the laurels, the FHS Band was doing just fine. Several members of the Band travelled to Caro to participate in the annual Solo and Ensemble Festival. Those participating were Erma Muchler, who played a baritone solo accompanied by Luella Beebe on the piano; a saxophone quartet comprised of Don Griswold Phyllis Roberts, June Wilson and Ed Louden; and a cornet quartet comprised of Ken Herrick, Leroy Young, Towner Buck and Tom Stephens.

In June, Leroy Young was selected for the All-State Band. The All-State Band met at the National Music Camp at Interlochen, Michigan for two weeks under the supervision of the University of Michigan. Leroy also played football and basketball at FHS.

For the third year in a row the Band was invited to play at the Michigan State Fair. This year, in addition to playing in the concert bowl, the Band marched in a parade. And luckily, for the first time, all members of the Ban had a uniform. They also wore "spats" donated and made by a group of ladies: Mrs. Arthur Bush, Mrs. Luther Anderson, Mrs. Allen Moyer, Mrs. Ralph Baker, Mrs. Lowery Nash, Mrs. Earl Smith, Mrs. James Chapman, Mrs. Arthur Sorenson and Mrs. Tom Woodworth.

Mr. Howard Park, the Band Director, made a special announcement urging those attending the final football game to recognize the Senior Majorettes Lois Torrey, Jane Hodgman and Joyce Orritt. The three Majorettes had been with the Band for the last five years,

Joyce Orritt   Jane Hodgman Lois Torrey

198 The Village Players Post War

Front Row: Conrad Krankel, Marion Nash, Joyce French, Charles Turner, Marjorie Hoyle: Second Row: Martha Moyer, Dorothy Hoyle, Luella Beebe, Don Dexter, Carolyn Fisher, Dave Firestone, Eva Mae Calkins, Roberta Van Norman, Ed Louden, June Wise, Phyllis Roberts, Don Griswold: Third Row: Freda Anderson , Calrice Harper, Darlene Smith, Beverly Bush, Helen Austin, Carl Miller, Erma Muchler, Lyle Harper, Paul Dorland, Back Row: Mr. Howard Park, Ivan Muchler, Betty Watkins, Raymond Muchler, Lennard Smith, Fred Holtslander. Warren McKenzie.

The Band was generous with its time, performing at several civic functions, Halloween and Christmas parades and concerts. The first performance of the year was the Spring Concert on April 8th. The concert was well attended and raised funds to support the Band's travels to music festivals. The Band presented two Christmas concerts on December 11th and 18th and ended the year with their annual Band Banquet on Demeter 12th.

In June, at the school awards assembly, the Marc Peck was presented. As *The Independent* reported: *"In memory of Marc Peck, a former FHS student whose tragic death was felt deeply by Fenton, a memorial was instituted...to honor the senior most outstanding in scholarship and the one excelling in sports..."* the awards were given ti Carol Alchin for Scholarship and Pat Foley nfor Sports.[10]

---

[10] Marc Peck died in a dormitory fire at Kenyon College. He was the son of J.C. Peck, owner of the Rowena, the townŇ movie theater. It was reported that actor Paul Newman was his roommate at the college.

Scene Seven...Alumni, PTA and the Board

The Alumni of Fenton High School continued to be active in 1949 and held their annual reunion and banquet on June 10th at the Community Center. The High School building was open during the day for those who desired to stroll through the building . Many classes gathered together during the day before attending the banquet that evening.

The Alumni Association President, George Paine was assisted in planning and conducting a very successful affair by Than Chesnut, Mrs. Perry Brunson, Elton Austin, Raymond Hunt, Emerson Stiles, Elmer Westman, Van Hillman, Wilbur Strom, Grant Wright, Mrs. Clark Thompson, Mrs. Marjorie Lee, Mrs. Leslie Whittle, Elmer Hunt, Russell Haddon, Warren Roberts, Mrs. Donald Phillips, Mrs. Thomas McKinley, John Cox, John Jennings, J. C. Peck and Miss Thelma Clement.

The banquet program included the singing of Harriet Mortimore Toomey; the songs of a quartet composed of Lee Kelley, Ryan Strom, Lynn Welch and Grant Wright; and the Harp music of Shirley Brower

Later in June, an election of officers was held and the following persons were elected: President Burns Fuller, 1st VP Wilbur Strom, 2nd VP Kenneth Pettis, Secretary Thelma Clement and Treasurer Warren Roberts.

The fourth reunion of former Fenton school teachers was held at the home of Mrs. Floyd Stehle on July 21st. Among those attending were: Madeline Cooper, Margaret Gundry, Edna Armstrong, Florence Lyons and Alice Hillman. *(all married, except for Alice, but only maiden names listed here)*

In early March, after 15 years as Superintendent of the Fenton schools, Clarence Heemstra tendered his resignation. The Board didn't hesitate in naming C. D. Arrand, FHS Principal from 1934 to 1943 and then serving as Superintendent of Dye Schools, west fo Flint., as the new Superintendent.

At the same time the Board had been studying a proposal to build a new ten room building to accommodate elementary grade students. The elementary grades had experienced overcrowding for some time and were using the classrooms at the Methodist Church for many of the students. It was obvious that the new building was needed. At the June election, the public agreed and approved a $160,000 Bond issue

Those serving on the Board at the time were: President Harry Lowe, Bristol, Buchanan, Dager, Strom, Tirrel and Westman. Harry Lowe resigned and after the election in July, H.K. Schaefer was elected as the President of the School Board.

In the general election, the voters approved the Board's proposal to extend the school bus service to students living more than one mile outside the village limits

The new school building was completed ahead of schedule and was available for the new school year. The new building was built west of the existing building and facing Ellen Street. The total enrollment of 1184 students was an increase of 55 students over the last year. The enrollment for the grade school was 580 and for the upper six grades 584.

The first meeting of the Parent-Teachers Association in January was a very good start for the organizations as they experienced record attendance. At their meeting May they elected officers for the coming year. Those elected were: President John Dolza, father VP Charles Walker, Mother VP Mrs. Russell Lince, Teacher VP Mrs. Carlton Brown, Secretary Mrs. David Limbach and Treasurer Mrs. Clark Sanford.

Wiith the beginning of the new school year in September, the P,T. A. announced their theme of the 1949-1950 year: *"The Home , the School and the Community"*.

In December, the P.T.A. raised some finds by sponsoring a movie at the *Rowena* theater. J. C. Peck, the owner of the theater, provided the movie *"The Crusades"*, Cecil B. Demille production, and the Junior and Senior Hugh School students were charged with selling admission tickets.

Scene Eight...Let me Entertain You!

The "Dancing Dolls" seemed to be even more of an attraction in 1950 than in previous years. They were "booked" regularly by various and diverse organizations. They would dance for Union party in Flint and dance for the Howell High School students in their school auditorium.

Not all of the entertainment was "home-grown", in February, the Chevrolet Male Chorus, then a nationally acclaimed group, presented a concert at the Methodist Church that was enjoyed by an overflow audience.

But, of the entertainers, the Village Players, an established community theater group, provided their plays throughout the year and they were always well attended and well accepted.

In February, the Village Players' audiences were treated to three plays in which the leading actors in each of the plays, according to *The Independent's* review, will "be remembered" for their "characterizations". Those so acclaimed were Wilbur Strom in *"The Whole Town' Talking"* and *"Adam's Evening";* Mrs. J. A. Johnson in *"The Bride Regrets";* and Jacqueline Roberts in *"The Whole Town's Talking"*.

Even though the theater group had operated under several names since its inception in 1938, as an activity of the then new Community Center, the "Village Players" celebrated their 12th Anniversary with an "open house" at the Community Center.

As in past years, Fenton was the home of a group of ardent bowlers. Several leagues were organized for the fall-winter season and then bowled again in the summer. League. At the completion of each term, the traditional banquet was held and all the stories were rehashed and the Champions were presented their trophies.

Regardless of the season, the list of the top bowlers in men's leagues always seemed to include such names as Chet Hillis, Herb McKinley, Howard Craft, Harold Dode, Bill Dode, Shull Woodworth or Tom Woodworth.

Also as in the past years, the town was represented in both baseball and football. The Fenton Merchants were joined by the Fenton Legion team as members the Tri-County League. As in past years, The Merchants always seemed to be in contention for the league leadership with Gaines. Among the players, again this year, was the former POW

Jack Hartley. Jack Hartley was one of their leading hitters again this season, along with Vince Messinger, Jackson, Huskinson and Bumstead.

With the approach of autumn, the Fenton Independents were organized and again found the majority of their players had in recent years played high school football for the FHS Tigers. They played their games at Phillips Field on Saturday nights with sn occasional afternoon tilt.

For the opening game, the Village President Harry Lemen "kicked off" to School Board President Harold Schaefer. President Lemen entered the field in a yellow Buick convertible driven by Ray O'Reilly, the owner of th Fenton Hotel.

In the past season one of the players, Charles "Chuck" Franks, had been injured and required surgery and extensive hospitalization. Franks' insurance fell short of paying his hospital bill, so the Fenton Concrete Block team of the City Basketball League played a two of their games as fund raisers to help Franks pay his hospital bill.

It is interesting to note that after Franks' insurance paid $500, a balance of $250 remained on his bill. Franks had been hospitalized for a couple of weeks and had undergone surgery. Here in 2013, it is astounding how things have changed!

The Basketball season found the City Basketball League back in action. Again, as with the amateur football team, the league's players were, for the most part, former FHS players

The programs conducted at the Fenton Community Center were a major source of entertainment. For years the World Adventure Series had been one of the most popular programs, beginning in February and ending in April.

The first program of the winter series was on January 23^{rd,} when Julian Gromer presented his lecture on the "Hawaiian Paradise". Mr. Gromer was making a return visit after speaking on "African Life" the previous year.

Dennis Glen Cooper was the second presenter in the series with "This is Michigan". Miss Alberta Worden was next with an illustrated lecture on "Alaska". The last speaker in the series was Mr. Vincent Palmer. Mr. Palmer's topic was the "World Below the Waves".

It wasn't always the serious "stuff" at the FCC. In February, the New York production of "Craig's Wife" was performed. New York stage actress Miss Loree Marks starred in the play.

Scene Nine...Items of Interest

- For decades the townsfolk enjoyed getting a drink of cold water from one of the two flowing water fountains located on the opposite corners of Leroy and Caroline Streets. In August, the Water Department attached a faucet to each fountain. The "gadgets" were difficult to use and many frustrated citizens gave up their attempt to "get a drink". Once the gadgets were improved, the drinker found the water emitted to be "warm and sultry" unlike the cold refreshing water that once flowed to everyone's delight.
- Officer Bob Dode was on his way home early in the morning when he spotted three fellows walking near Gallagher's Sporting Goods Store. He parked his vehicle and walked toward the three men, who broke into a run, but stopped immediately when Officer Dode fired three shots into the air and ordered them to stop. The merchandise they had stolen was recovered along with other goods from a Flint Hardware store.
- From the "Believe it or Not" category! The Fenton Police published the names and the amount of their fine(s) in the November 3rd issue of the *Fenton Independent*. The list of forty-four offenders included three women. The names of many of the town's notables included the Village President Aldrich Locke who was fined $2.00 for some unspecified offense
- In October, the *Fenton Independent* reported a representative of the Optimist International was in town meeting with a few businessmen who had expressed an interest in establishing an Optimist Club in Fenton

What Things Cost in 1949:
Car: $1,650
Gasoline: 26 cents/gal
House: $14,500
Bread: 14 cents/loaf
Milk: 84 cents/gal
Postage Stamp: 3 cents
Stock Market: 200
Average Annual Salary: $3,600
Minimum Wage: 40 cents per hour

Pilot TV-37 3" Television $99.95 New

1949 Ford Tudor

Interlude Four...the Power Struggles Continue

As the great nations of the world continued to struggle for the control of people and lands, the young men and women of America were busy nurturing new families, completing their education, building new businesses or otherwise moving forward. However, many of the world's people were caught up in the upheaval of a changing power structure in their lands.

In China, the morale was low among the Nationalist Army of Chiang Kai-shek, with over 300,000 of the troops surrendering to the Communist forces. The Communists were pushing the regime of Chiang Kai-shek off of the mainland, where many "escaped" to the not consider themselves as Chinese. They resented the invasion, dictatorial impositions, and alleged "bullying and thievery" of the invading Chinese.

On October 1st, Communist leader Mao Zedong, stood before over 300,000 people in Tiananmen Square and pronounced the founding of the People's Republic of China. So, now there were two Chinas...the "Red" and the "Free".

The United States began the withdrawal of its troops from South Korea, which it had occupied since the surrender of Japan. The withdrawal was completed by the end of June.

The Dutch finally realized the futility of holding on to their colonies in the Far East...so the new Nation of Indonesia was born. In December, Sukarno was elected President of the Republic of Indonesia The French, however, stubbornly held on to their colony of Indochina, even as the revolutionaries became stronger.

In Europe the Soviets continued to consolidate their control over the eastern European nations, even while recognizing the futility of trying to isolate West Berlin...the Berlin airlift had succeeded!

Meanwhile, in the United Nations, the Soviets, possessing the veto power, were not in a cooperative mood as they acting strictly in their own self-interest. In this session of the UN, they vetoed the membership applications of Ceylon, Finland, Iceland, Italy. Jordan and Portugal.

Stalin was increasing the pressure on those governments who were not adhering closely to the Soviet way of looking at things. Yugoslavia was "expelled" from the Soviet sphere for their independent actions under Marshall Tito, the Bulgarian leader was removed from office and was later shot to death, the Hungarians were eradicating the "Trotskyites"[11] from their Communist party and set "trials" for the dissenters, who were found "guilty of treason" and summarily executed. Meanwhile, thousands of people from the Baltic States were "deported" to the eastern areas of Russia. The Soviet's "jewel", East Germany, was declared an independent nation and proclaimed "The Federal Republic of Germany".

The "free" nations of the West, in reaction to the apparent hostility of the Soviet Union, acted and formed a military alliance, the North Atlantic Treaty Organization, or more commonly referred to as NATO. The members were: Belgium, Canada, Denmark, France, Great Britain, Iceland, Italy, Luxembourg, the Netherlands, Norway, Portugal and the United States.

Not all of the nations and their people were totally engaged in the power struggles discussed here in, as some faculty members at Cambridge University in the United Kingdom developed the world's first Computer. This computer had a memory and could carry out a list of instructions and it could calculate. A 'glorified" calculator!

North Korea...the territory north of the 38th parallel, was occupied by the Soviets following the surrender of the Japanese and quickly organized as a Communist controlled zone of occupation. Later the occupied zone was proclaimed as the Democratic Republic of North Korea. On March 7th, the North Korean leader, Kim Il Sung, visited

---

[11] Leon Trotsky was a Russian Marxist revolutionary and theorist, Soviet politician, and the founder and first leader of the Red Army. He was a major figure in the Bolshevik victory in the Russian Civil War (1918–20). He was also among the first members of the Politburo. After leading a failed struggle against the policies and rise of Joseph Stalin, Trotsky was removed from power (1927), expelled from the Communist Party, and finally deported from the Soviet Union (1929) Trotsky continued in exile in Mexico to oppose the Stalinist bureaucracy,. His followers were referred to as "Trotskyites". .Trotsky was assassinated on Stalin's orders in Mexico, in August 1940. (Most of his family members were also killed.) *Wikipedia*

Stalin in Moscow, and suggested the time was right for the invasion and "liberation" of the people of South Korea. Stalin deferred at this time, fearing American intervention. Later, he would agree the time was "right" and his concern about American intervention proved to be well founded.

Stalin and his Korean lackey, may have been miss led by General MacArthur's remarks in which he described the United States line of defense in the Pacific and failed include South Korea in its sphere. His definition of America's interests in the Pacific was confirmed by the new Secretary of State, Dean Acheson. General MacArthur was then the Supreme Commander of the occupational forces in the Far East.

Douglas MacArthur

Japan continued to be under military occupation. Japan's economy was improving as stock prices doubled and food production increased but not enough for the U.S. to discontinue food aid, which was costing our country more than $1 Million a day.

Harry S. Truman began his first full term in office. The Armed Forces were reorganized into the "Department of Defense" and a "Joint Chiefs of Staff" was created with the Army, Navy and Air Force as its members. The Marine Corps was not given a full seat at table and were present but only voting on matters directly related to the operation of the Marine Corps

In February, Israel signed an armistice with Egypt, bringing hostilities to an end[12] and a hope for peace. Egypt maintained control of the Gaza Strip but was restricted to allowing the residents of the Gaza to become Egyptian citizens or migrate to Israel.

---

[12] The 1948 Arab–Israeli War or the First Arab–Israeli War was fought between the State_of_Israel and a military coalition of Arab states and Palestinian-Arab forces. This war was the second stage of the 1948 Palestine war As a result of the war, the State_of Israel kept nearly all the area that had been recommended by the UN General Assembly and took control of almost 60% of the area allocated to the proposed Arab state. Important demographic changes occurred in the country. Between 600,000 and 760,000 Palestinian Arabs fled or were expelled from the area that became Israel and they became Palestinian refugees. The war and the creation of Israel also triggered the Jewish exodus from Arab lands. In the three years following the war, about 700,000 Jews immigrated to Israel, residing mainly along the borders of the State. *Wikipedia*

Israel's defeat of the Arab forces led to a bloodless coup in Syria, reportedly backed the United States, since the new leader Husni-al-Ziams promised to sign a peace accord with Israel. During his short tenure in office Husni al-Ziam attempted to make several changes in the life of his country. He allowed the women the freedom of choice in wearing of a veil, raised taxes and worked with U.S. oil companies in the building of the Trans-Arabian pipeline...all of which made him many enemies. In August, his military colleagues turned against him. He and his Prime Minister were shot.

The Iraqis, having been defeated, withdrew their forces from Palestine and left Jordan in control of much of the territory on the West Bank of the Jordan River. Control of Jerusalem was divided between Israel and Jordon with Israel in control of the western section and Jordan controlling the rest of the city.

Even with all the turmoil in the Mideast, Israel became the 59th member of the United Nations.

In late September, President Truman told the nation the Soviets had tested an atomic bomb. The "Cold War" became even "hotter"!

Act Five...the Year 1950

Scene One...The Village Council

The Council's New Year began with their meeting on January 9th, with President Aldrich Locke presiding. The members Ernest Tirrell, Charles Dager, Dr. W. "Buck" Buchanan and Don Bristol were present...and only Elmer Westman was absent. Perhaps they knew what was to be on their agenda in the days ahead, for they were to struggle with many problems and controversial issues.

Like many part-time elected officials, they relied heavily on certain individuals to provide leadership on day to day basis. The Council had relied heavily on their Superintendent of Public Works (a title bestowed upon him in the recent past), Royce L. Downey for the past two years since he arrived on the job.

In early February, Mr. Downey informed the President and the Council of an offer he had received from the City of Clawson to become their City Manager. He added, at a "considerable increase in salary". According Mr. Downey, the Clawson officials had given him until March 1st to accept or decline their offer. He said that he was "very happy in Fenton", but "he must think of his family".

The Council took the matter under advisement and after two weeks of deliberation decided to offer Mr. Downey a substantial raise in pay, which he readily accepted and stayed on the job.

The Trustees hardly had time to reflect on the actions, when it was "Election" time again. The two local political parties ...the Citizens and the Peoples...met and presented their slate of candidates for the Village offices. They were as follows:

	Citizens	Peoples
President	Harry G. Lemen	Aldrich C. Locke
Clerk	Elton Austin	Mrs Susan White
Treasurer	Edgar Weber	Ed Martin
Assessor	Irving Gould	Lowell Swanson
Trustees	Henry Alchin	Wayne Townsend
	Bob Moyer	Charles Wyman
	Walter Walker	Tom Wild

It is interesting to note that at the Citizens Party Caucus, Harry Lemen was named after the nomination had been declined by both Elton

Austin and D.R. Stiles. There was further turmoil when Harry Lemen informed the Party that he declined to accept the nomination.

The Caucus Committee, composed of Francis Gray, Harry Wykes and Sid Smale met and named Raymond Forsyth to fill the vacancy. Bob Moyer also refused to run and he was replaced on the ticket by James Bigelow. The *Independent* reported it had been rumored for several days that Lemen would not run again

There was a relatively small turnout of voters for the March election which resulted in Aldrich Locke's re-election as he defeated Ray Forsyth with 548 to 195 votes. The Peoples Parry swept the Trustee contest with Charles Wyman, Tom Wild and Wayne Townsend defeating Henry Alchin, Walter Walker and James Bigelow. Mr. Townsend returned to the Council after a one year's absence. Citizen's candidates for Clerk, Treasurer and Assessor, respectively Elton Austin, Ed Weber and Irving Gould were returned to office.

In one of their first actions in June, the new Council created the office of Dog Warden and named David Boyden to fill the position. At the same meeting Trustee Tirrell reported on the financial condition of the Village at the end of the 1st Quarter. He happily reported the receipts were running higher than projected and the expenditures, in general, were slightly less than anticipated.

The time came when the newly formed council had to face up to several issues, some very controversial. Undoubtedly, the proposal to install parking meters downtown along Leroy Street was the one that drew the most attention. When the parking meter plan was extended to include part of the side streets, the "noise" became louder.

However, the plan was implemented, the meters installed and the Parking Meter Law became effective as of June 5th. President Locke stressed the installation of meters was not intended to penalize or hurt the motorists. "They're going to alleviate parking tie-ups and help create a parking turnover".

After eight weeks of operation, the collections from the parking meters exceeded the national average per meter. During that period the meters collected $1,311 or an average of $163 per meter, while the national average was $76 per meter

These revenues were earmarked to establish an off-street parking lot for those who didn't (or wouldn't) use the metered spaces.

Soon thereafter, the village was offered an off-street lot to use for parking. Don McQuire, proprietor of a downtown hardware store, offered a vacant lot he owned to be used for free parking for a period of three years. The village, in accepting his offer, agreed to grade the lot , fence it in and maintain and clean the lot. After the first year, Mr. McQuire was to receive an annual fee of $100 for the use of his property at Walnut and Roberts Streets. (If it could exist, Roberts would now be an easterly extension of Silver Lake Road).

Further evidence of the town's growth was provided when the findings of a State Traffic Survey resulted in the installation of a new traffic light at the corner of North Leroy and First Streets (the corner with the Fenton Hotel). This light replaced a "blinker" at that location. The light was to be synchronized with the traffic light at North Leroy and Roberts (now Silver Lake Rd.).

Early in the year, the town experienced what the *Independent* termed a "minor crime wave". Policeman Gilbert Hatfield reported there had been 23 car robberies over the weekend and one house invasion. Councilman Don Bristol, upon arriving home, found some intruders in his house. They ran from the house and Don Bristol reported no loss or damage of property. Officer Hatfield believed the car robberies were the act of youngsters, not professional criminals.

Joe Rogers, owner of Joe's Standard Service at the corner of Ellen and Leroy Streets, suffered the greatest loss. The thieves broke into his station office, forced open his cash drawer and stole $82 and a wrist watch.

Whether or not this crime spree triggered this action by the Council in June is doubtful, but the Village did add an officer to the Police force, when they employed Officer George Dobney to monitor the parking meters.

There were no major incidents until late December when both Larry Hamady's Food Market and Schupbachs Department Store, both on Leroy Street , just beyond the Village limits were looted. The Sheriff Deputies investigated the robberies which they attributed to professional thieves. The robbers took hams, canned goods, several cases of cigarettes and $1645 in cash. The total loss was estimated to be between $5,000 and $6,000.

Mr. Schupbach's loss was about $800 in merchandise. Mr. Schupbach said the thieves were "choosey" since they took only clothing of a better grade.

In mid-May the *Independent* article read "The Village of Fenton's modernization program took another step forward when the police radio sending and receiving sets were installed in the office and the car."

Yes. Fenton's police car could now communicate via radio with the home base. Officer Bob Dode and office employee Mrs. Betty Sarosky remarked that the system was "very good" and "very convenient" and could operate within a ten mile radius.

Another brief "citizen uprising" occurred when the Council employed an outside assessor to reevaluate the personal property subject to the Village's Personal Property Tax. Many of the citizens were "up in arms" about taxing their personal property. However the turmoil subsided when it was understood that only those who owned or operated a business in Fenton were subject to the tax on their inventories, furniture, and fixtures. (Guess it depends on whose Ox was being gored?)

While many of the streets in Fenton still remained unpaved, the Village's paving program was making progress each year to improve the condition of the town's streets. The Council's action this year was to limit the permanent paving program to two blocks a year in favor of moving forward with their "triple seal " program.

For years, the Village's efforts to provide "dust-laying" materials to the many dirt streets in the town, required a costly yearly expenditure. An application of liquid calcium chloride to cover 10 miles cost $2,160.

The Village began a "triple seal" program three years before which cut six miles from the total of unpaved roads which required "dust-laying" each year. This program sealed two miles of streets each year. Councilman Wayne Townsend remarked "The sooner our triple seal program is completed, the sooner we can eliminate the year after year payment for dust-laying".

The Village did have a "Curb and Gutter" program underway which this year completed the work on River Street between Adelaide and Roberts (now Silver Lake Road) and First Street between Oak and Lemen Streets. The side walk construction program completed walks on West Shiawassee Avenue and North Gruner, Sinclair and Henry Streets.

The end of 1950 marked the half-way point in the street surfacing program with eight miles of streets completed with the other eight miles to be completed by 1954.

Another Community improvement occurred when the Consumers Power Company replaced the old street lights with new (and brighter!) lights.

These programs were evidence of the fact the town was making real progress in improving its facilities.

Fenton is surrounded by many lakes; in fact some reports have over fifty lakes within a ten mile radius of the town. These lakes provided the townsfolk with many recreational opportunities, such as swimming, boating, skating and fishing. However, along with these "fun" things, the possibility of an accident was always present. The need for a "rescue " unit, capable of promptly responding to those in distress on the lakes, was becoming more apparent as a result of several drownings and near drownings in the nearby lakes.

In May, an independent group of citizens organized a Rescue Unit, and was permitted to locate at the Fenton Fire Hall. This group was successful in obtaining the support of many local businesses and other villagers who provided the funds to obtain a truck and other essential equipment.

In August, the Rescue Squad, under the leadership of Officer Gil Hatfield and William Dode, asked the Village Council to place the Unit under Village control. The Council favored the proposal and agreed to provide the oil and gas for the truck, accept the other equipment (valued at over $500) and purchase additional oxygen bottles to supplement the two on hand.

There weren't many holidays that inspired the Villagers to have a parade. However, Memorial Day was always recognized with a parade from the downtown area , usually from the American Legion hall, down South Leroy Street, a pause at the bridge over the Shiawassee River and then on to the Oakwood Cemetery. This year the parade route was changed and the parade crossed the river as it moved down Caroline Street toward Phillips Field on Ellen Street.

The parade halted at the bridge where the Women's Relief Corps honored the sailors by placing flowers on the river. Next, the parade stopped at Phillips Field. Here a firing squad fired three volleys over the top of a group of trees which had been planted in Phillips Field in honor of the men from Fenton killed in World War II.

The units in the line of March demonstrated the wide community interest in honoring those who died in our past conflicts. The individuals organizing the parade were General Chairman Walter

Lawson, Donald Clark and Earl Robinson. The Line of March was as follows: Village Council and Speakers in Automobiles, the Colors, W.R.C., DUV, VFW and Auxiliary, the Band, more Colors, American Legion and Auxiliary. the Eagles and Auxiliary, the Boy the Girl Scouts.

The Memorial Service was highlighted by an address by President Aldrich Locke and the playing of "Sleep Soldier Sleep". Others present were Rev. A. H Hanson, Bryant Hanbey, Richard Keist and Rev. R. H. Harper.

The *Independent* took special note of the outstanding appearance of the cemetery. Only a few years before, the Village assumed ownership of the cemetery, which at that time was in a very poor condition. Citizen groups and the Village employees had worked diligently to restore the Cemetery and the newspaper heralded their success.

As the year was drawing to a close, the question of the Village becoming a City became an issue of public discussion. The Pros and Cons were presented in the newspapers and it was an issue that would not be settled in the year 1950, but certainly, sometime in the coming years.

Scene Two...Doing Business Downtown

There were several positive signs in both the retail and manufacturing businesses during the year 1950.

The Industrial Machine Tool Company was well established in the town and their plant on South Leroy Street had been operating for years. It probably was one of the most unlikely locations for a manufacturing plant. Its loading area was on the sidewalk directly across the street from the Fire Hall, its immediate neighbor to the north was the Community Center, it was snug up against the bridge across the Shiawassee River and the building extended from the curbside in a westerly direction along the river.

Several years before, Industrial had built an additional facility on North Leroy Street just next to the Fenton Hotel...another very unusual location for a manufacturing facility. Now, in 1950, the company sought rezoning to allow them to build on to the rear of this building, extending it to Walnut Street.

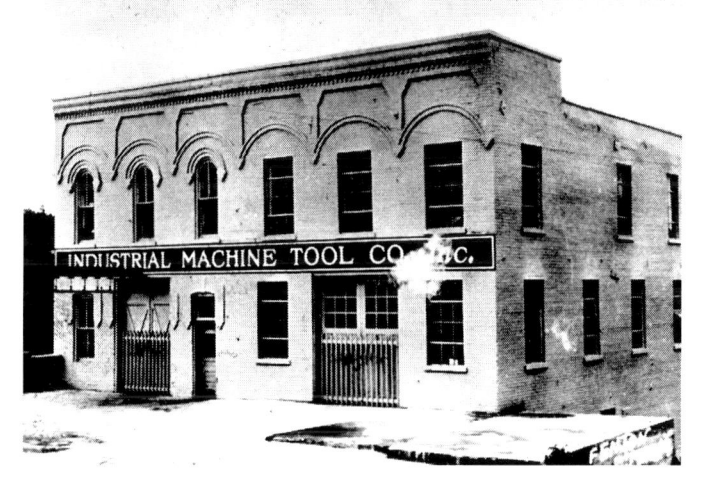

Arnold Westman, representing the company, informed the Council the company had already contracted for the addition and both the building and the equipment had been ordered and would be delivered in two weeks. When taking this action the company was unaware that the property had been rezoned and it was no longer zoned for industrial use. Well, what were the trustees to do? After some deliberation, the property was rezoned and the construction of the addition proceeded.

"We need more room for current operations". Hector Rabezzana stated as he announced plans to add 6,000 square feet of floor space to his factory, the Rado Manufacturing Company at 309 South Leroy Street. (the current location of the Fenton City Hall). At the same time, Mr. Rabezzana announced the change in the company's name to Rado. The company had been doing business as the General Research and Development Company. The zoning was correct and the construction of the new addition proceeded without difficulty. Rado's work force included a large number of women and their products were used by the automobile industry.

In the first seven months of the year, the number of building permits issued by the Village exceeded the number issued in all of 1949. As the community was experiencing a boom in housing starts, the downtown merchants were making efforts to better serve the growing population

After eighteen years of doing business in Fenton, the Byerly's Grocery closed down for over a month to do a complete remodeling of its store. The remodieling included a new front, lowered ceilings, new lighting and new fixtures. The store now had a section for frozen foods and ice cream. Fruits and vegetables were now kept garden fresh in a new crushed ice rack. A complete meat department was also included. There was a major change in serving the customers....Byerly's was now a "self-service" store. No more coming into the store with your grocery list and having a clerk scamper around the store gathering the items on your list. It is now "self-serve" ...you do the scampering and the picking.

Several of the downtown businesses changed ownership. The Obenshain Grocery was sold to one of their employees, James Shutt of Holly and Mickey's Dairy, then owned by Mr. and Mrs. Hathaway was sold to Mr. Harold Dyer of Muskegon.

Charles E. Rolland operated his dry goods store on North Leroy for thirty-nine years before selling the business to Aldrich Locke. He held the record for the time of being in business on Leroy Street. He was instrumental in obtaining the grants from the Rackham Foundation to build the Community Center and the Fire Hall. He also served as Chairman of the State Bank Board for over thirty-three consecutive years.

The Rolland Dry Goods store operated much like a store of the 1800s. The merchandise was displayed on tables throughout this L shaped store. (the main entrance was on Leroy Street and a back entrance on Caroline Street...the streets are at a right angle). Mr. Rolland's office was on an elevated platform, where he could observe the entire store. The store was equipped with a system of overhead tracks upon which small containers could travel to and from the office and the point of sale. The salesclerk would place the customer's money in the container, along with the bill for the merchandise, and send it to Mr. Rolland. Mr. Rolland would register the sale, place any change in the container and return it to the salesperson. Sounds like 1800s to me!

Arthur G. Becker, longtime downtown merchant, returned to the retail world, after losing his old store on South Leroy when the D & C store expanded their presence on the street. Mr. Becker and his son Tom acquired the former A & P store in the first block of South Leroy Street. The old building was completely remodeled to accommodate a modern department store. Now, after first entering business some 28 years before, Art Becker was back in the game!

Kleber Merrick announced the Merrick's Motor Sales had acquired an exclusive agreement as a Mercury dealer. Generally, the Mercury automobile was sold by dealers who also represented the Lincoln cars. The Merricks operated a Sunoco gasoline station on the site and previously sold Buick automobiles.

One of the most likeable young men in town, Johnnie Nierescher, moved his greenhouse business from its location on Poplar Street (now Silver Lake Road) to newly constructed greenhouses behind his residence at 888 North Leroy Street. He had been in business at the Poplar Street location for three years.

Another prominent fellow in town, D. R. Stiles, with over thirty years in the insurance business in Fenton, formed a partnership with his son Edison, and assumed the name of Stiles Insurance Agency. His business had been located at 106 East Caroline Street since 1935. Young Kenny Segar, who walked by this office quite frequently, said that at the time, he thought it was the office of "Doctor" Stiles....D. R. Stiles!

Any discussion about Fenton businesses should not be completed without some mention of a usual business that flourished during this period in our history. Dan Haddon, purchased furs from the local trappers and shipped them to a buyer in New York. The harvest for the winter of 1949-1950 was quite bountiful and Mr. Haddon reported the largest shipment he had made in many years. Muskrats and Raccoons provided most of the hides collected and shipped.

One of the most important institutions in the business community was the State Savings Bank of Fenton. At their annual meeting in

January, they reelected all their officers to their previous held positions, except for Otis Furman, who was promoted to Assistant Vice President from Cashier.

The members of the Board of Directors of the Bank were: George W. Cook, H. W. Hitchcock, J. H. Jennings, D. E. Kelleher, G. W. Pellett, L. A. Riedel and E. C. Reid. The officers of the Bank were: John H. Jennings, Chairman of the Board; E. Clair Reid, President; Horace W. Hitchcock, Vice Pr4esident; D. E. Kelleher, Vice President; Otis E. Furman, Assistant Vice President; Robert F. Smith, Cashier; and Mary A. Hill, Assistant Cashier.

What Things Cost in 1950:
Car: $1,750
Gasoline: 27 cents/gal
House: $14,500
Bread: 14 cents/loaf
Milk: 82 cents/gal
Postage Stamp: 3 cents
Stock Market: 235
Average Annual Salary: $3,800
Minimum Wage: 75 cents per hour

1950 Motorola 12" B&W Television - Model 12K2

1950 Zenith

Scene Three...The Town's Churches

The people of Fenton were church going people. The distractions of Televised Football games had not yet taken a toll on church attendance. On Good Friday, most of the stores and business places closed their doors from Noon to 3PM.

The Church year was very much as it had been decades. All denominations came together for a joint service on Easter and Thanksgiving and for the High School Graduates' Baccalaureate services

The Church pastors remained the same in 1950 as in the previous year except for the First Baptists and the Free Methodists who experienced changes in their leadership.

The Reverend Hugh Woodside resigned as Pastor of the First Baptist Church in late February, proclaiming his resignation was voluntary. The Reverend Woodside had been with the church since September of 1947.

About a month later, the Reverend Louis L. Kalinchak, a native of Richmond, Virginia accepted the call of the First Baptists. However something must have gone wrong because in July, the Reverend Kalinchak was history and the Reverend Elvin K Mattison was announced as the Church's new Pastor.

The Reverend H. E. Leininger had pastored the Free Methodist Church for the last five years, when he was reassigned to the Church in Durand. He was replaced by the Reverend Henry Powell.

So, as the year ended, the "lineup "for the pastors of Fenton's major churches was as follows:

St. Jude's Episcopal	Alvin H. Hanson
Methodist	Ralph D. Harper
First Presbyterian	Harley H. Stockham
First Baptist	Elvin K. Mattison
St. John Catholic	Dennis P. Tighe
Trinity Lutheran	A.A. Klein
Free Methodists	Henry Powell

Father Dennis Patrick Tighe finally had his school. After years of dreaming and planning, the St John Catholic Church opened their school. A formal dedication dinner was held on March 19th at which Village President Aldrich Locke and the Reverend William O'Regan of the University of Detroit were the guest speakers.

The St. John school opened in the Fall with an enrollment of 186 students in grades from one through eight. The Sisters of the Immaculate Heart provided the faculty for the school.

St. John provided another major event in Fenton's church world, with its annual Barbeque in July. A prime beef dinner highlighted the outing which was very well attended by parishioners and the public in general. There were pony rides for the youngsters and games for all ages.

The Episcopalians announced their intention to build a "Parish House and Recreation Center" directly behind the Church. In order to defray some of the costs, the congregation worked diligently to raise some funds. One of their "big" fund raisers was an "authentic" Italian dinner. It was held at the Community Center in April and drew a large number of diners. Mrs. Elmer Westman and John Millington were co-chairs for the event and Edmund Gould was in charge of the ticket sales.

There were fund raising events scheduled for each month during the year. The "Cotton Ball" in May; an Antique Auction in June; A Swedish Smorgasbord in July; the Rector's Birthday Party in September and the Annual Bazaar and Dinner in November.

The officers of the St. Jude's Guild for the year were President Mrs. Warren Roberts. VP Mrs. J. C. Phillips, Corresponding Secretary Mrs. Fay E. Emerson, Treasurer Mrs. Edmund Gould and Secretary Thelma E. Clement. In December, as the end of the term in office was approaching, a new slate of officers for 1951 was elected. Those elected were President Mrs. J. C. Phillips, VP Mrs. Warren Roberts, Secretary Mrs. H. I. Miller, Corresponding Secretary Mrs. Fay Anderson and Treasurer Mrs. Edmund Gould.

Both the St. John Alter Society and the Trinity Lutheran Church's Ladies Aid held events honoring their children.

The Altar Society sponsored a Mother-Son dinner in May at their new school building. As was the tradition, the Toast to the sons was offered by the Chairman Mrs. Ben Krankel; the Toast to the Mothers by Pat Auker; and Greetings by Mrs. Emmanuel Boilore. Ed Louden, Rodney Bly and Don Griswold presented their act "Re-Cords" and Betty VanGuilder was their accompanist.

The Lutherans held a Mother-Daughter Party on June 1st. The program was musical. Those presenting were: Susan Bachtel, Sandra Klein, Kay and Jane Buta, Shirley Tisch, Lois Courtwright, Beverly Tisch, Luella Tisch and Mrs. Lucille Buta. The accompanist was Mrs. Peter Parish.

The women of all the Churches were the most active "workers" for the Church. The names of the women's groups varied from one church to another. The Presbyterian ladies were organized as "Cornerstones" and the Methodists were in "Bands". Some of the women active in their organizations were: Presbyterians-Mrs. Nora Almquist, Mrs. David Limbach, Mrs. Peter Morea and Mrs. A. H. Fessler. Methodists-Mrs. Clara Dittslock and Mrs. Harry Durant.

Pictured here are the "twin" churches....Jude's Episcopal (above) and the First Presbyterian Church...both located on opposite corners of South Leroy and East Elizabeth Streets.

Quadrille

California COBBLERS

Sing while you work or play! For here's real carefree California comfort . . . street-groomed for town-careering, supple-snugged for country capers, cushion-platformed for square-dance-dating! Yes, hours of wear and hours of comfort in smooth red leather, and at such a light little price it hardly makes a dent in your budget.

AAAA to B Widths

$6.95

Many Other Styles to Choose From.

Saturday Store Hours: 8:30 a. m. to 9:00 p. m.

BOBIER'S FAMILY SHOE STORE
FENTON

103 North Leroy Street   Phone 4643

Scene Four...FHS Sports

As the 1949-1950 Basketball season arrived, Coach Ivan Williams found the situation similar to the one in football...only two lettermen, Frank Wegner and Mike Harrison, were returning. The new players had the benefit of playing with the Reserve in the past years. Consequently, the team came together and lost only three games and tied for second place in the County league. The teams won their first tournament game, but lost to Flint Tech in a close game and were eliminated.

Jerry Bassler set a new FHS record by scoring 30 points against Hoover High School. Mike Harrison led the team in scoring for the season with 242 points. Mike also was placed on the All County Second Team.

In November as the team prepared for the 1950-1951 season, all of the players except Harrison, Wegner and Judson were returning. They were joined by Dean Moore, Dave Stockham and Bill Bass. Hopes for a successful season ran high for the new edition of FHS Basketball.

FHS Basketball Team 1949-1950

1st Row L-R John Judson, Frank Wegner, Glen Anderson, Jerry Bassler, Paul Petty, Mike Harrison. 2nd Row L-R Coach Bill Cowan, Jerry Palmer, Darwin Dager, Bill Sprague, Dave Thorton, Lyle Harper, Tom Stephens, Elton Cull, Coach Ivan Williams

With the coming of Spring, the Baseball and Track athletes began training for the upcoming completion. It was a miserable springtime. It was unseasonably cool and it rained and rained. The track team had very few days to exercise out-of-doors and the ball players threw the ball around in the gymnasium with few occasions to practice on a soggy diamond.

In spite of the foul training conditions, Coach Ivan Williams entered four members of his track team in the River Rouge Relays, an indoor track event held in mid-April, almost a month before the league track season began.

He selected Jim VanCleve for the 60 yard dash; Dave Simpson for the 65 yard low hurdles; Lyle Harper for the High Jump and Richard Kiest for the Mile Run. It was too much to expect any of the participants to win, but they did compete and they enjoyed and profited from the experience.

Because of the inclement weather, Coach Williams was not yet able to access the ability of the new members of the team, so at the first dual meet of the year, his entries were mostly from the returning lettermen. Against Bendle, the team had three firsts and a smattering of seconds to amass a winning score of 26 points.

Jim Van Cleve ran the 100 yard dash in 10.6 seconds, Richard Kiest was all alone in winning the Mile in 4.54 minutes and newcomer Larry Lisk did the ½ Mile in 2.13 minutes to finish in First Place.

Two of the Fenton trackmen used the Regional meet for their "ticket" to the State Champion Track Meet. Jim Van Cleve and Larry Lisk earned the coveted bids. Unfortunately, there was no gold to bring home!

The Baseball team held their first outside practice on March 28th, only two weeks before the opening game of the season. The pitchers and the catchers were in better condition since they had two weeks of indoor practice in the gymnasium. Thirty candidates answered the first call and Coach Cowan said he expected to reduce the squad to about twenty players by the time the season opened.

The County Championship team of the past season lost an outstanding pitcher in Pat Foley, who had signed a contract with the New York Yankee organization and was now pitching in the one of their minor league clubs. In addition, the team also lost catcher Max Bottecelli, shortstop Vince Messenger and outfielder Bill Freeman.

These four players were excellent in the field and provided most of the hitting power of the last year's team.

Among the returning letterman were Mike Harrison, Darwin Dager, Glen Anderson, Dean Moore, Jerry Palmer and Ray Durant. Others joining the letterman with promise were Paul Petty, Bill Edinger, John Judson, Dave Thornton, Al Archer, Floyd Leuneberg and Dick Ruddick.

The Tigers went undefeated and won the Genesee County League title for the second year in row. A look at the record book shows that it was a "Mike Harrison" year. Harrison's pitching record was 5-0 while hitting a .483 average. Harrison gave up 11 hits in his five victories which included three shutouts and one no hit game.

The other four wins in the season were pitched by Darwin Dager. Dager posted two shutouts in his 4-0 season. Dager second in team batting with a .374 average. The team batting average was .312.

. FHS 1950 Baseball Team

Front L-R Mgrs. Rex Roberts Gary Zoll 1st Row L-R Darwin Dager, Glen Anderson, Bill Edinger, Mike Harrison, Jerry Palmer, Paul Petty, Dean Moore 2nd Row L-R Dave Thornton, Harry Schulte, Dick Rudduck, Gil Moran, Lowell Newton, Doug Rayment, Coach Bill Cowan 3rd Row L-R Allen Burdick, John Judson, Bill Bass, Floyd Leuneberg, Al Archer, Ed Moore

Football practice started two weeks before the school year began, and Coach Ivan Williams was very optimistic as 64 boys responded to the call. With thirteen lettermen returning from last year's team which finished in a second place tie in the Genesee County Conference, Coach Williams would have a nucleus of experienced players at the key positions.

The returning lettermen were: Centers Paul Petty and Tom Stephens; Guards Martin Foley and Bob Cutler; Tackles Tom Morrison and Ron Rounds; Ends Lyle Harper, Dave Thornton and Darwin Dager; Backs Glen Anderson, Jerry Palmer, Jim Van Cleve and Dean Moore.

For the first time in FHS football, all nine of the games on the schedule were played under the lights. The Tigers kicked off the season at Phillips Field by defeating Howell 7-0 in a contest marred by numerous penalties. For the first time in over a decade, the Tigers ended the season undefeated and untied...and the League Champions.

FHS 1950 Football Team

1st Row L-R Elton Cull, Jim VanCleve, John Judson, Dick Burley, Paul Dorland, Rick Perry, Don Hatfield-Mgr. 2nd Row L-R Jerry Peterson-Mgr., Martin Foley, Lyle Harper, Glen Anderson, Bob Cutler, Larry Young, Jerry Palmer, Paul Petty, Jim Chene-Mgr. Coach Warren Cottle, Dean Moore, Tom Moorman, Darwin Dager, Bud Pittman, Tom Stephens, Dave Stockham, Rod Bly, Dave Thornton, Ron Rounds, Coach Ivan Williams. 4th Row L-R Jerry Bender, Dick Rudduck, Harry Schultz, Bill Bass, Lowell Newton, Dick Keist, Bruce O'Berry, Bob Zankl.

Scene Five...FHS Activities

For several years, Fenton High School had been recognized for their outstanding vocal music program, especially since Mrs. Lucille Buta had been its director.

The two productions in the spring of the year, demonstrated her ability to develop talent and produce enthusiastic, disciplined, professional-like performances. Student participation in the vocal music curriculum was much larger than one would expect in a relatively small high school...largely because of the respect the students had for Mrs Buta

In late February, the A Cappella Choir performed the operetta "Chimes of Normandy" to a "packed house" at the Community Center. The *Independent* review of the performance remarked about how "the people responded enthusiastically" and how the students "with mature poise they delivered" an outstanding performance. Cast picture below.

The story, based on an old legend of Normandy, revolved primarily around six characters played by Ron Millington, Conrad Krankel, Jerry Hatfield, Jane Hodgman, Esther Barton and Bill Edinger. The piano accompanist was Betty VanGilder.

A short time later, in April, the school held their annual "Spring Festival" in which the A Cappella Choir was augmented by two newly organized Boy's and Girl's Glee Clubs. Again, the groups' presentations were exceptionally well received.

Under the direction of Mr. Howard Park, the FHS Instrumental program also flourished. While it didn't have anything to do with the Band's performances, probably the most significant event that occurred relative to the Band, was the forming of a Band Boosters Club.

A group of parents of band members formed the nucleus of the new club, but the effort was also supported by other interested citizens and tone business community. At one of their early meetings they elected Paul Cotcher as their President and the following officers: VP Mrs. Earl L. Smith, Secretary Mrs. Lowery Nash, and Treasurer Mrs. T. B. Ross.

One of the interesting programs sponsored by the Boosters was in the summer of 1950. Classes starting with "toneties", progressing to beginner's classes, then to advanced instrumental instruction. These classes were conducted by Howard Park. This essentially provided a year-round program for FHS.

The Boosters completed their year of activities with a banquet honoring the FHS Band. The affair was held at the Community Center and Assistant Band Director of Michigan State College's Marching Band was the guest speaker.

During the school year the band performed at the football games and most other school events. In September the band performed at the Michigan State Fair. The 35 member band presented a half hour concert at the Music Shell at the Fair.

In April, the Band's clarinet quartet participated in the State Solo and Ensemble Festival at East Lansing. Members of the quartet were Conrad Krankel, Marion Nash, Joyce French, Chuck Turner and alternate Helen Austin. They received a "Superior" rating at this event.

In June, a group of school musicians led by Howard Bacon and Don Griswold formed an orchestra to play for the summer Friday night dances

The FHS students' skills in the arts weren't limited to music. The students were in profound agreement with Shakespeare's saying "the plays the thing". The FHS theatre season featured two productions...the Junior play and the first production of a newly formed Drama club

The Juniors presented three one-act plays in the spring. The program was held at the Community Center and was attended by a sell-out audience. The Juniors selected two comedies: "Cupid's Bow" and "Junior Buys a Cat" and a mystery "House Next Door".

The "Cupid's Bow" players were Sharon Kelley, Rosslyn Conrad, Jim VanCleve, Richard Smith and Brad Omick.

"Junior Buys a Cat" cast found Duncan MacDonald, Jean Millington, Lee Merrick, Marilyn Piddington, Rodney Bly, Richard Kiest, Carl Huebschle, Valderine Long, Collette Weesner and Miles House.

"The House Next Door" cast included Amata Cook, Judy Omick, Ann Boilore, Phyllis Roberts, Matilda McKenna, Lucile Hubert, Don Griswold Jerry Bassler and Ed Louden.

The newly formed Drama Club at FHS performed the action-packed two act play "Nine Girls" at the Community Center in April. The cast included Martha Limbach, Elizabeth Dunn, Nora Henderson, Sandra Seal, Doris Cecil, Virginia Wieland, Carol Adams, Jean Bradsher, Janet Miller and Martha Moyer.

The "behind the scene" group included Mary Hillis (Stage Manager), Lillian Rasmussen, Cathy Lince, Bill Bass, Don Moore Dick Ruddick, Tom Moorman, Bob Zankl, Ann Kiesling, Louise Turco, Barb Bender, Sue Furman, Marnie Hartley and Nanette Stiff.

The "BIG" activity for the Class was their Graduation and all the events associated with the commencement. The traditional Baccalaureate services were held at the Methodist Church with the Reverend Harvey Stockham (Presbyterian) delivering the class,. He was assisted by Rev. Ralph Harper (Methodist), Rev. Dennis Tighe (Catholic), Rev. Alvin Hanson (Episcopal) and Rev. H. E. Leininger (Free Methodist).

The Commencement exercises were held at the Community Center on June 15th. The Invocation and Benediction was delivered by the Revered Alvin Hanson, The Senior Boy's Quartet, with Mrs. Buta as accompanist, sang "The Lord's Prayer" and Chaplain Eli Richards delivered the Class Address. Principal August Arndt presented the class and Superintendents Charles D. Arrand presented the Diplomas to the Graduating Seniors. See Appendix Two for list of Graduates.

The top eleven Honor Graduates for 1950 were Ronald Millington, Mary Jean Elrich, Jerry Hatfield, Betty Van Gilder, Carol Walden, Jackie Roberts, Nancy Bly, Marilyn Bass, Janet Breckenridge, Norma Bauer and John Danko.\

"No more homework, no more books...No more Teachers dirty looks" On their Senior Trip, the graduates went on a 3 day cruise to Mackinac Island. Those on the trip had maintained proper standards in scholarship and citizenship and had earned their share of the money to defray the expenses. Mr. and Mrs Arrand and Mrs. Buta accompanied the group.

Class of 1950 celebrating their 50th Reunion

Top Photo: L-R Nelson ÈBudŠ Curtis, Marcia (Schupbach) Freeman, William ÈBillŠ Freeman, Virginia (Hall) Roche, Betty (Van Gilder) Herrick, Eleanor (Dunn) Frost. Painters (L-R) Joan (Dreyer) Millington and Joan (Steward) Kean with Joyce (McMichael) and Elmer Schupbach, partially hidden to the rear.)

Bottom Photo: Bill Freeman painting the Class Numeral

Photos by Ken Herrick.

Scene Six... FHS Items of Interest

- August Arndt, FHS Principal, resigned at the end of the school year to accept the position of Assistant Professor in Mathematics at Central Michigan College.
- Carol Walden was chosen as FHS "Good Citizen Pilgrim"... a program of the Michigan D.A.R...
- Coach Ivan Williams was honored by the Century Sports Club for his ten year record in Basketball. In the ten years his record was 101 wims-37 losses a .732 win average.
- The Alma College A Cappella Choir performed at a FHS assembly. The ladies of the Presbyterian Church provided the lunch for their fellow "Scots".
- The FHS athletes formed a Varsity Club and elected President Frank Wegner, VP Jim Van Cleve, Secretary/Treasurer Don Thornton and Historians Martin Foley, Bill Edinger and Ken Herrick.
- Superintendent C. D. Arrand hired 41 faculty members for the 1950-1951 school year. New members included Mr. and Mrs. Derby Dustin, Mrs. Thelma Barker Crane, Richard Feusse, Mrs. Helen Varnum and Miss Jacqueline Watson.
- The Parent-Teacher Association was active during the year. A program "Youth of Fenton" was discussed by a panel with members Rev. Alvin Hanson, Mrs. Ward Goodrich, Mrs. Floyd Hartley, Aldrich Locke, Robert Dode, Robert Edwards, Dr. R. N. Peckham and Dr. D. L. Hogan.
- Six members of the FHS '40 and their spouses held a reunion. Those attending were Lucella (Reynolds) Wright, Dorothy (Austin) Smale, David Dawson, Ilda (Foust) Sleeman, Robert Schleicher, Katherine (Dode) Helmboldt and Arlra Ellsworth.
- The FHS Alumni Association elected officers in June.. Those elected were President Burns Fuller, 1st VP Wilbur Strom, 2nd VP Ken Pettis, Secretary Thelma Clement and Treasurer Warren Roberts.
- FHS Senior Jacqueline Roberts was one of 375 to receive a scholarship from Michigan State College.

- Mr. D. A. O'Dell Fenton Pharmacist was appointed to the School Board to fill the vacancy created by the death of Mr. Harold Schaeffer.
- Dave Thornton defeated Don Griswold for President and Dave Stockham won over Barbara Bender for VP. of the Student Council.
- After three and one-half years. 75 of the Phillips Field Building Fund Certificates were redeemed. Each if the 150 outstanding certificates were subject to a drawing for the 75 certificates to be redeemed. The $10 certificates earned 35 cents in interest.
- The Fenton School enrollment for the fall of 1950 reached 1,215. The 9th Grade enrollment was highest with 120 students.
- The Fenton Teachers Club met in January to discuss the National Education Association (NEA) position on "Salary Scheduling".
- Allen E. Lewis replaced N. H. "Than" Chesnut as Director of the Fenton Community Center. "Than" had been serving as Director for the last two years and had served as the Interim Director 1944-1948 while Russ Haddon was in the U.S. Navy.

Scene Seven...Clubs, For Men Only!

The male population of Fenton had a wide range of organizations available to them. Most of the clubs had an agenda that included projects in support of the community, even if the activity was not identified with their specific mission.

The most obvious "civic minded" were the Jaycees and the Kiwanis. The Jaycees, with the youth and vigor of their members, took on many projects that required the "hands on" participation of the members. The Jaycees were very willing to join with the Village or other clubs, to "get the job done".

In March, the President of the National Junior Chamber of Commerce addressed a joint meeting of the Fenton Jaycees and the Kiwanis at the Community Center. The Fenton Jaycees were honored since the National President made only four stops in Michigan during his speaking tour.

The Jaycess organized and conducted the town's festivities for the 4th of July celebration. With Paul Bottecelli and John Schroeder acting as Co-Chairmen the program included a children's parade, a double-header baseball game followed by a parade and fireworks at dusk. J. C. Peck, who was serving his last months as a Jaycee, organized the street dance on East Caroline Street. It was there the "Queen of the Fourth" was crowned. Amata Green was the 1950 Queen and her court included Joyce French, Betty Walraven and Rosalyn Conrad.

Ryan Strom was in charge of the "First Annual Holly to Fenton Canoe Race". The concession stands and the construction of stands downtown and at the school was handled by Evar Strom, Harold Dode, John Conway, Leo Miner and William Dode Jr..

The Jaycees assigned all profits from their enterprise to the civic improvement of the Village of Fenton.

One of the less spectacular projects conducted by the club was the installation of "Welcome to Fenton" signs at four of the main streets entering Fenton. This project was done in partnership with the Kiwanis and under the direction of Jaycee Charles Walker.

For years the Village Council had received complaints of "high Pressure" salespeople coming through the town's neighborhoods. The Jaycess set a "Solicitation Board" which would furnish legitimate solicitors with written Jaycee approval. The Board, headed by Paul

Bottecelli, provided any solicitor a questionnaire which served as the basis for a review by the Board. Over 50 solicitors were processed in the first year.

The officers serving during the year were President Edison D. Stiles, 1st VP Robert Ganshaw, 2nd VP Roger Bass, Secretary Thomas B. Merrill, Treasurer George Smith, Board Members: William Bedford, William Dode Jr., Charles Leighton and Paul Bottecelli.

The members of the Fenton Kiwanis were older men who, most likely the decision makers of their businesses in town. They were engaged in a wide range of projects and were very willing to cooperate with other organizations needing their support for their community based programs.

The Kiwanians sponsored the scouting program in Fenton, sent two boys to Boy's State at Michigan State College, hosted the FHS Baseball team and worked with the Jaycees in placing "Welcome" signs a the village's entrances.

Lyle Harper, son of the Reverend Ralph Harper and Mrs. Harper and Roger Verrell, son of Mr. and Mrs. Lloyd Verrell of Linder were selected to attend the Boys' State at MSC. Boy's State conducted a model government and provided the young men an experience in governance.

At the Baseball banquet for the FHS team, Gene Desautels, the manager of the Flint Arrows and a former "big league" player was the guest speaker.

The Kiwanians hosted their ladies at their "Annual Ladies Night" in November where Mr. Jack White, popular WJR radio personality was the guest speaker.

Over 125 were in attendance at the Fenton Community Center were the Master of Ceremonies was Bill Gallagher. Mr. Gallagher introduced the Club President Carl Lind and Aldrich Locke who were honored for perfect attendance. Both Kiwanians had not missed a meeting since the inception of the club

November was a busy month for the club as they hosted a meeting of Kiwanis Clubs from Mt. Pleasant, Bay City, Owosso, Midland, Clare Saginaw, Flint, Holly, Brighton, Lansing and East Lansing Over 200 Kiwanians were in attendance. Professor Paul Bagwell of Michigan State College was the guest speaker at the conclave held at the Fenton Community Center.

Scene Eight...The Ladies and their Clubs

Any discussion of Fenton's women clubs has to start with the Bay View and Entre Nous, by far the oldest clubs in Fenton, with both having been in existence over a half-century.

As it occurred on several occasions, the two clubs came together when one or the other had a special program. Such a program was sponsored by the Bay View ladies in January when Mrs. Arthur Smith of Dearborn presented "American History in Glass" With over eighty pieces of sculptured glass to accompany her lecture, her presentation was delivered to group of over 100 women at the Community Center.

Both clubs had essentially the same format for thief club meetings. At each meeting, generally at the home of one of the members, the discussion would be led by one or more of the ladies. The presenters would have studied the subject for discussion and prepared a thoughtful paper based on the research.

A typical meeting of the Entre Nous occurred in January at the home of Mrs. Frank B. Mytinger when papers entitled "Early History of Michigan" and "Early History of Fenton" were presented by Mrs. Elroy Herrick and Mrs. Than Chesnut, respectively. As reported in the *Independent,* the members also viewed a goodly number of fascinating old photos of Fenton buildings from the collection of Mrs. A. Damon. Others mentioned as members were Mrs. D. S. Frackelton, Mrs. Ernest Hungerford, Mrs. Clifford Phillips, Mrs. Walter Walpole, Miss Maude Morris, Mrs. H. I. Miller and Mrs. Kleber Merrick.

The Bay View members included Mrs. W. H. Alexander, Mrs. W.N. Richards, Mrs. A. E. Walcott, Mrs. W H. Skillen, Mrs. E. E. Crane and Mrs. W. D. Knapp.

The Child Study Club movement was still very strong in Michigan, and the largely "stay-at-home moms" of Fenton were active in the village's four Child Study Clubs. On occasion, the four clubs would come together for a special program. One such program occurred in April, when over 100 ladies gathered at the Community Center to hear Herbert L. Bodwin of the State Department of Mental Health.

The format for the CSC's meeting was essentially the same as the other women's clubs. The meetings were held at the home of one of the members and one or two of the members would present a "paper" on some subject of interest or an occasional guest speaker would hold forth. The meeting would conclude with a tea and a light lunch.

Illustrative of the programs are two of the meetings of the Senior CSC in January. Mrs. G. C. Walcott hosted the members at her home and Mrs. Don Alchin presented her paper on Mental Health and Mental Attitudes", then Mrs. Maurice Kiest offered her research on "Care of the Convalescent Child". The *Independent* reported those in attendance: Mrs. Ellwood Hagerman, Mrs. Jim Bachus. Mrs. Fred Ulch, Mrs. Charles Elrich, Mrs. Woodrow Wilking, Mrs. Ken Latta, Mrs. Carl Tisch, Mrs. Milton Bobier and Mrs. Dwight Fisher.

The following week the club met at the home of Mrs. Fisher and the Reverend Alvin H. Hanson of St. Jude's Episcopal Church delighted those in attendance with a review of the book "Three to Make Ready". The subject of the book was the problems of a family raising three teen age daughters. The *Independent's* article named the following in attendance: Mrs. Ivan Williams, Mrs. Kleber Merrick, Mrs. Arnold Westman Jr., Mrs. David Frew, Mrs. Dorothy Hodgman, Mrs. W F. Buchanan and Mrs. Ross Hagerman.

In April, the Senior CSC sponsored their annual Mother-Daughter Banquet with the support of the other three clubs. The Banquet was held at the Community Center on the evening of May 4thand was very well attended. Mrs. Jack Lea and Mrs. Elmer Nellett were in charge of the ticket sales.

The Junior CSC met regularly and was very active in the community. One of the more interesting of their projects of the club was when they dressed a large number of dolls which had been purchased by the Kiwanians for distribution to needy children at Christmas time.

In June, the Junior Study Club President Mrs. Robert Lutz appointed her committee members: Margaret Hoeksma, Pat Hedford, Phyllis Locke, Nada Stiles, Johnnie Stafford, Olive Moyer, Jean Harris, Sue Jarvis, Dorothy Peckham, Ona Field, Jean Walker, Jean Nierescher, Pat Strom, Elsie Dunn and Dorothy Williams. Other members identified were: Mrs. Bob Locke, Mrs. Doug Savage, Ethel Millington, Mary Phillips, Marjorie Nierescher and Mrs. Lynn Welch, Mrs. Clair (Ona) Field, Mrs. Ken (Jean) Harris

In April, the Novus CSC, elected the following officers President Mrs. John Conway, 1st VP Mrs. Norman McNeil, 2nd VP Mrs. William Dode Jr., Rec. Secretary Mrs. R. C. Covert, Corres. Secretary Mrs. Dale Bachtel, Treasurer Mrs. Robert Hunt and Auditor Mrs. Jon Block.

Scene Nine ...the Veterans and their Ladies

The Fenton American Legion and the Veterans of Foreign Wars Posts continued to prosper from the influx of the young veterans of World War II.

The V.F.W. election of officers in March illustrated how the younger veterans were being to assume positions of responsibility in the organization. "Old Timer" Emanuel "Dick" Boilore was elected Post Commander; however the Senior and Junior Vice Commanders were veterans of WW II. Leo Alvesteffer and Junior Huff were elected to those offices. Others elected were John Banfield, Sam Casazza, Henry Rosbury, Frank Mytinger and Earl Robinson.

The V.F.W. Post and the Auxiliary held a joint installation of officers in May. The Ladies elected Doris Huff as their President and the following officers: VP Lillian Goodrich, JrVP Leda Hanbey and Treasurer Zola Simmons,. Others serving were Naomi Bennett, Irene Boilore, Ilda Faust, Bessie Taylor, Hazel Crystal, Pauline McNeil, Alice Locke, Geraldine Carson, Katherine Watters, Mae Martin, Lelah Stiff and Violet Harley.

In January, Mrs Irene Boilore hosted a gathering of the Auxiliary's Past Presidents and their husbands. Those attending were Mr./Mrs. Aldrich (Alice) Locke, Mr./Mrs. Walter (Lelah) Stiff, Mr./Mrs. Don (Naomi) Bennett, Mr./Mrs. Harry (Edna) Pokorny, Mr./Mrs. Fred (Fannie) Schleicher, Mr./Mrs. Henry (Hazel) Crystal, Mr./Mrs. William (Myrtle) Harris and Mrs. Hattie Rohm.

The Ladies of the Auxiliary's programs included visits to the Veterans in the Michigan VA Hospitals, support for the VFW Children's Home in Eaton Rapids and the selling Poppies to support their charitable work. During this period, the ladies also sponsored a Children's Picnic at Myers Lake each summer.

The Ladies Auxiliary of the American Legion Post held their installation of officers for the year 1950-1951 in September. The new officers were: President Elsie Brancheau, Sr. VP Marguerite Stanley, Jr. VP Gertrude Banks, Secretary Betty Horton, and Treasurer Betty Goodrich. Others serving were: Goldie Cecil, Anna Rasmussen, Lillian Goodrich, Jeanette Hathaway, Jacqueline Steffey and Ilda Foust.

A Lot of Pleasant Evenings AT HOME with...
TELEVISION

Now On Display

ZENITH, WESTINGHOUSE, GENERAL ELECTRIC, CAPEHART

These Fine Makes On Display In Our Annex,
Next to the Locker Plant, 113 Walnut Street

Open Monday, Tuesday and Wednesday Nights

STOP IN — SEE THEM WORK

—— OR ——

LET US GIVE YOU A HOME DEMONSTRATION

WINGLEMIRE'S
FENTON   HOLLY

Scene Ten...Clubs...Don't Forget the Youngsters

The Boy Scout program in Fenton offered a very active scouting experience for the young boys in the town and surrounding area. The Boy Scouts were sponsored by the Kiwanians and in their Scouts' annual report to their sponsors the following information was presented.

During the past year, the number of Scouts in Troop 112 doubled. The Troop began with 31, added 40 and dropped 9 to leave a total of 62 active Scouts. Further, two overnight camps were held with 44 Scouts participating. In service to the community, the scouts assisted at parades, directed traffic and helped with the Community Chest and the Cancer Fund drives. At the time, Ross Hagerman was the Scoutmaster and his assistants were Harold Roshaven, Lloyd Steffey and Elmer Munson. Later, Phil Savage replaced Mr. Hagerman as the Scout Master.

The Annual Scouts National Jamboree held a Valley Forge, Pennsylvania in June, was attended by five Fenton Scouts in 1950. They were: Rex Roberts, Warren McKenzie, Tom Shepherd, Karl Bruder and Tom Webb.

In late February, the P.T.A. held a public meeting to discuss the founding of a Cub Scout pack in the town. The response was "overwhelming" and soon the group organized seven "dens" of Cub Scouts. Owen Meier was named as the Cubmaster for this new venture in scouting. The initial group of Cub Scouts, 56 in number, received their "Bobcat" pins in April. Their names will be found in Appendix Three.

Some of the Den Mothers were Mrs. Douglas Gould, Mrs. Eugene Sergeant, Mrs. Harold Graham, Mrs. Leroy Neil, Mrs. C. E. Ross, Mrs. Roger Bass and Mrs. William Hathaway.

The Girls Scouts had been organized and active for some time. Fenton sported two "Troops", numbers 50 and 109. Some of the adult leaders were Mrs. D. A. O'Dell,, Mrs. Don Alchin, Mrs. Alvin Hoeksema and Mrs. Verl French. Among the girls active in the troop activities were: Troop 50 - Sara Hunt, Carla Sue Walcott. Claudia Snider, Mary Jane Soper, Ann Hopkins, Yvonne Myers, Patty O'Dell, Patsy Collins, Virginia "Skippy" Richmond and Sandra Perish; Troop 109 - Freda Hoeksema, Donna Verbensky, Barbara Bretzke, Gail Adams, Dorothy Lauer, Becky Alchin, Nancy Jarvis, Mary Muchler, Mary Jean

Dunn, Patsy Haviland, Nancy Sorg, Shelva Reed, Carol Stone and Danean Haviland

The Rainbow Girls[13] continued to be a viable organization for teen age girls. In May, the Rainbow Girls installed their officers. Joyce French and Luella Beebe were elected Worthy Advisor and Associate Advisor respectfully. Others elected to serve were Janet DuBois, Betty Marsh, Patricia Moyer, Darlene Jarvis Beth Richmond, Beth Walraven, Shirley Gillespie, Pat Aldrich, Janice Nash, Susan Kelley, Lona Dixon, Donna Burdick, Marcia Welch, Barbara Bender, Ann Zankel, Lillian Bly and Beverly Griswold. The installing officers were the Worthy Advisor Miriam Bruder assisted by Beth Gordon, Arlene Thompson, Nancy Bly and Lona Dixon.

In October, a second installation occurred and Luella Beebe moved to Worthy Advisor and Patricia Moyer became her Associate Advisor. Others named to serve, not listed previously, were Joan Parkin, Joy Russell, Janine Ziebig, Charlene Raske, Patricia Elrich, Carol Kelsey, Jane Helbin, Anne Bush, Freda Anderson, Jane Bentley, Patricia Robinson, Dorothy Barnes, Barbara Butcher and Kathleen Miller.

The DeMolay[14] chapter, sponsored by the Masonic Blue Lodges of Fenton, Linden and Holly was composed of young men the area, The chapter held a public installation of officers at the Fenton Community Center in January. The officers from Fenton who were installed were Bruce O'Berry, Roger O'Berry, Tom Stephens, Jerry Bassler, Reynold Kordatsky, Rodney Bly, Jesse Moyer, Dick Burly, Jim VanCleve, Bob Strom and Allan Burdick.

The event was "grandiose" as these events go, in that the Chevrolet Chorus of Flint, a nationally recognized group, provided the entertainment.

---

[13] The order came into existence in 1922. The original name was "Order of the Rainbow for Girls" Girls can hold many different offices (also called Stations) in the local Assembly; all but two serve for one term (4 to 6 months out of the year). Some offices are elected by the other girls in the assembly. These offices include Faith, Hope, Charity, Worthy Associate Advisor, and Worthy Advisor. *Wikipedia*

[14]. A local DeMolay body is known as a Chapter and is headed by the Master Councilor. DeMolay International (aka, the Order of DeMolay), was founded in Kansas City, Missouri in 1919, it is an international organization for young men ages 12 to 21. *Wikipedia*

Scene Eleven...The Fraternal Orders...Plus!

The Masons, Oddfellows and Eagles are included in this category and a little stretch to include the XX Club

The XX Club became a local group, when, during the depression years, the members of the local Chapter of the Exchange Clubs of America, decided to forego the international organization and keep their dues money at home. They limited their membership to twenty members (recall the Romans used XX for the number twenty!). What they lacked in numbers they made up in action. They eagerly cooperated with the Kiwanians and other town organizations in a variety of programs form community improvements to entreating the high school athletic teams, as they did in hosting the FHS football team to a dinner at the VFW hall in December.

The officers serving in 1950 were President Clifford J. Phillips, 1st VP Charles E. Wyman, 2nd VP Robert F. Smith, 3rd VP Maurice R. Matthews, Treasurer E. C. Reid and Secretary Clark Thompson.

The "big" thing for the Independent Order of Oddfellows was the opening of their new meeting hall in November. The old I.O.O.F building was vacated when Pellett's Department store expanded their store on South Leroy Street. The new two story building was located just north of the river where it passed under Poplar Street. (Poplar is now Silver Lake).

The companion organization, the Rebekahs, the Favorite Rebekahs, held their installation of officers in January with the retiring Noble Grand (NG) Margaret House conducting the ceremonies. The new officers included NG Grace Russell and her staff as follows: Maud Reed, Lena Barnes, Emily O'Berry, Ruby Anglen and Minnie Moore.

In December, the Rebekahs now ensconced in their new hall, elected the leadership for the upcoming year. Those elected were NG Jacqueline Steffey and VG Marjorie Petty. Others elected to serve were Violet Vandercook, Marie Morea, Betty Horton, Esther Lord and Minnie Moore.

The Fraternal of Eagles...the Fenton Aerie and their Auxiliary...continued to enjoy success in attracting new members and conducting several programs in support of the general public. They occupied a second floor hall on the west side of the first block of North Leroy Street.

In March of the year, there was a period in which coal was in very short supply. The shortage caused the closing of several public buildings as well other private businesses. Since coal was still the primary fuel for heating of the homes and buildings, many citizens suffered discomfort as their homes went without heat.

During this period, when the schools were closed because of the coal shortage, the Eagles stepped up and offered their "oil heated" hall for the FHS Band to practice.

In May the Auxiliary elected officers for the coming year. President Mrs. Lowery Marsh and VP Mrs. Dewey Barnes and the following officers were elected: Mrs. George Roberts, Mrs. Earl Carmer, Mrs. Ella Sisco, Mrs. Bessie McCormick, Mrs. Ed Youngs, Mrs. Mae Martin and Mrs. Harry Pokorny,

On Sunday, November 5th, the Aerie celebrated their fifth anniversary at the V.F.W. Hall in Linden. A turkey dinner was served and dancing and entertainment followed.

The "daddy" of the fraternal organizations, the "Masons", with their array of groups, continued to occupy the second and third floors of the building on the northwest corner of Leroy and Adelaide Streets. During the year, the Knights Templar attracted most of the public attention. Their splendid uniforms and their military drills were fine spectacles to behold.

In April, the Knights Templar elected their officers for the year. Ken Wood was tapped as the Eminent Commander. Others serving were Stanley Kirshman, George Taylor, Clifford J. Phillips, D. R. Stiles, Ed Weber, Clifford Fonger, Sennet West, Leland Dooley, Charles Raske, Graham Paterson and Earl Haves.

In early June, the Fenton Knights attended the Grand Conclave in Flint and joined with others from Durand and Owosso in exhibition drills and a parade as part of the Central Michigan Battalion.

The Fenton Lodge of the F. & A. M., the Free and Accepted Masons, installed their officers in late December. The newly elected Worshipful Master was Charles J. Phillips. Others elected were Harold Otto, Sidney Smale, D. R. Stiles, Ed Weber, Graham Paterson, Burdette Graham, Ervin Anderson, Fred Raper, Lynn Avery, Chester Cecil and Leon Brown.

So much for the "fraternals" ...And now the Plus!

Surrounded by over fifty lakes and streams, fields with deer, rabbits and pheasants in abundance, the outdoorsmen of Fenton were naturals for membership in the Izaak Walton League. In January, they reelected one of the town's most recognizable sportsmen as their President. Bill Gallagher, who grew up in Byron, had been operating a sporting goods store in Fenton since his return from service in World War II. The store specialized in taxidermy and processing hides. Bill Gallagher often went on hunting excursions for some of the more exclusive animals...moose hunting in northern Canada for example. With his return to office, he had VP George Baker, and Secretary/Treasurer Bob Baker. The Trustees serving were Charles Wyman, Willard Hatfield and Jay Welch. The members enjoyed a "Marsh Hare" supper following the

The Izaak Waltonions had a cabin in Tyrone Township, south of Fenton, which they substantially improved in early 1950. With members Wes Goss and James Bentley leading the way, the members rebuilt the kitchen and interior of the clubhouse, providing a more hospitable place for the membership.

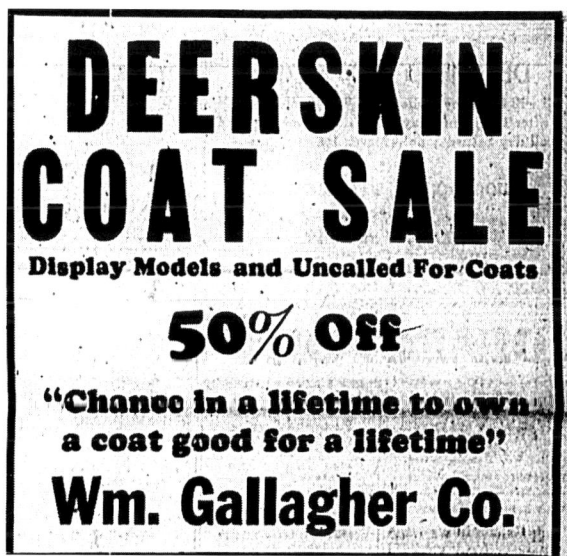

DEERSKIN COAT SALE

Display Models and Uncalled For Coats

50% Off

"Chance in a lifetime to own a coat good for a lifetime"

Wm. Gallagher Co.

Bill Gallagher's Ad in *Fenton Independent* 2/16/50

On April 26th, the local Waltonions celebrated their 25th Anniversary with a public dinner of wild game and rededicated their commitment to the conservation of our natural resources.

The Men's Fellowship experienced another fine year, completing their series of Dinner/Programs with a "Ladies Night" at the Fenton Community Center on March 23rd. The program for the event was provided by General Motors and featured the latest advances in science. The renowned Charles Kettering developed the presentation entitled "Preview of Progress".

The series, all held at the Fenton Community Center, was well subscribed and the variety of programs were of interest to the townsfolk. A famous clown provided the entertainment for the Father-Son affair on one occasion and the more serious folks learned more about the State's Conservation efforts from Mr. E. D. Burroughs, State Director on another.

Any discussion of clubs and their activities would not be complete without considering the importance of the Fenton Community Center to these organizations.

Since its inception in 1938, the FCC had provided the space for a multitude of club meetings, social events, dances, conferences, recitals, concert, a graduation ceremony and all sorts of group activities requiring small rooms, a large hall, a theater stage and/or kitchen facilities, to name only a few of the assets needed to successfully conduct an event...and all l of which were available at the FCC.

Not only the physical assets were available to the pubic but, from the very beginning under its Director Russell Haddon, there was a staff ready and willing to assist the "customers" plan and execute their events.

It took a general coal shortage in the community to cause the cancellation of four events at the Center in March, but soon thereafter, as a new supply of coal arrived and heating of the facility was renewed, the FCC was the scene of gathering of the States Farm agents at which time the President of Michigan State College, Dr. John Hannah, addressed those assemble. In September, the Farm-Merchant Coop filled the hall with their exhibits and meetings. With coming of summer, the FCC offered its eight week children's playground program for another year.

Scene Twelve...Let Me Entertain You...Again!

As they had been doing for decades, the townsfolk found a myriad of ways to entertain themselves...the clubs, of course, the programs at the FCC of course... but they found many other outlets...the town sports...baseball, basketball, bowling...amateur theatre, and swimming, boating, skating, hunting and fishing. With so many lakes and streams in the nearby countryside, Fenton was an ideal location for the outdoorsman...as Julia Sweeney, local realtor, often proclaimed in her ads in the *Fenton Independent*.

One of the first activities organized at the Community Center upon its opening in 1938, was the establishment of a drama club. Over the years the "drama" club operated under several different names, however. in recent years they had settled on the "Village Players" as their "nom de plume".

The players selected a well-worn, but well received play, "Blithe Spirit" as their first production for the year. Noel Coward's play was well directed and acted by a cast of actors for the most part unknown to the Fenton community. The play was directed by Mrs. J. A. Johnson and played before a small audience at the FCCC on February 12th. The principal players were Margaret Morrison, Ida Tice, Lynford Norton and Charlotte Lawson. Wilbur Strom, Jane Wilson and Mildred Moyer, veterans of the Fenton stage, were in the supportive roles.

Only two weeks later, the FCC stage was occupied by Edward Dunning, a baritone of the New York City Opera Company. The concert was sponsored by the Methodists Young Adult Fellowship and was arranged through Winifred Andrews Dunning, the singer's wife, who was the Director of the Chevrolet Male Chorus. Mrs. Dunning also served as the piano accompanist.

A popular vehicle for musical entertainment in Fenton for several years was the recital. The recital was often used as the opportunity for one of the local music teachers to present her students to the public.

Of the several respected music teachers in the town, the "premier" was Alice VanAtta. Miss Van Atta and her two siblings Mabel and Wallace, all unmarried, lived on High Street. Wallace passed away in May of the year. Alice was the organist and choir director for the St. Jude's Episcopal Church.

Beginning in the later part of 1949, Miss Van Atta offered a six part Music Appreciation program. While the Lecture-Recitals in this series were held at the Community Center, on the Sunday afternoon of January 15th, her subject was "Organs and Organists' and the venue was changed to the Presbyterian Church.

Miss Van Atta's Lecture-Recital series concluded on April 16th with an "American Music" presentation. American music from the earliest Pilgrim's hymn to the day's contemporary compositions were included in the program. The program and the series was brought to a close with the singing of the anthem "America" by Mr. Joseph Hunter of Flint. The *Fenton Independent* reported "The anthem ended the program on a truly inspirational note."

Dancing was still a popular form of entertainment. When advertising a dance, the sponsors were wise to identify the kind of a dance it would be....old time or modern or a bit of both. Most of the community wide dances were held at the Community Center, but some organizations, such as the VFW or the Eagles, held dance parties in their small meeting halls.

The "old time" dancers had their preferences as to who the "caller" was going to be. The St. John Alter Society held an "old time" dance at their Parish Hall in July and announced they had the "Hajek's Hoe-downers"... a local group...providing the music and they had engaged Harold Bacon of Flint as the "caller". In their announcement provided to the *Fenton Independent,* the sponsors stated Mr. Bacon "...has the knack of leading the couples through the various numbers with the minimum of pitfalls for the uninitiated."

Recall that in 1947, "Uncle Jack" Hutchkiss introduced his "Dancing Dolls". The "Dolls" were a group of children, at the beginning all under two years of age, whose specialty was "old fashioned" dancing. But later they performed a variety of dances and accepted children a few years older.

> The 1950 edition of the "Dancing Dolls" was well organized and very active. In fact, in December they elected officers for the coming year. Those elected were President Bobby Parkin, VP Sandra Nelson, Secretary Marcia Wise and Treasurer Mary Jean Dunn. "Blond, blue eyed Nancy Pray" headed the reception committee and instructed special dancing.

The "Dancing Dolls" entertained many of the townsfolk at variety of venues. There were several featured dancers. Betty Black's "number" was waltzing with a full glass of water balanced on her head. Patty Lou Bitten of Brighton did a "military dance" wearing a white satin costume with silver slippers. Other dancers were Bobby Parkin, Sharon Geister, Jimmy Chene, Mildred Geister, R. J. Luke, Dawn Pray, Jerry Chene and Nancy Pray.

Fenton had many parades and especially two of them were primarily for entertainment. The "Motorless Parade", held each year at the close of the summer playgrounds, was open to boys and girls of all ages. In 1950, the parade was divided as in the past, into four divisions: Tot Lot, Boy's Bikes, Girl's and Boy's Costumes and Vehicles.

Prizes were offered for the winners in each division and a Grand Prize of $10 was awarded to the best overall entry. Dennis and Fred Kirkey and Roger Bass won the Grand Prize with their entry of a giant "Giraffe"

The other "fun" parade was held at Halloween. The parade was led by the FHS Band and started at 6:30 pm. The early darkness seemed to add a bit of eeriness to the appearance of the costumed paraders.

The parade ended "under the lights" of Phillips Field were cider and donuts were in abundance. (The "treats" were provided by Stan Peabody, owner of the Grandview Orchards.) The younger children were under the supervision of their school teachers and the refreshments were served by members of the town's Child Study Clubs.

For those residents who desired to become more actively involved in their entertainment, they turned to such activities as bowling, basketball and baseball.

It seemed that the bowling season never ended in Fenton. The town bowlers had their big season during the winter months, but as soon as they had their awards banquets at the end of one season, they were hastily organizing for the next go around

A group of young men, and a few who wished they were a few years younger, organized four basketball teams for the City League Basketball and played on Thursday nights at the FHS gymnasium. The four teams were known as Sugden's, C.I.O., Schupbach's and Independents. Some the players were Larry Sugden, Al Turco, Charles Franks, Duane Loomis, Clare Whitman, Mel Schupbach, Curt Schupbach, Bill Freeman, Bob Hunt, Lyle Neely, Maurice Neely, Bill Brabon, Jim Thompson, Roger Bass, and Ted Stack.

After completion of their nine game season, the Schupbach's were on top with a 7-2 record. The Independents failed to win one game!

The town's baseball team, the Fenton Merchants, not only provided an outlet for the town's men to play baseball, but also provided a spectator sport for many of the townsfolk. The home games were played on the FHS diamond and were well attended.

The Merchants, as in recent years, played in the Tri-County League. The league had teams from Gaines, Holly, Durand, Byron, Swartz Creek, Flint and Ortonville.

The Merchants started the season with a string of losses before they found the winning combination and ended the season with a respectable record. One of the "highlights" of the season was when Fenton defeated Gaines for the first time in three years.

Lyle Neely carried the pitching load, with help from Charlie Conklin and Huskinson. Charlie Conklin, Dwight "Baldy" Lee and Bob Hunt were the hitting leaders of a group of very good batters. The team roster also included the following: Joe Shea, Claude Kirkey, Duane Loomis Clare Whitman, Al Turco, Bill Brabon, Mike Harrison, Verne Hunt, Lyle Bumstead, Ted Moore and Vince Messinger.

In the League All-Star game, West vs. East, found Bob Hunt managing the east team. Fenton had five players selected for the East team. Those selected were pitcher Lyle Neely, First Baseman Charlie Conklin, Shortstop Mike Harrison, Catcher Joe Shea and Outfielder Dwight "Baldy" Lee . Conklin, Shea and Lee were named as starters. Bob Hunt's East team overwhelmed the West team 10-6, however both Conklin and Lee were injured in the game.

Bob Hunt was one of the town's better athletes, playing on both the baseball and basketball town teams. When asked why he didn't play sports when he was a student at Fenton High School, he remarked that he was a "farm boy" and he had "chores" to do after school.

The team was honored t the conclusion of their regular season with a n invitation to play in the Southeastern Michigan Annual Tournament. The tournament was played in Durand several League Champions from Southeastern Michigan. The Merchant's season record was 15 wins and 4 defeats. Lyle Neely won 10 and lost only 2 games as the team's leading pitcher.

Scene Thirteen...Items of Interest

- Mr. and Mrs. Bernard Schmuk were struck down by an auto while crossing Caroline Street...suffered only bruises and soreness.
- Judy Ann, daughter of Mr. and Mrs. Arthur Smithingall was the first baby with a Fenton mailing address born in 1950.
- James J. Cohoon, a Fenton Jaycee, was named the Outstanding Young Man for 1949 by both the Flint and Fenton Junior Chambers of Commerce.
- Fenton Pioneer, John H. Jennings died and left the bulk of his estate to his housekeeper, Mrs. Nellie M. Young.
- Gary Wilkins, son of Mr. and Mrs Woodrow Wilkins and Charles Carmer, son of Mr. and Mrs. Earl Carmer, were stuck by an auto as they ran across the street. They suffered minor bruises and cuts. They were treated by Dr. Fred Bostick.
- Mr. Don Smale was named head of the Genesee County Historical Society.
- In February, Duane Kelley and C. H. King narrowly escaped drowning as they fell through the ice as they attempted to remove their fish shanty from Bennett Lake.
- Earl Humboldt's Garage and Paint Shop on Silver Lake Road was completely destroyed by fire.
- Don Carnegie escaped serious injury when his plane failed to clear some trees at the end of the runway while taking off at Dauner Field.
- Police Officer Bob Dode was recuperating from surgery at Hurley Hospital and substitute Placemen Lloyd Kelley and Harold Dode filled in for him, reported Officer Gil Hatfield.
- Charles E. Rolland was named Chairman of the Board of the State Savings Bank.
- Lee Lanning suffered severe head and internal injuries as a result of a head on collision near Ripley Road , east of Linden.
- Bill Gallagher's store was was robbed for the second time, with the thieves taking over $3,000 in merchandise.
- Irving Gates, a Fenton village employee, was seriously burned while working at the gravel pit.

- Emery Golden of Indiana, spending the summer at a nearby lake, turned into an oncoming Grand Truck train at the Leroy Street crossing. The collision totaled his car, and sent him to the hospital with a broken shoulder and lacerations to the his body.
- Arthur R. Fitzpatrick was killed when he was ejected from his car when it went off Silver Lake Road and rolled over him.
- In August, the number of residential building permits had already exceeded the total for the previous year.
- Members of the FHS Class of 1940 held a reunion at Dodge Park Those classmates present were Luella (Reynolds) Wright, Dorothy (Austin) Smale, David Dawson, Ilda (Foust) Sleeman, Robert Schleicher, Katherine (Dode) Helmboldt and Arlra Ellsworth.
- Kenneth Bacon became Fenton's first casualty of the Korean War. PFC Bacon was listed as MIA.
- Two weeks later, 1st Lieutenant James F. Foley was wounded in the leg and sent to a hospital in Japan.
- Two Fenton men were Republican candidates for office. William R. Marshall ran for Genesee County Sheriff and Walter Lawson was on the ballot for the office of State Representative.
- George Anglen retired from 'running" the Grand Trunk depot in Fenton for the last 38 years.
- In August, PVT Max Fox, FHS '49, became Fenton's third casualty of the war in Korea. when he was seriously wounded in combat.

Epilogue

The United States in the 1950s experienced significant economic growth, with an increase in manufacturing and home construction in the post-World War II economic "boom". The United States was considered both socially conservative and highly materialistic during this period.

The year 1950 showed evidence of the problems that would plague the United States during the tremulous decade of the 50s.

The "Cold War" between the Soviet Union and their satellite states and the Western World, led by the United States, affected international relations throughout the world. The Cold War created a politically conservative climate in the country, as the confrontation with the Soviets continued throughout the entire decade

The "Cold War" turned "hot" when on June 25th, North Korea, armed with Soviet tanks and armament, invaded South Korea. The United States rushed Army units from Japan, where they had been enjoying their "barracks life" as Occupation Troops. The U. S. troops were not well prepared for combat and were unable to stop the North Korean offensive. They fell back into a small area...referred to as the Pusan Perimeter.

With the arrival of reinforcements and the landing of U. S. Marines at Inchon, behind the enemy lines, the tide was turned and the invaders were driven back into North Korea. The U. S. forces continued their offensive and reached the Yalu River, the border with Manchuria, before the Chinese entered the conflict. Unexpectedly, U. S. Marine Corps units in the north were surrounded in the area of the Chosin Reservoir and vastly outnumbered by the Chinese Army.

Some very intense fighting occurred as the Marines and other U.S. Army units fought their way out of the encirclement and to the sea to escape the Chinese. Marine General Oliver P. Smith, commanding the 1st Marine Division during the Battle of Chosin Reservoir, when questioned by the press about "the retreat", responded "Retreat, hell! We're not retreating; we're just advancing in a different direction."

Now joined by other combat troops from other member nations of United Nations, the U.N. forces established their positions along the 38th parallel, which is essentially the "boundary" between North and South today.

On the national scene, the period was marked by a series of Congressional investigations, notably named after their chairmen, Senators Estes Kefauver and Joseph McCarthy (Pictured to the left).

The Kefauver Committee became a "hit" on television as the pubic followed the televised committee hearings. The Kefauver committee was investigating "Crime in Interstate Commerce" and was successful in exposing organized crime in the country.

The "Cold War" created a climate of suspicion in the United States. There were many accusations about those conspiring against the nation and in a speech in February; Senator Joseph McCarthy claimed there were 205 Communists working in the State Department

On the domestic scene, there was a marked increase of the middle class in the 1950s. After going without during the war years, the people's need to have more and better goods was intense. People bought big houses in the new suburbs and bought new time-saving household appliances. This surge in "buying' was greatly influenced by television advertising and "easy" credit…"buy now, pay later" …programs from banks.

Another major program of the 1950's was the authorization and the beginning of the construction of the Interstate Highway System in June 1956. The system of highways took decades to complete.

The people of the United States were moving rapidly into the "television age". It was estimated that 77% of American households purchased their 1st Television set in the early 1950s.

In a televise speech in September, 1951, President Truman inaugurated the transcontinental television service. His address from San Francisco was viewed from the west coast to the east coast at the same time

With television's growing popularity, there was a decline in movie revenues. Hollywood was challenged to find new ways to attract audiences back to the theaters. New film techniques such as Cinemascope, Cinerama, and 3-D movies were developed. These new techniques were especially suited for grand productions such as *The Robe, The Ten Commandments and Ben-Hur*.

In the Computer world, a significant milestone was reached when IBM developed the programming language called FORTRAN.

FORTRAN may have been most important milestone in the development of programming languages.

Other scientific milestones were reached during the decade.
*   In 1953, the helical structure of DNA was announced at the University of Cambridge.
*   In 1957, the Soviets launched the *Sputnik* and the United States followed with their first satellite, the *Explore I*, three months later, thus beginning the space race
*   In 1955, the first polio vaccine, developed by Dr. Jonas Salk, was introduced.
..

The early 1950s also saw the beginnings of a strong Civil Rights movement. The right for all Americans to an equal and fair education regardless of race, creed or religion was a significant decision of the Supreme Court.

All was not "sweetness and light" on the political scene. In September of 1950, two Puerto Rican nationalists attempted to assassinate President Harry S. Truman. At the time of the assault, the White House was undergoing a major renovation and the President and his family was living in the Blair House, across the street from the White House.

The Presidential election of 1952 saw World War II leader Dwight D. Eisenhower defeat the Democrat candidate Adlai Stevenson, thus beginning his two term stay in the White House.

As was his custom, Congressman William J, Blackney provided his thoughts in a column in the weekly newspaper, the *Fenton Independent*. On January 12, 1950, he commented on President Truman's "State of the Union" address in which the President "emphasized that all is well with our nation. He meant not only for the present but painted a beautiful picture as far ahead as the year 2000". Blackney continued "our huge debt, now soaring toward the 200 billion dollar figure, our unbalanced budget with an anticipated 5 ½ billion dollar deficit for this fiscal year, our growing payrolls and the inclination of this administration to spend, certainly cannot reassure our people." Later in his column he concludes with "I simply cannot believe in a perpetual Santa Claus to everlastingly cure our ills, nor to our being on the job fifty years hence."

In the same publication, Representative Blackney offered the following discussion on "Tax Facts".

Tax Facts

In the United States each person's share of the national debt is approximately $1,700, larger by far than that of other leading nations, excepting Great Britain's-which stands roughly at $2,020. Canada's per capita debt is about $1,200.

The U. S. national debt recently totaled $250,000,000,000. In 4 years since V-J Day the U. S. gave or loaned to other countries more than $27,000,000,000 (up to last July 1) n That figures out to be $18,500,000 a day or- to bring it down fine-$200 for every tick of your clock since Japan capitulated.

Staggering. If everyone in the United States cashed in all of his life insurance policies, the total would amount to 44 billion dollars. This would not be enough money to run the government for one year.

Encore… A Buried Treasure?

The story I am about to relate probably doesn't belong in this book. The story began in 1950, however it has not ended…and it may never come to a conclusion. However, it is too fascinating not to be told.

While sitting in a Doctor's waiting room a few months ago, a fellow across the room from me said, "Are you Robert Harris"? I promptly affirmed that I was indeed that person. He then followed with "You're the fellow who has been writing books about Fenton"? I again, confirmed his inquiry. "Well" he said, "I have a story for you". And after hearing him out, I agreed, he had an amazing tale to tell.

This is the story as my new friend related it to me. It was in 1950 and he was newly married and he and his bride rented a small upstairs apartment on North Leroy Street in Fenton. It was a small apartment with a small bedroom, which was overpowered by an antique four poster brass bed which had a large brass ball adorning each of the four bed posts.

One afternoon his wife and her cousin were in the bedroom and one of them accidentally knocked one of the brass balls off one of the bed posts. They attempted to restore the ball to the post, but found the flange had been bent and it would need to be straightened to refit it to the post. It was a job for her husband, so when he returned to the apartment he was presented with the brass ball for him to repair.

As the fellow began to work on the flange on the ball, he noticed that the ball was hollow and there seemed to be some paper lodged inside of the ball. With some tweezers, he carefully removed the paper from the ball's interior. The "paper" turned out to be an envelope. On the front of the envelope there was some faded writing in ink. On closer examination, he deciphered the writing as "To Whom It May Concern" and it was signed "John H. Seretta III".

Upon opening the envelope he found a small half sheet of paper. On one side of the paper was a handwritten note, and on the reverse side, a hand drawn map. The "map" consisted of a horizontal line running across the page. It was labeled US 23 Highway on the left and the house number on N.Leroy St. appeared above the line on the right. Below this line was the outline drawing of a house, complete with sidewalk. It showed a rectangular house parallel to North Leroy Street. On the left of the house there was a drawing of a tree and intersecting lines from the tree and the corner of the house. In the lower left corner of the "map" there was a circular "compass" showing the direction to the north, south, west and east.

The note read as follows.

> *If you will measure out carefully 5 ½ ft north west from tree and parallel to the house, starting at the house base measure 4 ft and where these lines intercept, you will dig approx 3 ½ ft and buried find a gallon jar You will find one hundred and thirty one and a half thousand dollars.* <u>*$131,500.00*</u>
>
> *Aug. 16, 1921   Sign   John H. Seretta III*

My friend could not recall, what he told his landlady about finding the note and map, as he asked her permission to dig up her yard. But whatever was said was sufficient to obtain her acquiescence. So, he measured as the note had prescribed, dug a hole about 4 ft in depth and to his chagrin found nothing! Was this just a hoax? Was John H. Seretta III having a good laugh...wherever he was? Or did he dig in the wrong place?

He re-examined the map and recognized that the house on the map, rectangular in shape, was parallel to the street. However, now the house was still rectangular in shape, but it was perpendicular to the street. The landlady confirmed that several years ago, her late husband had built an addition to the rear of the house. My friend then knew he had measured from the wrong corner of the house. He found the "old Corner" and re-measured. This must be the spot!

He again approached his landlady for her "OK" to dig another hole. For some unknown reason, the lady refused to allow him to dig. Perhaps the large scar in her lawn from the previous dig was the reason, but she did ask for the map. My friend had sent the map to a famed "treasure hunter" in Florida and he truthfully answered that he no longer had the map Incidentally, the "treasure hunter" indicated that he thought the map was authentic and agreed to recover the "loot" for one half of the finding. He could not accept the proposal since he was not the owner of the property and had no claim on the buried jar or its contents.

It is here that the story should end. My friend bought some property, built a new house and moved from the North Leroy Street apartment. He put the envelope and the note with the map into his safe keeping and never tried to recover the gallon jar with the $131,500.

Sometime later, he found the urge to revisit the issue. He had listened to a radio broadcast about the assassination of President Lincoln and he heard something that triggered his memory and stirred his curiosity. In the radio program they had mentioned a John H. Surratt as one of the conspirators in the assassination. John H. Seretta? John H. Surratt? It sounded too close to ignore....are they the same man?

So who was John H. Surratt? John was the son of Mary Surratt and John Surratt, who after the death of her husband, ran a boarding house in Washington, D.C. Mary, like many from the State of Maryland was in sympathy with the rebellious southern states. Consequently many of the conspirators in the assassination of President Abraham Lincoln met and conspired at her boarding house. This group included John Wilkes Booth and her son John Jr.

Weeks before the assassination, this group had planned to kidnap the President on his way to the Old Soldiers home, which he frequented to gain some "quiet time" away from the White House. On the day of the planned kidnap attempt, the President changed his itinerary and the group, that included son John H. Surratt Jr., was unable to carry out their dastardly deed.

John Harrison Surratt Jr., a Confederate sympathizer, had acted as a courier for the South on many occasions and as such made several trips to Montreal, Canada on behalf of the Confederacy. The Confederates had moved a large amount of gold to Montreal to be used by their agents in the north and to support their subversive activities.

John H. Surratt Jr. was on one of those trips to Montreal and was in Elmira, N.Y. on his way home, when he learned of the assassination of President Lincoln. He knew that if he returned home, he would be arrested since he would be identified as an associate of the assassins.

Consequently, John went to England to escape arrest. Later he traveled to Italy, where it was reported he attempted to join the Pope's Swiss Guard. He then moved to Egypt, where eventually U.S. agents found him and returned him to the United States to stand trial. During his absence, his mother, Mary Surratt had been found guilty of conspiracy in the assassination and, along with four men of the group, she was hanged. Mary Surratt was the first women to be executed by the Federal Government.

John H. Surratt Jr. was put on trial years after the assassination. The trial ended with a hung jury and John was set free. He moved to Baltimore where he clerked for a shipping company. He married and fathered seven children, one of which was named John H. Surratt III.

My friend wrote to the national archives and other sources attempting to learn more about John, the III, especially seeking a copy of his signature to no avail. Other searches indicate that John H Surratt III died in Baltimore before the Census of 1920. His wife remarried a German immigrant, twenty years her junior, almost immediately in 1920.

If John Jr.'s mission to Montréal was to bring gold back into the United States to support Confederate subversive activities in the North, it would account for his ability to live and travel abroad for several years. What if he secreted some of the gold before he left for England and retrieved it after he was set free by the trial jury. He would not have been able to openly display his wealth, since the name Surratt was well known and associated with the assassination of President Lincoln...In fact; John Jr. gave several lectures during which he proclaimed his innocence and that of his mother. It would behoove him to keep the gold in a secret place. It is possible that John Jr., before his death disclosed the treasure to his son John H. Surratt III. Now, with this huge sum of money, John III faked his death, moved to Fenton, Michigan and changed the spelling of his last name. While it is spelled differently, it would sound the same and he would avoid any "slip up" that might expose his true identity. But now, what does he do with $131,500 in gold in Fenton, Michigan? In 1921, $131,500 is a HUGE sum of money...and it may be in gold...!! John III decides to bury it and leave a note that someone may accidentally come across years later.

If the $131,500 was in paper money, it may have decorated if the jar was not tightly sealed. If it is found to be in acceptable condition, the bills could be surrendered for a like amount of the paper money of today. However, if the treasure is in gold, the value of the find would be considerably greater. What would $131,500 in gold weigh in 1865...or 1921? The buried treasure could be worth millions!

Today, at the address on North Leroy Street, the tree is gone and the likely location of the buried jar is under several layers of asphalt paving. My friend has held this note and the map for over 60 years and all he has for his efforts and concern is a bit of frustration and a helluva good story! The End...or not?

Appendix One...World War II Honor Roll

The original World War II Honor Roll listed the following as serving:

Clifford Abbey	Jack Brooks	Dominie Conklin
William Abbott	James Brown	Walter Conrad
Garl Alber Jr.	William Brown	Robert Cooper
Earl Alberts	Kenneth Bump	Bruce Cox
Don Alexander	Max Bump,	Harold Covert
Gerald Alexander	A.D. Burdick	Claude Covert
Alger Jr	**Keith Burdick**	Roland Covert
Harry Amsink	Wesley Burgess	Dean Cox
Harold Annis	William Burkett	Roy Cox
Robert Atkins	Walter Burow	Joseph Craft
Lloyd Ayliffe	Ronald Butler	Earl Crane
Wilbur Bachus	Carroll Butts	Phillip Crane
James Bachus	Robert Carlson	Ralph Crane
Almarion Bacon	W.M. Carlson	Ralph Crawford
Joseph Bacon	Earl Carmer	Norman Crego
David Bard	William Carmer	Stewart Crego
George Bard	Don Carpenter	George Crocker
Earl Barden	Marvin Carpenter	Richard Cronk
Ross Baxter	Raleigh Carpenter	Kenneth Crumer
Robert Beach	Ross Carrick	Woodrow Crump
Thomas Becker	Wilbur Case	Clifford Crystal
Murray Bell	Joe Casazza	Llelwyn Crystal
Harry Bender	John Chapman	Kenneth Cummings
Max Bennett	Eugene Chappelle	Norman Cutler
Jack Bidelman	Thomas Chappelle	John Dagan
Donald Biggs	Clair Cheesebro	Edward Covert
Robert Biggs	Arthur Cheesebrough	Harry Daniels
Robert Black	John Christman	Jack Davies
Edward Black	Carter Churchill	James Davis
Warren Boilore	Robert Clark	Lyle Davis
Paul Bottecelli	Donald Clark	David Dawson
Ralph Bower	Dwayne Clark	Kenneth Day
Thomas Bowman	Harvey Clement	William Dean
Lewis Brabon	Maurice Coates	Eugene
Harold Bradley	Luther Cobb Jr.	Walter Denker
Max Bretzke	Ras Cole	Clyde Dean
William Brewer	Vincent Collins	Conrad Dery
Harold Bristol		

Robert Devereaux	Eugene Hall	Howard Kirschman
Theodore Diott	Clifford Harding	James Klein
Willis Doan	Roswell Harding	Jack Klinger
Leo Doan	Fred Harper	Jack Koeger
Loren Doan	Burton Harris	Louis Kordatzky
William Dode	Robert Harris	Max James
Donald Dormire	John Hart	Bruce Langley
Donald Edwards	John Hartley	Dave Lathrop
Joseph Edy	Paul Haskell	George Lathrop
Lowell Ellsworth	William Hathaway	Kenneth Lawless
Ralph Ellsworth	Sydney Hay Jr	Orville Lawson
Kenneth Faust	Byron John	Cassius Lea
Ted Filkins	James Heffner	Jack Lea
James Foley	Walter Hill	Joseph Leeper
Harold Fowler	Richard Hiscox	Edward Leeper
Earl Fredenburg	Samuel Hobbs Jr.	Jack Legg
Donald Freeman	Harold Hoffman	Harry Lewis
Lee Freeman	William Holdsworth	Orville Lewis
Robert Freeman	Crane Horrell	William Lewis
James Frew	**Frank Howes**	John Longworth
Glen Gale	Gerald Hoyle	Ronald Longworth
Charles Gannon	Carl Hudson	Duane Loomis
Phillip Garvey	Junior Huff	Jack Looze
Robert Gearhart	Orrin Huffman	Edward Love
Fred Gilbird	Kenneth Hulet	Harold Lyons
Glen Gilbird	Clarence Hull	Robert Lyons
William Giles	Glen Hull	C.M. Lyons
Howard Goodrich	Arthur Hull	Clifford Macmillan
Roy Goodrich	**Donald Hunt**	Don Macmillan
Floyd Gordon	Verne Hunt	George MacNeal
Howard Gordon	William Irish	James Madden
Lee Gordon Jr	Johndean Jacobs	Madden, Harold
Gene Goss	Gordon Jennison	DeForest Marshall
Robert Gould	Edward Johnson	Garwood Marshall
Earl Granger	George Judson	John Martin
William Gray Jr.	John Kean	M.W. Marwede
Ralph Gray Jr.	Arthur Keeling	Robert Matkin
Clifford Green	William Keist	Dana MaWhinney
Charles Groover	Edward Kelleher	Lester McAllister
Ross Hagerman	Jack Kimball	Robert McArthur

Ralph McAvoy
John McCann
Virgil McDowell
Burton McGarry
Myron McGlynn
Fred McKenzie
Charles McKeon
DeForest McKinley
Norman McNeil
Earnest Meadows
Richard Measles
Thomas Merrill
William Merrill
Robert Mertz
James Meslo
Stephen Milewiki
Jack Miller
Noel Miller
Gorton Milliken
Charles Mills
Leo Miner
Arthur Miner
H.J. Miner
Jack Mitchell
Robert Moffett
Julian Moore
John Moore
Robert Morea
Roy Morris
Charles Morton
Matthew Morton
L. Mossholder
Malcolm Murray
Anton Nakovic
Ernest Neely
Gerald Neil
James Nierscher
J.G. Obenshain
Robert Obenshain
Russell O'Berry

Pat O'Connell
George O'Neil
Wilbur Orthner
Robert Page
Glen Palmer
Stanley Parker
Charles Parker
James Pasco
Gerald Pasco
Douglas Patton
William Payne
Charles Pearsall
Dudley Pease
George Pellett
Robert Perry
Oliver Perry
Theodore Perry
Clare Pettis
Kenneth Pettis
George Phile
Charles Pinkston
Dallas Powell
Lisle Pratt
Chet Przewciznik
Donald Randolph
Don Rasmussen
Julius Rasmussen
Jack Reardon
George Reardon
Jack Reed
Norman Reed
Gerald Reed
Cleon Reedy
William Renwick
Frank Rertaino
George Reynolds
Lyman Reynolds
John Rhodes
Douglas Ridholls
Richard Riedel

Ronald Riegle
Jack Riegle
Marvin Roberts
Elvin Robinson
Harold Robinson
Albert Rogers
Burnette Rogers
Jack Rolland
Ted Rolls
Donald Rounds
Gerald Rounds
Evart Runyan
Robert Runyan
Walter Runyan
Edward Rusinski
George Rusinski
Gerald Russell
Lazarre Russell
William Rynearson
Claude Sansam
John Schaefer
Harold Schaefer
Richard Schaefer
Arnold Schutt
Ralph Schillinger
Fred Schleicher
Robert Schleicher
Leo Schleicher
Kenneth Schultz
Curtis Schupbach
Elmer Schupbach
Harold Schupbach
William Searight
Leon Shelby Jr.
J. B. Shinnabarger
Clifford Sifford
Earl Silvers
Donald Sinclair
Bruce Sinclair
Joseph Skinner

261

Delmar Skutt	Robert Trimmer	Dr. C.H. White
Richard Smale	Vincent Truchan	Cedric Whitman
Sidney Smale	Albert Turco	Chester Willing
Don Smedley	Donald Vincent	Ronald Wilson
Millard Smith	John Vincent	Stanley Wilson
Leo Smith	Charles Vining	Russell Wilson
Lester Smith	Earnest Vining	Hollis Winn
Richard Smith	Grover Vorhies	Arthur Wolverton
Robert Smith	Howard Vosburg	Lloyd Wolverton
William Solomon	Tholund Vreeland	Ray Wolverton
Jack Soper	Dr. C.G. Walcott	
John Sortman	Walter Walker	Rex Woods
Donald Stehle	Neil Walker	Robert Woodward
Emerson Stiles	Herbert Walters	Neil Woodward
Howard Stocken	Verne Walters	Leslie Wright
Jack Stork	Harvey Walters	Max Wright
Howard Sutherby	Fred Walters	Carl Wyckoff
Stan Swartz	Glenn Ward	Earl Wyckoff
Stafford Swartz	Don Watters	Howard Yager
Robert Taylor	Rod Watters	Marvin Youker
W.M. Terwilliger	Herbert Watts	Austin Young
Leonard Thompson	Percy Way	Michael Zabich
J.K. Tippler	Robert Weise	Walter Zabich
Glen Townsend	William Wermuth	**Melvin Zabich**
Wayne Townsend	Arnold Westman	Russell Zoll
Francis Trimmer	Edwin White	Frank Zowilanski

Those names printed in **bold** are the names of those who lost their lives during the conflict.

From the information provided by Mr. Kenneth Seger, Curator of the Fenton Museum, 23 men from the Fenton community died during World War II. Mr. Seger has devoted several years to assembling the photos and personal information about those who gave their lives and all others who served during the most horrific war in the history of the world. The information was derived from the material he has collected.

Appendix Two...FHS Class Rosters 1946 -1950

Class of 1946

A-B-C-D-E-F	K-L-M-N-O-P-R
IRENE ALLISON LATHROP	PHILLIP KELLEY
KATIE ARMSTRONG THEISEN	DOROTHY KEMP
SHIRLEY BOILLAT BEACH	BURTON LA FAVE
SALLY BROWN MOSS	C.R. LAMB
DUDLEIGH BUCKINGHAM	MARJORIE LAWSON HARTLEY
ELVIRA BURKE HYYPIO	CAROLYN LEE HOOFFSTETTER
JOANN BURKHOLDER REDMAN	TED MOORE
BOBBY BUTTS	CLAYTON L MOORMAN
ANNE CAMP MATTHEWS	IRVING H NEGUS
JANE CHAPMAN SHARPE	DONALD S ORTHNER
DORA M CHENE YOUNG	EDNA PETRY HUEY
MAXINE CLARK TORREY	JAMES PIDD
ELEANOR COLLETTE BUCHANAN	MARY PRESTON HEISLER
GLENDORA N COLLINS SMITH	ANNA RATHBUN TESTER
DORIS CONARTY LATHROP	CLEVELAND RIDLEY
BRUCE CORNEIL	ANN RUSSELL CRAIG
RAYMOND CRAWFORD	MABLE RUSSELL PRIEUR
CHARLOTTE JEAN DE DOMINCES LAWSON	GRACE RYNEARSON JOHNSON
JOYCE P DEAN BARCEY	**S-T-V-W**
RODERICK DEXTER	GERALDINE SCHLEICHER THOMPSON
JANETTE EDWARDS BLACK	MARIAN E SCHUPBACH HARRIS
ROBERT FESSLER	FRANCES SHAW TONER
DORIS FIRESTONE VANDERCOOK	ROBERT G SMITH
ELIZABETH FOLEY MCGRAW	PAT SMITH LANDES
DONALD FORSYTH	RAY STEEDE
LAWRENCE W FRAZIER	NADICE STOKES FREDERICKSON
G-H-I-J-K	JAMES STRAYER
GEORGE L GRANGER	ROBERT TAYLOR
ESTELLE GUSHWA	ROBERT TORREY
MARION HABY PARNELL	ANNIE VINCENT COREY
J VINCENT HARRISON	GENE WARD
JOHN W HOWE	KENNETH WEGNER
JANE A JACOBS BUCKLER	DOROTHY WINTERS JAMES
	CHARLOTTE ZOLL RODENBO

Class of 1947

A-B-C	DUANE J. JONES
MARIAN G. ALCHIN NORTH	ROSEMARY KEAN LAWLESS
MARJORIE BACHUS GOSS	NORMA A. KELLET FOLEY
HOWARD BACON	MILDRED MILLER BUSH
RUTH ANN BAILEY BEELY	MARIE MOORMAN BEARDSLEE
ANNA MARIE BAKER TODD	LOIS JEAN NICHELS BENFIELD
PRASCILLA BAZELY SLATER	CLARIS NORTHRUP SUMMERS
JOYCE BELL BONES	BONNIE O'BERRY BJORLING
RICHARD BLACK	JACK R. ORRITT
JOYCE BUMP	JANICE PAINE WAITE
MERELYN BURTON BARNETT	MARC PECK
BERNARD CAMPBELL	JACK PELLETT
CAROLYN CHIDLAW	JIM PITT
FRANK E. CLARK	RICHARD D. PRATT
VERN W. CLARK	JOHN REED
JOAN CLARK CYPHER	RUSSELL C. ROBERTS JR.
BRUCE CLARKE	RICHARD ROCKMAN
CECELIA COLBURN TERRY	JULIEANNE ROUNDS SAMPSON
FREDERICK W. COLE	JOSEPH RYAN
BARBARA COMSTOCK STIFF	**S-T-W-Y**
SALLY COWAN DECARIE	SHIRLEY SCOTT MCKEON
MARY L. CUTLER PELTIER	WAYNE SEWELL
D-E-F-G	BETTY LOU SHIELDS DAVIES
ETHEL M. DAVIS MIESSNER	JOYCE SIFFORD FEENEY
GERALD DOUGHTERY	BERNARD SINCLAIR
JOYCE DURAND THOMPSON	WILLIAM J. SMITH
VIRGINIA EDWARDS WOODS	VENETTA STANDRIDGE BOLZ
NOEL M.FRANCIS	ROBERT STIFF
ALLEN GALE	WILMA STURGIS FRANCIS
ROBERT H. GLASPIE	DONALD SWANEBECK
BETH GORDON DRYER	MARTHA SWANSON DOLLEY
MARY ALICE GORDON POAG	JAMES THOMPSON
DALLAS GOSS	ARLENE THOMPSON KIDD
ROBERT J. GRAHAM	VIOLET THORNTON BAIRD
J. C. GREEN	JEAN THORP WESSENDORF
FLOYD GUERNSEY	WALTER S. TOBIN
HOWARD D. HARPER	ALVIN W. TORREY
CHARLES HELMS	BRUCE TRIMMER
MARILYN HOGAN WEGNER	JAMES WALTERS
BARBARA HOLTLANDER TARDIFF	ROBERT WESSENDORF
GEORGE HOWE	CLARE WHITMAN
BARBARA HYDE ASBURY	FRANK N. WINN
J-K K-M-N-O-P-R	PENROD WRIGHT
ARLENE L. JACOBS WRIGHT	OLIVIA YOUNG KERSHAW
NED R. JAGGI	

Class of 1948

A-B-C-D-E-F	I-J-K-L-M-N-O-P-
CAROL L. ANDERSON HALLER	BARBARA J. IRELAND GRAVES
WILLIAM E. AUKER	ROSEMARY JACOBS HUEY
JOYCE A. BAIRD SURA	HARRIETT JOHNSON STRIGGOW
NANCY L. BAUER KRAMER	JEANNE KELLEY CAIRD
FRED L. BECKER	CHARLES PAUL KEUHN
JAMES BOTTECELLI	STUART KING
DENNIS A. BRONSON	FRANCES LAUER PAULSEN
CELINE R. CAMP HOBAN	PHYLLIS ANN LOOMIS BLACK-WAGNER
RALPH S. CHESEBROUGH	WILLIAM A. MARSH
E. GEOFFREY CHIDLAW	JOYCE M. MERENESS WALTERS
JAMES CLARK	ALICE MAE MOORMAN FARNER
CLARE COOPER	MARVA ANNE NECUS BRENNAN
RAMON S. COYNE	JOANNE D. ORCUTT PORTER
FRANCES RUTH CURRIE GOSS	RICHARD G. PERRY
BRUCE E. DORLAND	**R-S-T-W-Z**
ANNE FOLEY DAY	BARBARA JEAN REED ADDIS
LEO ANTHONY FOLEY	JILL REED KUZILA
CHARLES FRANKS	MARGUERITE RICHMOND BERRY
PHILIP FRENCH	WALLACE L. ROBINSON
G-H-I-J	DON SCHUPBACH
LEO ROYCE GEARHART	NANCY LEE SCHLEICHER HANSHAW
GLORIA L. GORDON	WILLIAM PHILLIPS SCOTT
DALE GOSS	LORETTA JEAN SHELBY HELMBOLDT
GERALD GLEN GRAHAM	IRENE CHRISTINE SHERWOOD
VICTOR MARSHALL GUERNSEY	BETTY JANE SMITH SORG-STABLI
CLINE HAGERMAN	FRANCES J. STANLEY DANIELS
CAROL HARTLEY BOYER	NORMAN E. SPEAR
DONALD E. HELMBOLDT	PEGGY ANN TAYLOR HOLTSLANDER
WILLIS E. HILL	BETTY MAE TEEPLE BIDELMAN
ROSEMAY L. HOWE MODDERS	HOLLY ELIZABETH WALPOLE ALTHAVER
LOIS HUNGERFORD JONES	PATRICIA HELEN WATT HOWE
SAM J. HUNTER	RONALD WATTS
JANET M. HUSTON HAGERMAN	VIOLA E. WILHOIT CLARK
EMMA JEAN HUTCHISON PIERCE	CHARLES E. WYMAN
ROYCE DAVID HYDE	MAMIE RUTH YOUNG PETTIS
	EVELYN A. H. ZEIBIG GUSTIN

Class of 1949

A-B-C-	WILLIAM HAGOOD
CAROL A ALCHIN OTTO	ELEANOR HARPER EDINGER
JANICE ANDERSON PINER	FRANK HELMS
JOHN P. AUKER	BILL HOEY
KENT W. BENNETTS	DOROTHY HOYLE SPEAR
EUGENE BENTLEY	WALTER HUNGERFORD
CAROLUN BLAZIER KIRSHMAN	MADELINE BETH HUNGERORD BOURNE
MADALENE BLY WEGNER	LORRAINE HUNGERFORD LAHRING
MAX BOTTECELLI	**I-K-L-M-P-**
SHARON BRILL ATCHNER	ELAINE IRELAND KERESKY
MIRIAM BRUDER MILLER	LESLLIE KENT
ARTHUR BUSH	RICHARD LOCKE
BETHANY BUSH BADER	DIANE LOEHNE SCHUPBACH-SOVIS
EVA MAE CALKINS	LORENA MARSH JAGGI
MONICA CAMP DAHL	GARNER MERRICK
IDA COOK COOPER	VINCE MESSINGER
MARK CRANE	MARILYN PAINE GRAHAM
D-E-F-G-H	BARBRA PETTY NORTH
DONALD A. DUNN	ROSIE PRESTON SKIERA
JERRY DURFEE	JAMES PROPER
MARION EASTMAN EARON	**R-S-T-W-Z**
CAROLE EDDY FLICK	FRANK S. ROSS
MARVEL EDWARDS MULLEN	LEMAN SHELBY
GREG G. FAUTH	ROGER SMITH
JOHN FAUTH	RICHARD STANLEY
RICHARD FESSLER	MARI STEPHENS FRAZIER
DELORIS FINGER HYDE	NANCY STOCKHAM
DAVID FIRESTONE	BARBARA SWANEBECK POUGNET
CAROLYN FISHER MOYER	ROBERR SWANSON
FOLEY PAT	DOROTHY ELEANOR SWARTZ BAZZY
BETTY FOLLAND PARDEE	HAROLD TAYLOR
JANE GAMBLE REED	MARJORIE THORNTON SHANN
ROBERT GARDNER	BETTY WATKINS MAC DONELL
BRUCE E. GILLESPIE	DENISE WATSON DADDINO
EDITH GILLESPIE ZIMMERMAN	KATHRYN WIELAND DOMBEY
MARJORIE GREEN NORRIS	VELMA WOLVERTON BUTTS
MARJORIE GREEN NORRIS	JOHN R. WRIGHT
	NONA YOUNG GREINER

Class of 1950

A-B-C-D-E-F-G-H-J	MILDRED JACOBS
GILBERT BARR	HANS JOTHANN
ESTHER BARTON	KENNETH KIDDER
MARILYN BASS	CONRAD KRANKEL
NORMA BAUER	**L-M-O-P-R-S**
LUELLA MAE BEEBE	LARRY LISK
NANCY BLY	JOHN LOOMIS
JANET BRECKENRIDGE	BETTY MADDEN
PAT BRONSON	RONALD MILLINGTON
CHARLES CARMODY	JOYCE ORRITT
NELSON CURTIS	RAYMOND PESTA
JOHN J. DANKO	VIOLET PETRY
DONALD DEXTER	MARIAN REDD
JOAN DRYER	JACQUELINE ROBERTS
ELEANOR DUNN	JEANIE ROBERTS
RAYMOND DURANT	LORING ROSSMAN
WILLLIAM EDINGER	RUTH RUSSELL
MARY JEAN ELRICH	MARCIA SCHUPBACH
CLARA BELLE FOLEY	SHIRLEY STANLEY
DAN FOLEY	NORMA STEHLE
GRACE FOLLAND	JOAN STEWARD
PAUINE FRANCIS	PATRICIA STIFF
WILLIAM FREEMAN	**T-V-W**
DONALD FREW	ROBERT TINKER
LOIS GOODRICH	LOIS TORREY
VIRGINIA HALL	CHARES TURNER
MICHAEL HARRISON	BETTY VAN CILDER
JERRY HATFIELD	ROSSLIE VAN NORMAN
JOYCE HELMBOLDT	CAROL WALDEN
KENNETH HERRICK	ALICE WALPOLE
JANE HODGMAN	KENNETH WATTS
ANNA MAE HUBERT	FRANKLIN WEGNER
CLARA MAE HUBERT	MARILY WESTFALL

Appendix Three...Cub Scouts

Those receiving their "Bobcat" pins at the beginning of the Cub Scout program in Fenton in April, 1950.

Robert Alpaugh	Fred Levendoski
Charles Arrand	Avery Loucks
Kent Avery	Kim Lutz
Harold Barden	Richard McClure
Roger Bass	Ira Nell
Ronald Bauer	Donald Petts
Clark Book	Gerald Rawson
Bryce Brancheau	Ralph Rheingans
Donald Bristol	Thomas Robinson
Jim Buffmeyer	Wayne Roshaven
Carl Burdick	Robert Sergeant
James Churchman	John Sherman
James Cooley	Freeman Smith
Darwin Copeman	Neil Smith
Leroy Crummer	Jerry Snyder
Dean Curtis	James Soper
Buddy Dode	Ronald Steffey
John Fairchild	Kenneth Stocks
Lawrence Fisher	Larry Thomas
Ronald Florance	Richard Vosburgh
Terry Graham	Forrest Walpole
Lee Hempstead	Harry Warren II
John Hillis	David Watts
Jim Hough	Richard Weigant
Lewis Kieft	Leo Weigant
Dennis Kirkey	Dwight E. Wheeler IV
Michael Lauer	Danny Wilson

Appendix Four...About The Author

Dr. Robert G. Harris - graduated from Fenton High School in 1941. He married his high school sweetheart, Marie Durant in 1944 and together they have two children, Robert and Patricia. He received his B.A. (Mathematics) and PhD. from Michigan State University and a M.S. in Electrical Engineering from the U.S. Naval Postgraduate School. He retired as a Lieutenant Colonel from the United States Marine Corps after twenty four years of service, during which he distinguished himself in several areas. Most notably he was one of a small group who conceived, developed and combat tested an All Weather Close Air Support Radar Bombing system which became an integral part of Marine aviation. The combat evaluation of the new bombing system (the first Ground Directed Bombing (GDB) system) was conducted with the 1st Marine Division in Korea.
. During the Korean conflict, he was cited on two occasions for his outstanding performance of duty. He served with distinction with the Marine Corps Development Center and the Advanced Research Project Agency in the Department of Defense. Following retirement from military service, he was the founding President of Johnson County Community College in the Kansas City area. He later served as President of Middlesex County College, the largest community college in the State of New Jersey and President of McHenry County Community College in Illinois. . Returning to his hometown in 1980, Harris established the Harris Financial Corporation which provides investments, mortgages and other financial services. Harris, who first joined Rotary in 1968, was one of the founding members of the Fenton Rotary Club, serving as its President in 1999. He was inducted into the Fenton High School Alumni Associations Hall of Fame in 2003 and was honored to be selected as the Grand Marshall for Fenton's Freedom Festival in 2013. He has previously authored *"The Village Players"* and *"The Village Players At War"* both narrative histories of the Village of Fenton for the Years 1937-1941 and 1942-1945 respectively. He also wrote of his experiences as a Marine in his book "Many Come, Few Are Chosen". The book is available as an "e-book" at Amazon.com.

Our revels now are ended. These our actors,
As I foretold you, were all spirits, and
Are melted into air, into thin air
And, like the baseless fabric of this vision,
This cloud-capp'd towers, the gorgeous palaces,
The solemn temples, the great globe itself,
Yea, all which it inherit, shall dissolve,
And, like this insubstantial pageant faded,
Leave not a rack behind. We are such stuff
As dreams are made on; and our little life
Is rounded with a sleep.

William Shakespeare

Index

Abbey, Mrs. Clifford, 183
Abbott, William, 265
Abbott, Mrs. Clair, 102
Achin, Wilda, 88
Adams, Alice, 23
Adams, Carol, 144, 156, 183, 234
Adams, Don, 142
Adams, Doris, 144
Adams, Ellen 111
Adams, Gail, 244
Adams, Mrs. Edwin, 183
Adams, Mrs. Ellen, 156
Adams, Mrs. Harry (Ellen) 84, 155
Alber Jr., Garl, 265
Albers, Garl, 31
Alberts, Earl, 265
Alchin, Becky, 244
Alchin, Carol, 49, 84, 85, 113, 114, 115, 116, 156, 162, 163, 198, 200
Alchin, Don (Mildred) 82, 106, 180
Alchin, Henry (May) 3, 133, 190, 212
Alchin, Marian, 6, 47, 49, 114, 115, 116, 124
Alchin, Mrs. Don, 85, 185, 241, 244
Alchin, Mrs. Henry, 86, 102, 147, 182, 184
Alchin, Wilda, 183
Alden, Lucille, 144
Aldrich, Pat, 245

Alexander, Don, 265
Alexander, Gerald, 265
Alexander, Bethany, 154
Alexander, Mrs. N. H. Grace) 83, 240
Alger Jr, Ben, 265
Alger Jr, Mrs. Ben, 182
Algoe, Mr. and Mrs. Frank, 81
Allegner, Marie, 14
Almquist, Mrs. Nora, 226
Alpaugh, Donna, 144
Alpaugh, Robert, 274
Alvesteffer, Dorothy, 186
Alvesteffer, Leo, 191, 242
Amsink, Harry, 265
Anderson, Ervin, 247
Anderson, Freda, 200, 245
Anderson, Glen, 158, 159, 193, 194, 228, 230, 231
Anderson, Janice, 115, 116, 198,
Anderson, Mr. and Mrs. Warren, 90
Anderson, Mrs. Fay, 181, 184, 225
Anderson, Mrs. Luther, 199
Anderson, Warren, 28, 35

Anglen, George, 143, 144, 255
Anglen, Ruby, 153, 183, 185, 191, 246
Angus, Harriet, 154
Angus, Mrs. Sam, 147, 182
Anible, Francis, 14
Annis, Harold, 265 53, 54,111, 156
Anthes, Eleanor, 102, 114
Archer, Al, 230
Armstrong, Edna, 201
Armstrong, Gene, 95
Armstrong, Katie, 18, 23
Armstrong, Mrs. Clarence (Lulu) 18, 84
Arndt, August, 41, 53, 54, 111, 113, 155, 156, 234, 236
Arndt, Jane, 146
Arndt, Mrs. August (Louise) 18, 84, 85
Arnold, Walter, 190
Arrand, Charles D., 201, 234, 236, 274
Arrand, Mrs. DeForest, 84
Atkins, Robert, 265
Auker, Bill, 110
Auker, Charles, 9, 90, 190
Auker, Josephine, 91
Auker, Mrs. Charles, 10
Auker, Pat, 162, 198, 225

Austin, Elton, 3, 71, 81, 106, 175, 201, 212
Austin, Mrs. Elton (Helen) 200, 233
Averman, Mrs. Charles, 85
Avery, Kent, 274
Avery, Lynden, 145, 247
Avery, Mrs. Lynden (Marion) 84, 86, 87, 145, 146, 148, 181
Ayliffe, Lloyd, 33, 265
Ayliffe, Howard, 33
Azelton, Mrs. Orville 123
Azelton, Orville "Bud", 9, 90, 143
Bachtel, Mrs. Dale, 241
Bachtel, Susan, 225
Bachus, James, 265
Bachus, Wilbur, 265
Bachus, F., 60
Bachus, Marjorie, 47, 85, 117, 124
Bachus, Mrs. Frank (Violet) 18, 84, 183
Bachus, Mrs. Jim, 241
Bacon, Almarion, 265
Bacon, Joseph, 265
Bacon, Howard, 6, 40, 49, 84, 115, 116, 143, 233
Bacon, John, 8
Bacon, Kenneth, 255
Bailey, Ruth Ann, 124
Baker, Bob, 248
Baker, Charles, 190
Baker, George, 60, 248

Baker, Mrs. Burton (Annelle) 84, 115
Baker, Mrs. Ralph, 199
Baldwin, William "Billy", 133, 140, 142
Ballard, Bob, 33
Banfield, John, 242
Banks, Donna, 120
Banks, Gertrude, 242
Banks, Phyllis, 33
Barbour, Mrs. J. R., 83
Bard David, 154, 167, 265
Bard, George, 265
Bard, Mrs. Esther, 185
Barden, Earl, 265
Barden, Harold, 96, 274
Barnard, Arthur, 3
Barnes, Dewey W., 143
Barnes, Dorothy, 245
Barnes, Lena, 183, 246
Barnes, Mrs. Dewey, 247
Barton, Esther, 160, 162, 198, 232
Bass, Marilyn, 60, 160, 234
Bass, Mrs. Roger, 244
Bass, Roger, 239, 252, 274
Bass, William Bill" 195, 197, 228, 230, 231, 234
Bassler, Guido, 95
Bassler, Jerry, 187, 195, 197, 228, 234, 245
Bauer, Jimmy, 120, 166
Bauer, Nancy, 113, 114, 116, 162, 146

Bauer, Norma, 102, 198, 234
Bauer, Ronald, 274
Baxter, Ross, 265
Beach, Robert "Bob"8, 25, 71, 77, 92, 134, 137, 140, 153, 178, 265
Beach, Sol Faye, 13, 25
Becker, Arthur G. 57, 221
Becker, Esther, 53, 54
Becker, Thomas L., 63, 265
Bedford, William, 239
Beebe, Luella, 144, 183, 199, 200, 245
Bell, Murray, 265
Bell, Mrs. Robert (Nita) 87
Bell, Rev. Robert W., 22, 101, 137, 169
Bender, Harry, 265
Bender, Barbara, 144, 234, 237, 245
Bender, Jerry, 194, 231
Bender, Mrs. Buster, 147
Bender, Mrs. Delphin (Elizabeth) 19
Bennett, Max, 265
Bennett, Mr./Mrs. Don 242
Bennett, Mrs. Don (Naomi) 13, 93, 99, 186, 212
Bennetts, Kenneth, 110
Bennetts, Kent, 163, 198
Bentley, Eugene, 114, 159, 198

Bentley, James, 190, 248
Bentley, Jane, 120, 166, 245
Berry, Dick, 158
Bidelman, Jack, 265
Bigelow, Fred, 31, 33, 35
Bigelow, James, 213
Biggs, Donald, 31, 265
Biggs, Robert, 265
Billmeier, Arnold, 81, 94, 139
Bishop, Effie, 87, 101, 152
Bjorling, Edward, 110, 114, 116, 162
Black, Edward, 265
Black, Robert, 265
Black, Betty 166, 251
Black, Danna, 166
Black, Dick, 166
Black, Donna, 120
Black, Sandy, 120
Blackney, Congressman William, 10, 64, 168, 177, 258
Blazier, Mrs. Edward, 84, 86, 101, 181
Block, Mrs. John, 182, 241
Bloomer, Mrs., 149
Bly, Lillian, 245
Bly, Mike, 191
Bly, Mrs. Andrew (Edna) 13, 153, 186
Bly, Nancy, 144, 184, 234, 245
Bly, Rodney, 187, 225, 231, 234, 245
Bobier, Diane, 146
Bobier, Milton, 187
Bobier, Mrs. Milton (Mabel) 18, 241
Boilore, Ann, 150, 234
Boilore, June, 23
Boilore, Warren, 191, 265
Boilore, Emmanuel "Dick", 12, 98, 99, 154, 191, 242
Boilore, Mrs. Emmanuel (Irene) 13, 14, 99, 153, 154, 186, 225, 242
Book, Clark, 274
Bostick, Dr. Fred, 10, 187, 254
Bottecelli, Agnes, 14, 99, 154, 186
Bottecelli, Joe and Agnes, 6
Bottecelli, Joe, 154
Bottecelli, Mrs. Paul (Patricia) 183
Bottecelli, Paul, 6, 28, 89, 139, 238, 239, 265,
Bottecelli, James 42, 43, 48, 107, 108, 109, 113, 117, 155, 156, 157, 158, 162
Bottecelli, Max, 43, 108, 110, 113, 117, 141, 155, 156, 157, 158, 159, 194, 195, 197, 198, 229
Bousu, Huldah 111
Bowen, Mrs. Elva, 150
Bower, Ralph, 265

Bower, Nancy, 84, 85
Bowles, Bryan, 10
Bowles, Mrs., 92
Bowman, Thomas, 265
Bowman, Basil, 12
Bowman, Marcella, 63
Bowman, William, 63
Boyce, Esther, 184
Boyden, David, 213
Brabon, Lewis, 265
Brabon, Bill, 38, 39, 42, 43, 121, 166, 252, 253
Brabon, Stella, 183
Brackenridge, Mrs. Earl, 184
Bradley, Harold, 265
Bradley, Lelah, 97
Bradley, Lucille, 144, 183
Bradshaw, Ray, 95
Bradshaw, Rita, 95
Bradsher, Jean, 234
Brancheau, Bryce, 274
Brancheau, Elsie, 154, 186, 242
Brancheau, Mildred, 97
Brazier, Mrs. E., 23
Breckenridge, Janet, 156, 160, 197, 234
Breckenridge, Mrs. Earl, 181, 185
Brennan, Thomas, 98
Bretzke, Max, 265
Bretzke, Barbara, 244
Bretzke, Mrs. Ed, 147
Brewer, William, 265
Brill, Sharon, 162
Bristol, Don, 55, 133, 139, 176, 212, 214, 274

Bristol, Mrs. Don (Jean) 19, 112
Bristol, Mrs. Julian (Marian) 95, 144, 183
Britten, Harold, 143
Bronson, Donna, 116, 162
Bronson, Ida, 185
Bronson, Pat, 198
Brooks, Jack, 265
Brower, Shirley, 201
Brown, Art, 59, 121, 167
Brown, George, 78
Brown, Hazel 111
Brown, James, 265
Brown, Leon, 247
Brown, Marshall, 31
Brown, Mrs. Carlton (Hazel) 53, 54, 156, 202
Brown, Mrs. Robert, 146, 181
Brown, Ruby, 29
Brown, William, 265
Bruder, Edward, 144, 183
Bruder, Karl, 244
Bruder, Lillian, 144
Bruder, Miriam, 144, 163, 183, 245
Bruder, Ron, 193, 195
Brunson, Betty, 138
Brunson, Fred, 180
Brunson, Ida, 153
Brunson, Mrs. Perry, 201
Buchanan, Dr. W. "Buck" 27, 64, 77, 133, 141, 176, 187, 212

Buchanan, Mrs. W F. (June) 147, 182, 241
Buck, Towner, 199
Buckingham, Gene, 190
Buffmeyer, Jim, 274
Buffmeyer, Mrs. Roy (Ella) 85, 101, 182
Bump, Kenneth, 265
Bump, Max, 265
Bump, Don and Jim, 33
Bumstead, Charles, 154
Bumstead, Lyle, 59, 121, 167, 253
Burden, Maxine, 88
Burden, Mrs. Edgar (Marvel) 102, 144, 183, 185
Burdick, A.D., 265
Burdick, Keith, 265
Burdick, Allen (Alan), 156, 215, 230
Burdick, Carl, 274
Burdick, Donna, 245
Burdick, M., 122
Burdick, Mrs. Don (Jean) 147, 183
Burgess, Wesley, 265
Burke, Donald, 120
Burkett, William, 265
Burley, Dick, 193, 231, 245
Burow, Walter, 265
Burr, George, 133
Burrow, Walter, 31
Burton, Barbara, 162
Burton, Betty, 85, 198
Burton, Eldon, 112, 155
Burton, Merelyn 48, 116

Burton, Mrs. Eldon (Beatrice) 182
Bush, Ann, 150, 245
Bush, Art 38, 39
Bush, Arthur, 22, 110
Bush, Bethany, 150
Bush, Beverly, 200
Bush, Harry, 31, 35
Bush, Mr. and Mrs. Arthur, 150
Bush, Mr. and Mrs. Linus, 151
Bush, Mrs. Arthur, 199
Bush,Mrs. Harry(Doris) 87
Bussey, Charles, 73
Buta, Kay and Jane, 225
Buta, Mrs. Lucille, 52, 54, 111, 113, 114, 156, 161, 162, 198, 225, 232, 234
Butcher, Barbara, 245
Butcher, Donald, 115
Butler, Mrs. Aubrey, 84
Butler, Ronald J., 140, 265
Butt, Rev. Andrew, 22
Butts, Carroll, 265
Butts, Bobby, 37, 38, 39, 43, 166
Butts, Carl, 42
Butts, Mrs. Carl (Mary) 95, 144, 180, 183
Butts, Mrs. Caroll (Jane) 183
Butts, Wanda, 88
Calkins, Eva Mae, 200
Calkins, Virginia, 91

Camp, Ann, 150, 151, 152
Camp, Celine, 150, 151
Camp, Monica, 23, 151, 162
Cargo, Reverend Ira W., 22
Carlson, Robert, 265
Carlson, Howard, 35
Carlson, William, 191, 265
Carmer, Earl, 33, 265
Carmer, Mildred, 160
Carmer, Mrs. Earl, 247
Carmer, Rita, 185
Carnegie, Don, 33, 195, 254, 265
Carpenter, Marvin, 265
Carpenter, Raleigh, 60, 265
Carrick, Ross, 265
Carson, Geraldine, 242
Carter, Ann, 151
Casazza, Joseph, 14, 265
Casazza, Sam, 14, 191, 242
Case, Wilbur, 90, 265
Catsman, Raymond, 31
Cecil, Chester, 247
Cecil, Doris, 234
Cecil, Goldie, 242
Champlin, Bruce, 115
Chapin, Mrs. Floyd (Olive) 83, 101, 146
Chapman, John, 265
Chapman, Bertha, 95, 153, 185

Chapman, Mrs. James, 199
Chapman, Mrs. John (Mary) 123
Chappelle, Eugene, 265
Chappelle, Basil, 190
Chappelle, Thomas 60, 265
Chase, Mrs. Donald E., 84, 181
Cheesebro, Clair, 265
Cheesebrough, Arthur, 265
Chene, Jerry, 252
Chene, Jim, 193, 231, 252
Chesnut, Mrs. N. (Nina) H. "Than" 84, 240
Chesnut, N. H. "Than" 55, 93, 142, 168, 187, 201, 237
Chidlaw, Caroline, 47
Chonoski, Bob, 31
Christman, John, 265
Church, Carryl, 142
Churchill, Carter, 265
Churchill, Marion, 119
Churchman, Dayton, 81
Churchman, James, 274
Clark, Donald, 216, 265
Clark, Dwayne, 265
Clark, Dale, 120
Clark, Douglas, 55
Clark, Fred, 22
Clark, James, 156
Clark, Jim, 158, 163

Clark, Mrs. Douglas (Emma) 101
Clark, Robert, 265
Clark, Vern, 42
Clay, Lois, 111
Clement, Harvey, 265
Clement, Thelma E. 51, 101, 152, 201, 225, 236,
Cloud, Ben, 100
Coates, Maurice, 265
Coats, Hattie, 153
Cobb Jr., Luther, 265
Coe, Mrs. Floyd, 23
Cohoon, Claude, 8
Cohoon, James J., 139, 189, 254
Cohoon, Mr. and Mrs. James, 90
Cohoon, Mrs. Claude (Lena Mae) 19, 85, 147
Cohoon, Mrs. James, 88
Cohoon, Mrs. Linda, 182
Colburn, Cecelia, 116, 151
Cole, Ras, 265
Cole, Bob, 38
Cole, Bud, 39, 40, 41, 42, 43, 108
Collins, Vincent, 265
Collins, Bruce, 115, 198
Collins, Glendera, 23
Collins, John, 73
Collins, Patsy, 244
Comstock, Barbara, 124
Conarty, Doris, 23
Conklin, Dominie, 265
Conklin, Charlie, 167, 253
Conley, Rita, 148
Conrad, Walter, 265
Conrad, Rosslyn, 233, 238
Conway, John, 191, 238
Conway, Mrs. John, 241
Conway, Rita, 153, 186
Cook, Alyce R., 53
Cook, Amata, 150, 151, 234
Cook, George W., 222
Cook, Ida, 198
Cooley, Eugene, 57, 81
Cooley, James, 274
Cooley, Mrs. Eugene (Helen) 83, 84, 145, 147
Cooper, Robert, 265
Cooper, Clare, 114
Cooper, Madeline, 201
Cooper, Rev. H. G. 22, 101
Cooper, Verna, 144, 160
Copeman, C., 60
Copeman, Darwin, 274
Corneil, Bruce, 40, 41
Corneil, Mrs. Fred (Carrie) 29, 181
Cotcher, Mary Beth, 146
Cotcher, Mrs. Paul (Ruth) 84
Cotcher, Paul, 233
Cottle, Warren, 231
Courtwright, Lois, 225
Covert, Edward, 265
Covert, Claude 265

Covert, Harold 265
Covert, Mr. and Mrs. Rolland, 90, 241
Covert, Mrs. Rolland E. (Marjorie) 183
Covert, Rolland, 139, 265
Cowan, Hubert, 111, 110, 156, 157, 158, 159, 160, 193, 194, 228, 229, 230
Cowan, Sally, 47
Cox, Bruce, 265
Cox, Deane, 265
Cox, John, 22, 201
Cox, Mr. and Mrs. Deane, 151
Cox, Roy 265
Coyne, Raymond, 116, 162, 166, 198
Craft, Joseph, 265
Craft, Howard, 7, 8, 10, 59, 75, 135, 136, 203
Cramer, Bessie, 51, 53, 54, 111, 156
Crane, Earl, 265
Crane, Ralph, 265
Crane, Charles S., 106
Crane, Mark, 158, 195
Crane, Mrs. E. E., 83, 240
Crane, Mrs. Thelma Barker, 236
Crane, Phillip O., 9, 12, 90, 154, 266
Cranston, Claude, 140
Crawford, Ralph, 28, 117, 118, 121, 265

Crawford, Mrs. Ralph (Joyce "PeeWee") 118
Crego, Norman, 265
Crego, Stewart, 31, 265
Crocker, George, 265
Cronk, Richard, 265
Crummer, Kenneth, 265
Crummer, Leroy, 274
Crump, Woodrow, 265
Crystal, Llewellyn, 33, 35, 265
Crystal, Mrs. Henry (Hazel) 13, 35, 99, 144, 153, 183, 185, 186, 242
Crystal, Mr./Mrs. Henry 242
Cull, Elton, 228, 231
Cummings, Carrie, 95, 144
Cummings, Lewis, 35
Cummings, Ray, 89, 95
Cummings, Kenneth, 265
Curle, Mrs. Donald (Edna) 92
Curtis Jr, Nelson "Bud", 85, 142, 193
Curtis, Dean, 274
Curtis, Nelson, 190, 198
Curtis, Sharon, 184
Cutler, Norman, 265
Cutler, Bud, 193, 195
Cutler, Robert, 159, 195, 231
Dagan, John, 265
Dager, Charles, 175, 212

Dager, Darwin, 110, 158, 159, 193, 194, 228, 230, 231
Dalrymple, John A., 51
Damon, Mrs. C. A., 83, 84, 145
Daniels, Harry, 265
Danko, John, 234
Dart, Susie, 183
Davies, Jack, 265
Davies, Mrs. John (Mary Alice) 95, 144, 183
Davis, James, 265
Davis, Lyle, 265
Davis, Charles C., 168
Davis, Clara, 63, 123
Davis, Ethel, 47, 184
Davis, Marjorie, 184
Davis, Mrs. Jay (Jessie) 119
Davis, Mrs. Marjorie, 184
Davis,. Flora, 101
Dawson, David, 236, 255, 265
Day, Kenneth, 265
Day, Elizabeth, 95
Dean, Clyde, 265
Dean, William, 265
Denker, Walter, 265
Dennison, Harold, 166
Dery, Conrad, 265
DesJardins, Mrs. Leigh (Iola) 101
Devereaux, Cassie, 14, 154
Devereaux, Robert, 266

Deweese, Mrs. Beulah, 53, 54
Dexler, Roderick, 41
Dexter, Donald, 85, 200
Dexter, Mrs. Hilton O.(Myrtle) 112
Diott, Theodore, 266
Dittalock, Mrs. Cora, 102, 226
Dixon, Lena, 144, 245
Doan, Leo, 266
Doan, Loren 266
Doan, Willis, 266
Dobbs, Glenn, 35
Dobbs, Harry, 98, 191
Dobbs, Mrs. Harry (Gladys) 13
Dode Jr., Mrs. William (Ruth) 147, 183, 238, 239, 244
Dode, Buddy, 274
Dode, Harold, 6, 189, 203, 238, 254
Dode, Mrs. Harold (Mildred) 182
Dode, Robert "Bob" 6, 74, 122, 206, 215, 236, 254
Dode, William, 60, 140, 189, 203, 216, 266
Dollis, Jerry, 60
Dollis, Ruth, 60
Dolza, John, 3, 155, 202
Dolza, Mary Lynn, 186
Dolza, Mrs. John (Letha), 86, 87, 145, 148, 184, 185
Donald, Rev. Clyde, 21

Donaldson, Mr. and Mrs. E. M., 29
Dooley, Leland, 247
Dorland, Bruce, 42, 43, 110, 115, 157
Dorland, Paul, 200, 231
Dormire, Donald, 266
Dougherty, Gerald, 117
Dowling, Jack, 47
Downey, Royce L., 166, 178, 189, 212
Dreyer, Catherine, 91
Dreyer, Joan, 102, 150, 151, 160
DuBois, Diane, 166
DuBois, Janet, 144, 166, 183, 245
Dudgeon, Rev. Wesley, 10, 21, 22
Dunn, Don, 163, 197
Dunn, Eleanor, 102, 150, 151, 160
Dunn, Elizabeth, 234
Dunn, Mary Jean, 151, 154, 169, 245, 251
Dunn, Mrs. Donald (Elizabeth) 147, 155
Dunn, Mrs. Elsie, 182, 241
Dunton, Allen, 81
Durand, Gerald, 90, 143
Durand, Mrs. Gerald (Joyce) 113, 114
Durant, Mrs. Harry (Eleanor) 226
Durant, Ray, 193, 194, 230
Durfee, D., 60

Durfee, Jerry, 108, 110, 158, 159, 163, 186, 194
Durfee, Jim, 118, 166
Durfee, Margaret, 97, 153
Dustin, Mr. and Mrs. Derby, 236
Dye, Clifford B., 176
Eastman, Marion, 163
Eble, Dick, 62, 168
Eble, Howard, 12, 31
Eble, Mr. and Mrs. Howard 62
Ebmeyer, Dorothy, 91
Eddy, Carol, 114
Edinger, Bill, 158, 159, 193, 194, 195, 198, 230, 232, 236
Edinger, Dick, 33, 167
Edinger, Juanita, 189
Edinger, Mr. and Mrs. Richard, 150
Edinger, Nita, 183
Edinger, Mrs. Clarence (Marion) 19
Edwards, Donald, 266
Edwards, Janette, 18
Edwards, Jimmy, 47
Edwards, Marvel, 114, 162, 163
Edwards, Mrs. Robert (Marjorie) 84
Edwards, Robert, 236
Edwards, Virginia, 85
Eedy, Carol, 162
Eedy, Joseph, 266
Eldridge, Pat, 183
Ellsworth, Arlra, 236, 255

Ellsworth, Lowell, 266
Ellsworth, Ralph, 266
Ellsworth, Mrs. Elwood, 182
Elrich, Mary Jean, 160, 234
Elrich, Mrs. Charles, 241
Elrich, Patricia, 245
Embry, Mr. and Mrs. Arthur W., 82
Emerson, Mrs. Fay E., 225
Ephraim, Harry, 33, 34
Ettinger, Dr. Ralph, 10, 27, 33, 64
Fairchild, John, 274
Faling, Blanche, 153, 185
Faling, Mrs. Harry, 101
Faull, Mrs. Thomas, 181
Faull, Thomas, 139, 189
Faust, Ilda, 186, 242
Faust, Kenneth, 266
Faust, Mrs. Shard, 14
Feldman, Bill, 35
Fessler, Dick, 198
Fessler, Mrs. A. H. 84, 226
Feusse, Richard, 236
Field, Mrs. Clair (Ona), 147, 182, 241
Filkins, Ted, 266
Finger, Deloris, 114
Firestone, Dave, 198, 200
Fisher, Carolyn, 115, 144, 163, 200
Fisher, Donna, 144
Fisher, Dwight, 53, 54, 111, 156
Fisher, Lawrence, 274
Fisher, Mrs. Dwight, 241
Fisher, Walter, 166
Fitzpatrick, Arthur R., 255
Flick, Olin, 90
Florance, Ronald, 274
Foley, Ann, 150, 151
Foley, Barbara, 150
Foley, Bill, 193, 195, 198
Foley, Clare, 102
Foley, Dan, 159
Foley, Elizabeth, 150, 151, 152
Foley, Harold "Tar", 59, 60, 121
Foley, James F., 31, 94, 255, 266
Foley, Leo, 42, 43, 108, 110, 116, 117, 162
Foley, Martin, 159, 162, 193, 198, 231, 236
Foley, Norma, 114
Foley, Pat, 42, 107, 108, 110, 141, 157, 158, 159, 167, 169, 193, 194, 195, 198, 200, 229
Foley, Phillip, 142, 152
Folland, Alice, 31
Folland, Grace, 162
Fonger, Clifford, 247
Forsyth, Don, 142
Forsyth, Raymond, 71, 213
Foust, Ilda, 97, 242

Fowler, Harold, 266
Fox, Max, 162, 255
Frackelton, Mrs. D. S, 84, 240
Francis, Pauline, 85, 162
Frank, James, 115
Franks,Charles "Chuck" 39, 40, 41, 42, 43, 108, 110, 157, 158, 166, 204, 252
Fraser, Nancy, 120, 166
Fredenburg, Earl, 266
Freeman, Donald, 266
Freeman, Harold 154
Freeman, Lee, 266
Freeman, Robert, 266
Freeman,William "Bill" 42, 94, 114, 158, 162, 194, 229, 235, 252
French, Ann, 144
French, Beverly, 144
French, Clara, 183
French, Joyce, 115, 160, 183, 200, 233, 238, 245
French, Mrs. Verl, 244
Frew, Don, 159, 193
Frew, James, 266
Frew, Mrs. David (Beth) 18, 85, 182, 241
Fritts, Marjorie, 28
Fuller, Burns, 3, 201, 236
Fuller, Mrs. Burns, 84, 101, 152
Furlong, Clyde J., 45, 53, 155

Furman, Otis E. 93, 106, 222
Furman, Sue, 234
Gage, Louis, 105
Gale, Allan, 40, 41, 42, 43, 108
Gale, Bud, 108
Gale, Glen, 266
Gallagher,William "Bill" 26, 98, 119, 153, 187, 190, 191, 239, 248, 254
Galloway, Anna, 95, 185
Galloway, Mrs. Frank (Sadie) 95, 183
Gamble, Jane, 163
Gamble, Mrs. William (Catherine) 147
Gannon, Charles, 266
Ganshaw, Robert, 239
Gardner, Della, 111
Gardner, Mrs. Herbert R. (Willow) 86, 145
Garnett, Elda, 28
Garrow, W. M., 29
Garvey, Phillip, 33, 266
Gates, Irving, 254
Gearhart, Robert, 152, 266
Gearhart, Royce, 116, 158, 162
Geister, Beverly, 160
Geister, Mildred, 166, 252
Geister, Sharon, 166, 252
Gibney, Ann, 116
Gilbird, Fred, 266
Gilbird, Glen, 266

Giles, Ed, 180
Giles, William, 266
Gillespie, Bruce, 163, 195
Gillespie, Foster, 186
Gillespie, Shirley, 245
Glaspie, Hoyt, 72, 75, 97
Glaspie, Robert "Bob" 40, 41, 42, 48, 108, 113, 166
Gleason, Laverne, 144
Gleason, Mrs. Ray, 182
Goodell, Mrs. Laverne (Florence) 153, 185
Goodhue, Art, 31
Goodrich, Howard, 14, 266
Goodrich, Lois, 162
Goodrich, Mrs. Howard (Elizabeth) "Betty" 14, 154, 182, 186, 252
Goodrich, Mrs. Roy (Lillian) 13, 14, 97, 153, 154, 183, 186, 242
Goodrich, Mrs. Ward, 236
Goodrich, Roy, 266
Gordon Jr, Lee, 266
Gordon, Beth, 19, 47, 124, 184, 245
Gordon, Floyd, 266
Gordon, Gertrude, 144
Gordon, Gloria, 19, 155, 156, 163
Gordon, Jean, 156
Gordon, John, 154, 186
Gordon, Mary Alice, 47, 114, 124

Gordon, Mrs. W H., 182
Goss, Dallas, 47, 116
Goss, Darla, 160
Goss, Gene, 266
Goss, Wes, 248
Gosseaux, Emile, 42, 53, 54, 85, 107, 111, 117, 142, 156
Gosseaux, Mrs. Emile (Zella) 85, 90, 119, 166
Gould, Doug, 122
Gould, Edmund, 225
Gould, Irving, 3, 71, 72, 73, 79, 133, 175, 212
Gould, Luella, 154
Gould, Mrs. Douglas (Nellie) 182, 244
Gould, Mrs. Edmund (Luella) 101, 225
Gould, Mrs. William Ida) 23
Gould, Robert, 266
Graham, Burdette, 247
Graham, Gerald, 162
Graham, Henderson, 144
Graham, Mary Alice, 146
Graham, Mrs. Harold, 244
Graham, R. B. 10, 141, 187, 191, 247
Graham, Richard, 120
Graham, Terry, 274
Granger, Earl, 266
Granger, George, 38, 39, 167
Gray Jr, Ralph, 266

Gray Jr, William, 266
Gray, Francis, 95, 144, 213
Green, Clifford, 266
Green, Marjorie, 162
Gregory, Mrs. Bruce, 184
Griswold, Beverly, 245
Griswold, Donald, 115, 116, 156, 187, 195, 197, 198, 200, 225, 233, 234, 237
Griswold, Dorothy, 153, 185
Groll, Jack, 42, 43
Groll, Mary, 152
Groover, Charles, 266
Guernsey, Floyd, 47, 108
Guernsey, Victor, 116, 156, 162
Gulch, Gail and Pearl, 150
Gundry, Margaret, 201
Gurnes, Mrs. Grace, 17, 83
Gushwa, Estell, 38, 39
Haddon, Dan, 221
Haddon, Mrs. Russell (Sybil) 19, 83, 84, 116, 119, 145, 163
Haddon, Russell 3, 7, 28, 55, 71, 132, 133, 201, 237, 249
Hadley, Edith, 83
Hagerman, Cline G., 42, 110, 158
Hagerman, Gail, 150

Hagerman, Mrs. Clark, 181
Hagerman, Mrs. Ellwood, 241
Hagerman, Mrs. Ray (Mildred) 146
Hagerman, Mrs. Ross, 241
Hagerman, Ross, 244, 266
Haglund, Joyce, 53, 54, 111, 156
Hagood, Bill, 157, 158, 159, 193, 194
Hagood, Doris 183
Hajec, Betty, 150
Hajec, Walt, 158
Hall, Alma, 95
Hall, Emma, 13, 153
Hall, Eugene, 266
Hall, Fred, 3, 71, 135
Hall, Ida May, 183
Hall, Virginia, 114, 162
Halstead, Mildred, 23
Hamady, Larry, 180, 214
Hanbey, Mrs. Bryant (Leda) 13, 99, 153, 186, 242
Hanbey, Bryant "Slim", 12, 60, 191, 154, 217
Hanson, Rev. Alvin H., 152, 217, 224, 241, 234, 236
Harding, Clifford, 266
Harding, Roswell, 266

Harley, Mrs. Vinton (Violet) 13, 153, 186, 242
Harper, Calrice, 200
Harper, Charles, 150
Harper, Eleanor, 115, 163
Harper, Fred, 266
Harper, Lyle, 115, 159, 187, 193, 195, 200, 228, 229, 231, 239
Harper, Rev. Ralph and Mrs. Harper, 239
Harper, Rev. Ralph D. 22, 152, 217, 224, 234
Harrington, Rose, 154, 186
Harris, Burton, 266
Harris, Dr. Kenneth, 89, 139, 141, 187
Harris, Mr./Mrs. William G. 5, 45, 101, 242
Harris, Mrs. Ken (Jean), 241
Harris, Mrs. William G. (Myrtle) 13, 14, 99, 153, 154, 186
Harris, Robert, 261, 266
Harris, William, 12, 154
Harrison, Mike, 108, 113, 156, 157, 158, 167, 187, 193, 194, 195, 197, 198, 228, 230, 253
Harrison, Vince, 37, 38, 39, 40, 41, 59, 166, 167
Hart, John, 266
Hart, Mrs. Julia, 45
Harter, Stanley, 154

Hartley, Carol, 113, 117, 146, 156
Hartley, Floyd, 179
Hartley, Jack, 59, 167, 204, 266,
Hartley, Margaret, 150
Hartley, Marnie, 118, 234
Hartley, Mrs. Floyd (Royal) 18, 84, 146, 182, 236
Hartley, Pete, 118, 166
Hartsough, Ida, 120
Haskell, Paul, 266
Hatfield, Chester and Gilbert, 33
Hatfield, Don, 193, 194, 231
Hatfield, Gilbert, 76, 214, 216, 254
Hatfield, Jerry, 49, 94, 115, 116, 187, 198, 232, 234
Hatfield, Mrs. Willard (Martha) 95, 144, 183
Hatfield, Willard, 3, 95, 143, 248
Hathaway, Bill, 12, 190
Hathaway, C. F., 190
Hathaway, Charles, 81
Hathaway, Mr. and Mrs., 220
Hathaway, Mr. Charles, 26
Hathaway, Mrs. William (Jeanette) 97, 154, 242, 244
Hathaway, Verna, 81
Hathaway, William, 266

Hauritz, John, 154
Haves, Earl, 247
Haviland, Danean, 245
Haviland, Patsy, 169, 245
Hay Jr, Sydney, 266
Hedford, Pat, 241
Heemstra, Clarence R., 51, 53, 54, 111, 117, 156, 201
Heemstra,Mrs. Clarence (Marie) 84, 181
Heffner, James, 266
Helbin, Jane, 245
Helmboldt, Bruce, 141
Helmboldt, Joyce, 198
Helmboldt, Mrs. Leo (Katherine) 148, 182, 236, 255
Helms, Frank "Butch", 42, 43, 108, 110, 157, 158, 159, 163, 193, 194, 198
Helms,Charles Chuck" 42, 43, 107, 108, 113, 114, 116, 167,
Hempstead, Kate, 153, 185
Hempstead, Lee, 274
Henderson, Mrs. Wm. (Alma) 144
Henderson, Nora, 234
Henry, K., 60
Heron, Betty, 114
Herrick, Kenneth 107, 115, 116, 159, 187, 193, 197, 199, 235, 236

Herrick, Mrs. Elroy (Ethel) 181, 240
Hill, Bill, 42, 43, 110, 117
Hill, Harold, 9, 133
Hill, Mrs. Harold (Mary) 222
Hill, Walter, 266
Hillis, Chester D. "Chet" 91, 137, 140, 203
Hillis, John, 187, 274
Hillis, Mary Lou, 150, 234
Hillis, Mrs. Chester (Florence) 85, 92, 147, 182
Hillman, Alice, 111, 112, 201
Hillman, Van, 201
Hinkley, M. E., 61
Hiscox, Mrs. Alex (Mattie) 23, 95, 183
Hiscox, Richard, 266
Hitchcock, Horace W. 11, 222
Hixson, Mrs. Emily, 86
Hobbs Jr., Samuel, 266
Hodgman, Dorothy 111
Hodgman, Jane, 115, 199, 232
Hodgman, Mrs. Dorothy, 18, 85, 147, 181, 241
Hoekesma, Mrs. Margaret, 182, 241, 244
Hoeksema, Freda, 244

Hoeksema, Mrs. Alvin (Margaret) 244
Hoey, Mrs. William, 84, 88, 145, 184
Hoey, William "Bill" 158, 197
Hoffman, Bradley, 57, 71, 121, 133
Hoffman, Harold, 266
Hoffman, John B., 137
Hoffman, Mary, 111
Hogan, Dr. D. L., 236
Hogan, Gloretta, 150
Hogan, Marilyn, 47
Holdsworth, William, 266
Holtslander, Fred, 200
Hopkins, Ann, 244
Horrell, Crane, 266
Horton, Betty, 183, 186, 242, 246
Horton, Dexter, 106
Horvath Jr., Anton, 90
Horvath, Anton, 143
Horvath, Arlin, 115, 159
Horvath, Skip, 116, 157, 194
Hoskins, John, 9, 26
Hough, Avis, 95, 144
Hough, Jim, 274
House, Margaret, 144, 83, 246
House, Miles, 234
Howe, George, 37, 38, 40, 41, 42, 43, 47, 49, 107, 108, 113, 114, 166
Howe, John, 37, 38, 40, 41, 166
Howe, Rosemary, 97, 113, 116, 117, 155, 156,
Howell, Mrs. Emma, 168
Howes, Frank, 266
Hoyle, Dorothy, 115, 200
Hoyle, Gerald, 266
Hoyle, Marjorie, 115, 200
Hubert, Anna May, 151
Hubert, Clara, 102, 151, 160
Hubert, Lucille and Anna Mary, 150
Hubert, Lucille, 117, 160, 234
Hudson, Carl, 266
Huebschle, Carl, 234
Huet, Laquite, 144
Huff, Mrs. Harold (Doris) 99, 153, 186, 242
Huff, Harold, 191
Huff, Junior, 242, 266
Huff, Ruby, 13
Huffman, Orrin, 266
Hulet, Kenneth, 266
Hull, Arthur, 266
Hull, Clarence, 266
Hull, Glen, 266
Humboldt, Earl, 254
Hungerford, Beth, 162, 198
Hungerford, Lois, 114
Hungerford, Lorraine, 162, 198

Hungerford, Mrs. Ernest (Eva) 84, 145, 240
Hungerford, Mrs. L. E. (Frances) 146, 181
Hungerford, Walter, 108, 115, 116, 198
Hunt, Donald, 266
Hunt, Elmer F., 121, 201
Hunt, Mrs. Lloyd (Marion) 84, 145
Hunt, Mrs. Robert (Irene) 147, 182, 241
Hunt, Raymond, 3, 10, 71, 166, 187, 201, 253, 266
Hunt, Robert "Bob" 121, 167, 252, 253
Hunt, Sara, 244
Hunt, Verne, 59, 121, 167, 253, 266
Hunter, Samuel, 108, 110, 156, 158
Huston, Janet, 117
Hutchkiss,, 120, 251
Hyde, Barbara, 19, 47, 52, 116, 124
Hyde, Bonnie, 184
Hyde, Mrs. R, H., 83
Hyde, Mrs. Raymond, 23
Hyde, Royce, 40, 41, 108, 158
Imhoff, Mrs. Irene (Graham), 180
Ireland, Barbara, 60, 115

Ireland, Bob, 31, 33, 60, 121, 160
Ireland, Elaine, 144, 163
Ireland, Mrs,. Robert (May Thompson) 33
Ireland, Sis, 160
Irish, William, 266
Irvin, Joan, 144
Irvine, Dickie, 168
Irwin, Mrs. R., 149
Jacobs, Johndean, 80, 266
Jacobs, Marie, 102, 160
Jacobs, Mildred, 102, 160, 198
Jacobs, Rosemary, 116
Jaggi, Ned, 37, 38, 42, 43, 47, 107, 113,
James, Carol, 166
James, Max, 266
Jarvis, Darlene, 115, 144, 184, 245
Jarvis, Nancy, 244
Jarvis, Sue, 241
Jayne, Judge Ira W, 51
Jennings, John H., 51, 201, 222, 254
Jennison, Gordon, 266
Jeswick, Helen, 23
John, Byron, 266
Johnson, Barbara (Glaspie), 118
Johnson, Edward, 266
Johnson, Frederick H., 60, 63
Johnson, J. A., 119
Johnson, Mrs. Immanuel, 18

Johnson, Mrs. J. A., (Coral) 119, 166, 203, 250
Johnson, Nan, 144
Johnson, Oreanna, 153
Johnson, Pearl, 95
Johnson, Stanley, 187
Jones, Carol, 163
Joslyn, Marjorie, 120
Joslyn, Nancy, 120
Jothan, Hans, 158
Jubelt, Mrs. C., 150
Judson, George, 266
Judson, John, 158, 194, 228, 230, 231
Judson, Mrs. Russell, 148
Julie, Violet and Rose, 23
Justin, Margie and Nancy, 168
Kaas, Rev. H. C., 22, 101
Kalinchak, Rev. Louis L., 224
Kean, John, 266
Kean, Mrs. John (Ann) 156
Keeling, Arthur, 266
Keist, Richard, 195, 217, 231, 229, 234,
Keist, William, 266
Kelleher, D. E., 222
Kelleher, Edward W. 98, 266
Kelleher, Webster, 12, 153, 154
Kelley, Duane, 254
Kelley, Jean, 162
Kelley, Jeanne, 113
Kelley, Lee, 7, 8, 75, 94, 136, 140, 201
Kelley, Lloyd, 6, 190, 254
Kelley, Marge, 6, 28
Kelley, Norma 47, 113, 114, 116
Kelley, Phil, 37, 38, 41, 166
Kelley, Susan, 245
Kelly, Sharon, 156, 233
Kelly, Wilma, 144, 183
Kelsey, Carol, 245
Kent, Les, 163, 198
Kerton, Mrs. Lee (Florence) 101
Kessler, Robert, 41
Kidder, Kenneth, 198
Kidder, Mrs. George (Ella) 86, 182
Kieft, Lewis, 274
Kieft, Mary, 146
Kieft, Maurice, 47, 54, 111, 155, 156
Kieft, Mrs. Maurice (Matie) 18, 84, 85, 86, 87, 181, 185, 241
Kiesling, Ann, 183, 234
Kiesling, Chuck, 158
Kiesling, Mrs Thurman (Muriel) 155
Kimball, Jack, 266
King, C. H., 254
King, Stuart, 41
Kinne, Mrs. Brooks (Gladys) 153
Kinner, Evelyn, 156

Kinner, Mrs. Miriam, 54, 104, 111, 156
Kirk, Amuel M, 179
Kirk, George, 73
Kirkey, Claude, 121, 167, 253
Kirkey, Dennis and Fred, 252
Kirkey, Dennis, 274
Kirschman, Howard, 266
Kirshman, Stanley, 122, 247
Klein, James, 266
Klein, Mrs. A., 150
Klein, Rev. A. A., 149, 152, 224
Klein, Sandra, 225
Klinger, Dave, 135
Klinger, Jack, 266
Knapp, Mrs. W. D., 240
Knight, Gladys, 94
Koan, Mrs. George, 149
Koeger, Jack, 266
Kordatsky, Reynold 245
Kordatzky, Louis, 266
Kostka, Max, 31
Krankel, Conrad, 115, 116, 156, 193, 197, 198, 200, 232, 233
Krankel, Mrs. Ben, 225
Krieger, Mrs. Otto, 18
Kudlinger, Anna Marie, 150, 160
Kudlinger, Don, 34
Kuehn, Charles, 113
Kunk, Jean, 111
Kuzukos, Jean, 115
Langley, Bruce, 266

Lanning, Lee, 254
Lathrop, Dave, 266
Lathrop, George, 266
Lathrop, Jim, 42
Latta, Kenneth, 144, 190, 195
Latta, Mrs. Ken (Evelyn) 241
Lauer, Dorothy, 244
Lauer, Michael 274
Lauer, Mrs. Carleton, 184
Lawless, Kenneth, 266
Lawson, Charlotte, 250
Lawson, Orville, 266
Lawson, Walter, 190, 216, 255
Lea, Cassius, 266
Lea, Jack, 266
Lea, Mrs. Charles (Anne) 84, 87, 181
Lea, Mrs. Jack (Carol) 29, 147, 84, 181, 241
Lee, Carolyn, 23
Lee, Dwight "Baldy" 60, 63, 253
Lee, Mrs. Marjorie, 14, 201
Lee, Rosemary, 23
Leeper, Edward, 266
Leeper, Joseph, 266
Leese, Doris, 23
Leetch, Mrs. C. A. (Alta) 82, 101
Legg, Jack 266
Legg, Mrs. John, 86, 87, 185
Leggs, Jimmy, 154

Leighton, Charles, 54, 111, 112, 140, 156, 163, 189, 239
Leighton, Mrs. Charles, 147
Leininger, Rev. H. E., 22, 152, 224, 234
Lemen, Harry, 3, 4, 9, 10, 13, 61, 62, 71, 106, 133, 175, 204, 212
Lemen, Shelby, 108
Leonard, Mrs., 101
Leslie, Mrs. Earl, 184
Leuneberg, Floyd, 230
Levendoski, Fred, 274
Levendowski, C., 60
Lewis, Allen E., 237
Lewis, Harry 266
Lewis, Orville 266
Lewis, William 266
Limbach, Martha, 234
Limbach, Mrs. David, 181, 202, 226
Lince, Cathy, 234
Lince, Katheryn, 150
Lince, Mrs. Russell (Joanne) 84, 119, 202
Lince, Russell, 119
Lind, Carl, 141, 187, 239
Lind, Mrs. Carl, 184
Lipp, Fritz, 111
Lisk, Larry, 193, 195, 229
Little, Jane, 144
Locke, Aldrich C. 10, 11, 23, 90, 92, 96, 99, 138, 175, 176, 178, 186, 206, 212, 213, 217, 220, 224, 236, 239

Locke, Mr./Mrs. Aldrich, 242
Locke, Mrs. Aldrich (Alice) 13, 99, 101, 153, 184, 242
Locke, Mrs. Robert (Mary Thompson) 31, 35, 241
Locke, Phyllis, 241
Locke, Richard "Dick" 110, 114, 159, 195, 198
Lodgman, Jane, 198
Loehne, Diane, 163, 198
Logan, Carrie, 95
Logan, Mrs. Warren, 183
Logan, Warren, "Bones" 95, 142
Londul, Lilly, 144
Long, Valderine, 234
Longworth, John 266
Longworth, Ronald 266
Lonsbury, Donald, 168
Loomis, Ann, 116, 160
Loomis, Duane, 60, 121, 252, 253, 266
Loomis, Howard 60
Loomis, John, 187
Loomis, Mrs. Russell, 185
Looze, Jack 266
Lord, Mrs. Edward (Esther) 88, 144, 153, 183, 246
Lorenz, Bob, 31, 33
Loucks, Avery, 93, 95, 142, 187, 274

Louden, Edward 113, 115, 99, 187, 200, 225, 234, 266
Lowe, Harry A., 53, 71, 111, 155, 202
Lowe, Mrs. Charles, 181
Lowe, Sue, 119
Luke, R. J., 252
Lutz, G. C. "Gus", 133
Lutz, Kim, 274
Lutz, Mrs. Robert (Elizabeth) 85, 147, 241
Lutz, Robert "Bob" 89, 112, 94, 154
Lyons, C.M. 266
Lyons, Florence, 201
Lyons, Harold 266
Lyons, Robert 266
MacDonald, Duncan, 234
Macdonnell Jr., Alan, 119
Macdonnell, Peggy, 119
MacKenzie, Walden, 35
Macmillan, Clifford 266
Macmillan, Don, 266
MacNeal, George, 266
MacNeal, Mrs. George (Ada) 84
Madden, Bud, 121, 167
Madden, Harold 266
Madden, James, 266
Maehese, Francis, 191
Manns, Kenneth, 35
Marklund, Mrs. Lawrence, 102
Marsh, Betty, 144, 183, 245
Marsh, Bill, 158
Marsh, Bruce, 59, 71, 95, 121, 143
Marsh, Lorena, 160, 163
Marsh, Mrs. Lowery, 247
Marshall, Alton G. "Fuzz", 63, 266
Marshall, DeForest, 266
Marshall, William R. "Bill", 60, 64, 180, 255
Martin, Ed, 212
Martin, John, 105, 266
Martin, Mrs. Mae, 242, 247
Martin, Mrs. Wesley, 19, 84, 146, 184
Martin, Mrs., 87
Martin, Sue, 183
Martin, William, 31
Marwede, M.W., 266
Mathews, Mary, 144
Matkin, Robert, 266
Matthews, Kathryn, 102
Matthews, Maurice R., 79, 246
Matthews, Mrs. Maurice (Mary) 183
Mattison, Elvin K., 224
MaWhinney, Dana, 266
McAllister, Lester, 266
McArthur, Robert, 266
McAvoy, Ralph, 267
McBroom, Mickey and Dorothy, 26
McCann, John, 267
McCarty, Carolyn, 150, 151

McClure, Frank, 33, 34
McClure, Richard, 274
McCormack, Mrs. W.E., 23
McCormick, John, 190
McCormick, Mrs. Bessie, 247
McCormick, Mrs. Lyman (Lydia) 99, 153
McCormick, Phyllis, 23, 114, 162, 198
McCullan, S. A., 155
McDaniel, Mr. and Mrs., 80
McDevitt, Mrs. James (Mary) 147, 182
McDowell, Virgil, 267
McGarry, Burton, 267
McGarry, Chris, 119
McGarry, Mrs. B. G (Hazel) 83
McGlynn, Mrs. Myron (Hazel) 83, 88, 146
McGlynn, Myron, 267
McGuire, Mr. and Mrs. Don J., 151
McGuire, Mrs. Don (Elizabeth) 181
McKenna, Matilda, 234
McKenzie, Fred, 267
McKenzie, Robert, 115
McKenzie, Warren, 200, 244
McKeon, Charles, 267
McKeon, Jack, 38, 39
McKeusir, Warren, 166
McKinley Jr., Mrs. James (Anna) 87, 101
McKinley, DeForest, 60, 267
McKinley, Herb, 122, 203
McKinley, Jim, 89
McKinley, Mrs. Tom (Georgia) 23, 101, 201
McKinley, Tom, 60
McLenna, Bruce, 59 121
McMicheal, Donna, 150
McNab, Jean, 160
McNeil, Norman, 12, 191, 267
McNeil, Mrs. Norman, (Pauline) 99, 147, 153, 183, 186, 242, 241
McQuire, Don, 213
Mead, Mrs. E (Neva) 149
Meadows, Earnest 267
Measles, Richard, 267
Meier, Mrs. Owen, 85, 181
Meier, Sally Jo, 146
Merrick, Garner, 42, 110, 113, 121, 156, 157, 158, 159, 163, 193, 194, 197, 221
Merrick, Leah, 86
Merrick, Lee, 115, 60, 234
Merrick, Mrs. Kleber (Alice) 84, 145, 147, 182, 240, 241
Merrill, Mrs. Lowell (Hazel) 183
Merrill, Thomas, 12, 239, 267

Merrill, William, 267
Mertz, Robert, 267
Meslo, James, 267
Messinger, Vince, 108, 110, 157, 158, 167, 194, 195, 198, 204, 229, 253
Meyer, Burt, 119
Meyer, Russell, 73
Milewiki, Stephen, 267
Miller, Carl, 200
Miller, Elizabeth, 183
Miller, Ida Mae, 95, 114
Miller, Jack, 267
Miller, Janet, 234
Miller, Kathleen, 245
Miller, Mildred, 48, 114, 115, 124
Miller, Mrs. Clarence, 183
Miller, Mrs. H. I., 225, 240
Miller, Noel, 267
Miller, Susan, 154
Milliken, Gorton, 267
Milliken, Mrs. Gorton (Dorthy) 146
Millington, Jean, 197, 234
Millington, John, 92, 140, 141, 187, 225
Millington, Mrs. John (Ethel) 182, 241
Millington, Ron, 113, 120, 156, 163, 187, 194, 197, 198, 232, 234
Mills, Charles, 267
Miner, Arthur, 267
Miner, H.J. 267
Miner, Leo, 238, 267

Miner, Martha, 91
Miner, Mrs. Leo (Agnes) 181
Miner, Stanton, 89, 139
Mitchell, Jack, 267
Mitchell, Mary, 153, 185
Mitchell, Rev. Dr. J. Stanley, 21
Mitts, Ed, 92, 93, 141
Mitts, Mrs. Bensen, 146
Mitts, Mrs. Scott, 146
Moffett, Robert 267
Moore, Dean, 193, 194, 228, 230, 231
Moore, Don, 234
Moore, Ed, 230
Moore, Harry, 8, 136
Moore, Holly, 185
Moore, John, 267
Moore, Julian, 267
Moore, L.F., 133
Moore, Mrs. Don (Buelah) 183
Moore, Mrs. Harry (Minnie) 88, 183, 246
Moore, Mrs. Marion, 101, 152
Moore, Rolla, 153
Moore, Ted, 38, 39, 253
Moorman, Alice, 162
Moorman, Clayton, 189
Moorman, Dick, 159, 194
Moorman, Pete, 141
Moorman, Tom, 141, 193, 195, 231, 234
Moran, Gil, 230

Morea, Mrs. Peter (Marie) 144, 183, 226, 246
Morea, Robert, 267
Morehouse, Mrs. C. G., 83
Morehouse, Mrs. Dora, 84, 145
Morris, Maude, 84, 146, 181, 240
Morris, Roy, 267
Morrison, Margaret, 250
Morrison, Tom, 231
Mortimore, Carolyn, 153
Mortimore, Mrs. John (Caroline) 150
Mortimore-Toomey, Harriet, 94, 184
Morton, Charles, 267
Morton, Matthew, 267
Moss, B., 60
Mossholder, L., 267
Moyer, Bob, 212
Moyer, Burt, 119, 166
Moyer, Jesse, 245
Moyer, Martha, 115, 144, 200, 234
Moyer, Mildred, 95, 250
Moyer, Mrs. Allen (Olive) 199, 244
Moyer, Pat, 144, 183, 245
Muce, Katherine, 99
Muchler, Erma, 115, 199, 200
Muchler, Ivan, 200
Muchler, Mary, 244
Muchler, Raymond, 200

Munn, Clarence Biggie", 140
Munn, Eleanor, 111
Munson, Elmer, 244
Murray, Malcolm, 267
Murray, Mr. and Mrs. Dick, 81
Myers, Yvonne, 244
Mytinger, Frank, 12, 98, 191, 242
Mytinger, Mrs. Frank (Jean) 14, 19, 87, 101, 145, 146, 181, 184, 185, 240
Nakovic, Anton, 267
Nash, Janice, 183, 245
Nash, Jessie, 91, 191
Nash, Lowery, 9
Nash, Marion, 49, 115, 160, 184, 200, 233
Nash, Mrs. Lowery, 10, 199, 233
Nateria, Warren, 187
Neely, Ernest, 267
Neely, Lyle "BoBo" 59, 121, 252, 253
Neely, Maurice, 40, 41, 252
Negus, Marva, 162
Negus, Mrs. Irving, 23, 86, 87, 185
Neidermeier, Clark 71
Neidermeier, Mrs. Clark (Edythe) 182
Neil, Gerald S., 33, 267
Neil, Mrs. Leroy, 244
Nell, Ira, 274
Nellett, Elmer, 57

Nellett, Mrs. Elmer, 85, 147, 181, 241
Nelson, Mr. and Mrs. J. O., 80
Nelson, Sandra, 120, 166, 251
Newcombe, Mr. and Mrs. D. E., 151
Newton, Lowell, 230, 231
Nichols, Lois Jean, 114
Nielsen, Mrs. Thor (Phyllis) 84, 147, 150, 181
Nierescher, James, 12, 267
Nierescher, Jean, 241
Nierescher, Mrs. John (Marjorie) 86, 147, 181, 182, 241
Nierescher, William J. (Johnnie), 19, 81, 89, 155, 221
Niskanan, Alan, 40, 41, 42, 46, 113
Northrop, Evelyn, 18, 54, 111
Norton, Lynford, 250
O'Berry, Bonnie, 19, 47, 184, 188
O'Berry, Bruce, 231, 245
O'Berry, Emily, 183, 246
O'Berry, Roger, 159, 193, 245
O'Berry, Russell, 60, 267

O'Dell, D. A. 10, 26, 141, 187, 237
O'Dell, L.M, 26
O'Dell, Mrs. D. A. (Margaret) 88, 112, 244
O'Dell, Patty, 244
O'Grady, Mrs. Harold (Betty) 148, 182
O'Heron, Mrs. Champ, 86
O'Neil, Dorothy, 144
O'Reilly, Ray, 92, 140, 143, 187, 204
Obenshain, J.G., 267
Obenshain, James H. and Robert W., 82
Obenshain, Mr. and Mrs. Robert, 90
Obenshain, Mrs. J. B. (Virginia) 5, 87, 146, 148, 184
Obenshain, Mrs. Robert (Carol) 101
Obenshain, Robert, 89, 139, 175, 267
O'Connell, Pat, 267
Omick, Brad, 233
Omick, Judy, 234
O'Neil, George, 267
Orcutt, Frances, 160
Oren, Joseph D., 90, 143
Oren, Mrs. Joseph, 10, 119
Oren, Thelma, 91
Orritt, Jack, 108
Orritt, Joyce, 115, 117, 199

Orthner, Don, 37, 38, 39, 41, 121, 167
Orthner, Wilbur, 267
Otto, Harold, 95, 143, 247
Page, Robert, 267
Paine, George C., 51, 106, 168, 201
Palmer, Delia, 13, 99, 153, 186
Palmer, Glen, 267
Palmer, Jerry, 159, 193, 195, 228, 230, 231
Pardee, Jim, 195
Parish, Irene, 147
Parish, Mrs. William, 87
Park, Howard, 6, 111, 113, 115, 54, 156, 199, 200, 233
Park, Mrs. Howard (Alberta) 147, 181
Parker, Allie, 88, 153, 185
Parker, Charles, 267
Parker, Mrs. Hazel, 29
Parker, Mrs. W. J. (Thelma) 88
Parker, Olive, 153, 183
Parker, Stanley, 267
Parkin, Bobby, 251, 252
Parkin, Joan, 120, 166, 245
Parrish, Mrs. P. W. (Irma) 88, 145, 147, 148, 183, 185, 225
Parrish, Sandra, 244
Pasco, Gerald, 267
Pasco, James, 267

Pasco, Jerry, 122
Pasco, Jesse, 59
Pasco, Mary, 13, 99, 153, 154, 186
Pasco, Mrs. Jerold (Iola) 104, 111, 155
Pasco, Mrs., 57
Paterson, Graham, 35, 143, 247
Patten, Mr. and Mrs. C. L, 29
Patten, Mrs. Mort, 85
Patterson, Luella, 95, 144
Patton, Clark, 114
Patton, Douglas, 267
Patton, Mrs. William, 147
Pavey, Leon J., 63
Pavey, Mrs. Leon (Geneve) 83, 84
Payne, William, 267
Paynich, Ann, 47, 54, 111
Peabody, Jeanne, 147
Peabody, Mrs. Stanley, 148, 182
Pearsall, Charles 267
Pease, Dudley, 267
Peck, J. C., 10, 51, 57, 119, 139, 166, 201, 202, 238
Peck, Marc, 37, 38, 41, 46, 47, 107, 108, 200
Peck, Mrs. J. C. (Harrie) 19
Peckham, Dr. R. Noble, 27, 62, 141, 155, 236

Peckman, Mrs. Noble (Dorothy) 182, 241
Pedersen, Elizabeth, 119
Pellett, George P., 140
Pellett, George W. 25, 57, 79, 80, 143, 222, 267
Pellett, Jack, 113, 114, 115, 142
Pellett, Mrs. George W. (Carolyn) 84, 85, 95, 145
Percival, Mrs. Edward (Rosella) 10
Perkins, Mrs. Harold, 88
Perry, Dick, 40, 41, 42, 108, 110, 231
Perry, Oliver, 267
Perry, Robert, 267
Perry, Theodore, 267
Peterson, Alice, 94
Peterson, Arch, 95
Peterson, Graham, 33
Peterson, Jerry, 231
Peterson, Moreen, 94
Peterson, Gladys Abbey, 124
Petry, Violet, 113, 117, 156
Pettis, Kenneth 267
Pettis, Kenneth, 51, 201, 236, 267
Pettis, Mrs. A. J., 184
Petts, Donald, 274
Petts, George, 22
Petts, Mrs. George, 150
Petts, Mrs. Marguerite 14, 59, 193, 228, 230, 231
Petty, Barbara, 113, 117, 160, 163, 198
Petty, Marjorie, 246
Phile, George, 267
Phillips, C. Judson, 6, 76, 95, 120, 143, 247
Phillips, Clifford J., 188, 246, 247
Phillips, Martin J., 60
Phillips, Mr. and Mrs. E.A, 45
Phillips, Mrs. C. Judson (Mary) 241
Phillips, Mrs. Clifford (Mabel) 181, 185, 240
Phillips, Mrs. Donald 88, 201
Phillips, Mrs. Judson (Mary) 85, 147, 225
Piccinni, Frank, 186
Piddington, Marilyn, 234
Piddington, Marjorie, 144
Pinkston, Charles, 267
Pittman, Bud, 231
Pokorny, Harry, 12, 99, 154
Pokorny, Mr./Mrs. Harry (Edna), 242
Pokorny, Mrs. Harry (Edna) 13, 14, 99, 153, 154, 186, 247
Pollidan, Elise, 150
Polson, Mrs. Roy (Bertha) 86

Powell, Dallas, 267
Powell, Rev. Henry, 224
Powlison, Eugene N., 63
Powlison, Mrs. Jesse (Irene) 145
Pratt, Bessie, 185
Pratt, Lisle, 267
Pratt, Richard, 41, 47, 116
Pray, Dawn, 252
Pray, Myron, 6, 76
Pray, Nancy, 251, 252
Preston, Mary and Rose, 150
Preston, Rosie, 23, 162, 198
Przewciznik, Chet, 267
Putnam, Mrs. Ray (Lois Searight), 118
Putnam, Ray, 118
Pyne, Zella, 111
Rabezzana, Hector, 72, 220
Rackham, Horace, 106
Rackham, Mrs. Horace (Mary) 73, 106
Randolph, Donald, 267
Raper, Fred, 25, 247
Raske, Charlene, 245
Raske, Charles, 247
Rasmussen, Anna, 242
Rasmussen, Don, 267
Rasmussen, Julius, 267
Rasmussen, Lillian, 234
Rawson, Gerald, 274
Rayment, Doug, 230
Reagan, James, 73, 123, 135

Reardon, George, 267
Reardon, Jack, 267
Reasner, Mrs. Howard (Bertha) 85, 147, 155, 182
Rector, Lou, 8, 225
Rector, Mrs. Lou (Phoebe) 88, 144, 153, 183, 185
Reed, Barbara, 114
Reed, Gerald, 267
Reed, Harry, 12
Reed, Jack, 41, 107, 267
Reed, Mrs. Harry (Maud) 186
Reed, Norman, 191, 267
Reed, Shelva, 245
Reed, Mrs. Russell (Maude) 183, 186, 246
Reedy, Cleon, 267
Reeves, Tamara, 54, 91
Reid, E. Clair 57, 83, 135, 188, 222, 246
Reid, Mrs. E. C. (Desa) 181, 185
Reinke, Beth, 150
Renwick, Ed, 3
Renwick, Mrs. Ed (Margaret) 85, 147
Renwick, William, 267
Rertaino, Frank, 267
Reynolds, George, 267
Reynolds, Lyman, 267
Reynolds, Russell, 33, 166
Rheingans, Mrs. Ralph (Cleo) 86
Rheingans, Ralph, 274
Rhodes, John, 267

Richards, Mrs. W.N., 240
Richmond, Beth, 245
Richmond, Eldon, 22
Richmond, France, 144
Richmond, Mrs. Myron (Helen) 95, 144
Richmond, Marguerite, 162
Richmond, Mrs. Ralph (Virginia), 19, 147, 182, 244
Richmond, Myron, 95, 144
Richmond, Peg, 116
Richmond, R., 122
Ridholls, Douglas, 267
Riedel, Louis, 180, 222
Riedel, Mrs. Louis (Irma) 23, 84, 85, 146, 181,
Riedel, Richard, 267
Riegle, Jack, 267
Riegle, Ronald, 267
Robbins, Mrs Kenneth (Florence) 144, 183
Robbins, Mrs. Gordon (Lillian) 19, 182
Roberts, George, 143
Roberts, H., 122
Roberts, Jackie, 234
Roberts, Jacqueline, 166, 203, 236
Roberts, Marvin, 267
Roberts, Mrs. George, 247
Roberts, Mrs. Herb (Lillian) 101
Roberts, Mrs. Warren (Thelma) 225
Roberts, Phyllis, 115, 199, 200, 234
Roberts, Rex, 120, 230, 244
Roberts, Russell, 41
Roberts, Stella, 88, 183
Roberts, Warren, 51, 78, 92, 93, 140, 141, 142, 152, 187, 190, 201, 214, 236
Robertson, Mrs. Ralph, 10
Robinson, Earl, 191, 216, 242
Robinson, Elvin, 267
Robinson, Harold, 267
Robinson, Mrs. Leon(Elizabeth), 86
Robinson, Patricia, 245
Robinson, Thomas, 274
Robinson, Warren, 110
Rockman, Harold, 114, 115, 166
Rockman, Rick, 110, 166
Roddy, Mr. and Mrs. Wayne, 150
Rogers, Albert, 267
Rogers, Burnette, 267
Rogers, Joe, 29, 214
Rogers, Mrs. Burnette, 84, 184
Rohm, Hattie, 186, 242
Rohm, Mrs. Hal (Henrietta) 13, 14
Rolland, Charles E., 220, 254

Rolland, Jack, 267
Rolland, Mrs. Charles . E. (Grace), 83
Rolland, Mrs. Frederick G (Margaret), 106
Rolland, Mrs. Ivah, 84, 106, 181,
Rolland, Patricia, 146
Rolland, Thelma, 166
Rollins, Bert, 13, 97
Rollins, Mrs. Fred, 119
Rolls, Ted, 267
Rosbury, Henry, 12, 191, 242
Rosbury, Joe, 99
Rosenburg, Joe, 154
Roshaven, Harold, 3, 22, 133, 244
Roshaven, Mrs. Harold (Benita) 95
Roshaven, Wayne, 274
Ross, Barbara, 145
Ross, C. E., 132, 133
Ross, Mrs. C. E., 244
Ross, Mrs. T. B., 233
Rossman, John, 95
Rossman, Mrs. Ralph (Claire) 95
Rossman, Patricia, 186
Rossman, Ralph C., 53, 95
Rossman, Sheila, 160
Rounds , Gerald, 267
Rounds, Charles S. 3, 13, 47,71, 133, 134, 175,
Rounds, Donald, 267
Rounds, Ron, 193, 231
Ruckel, John, 144

Rudduck, Dick, 194, 230, 231, 234
Runyan, Bruce, 31, 60
Runyan, Evart, 267
Runyan, Kathleen, 63
Runyan, Mrs. W., 149
Runyan, Robert, 63, 267
Runyan, Walter, 267
Rusinski, Edward, 267
Rusinski, George, 267
Rusinski, Jeri, 154
Russell ,Gerald, 267
Russell, Grace, 88, 183, 246
Russell, Joy, 150, 245
Rynearson, Dick, 110, 158, 159, 169
Rynearson, Dr. W. J. 10, 27, 64, 140, 267
Salmers, Mrs. A., 149
Sanders, Lucille, 3, 71, 134
Sanford, Mrs. Clark, 202
Sansam, Claude, 267
Sarosky, Mrs. Betty, 215
Savage, Mrs. Doug (Margaret) 241
Savage, Phil, 244
Schaefer, Harold K., 53, 155,202, 204, 267
Schaefer, John, 267
Schaefer, Mrs. Harold (Elizabeth) 87
Schaefer, Richard, 267
Schillinger, Ralph, 267
Schleicher, Fred, 267
Schleicher, Leo, 267

Schleicher, Mr./Mrs. Fred (Fannie), 242
Schleicher, Mrs. Harold (Jean) 182
Schleicher, Nancy, 116, 162
Schleicher, Robert, 236, 255, 267
Schmuk, Mr. and Mrs. Bernard, 254
Schoemaker, Bernice, 150, 152
Scholten, Alfred, 54, 117
Schroeder, Carl, 154
Schroeder, John, 238
Schucter, Mrs. Emile, 86
Schulte, Fred, 120
Schulte, Harry, 194, 230, 231
Schultz, Kenneth, 267
Schupbach, Mrs. Curt (Lillian) 118
Schupbach, Curt, 28, 100, 118, 121, 252, 267
Schupbach, Curtis and Elmer, 138
Schupbach, Don, 42, 110, 138, 167
Schupbach, Elmer, 118, 267
Schupbach, Harold, 267
Schupbach, Linda, 186
Schupbach, Marcia, 85, 186
Schupbach, Mel, 166, 252
Schuster, Mrs. Emille, 185

Schutt, Arnold, 267
Schutt, Donna, 162
Schutt, Mrs. Otto, 150
Scott, Mrs. M., 83
Scott, Mrs. William (Nellie) 101, 152
Scott, Phil, 42, 43, 110, 166
Scott, Phyllis, 162
Scott, Shirley, 13, 47, 113, 124
Seal, Sandra, 145, 197, 234
Searight, William, 89, 90, 139, 189, 267
Seelye, Mrs. Al, 182
Seger Kenneth, 5, 111, 221, 268
Seger, Earl, 144
Seger, Frank, 75
Senecal, Mrs. Arthur (Josephine) 146
Sergeant, Mrs. Eugene, 244
Sergeant, Robert, 274
Severance, Clare, 22
Sewell, Rolland, 9, 90, 143
Sexton, J. W., 51
Shaw, Frances, 47
Shaw, Hazel, 154
Shea, Joe, 253
Shelby Jr, Leon, 267
Shelby, Leman, 94, 110, 157, 158, 159
Shelby, Loretta, 117
Shepherd, Tom, 244
Sherman, John, 274
Sherwood, Irene, 114

Shields, Betty Lou, 47, 124
Shields, Robert, 119
Shinnabarger, J. B., 267
Shivile, Deke, 8, 75, 136
Shiville, Beatrice, 91
Shiville, Earl, 90
Sifford, Clifford, 267
Silvers, Earl, 267
Silvers, Jr , Earl, 12
Simmons, Mrs. Guy (Zola) 88, 183, 242
Simons, Charles A., 6
Simpson, Dave, 193, 195, 229
Sinclair, Bernard, 6, 42, 43, 47, 49, 114, 168
Sinclair, Bruce, 267
Sinclair, Donald, 267
Sinclair, Mrs. Claude (Ruth) 57, 85, 95, 181, 182, 183, 184
Sisco, Mrs. Ella, 247
Skillen, Mrs. William (Elsie) H. 87, 145, 148, 181, 240
Skinner, Joseph, 62, 267
Skutt, Delmar, 31, 35, 268
Sleeman, Dr. 178
Sleeman, Ilda (Foust), 236, 255
Sleeman, Mrs. Robert (Clarinda) 86
Slover, Fred, 144
Slover, Mrs. Fred (Zelma) 14, 99, 154, 186
Sluyter, Mrs. E. R., 83

Smale, Donald 254, 268
Smale, Mrs. Donald (Leonnabelle) 86, 87, 148, 181, 184, 185,
Smale, Mrs. Sidney (Dorothy Austin) 147, 236, 255
Smale, Richard "Dick" 57, 105, 268
Smale, Sidney, 95, 144, 187, 213, 247, 268
Smith, Betty Jane, 151, 162
Smith, Bob, 119, 166
Smith, Darlene, 200
Smith, Fred, 79
Smith, Freeman, 274
Smith, George, 239
Smith, Lennard, 200
Smith, Leroy, 193, 194
Smith, Lester, 268
Smith, Millard, 268
Smith, Mr. and Mrs. Fred, 81
Smith, Mrs. Arthur, 23
Smith, Mrs. Earl (Mary) 199, 233
Smith, Mrs. Howard, 10
Smith, Mrs. Robert, 119
Smith, Neil, 274
Smith, Richard, 233, 268
Smith, Robert F. 3, 188, 216, 222, 246, 268
Smith, Tim, 166
Smith. Jim, 80
Smithingall, Mr. and Mrs. Arthur, 254
Sneath, JoAnn, 119

Snider, Claudia, 244
Snyder, Jerry, 274
Solomon, William, 268
Sommers, Edna, 153, 185
Soper, E., 60
Soper, Jack, 268
Soper, James, 274
Soper, Mary Jane, 244
Sord, Esther, 185
Sorenson, Mrs. Anton, 150
Sorenson, Mrs. Arthur (Marian) 85, 147, 199
Sorg, Nancy, 245
Sortman, John, 268
Spear, Norman 42, 43, 110, 162
Sprague, Bill, 228
St. Martin, Mr. andMrs. Herman, 151
Stafford, Johnnie, 241
Standridge, J. L., 142
Standridge, Jim, 150
Standridge, Junnie, 166
Standridge, Venetia, 114, 116
Stanley, Clifford, 75
Stanley, Dick, 159, 198
Stanley, Kathryn, 186
Stanley, O., 60
Stanley, Shirley, 198
Stanley,Marguerite, 242
Stanovich, Jane, 114
Stedman, Paul N., 53, 155
Steede, Ray, 40, 41
Steele, Daniel, 9
Steele, Mildred, 91

Steele, Mrs. Daniel, 10
Steffey, Jacqueline, 97, 183, 242, 246
Steffey, Lloyd, 34, 244
Steffey, Ronald, 274
Stehle, Donald, 268
Stehle, Esther 111
Stehle, Mrs. Esther, 54
Stehle, Mrs. Floyd, 201
Stehle, Mrs., 156
Stephens, Marie, 163
Stephens, Mary, 144
Stephens,Thomas 115, 187, 193, 195, 199, 228, 231, 245
Steward, Jean, 198
Steward, Mrs. Cleo (Marie) 13, 91, 153, 185, 190
Steward, Ralph, 161
Stewart, Joan, 189
Stewart, Mrs. James (Jessie) 83, 181
Stiff, Bob, 40, 41
Stiff, Isaac, 99
Stiff, Mrs. Walter (Lelah) 14, 99, 154, 186, 242
Stiff, Nannette, 144, 234
Stiff, Walter, 12, 98, 99, 154, 191
Stiff,, Mr./Mrs. Walter, 242
Stiles, D. R. 3, 95, 143, 213, 221, 247,
Stiles, Edison, 57, 133, 139, 189, 239
Stiles, Emerson, 201, 268

Stiles, Mrs. Edison (Nada) 241
Stocken, Howard, 268
Stocken, William, 168
Stockham, David, 197, 228, 231, 237
Stockham, Mrs. Harley, 18
Stockham, Nancy, 163, 197, 198
Stockham, Rev. Harley H., 12, 21, 22, 23, 112, 152, 154, 224, 234
Stocks, Kenneth, 274
Stoll, Carl, 163
Stone, Carol, 245
Stoner, Mr. and Mrs. E., 28
Stork, Jack, 268
Strayer, James, 41
Strayer, William, 9, 138
Strom, Bill, 90, 166
Strom, Bob, 245
Strom, Elmer, 119, 166
Strom, Emil, 144, 189
Strom, Evar, 133, 139, 176, 190, 238
Strom, J. R, 60
Strom, Lois, 111
Strom, Mary, 153
Strom, Mr. and Mrs. Evar, 90
Strom, Mrs. Arthur, 19, 86, 87
Strom, Pat, 241
Strom, Ryan, 94, 119, 140, 166, 201, 238
Strom, Seigrid, 153, 185
Strom, Wilbur, 119, 139, 166, 201, 203, 236, 250
Sugden, Larry, 121, 252
Sutherby, Howard, 268
Swanebeck, Barbara, 23, 113, 117, 151, 155, 156, 163
Swanebeck, Harvey, 190
Swanebeck, Helen, 95
Swanebeck, Mrs. Harvey (Myrtle) 88, 144, 183
Swanson, Lowell, 212
Swanson, Martha, 85, 114, 116
Swanson, Mrs. Lowell, 85
Swartz, Dorothy, 160, 162, 163
Swartz, Ronald, 166
Swartz, Stafford, 268
Swartz, Stan, 268
Swartz, Virginia, 114
Sweeny, Julia, 79
Symons, Charlie, 76
Syring, Byron, 86
Syring, Mrs. Byron Syring (Barbara Barnes), 86
Tamlyn, George, 9, 29, 71, 81, 142
Tanner, Ian, 12
Taylor, Dr. William M, 140
Taylor, George, 247
Taylor, Harold, 156, 157, 163, 197

Taylor, Mrs. Glenn (Bessie) 242
Taylor, Mrs., 92
Taylor, Robert, 268
Terras, U., 122
Terwilliger, W.M., 268
Theisen, Duane, 122, 141
Theisen, Hugo, 73, 135, 179
Thomas, Larry, 274
Thompson, Alice P., 29
Thompson, Arlene, 245
Thompson, Clark, 76, 188, 246
Thompson, Gene, 35
Thompson, Jim 61, 167, 252
Thompson, Leonard, 268
Thompson, Mr. and Mrs. Clark, 61
Thompson, Mrs. Clark (Helen) 83, 181, 201
Thompson, Mrs. James, 83
Thornton, David, 159, 193, 195, 197, 230, 231, 237
Thornton, Don, 236
Thorpe, Elsie, 95, 144
Thorpe, Jeanne, 19, 47, 116, 124
Thorpe, Mrs. Nelson, 183
Thorpe, Nelson, 144, 183
Thorton, Dave, 187, 228
Tice, Ida, 250

Tice, Leon, 78
Tiefer, Jackie, 14
Tighe, Rev. Daniel Patrick, 22, 102, 152, 224, 234,
Tinker, Robert, 162, 198
Tippler, J.K., 268
Tirrell, Earnest, 85, 119, 175, 212
Tirrell, Julie, 146
Tirrell, Mrs. Ernest, 84, 86, 147, 148, 181, 185
Tisch, Beverly, 225
Tisch, Carl, 112
Tisch, Luella, 225
Tisch, Mrs. Carl, 150, 181, 241
Tisch, Shirley, 225
Tobin, Walter, 107, 108
Toomey, Harriet Mortimore 201
Torrey Jr., Harold, 191
Torrey, Bob, 37, 38, 121, 166
Torrey, Harold, 9, 90, 143
Torrey, Lois, 115, 199
Torrey, Margaret, 91
Torrey, Mrs. Sterling, 181
Townsend, Glen, 268
Townsend, Wayne 3, 63, 71, 72, 175, 212, 215, 268
Tribbey, Mrs. James (Irene) 13, 14, 154, 186
Trimmer, Bruce 48

Trimmer, Francis, 60, 63, 268
Trimmer, Jean, 118
Trimmer, Kenneth R., 63, 118, 167
Trimmer, Louis, 118
Trimmer, Robert, 268
Trollman, Catherine, 152
Truchan, Charles and Vince, 137
Truchan, Charles, 144
Truchan, Mrs. Charles, 144
Truchan, Vincent, 268
Turco, Albert 59, 167, 252, 253, 268
Turco, Bob, 118
Turco, Louise, 150, 234
Turco, Mrs. John (Virginia) 154
Turco, Robert, 100, 118
Turner, Charles, 115, 187, 198, 200, 233
Turner, Jeannine, 160
Tuttle, Lyle, 78
Ulch, Mrs. Fred, 145, 241
Unger, Wilma, 95
Utt, Bob, 99, 154
Utt, Orville "Bob", 12, 98 99, 154
Utt, Osweald, 98
Van Atta, Alice 86, 87, 148, 184, 205, 250
Van Atta, Mabel, 87
Van Gilder, Betty, 144, 150, 198, 225, 232, 234

Van Norman, Roberta, 200
Van Wagoner, Don, 35
VanAlstine, Ruth, 186
VanCleve, Jim, 158, 159, 163, 193, 195, 229, 231, 233, 236, 245
Vandercook, Mrs. Lawence (Violet) 153, 185, 246
VanDoorn, Mrs. J. C., 101
Varnum, Mrs. Helen, 236
Verbensky, Donna, 244
Verbensky, Mrs. John (Vera) 182
Verrell, Roger, 239
Vincent, Ann, 102
Vincent, Donald, 268
Vincent, John, 268
Vining, Charles, 268
Vining, Earnest, 268
Vorhies, Grover, 268
Vosburg, Frank, 137
Vosburg, Howard, 268
Vosburgh, Richard, 274
Vrbensky, Jon, 154
Vreeland, Tholand, 154, 268
Wagner, Marie, 99, 154
Waite, Mr. and Mrs. Ward, 90
Waite, Ward, 89, 139
Walcott, Carla Sue, 244
Walcott, Dr. Carter G. 9, 10, 27, 64, 188, 268
Walcott, Mrs. Anson, 181, 240

Walcott, Mrs. C. G. (Winifred) 147, 181, 241
Walden, Carol, 144, 163, 198, 234, 236
Wales, Bob, 60
Walker, Charles, 175, 202, 238
Walker, Mrs. Charles (Jean) 147, 182, 241
Walker, Mrs. Walter (Evelyn) 87
Walker, Neil, 268
Walker, Walter, 212, 268
Walpole, Alice, 197
Walpole, Forrest, 274
Walpole, Holly, 116, 156, 162
Walpole, Mrs. Walter (Elizabeth) 146, 181, 184, 240
Walpole, Walter E., 53, 155
Walraven, Beth, 245
Walraven, Betty, 238
Walraven, Peggy, 144, 156
Walsh, Robert, 114
Walter, Jim, 42, 43
Walters, Fred, 12, 31, 268
Walters, Harvey, 268
Walters, Herbert, 268
Walters, Jim, 166
Walters, Katherine, 13, 99
Walters, Mrs. Harvey, 190
Walters, Verne, 268

Ward, Glenn, 268
Warner, Phyllis, 88
Warren II, Harry, 274
Warren, Red, 31
Watkins, Betty, 115, 200
Watson, Dennis 9
Watson, Jacqueline, 236
Watson, Mrs. Dennis (Elaine) 10, 147
Watt, Pat, 155, 160
Watters, Don, 268
Watters, Katherine, 242
Watters, Marjorie, 144
Watters, Rod, 268
Watts, David, 274
Watts, Herbert, 268
Watts, Ken, 158
Watts, Mrs. Arthur (Marjorie) 181, 184
Watts, Mrs. Sue, 182
Watts, Ron, 158
Way, Percy, 31, 268
Webb, Richard, 154
Webb, Tom, 244
Weber, Bernard, 12
Weber, Edgar, 71, 95, 133, 143, 175, 212, 247
Weber, K., 95
Weesner, Collette, 234
Weesner, Lea, 117
Wegner, Frank, 158, 187, 193, 194, 228, 236
Wegner, Ken, 37, 38, 40, 41
Weidman, John J. 71, 133, 175
Weigant, Richard, 274
Weigant, Helen, 23
Weigant, Leo, 122, 274

Weigant, Robert, 100
Weise, Robert, 268
Welch, Jay, 248
Welch, Lynn, 94, 140, 201
Welch, Marcia, 144, 245
Welch, Martha, 183
Welch, Mrs. Lynn (Lavina) 85, 95, 182, 241
Welch, Mrs. Roy (Thursa) 144
Welch, Ray, 3, 122
Wells, Tyler and Harold, 144
Wenderlein, Betty,, 48
Wermuth, William, 268
Werner, Franklin, 85
Wessendorf, Bob, 49, 116
Wessendorf, Herman, 33, 34,
Wessendorf, Madeline, 166
Wessendorf, Mrs. Herman, 119
Wessendorf, Mrs. Wayne, 147, 182
Wessendorf, Robert, 115
Wessendorf, Wayne, 31, 89, 139
West, Eleanor, 95
West, Merton, 175
West, Sennet, 247
Westman Jr , Arnold "Sonny", 29, 81, 94

Westman Jr., Mrs. Arnold (Jean) 18, 181, 241
Westman Mrs. Elmer (Nancy) 225
Westman, Arnold, 107, 166, 219, 252, 253, 268
Westman, Elmer, 92, 140, 175, 201, 212
Westman, Mrs. Arnold (Esther) 85, 87
Wheeler, Dwight E., 274
White, Dr. Carl H. 28, 140, 268
White, Edwin, 268
White, J. C., 186
White, Mrs. Arthur, 146
White, Mrs. Carl H. (Bess) 83, 87, 88, 146, 148, 184
White, Mrs. J. C. (Zella) 14, 95, 183, 186
White, Mrs. Susan, 212
Whitehead,, Erwin, 31
Whitman, Cedric, 28, 268
Whitman, Clare "Junior" 37, 38, 39, 42, 43, 47
Whitman, Mrs. Grant W. (Maude) 83
Whittle, G. Leslie "Duke" 92, 140, 187
Whittle, Mrs. G. Leslie (Rose) 83, 88, 92, 146, 201,

Wieland, Virginia, 234
Wiggins, Mrs. Frank (Charlotte) 19, 87, 148
Wild, Tom, 187, 212
Wilhoit, Mrs. Kenneth (June) 85
Wilhoit, Odie, 59, 111
Wilhoit, Walter, 99
Wilking, Mrs. Woodrow, 241
Wilkins, Gary, 254
Willard, Mrs. Fred, 184
William, James, 9, 111, 154, 266
Williams, Bob and Jack, 81
Williams, Donald, 168
Williams, Dorothy, 241
Williams, Dr. Paul, 27, 62, 92, 140, 187
Williams, Fred, 8, 75, 135
Williams, Ivan 11, 27, 38, 42, 43, 53, 54, 91, 92, 107, 108, 109, 121, 156, 157, 159, 193, 194, 195, 228, 229, 231, 236
Williams, Mrs. Ivan (Erta) 85, 181, 241
Williams, Mrs. Paul, 182
Willing, Chester, 31, 33, 60, 268
Wilson, Danny 274
Wilson, June, 199
Wilson, L. A., 75, 97, 154
Wilson, Mrs. L. A. (Jane), 119, 166, 250
Wilson, Ronald, 268
Wilson, Russell, 268
Wilson, Sherman, 81
Wilson, Stanley, 268
Winacuff, Mrs. Morris, 183
Winn, Frank, 38, 39, 41, 42, 43, 47, 107, 108, 115, 116
Winn, Hollis, 12, 98, 191, 268
Winn, Mrs. Hollis (Florence) 97, 154
Winter, Lynn, 119
Winter, Alfred "Frosty", 12
Winters, Dean, 31, 119
Winters, Dorothy, 23
Wise, Edith, 162
Wise, June, 200
Wise, Marcia, 251
Wise, Roy G., 63
Witherell, Mrs. Ervin (Alice), 13
Wolcott, Mrs. A. E., 83
Wolverton, Arthur, 191, 268
Wolverton, Lloyd, 268
Wolverton, Ray, 268
Wolverton, Velma, 198
Wood, Mrs. Albert, 149
Wood, Mrs. Kenneth (Nettie) 119, 166
Wood, Mrs. Roy (Florence) 85
Wood, Patsy, 166
Wood, Roy, 135
Woods, Rex, 268

Woodside, Rev. Hugh 101, 152, 224
Woodward Jr., Mrs. H., 150
Woodward, Mrs. Ann, 185
Woodward, Neil, 268
Woodward, Robert, 268
Woodworth, Carol, 49
Woodworth, Mrs. Shull (Della) 14, 188, 54, 183, 186
Woodworth, Mrs. Charles, 86
Woodworth, Mrs. Tom (Gladys) 199
Woodworth, Shull 8, 71, 74, 75, 136, 203
Woodworth, Tom 8, 135, 203
Wortman, Ward, 135
Wright, George, 179
Wright, Mrs. Warren (Grace) 88, 186
Wright, Grant 4, 94, 119, 140, 142, 201
Wright, Janice, 144, 183
Wright, John, 41, 46, 110, 142, 158, 159, 163
Wright, Leslie, 268
Wright, Lucella (Reynolds) 236, 255
Wright, Max, 268
Wright, Mrs. A. G., 83
Wright, Mrs. Elaine, 182
Wright, Mrs. Grant L (Elizabeth) 55

Wright, Penrod, 41, 42, 47, 48, 116, 117
Wyckoff, Carl, 268
Wyckoff, Earl, 268
Wykes, Harry, 175, 213
Wyman, Charles E. 95, 144, 188, 212, 246, 248,
Wyman, Mrs. Charles (Elvira) 82, 183
Yager, Howard, 268
Youker, Marvin, 268
Young, Austin, 268
Young, Edward, 9, 23
Young, Frank, 81
Young, Larry, 231
Young, Leroy, 115, 116, 158, 199
Young, Mamie, 160
Young, Mary, 91
Young, Mrs. Nellie M., 254
Young, Nona, 198
Young, Ruth, 160, 162
Youngs, Edward, 90
Youngs, Mrs. Ed, 247
Zabich, Melvin, 100, 268
Zabich, Michael, 268
Zabich, Walter, 268
Zamble, Ann, 120
Zankl, Anne, 120, 245
Zankl, Bob, 194, 231, 234
Zankl, Mrs. Rebecca, 156
Zeibig, Evelyn, 162
Ziebig, Janine, 245

Zimmer, Mrs. Floyd (Clarisa) 144, 183
Zimmer, Maxine, 88
Zoll, Mrs. Virgil (Florence) 144
Zoll, Gary, 150, 230
Zoll, Russell, 268
Zoll, Virgil, 60
Zowilanski, Frank, 268